Jann Turner was born in France to South African parents, raised in the Cape and educated in Britain and the United States. She is an award-winning film-maker and journalist who spent two years covering the Truth Commission for SABC TV's *Special Report*. She is the author of *Heartland* and *Home is Where You Find It*. She lives in Johannesburg.

SOUTHERN CROSS

JANN TURNER

ORION

An Orion paperback

First published in Great Britain in 2003
by Orion
This paperback edition published in 2004
by Orion Books Ltd,
Orion House, 5 Upper St Martin's Lane,
London WC2H 9EA

A CIP catalogue record for this book
is available from the British Library.

ISBN 0 75285 918 8

Printed and bound in Great Britain by
Clays Ltd, St Ives plc

www.orionbooks.co.uk

For Anneliese.
In honour of a friendship forged through fire.
In memory of a time we shouldn't forget.

In 1996 South African President Nelson Mandela appointed a governmental body called the Truth and Reconciliation Commission. Its task was simple, yet massive: to sift through the debris of a past shattered by racism. Its mission: to safeguard the present and future against such evil.

Chaired by Nobel Peace Laureate Archbishop Desmond Tutu, the Commission conducted a many years long inquiry into gross human rights violations committed in the struggles for and against apartheid. Its findings were published in a huge five-volume Final Report in 1998. The Report documents thousands of stories of torture, murder and disappearance. It records the extraordinary courage and dignity and even forgiveness of the victims and their families. And it recounts the confessions and remorselessness and repentance of the perpetrators.

The story that follows is not one of those documented by the Truth Commission, but it could have been.

A glossary of colloquial and Afrikaans phrases is at the back of the book.

part one

Love is, above all, the gift of oneself
JEAN ANOUILH

1987

one

The air was too still that day. Anna stared out across the city, numbed by daydreams and overheating in the stuffy conference room where she and her comrades were banging out the framework for an upcoming wage negotiation. Outside, the late summer sun glared down on Johannesburg. It seemed to have baked everything flat.

Anna ran her hands through her hair, shaking it out in the hope that might sharpen things. There were puddles of coffee and scatterings of sugar on the Formica tabletop in front of her. Cigarette smoke curled through the air, ashtrays overflowed. A film of grime covered everything.

All Anna wanted was an ordinary life. And all the wishing in the world, she reflected wearily, wasn't going to get her one. Hers was the ache of one caught in the vise of time and place. We are all shaped, to some extent, by our time and our country. Anna was moulded brutally by hers. She had no choices, or that was how she saw it. Life under apartheid offered only the narrow path of resistance. Her longing for that ordinary life of nine to five and family and Sunday-supplement gardening articles was a longing for freedom from struggle.

She sighed wearily, looking down at the black hole of a doodle on the notepad in front of her. A tap on her shoulder brought her back to the moment. Anna turned to find the strained face of a colleague at her shoulder.

'Phone call,' she whispered. Anna frowned quizzically. 'It's Willem Swanepoel.' Zabeida's dark eyes glittered with what could have been fear. There was an agitation about her that made Anna instantly uneasy.

'What's happened?'

Zabeida shook her head, and her frizzy hair bounced around her face. 'Dunno, but he said it's urgent.'

Anna stood up and padded out of the room in Zabeida's patchouli-scented wake.

Her mouth was dry as she approached the front desk and the telephone that had been left there with its handset off, like a grenade with its pin out. Her palms were slippery with sweat as she reached for the instrument and jerked it to her ear.

'Willem?' The question was there, compressed in the layers of terror and anticipation in her voice. She didn't need to say it; he heard her voice asking – is Paul okay?

Swanepoel's triumphant voice bellowed back down the line. 'They're releasing him this afternoon.'

Anna felt the relief violently, like a taut rope snapping, like a shot firing. Willem sounded drunk with elation. In a while she would be too – when at last she set eyes on Paul.

'You better get home. Wait there.' Willem's voice rose against the background din of what sounded like a bar. 'You *sure*?' Anna breathed.

'Hundred per cent!' He whooped. 'Listen, go home. I'll come by the house later, okay?'

'Okay,' she nodded. The unfamiliar sense of a smile spread across her lips as she hung up.

She'd waited for this moment so long, she hardly knew how to absorb its having arrived. In her fantasy his release had clamoured with every wonderful thing imaginable, like Freedom Day itself, all butterflies and rainbows and bells pealing out into sunshine and a sapphire sky. In reality there was an edge to this triumph. There was a shimmer of anxiety all around it.

Anna laughed out loud and flung her arms around her colleague, who'd been staring at her with some concern. 'They're releasing him today!' she shouted and Zabeida squealed with excitement and hugged Anna tight, twirling her across the carpet tiles.

She burst into the stuffy conference room and made an ecstatic announcement. It was as if she'd launched a firework into their midst. Her comrades lit up in Catherine wheels and rockets of delight. Anna laughed happily amid the shower of raised fists and hugs and kisses. The sound gurgled out from her like water cascading into parched earth.

They celebrated by reaching their first decision of the day – to call a halt to discussions and get an early start on the Easter-weekend celebrations. Anna said it was unlikely she'd join them and they jovially insisted she stick to that plan. Paul would need her all to himself tonight.

Anna grabbed her jacket and bag from her office, clattered down the stairs to the parking lot, jumped into her rusty Fiat and chugged out into the humid afternoon. The day was Thursday 16 April nineteen eighty-seven. The following would be Good Friday. Johannesburg was emptying out for the holidays.

Turning into the glare of Jorissen Street the world seemed suddenly intensely colourful, like an over-exposed photograph. The sky was a brilliant, headachy white. Anna drove in a bubble of anticipation; the straining and grinding of the overheated city muted by her elation.

Paul had been in detention for seventy-three days. Seventy-three interminable nights that had scalded her with longing. This detention had been his second. The first had *felt* like for ever, but in fact had been a mere eleven days. He'd come out from that one thinner, but relatively unscathed. Or so it had seemed to Anna. He was white after all and sometimes they treated their own, even those who'd betrayed them, with more care. The second time Anna and Paul were picked up together. That was 2 February, just months ago, though it felt like decades.

Anna had been released within a week. No explanation, no charge, and no apparent cause either – she hadn't been operational in a long time. Nor, as far as she knew, had Paul, so the reason for this detention was unclear. It was possible that the Security Branch had acted on poor intelligence, or on none at all. It could also have been a simple scare tactic. It didn't matter, the result was fear and disruption and that was what they wanted. The law gave them the right to hold a person indefinitely without charge anywhere in South Africa; there was no obligation to disclose the location. The detainee was entitled to no visits, no letters, and no phone calls.

It was during those nights of Paul's absence that Anna had found a way to restore his presence. It was so simple, she'd almost wept with relief when she discovered it. She'd begun to talk to him. It wasn't hard to summon the presence of one whose body she knew as intimately as she knew her own, one whose voice was as familiar as her own. By being with her in that way he had given her the strength to endure, the strength for which she was so much admired and so frequently commended among the families and friends of the hundreds of other detainees.

She often wondered how it was for him, not seeing or even hearing anyone he knew in months. No one, not even Willem Swanepoel, his attorney, had been granted access to him. By law he'd been entitled to a twice-monthly visit by a magistrate and a twice-monthly check-up by the district surgeon, but that was the only contact he would have had with anyone from the world beyond the prison or the police holding cell or wherever it was they were keeping him.

Now the waiting was almost over. Anna wanted to blast her hooter, to scream at the slow-moving cars blocking her way. She rolled down her window, but the fumes from the Easter weekend traffic were worse than the sweltering air inside the car, so she rolled the window back up again and bit hard on her anticipation. It took an excruciating half-hour to get home.

Home was an unremarkable, solid, nineteen-forties detached house on Valley View Road in the east of the city. Kensington was a genteelly crumbling suburb of spacious houses with incredible views over Johannesburg, and over the glittering ochre heaps of the mine dumps that encircle it and give it its other name – Egoli – the city of gold.

Paul had found the house a couple of years before and rented it on the spot from an owner who couldn't wait to leave, so anxious was he to emigrate to Australia and avoid the inevitable decline of his country towards black rule. At the time Kensington was zoned for whites only. Technically black people, or 'non-whites' as the state preferred to call them, could only overnight in such an area if they had permission to be working there as domestic servants. In reality, by then the Group Areas enforcement was lax. An important factor for Anna who was classified as 'Coloured', meaning she was of mixed race, and even more so for their housemates Rachel and Jacob Oliphant – who were black.

Anna pulled her car up onto the pavement in Valley View Road. She slammed through the front gate and raced up the path on jelly legs, her heart pounding. 'Paul?' Her voice quivered as she called out his name, but the house echoed disappointingly. He wasn't there. Not yet. Damn! Anna dropped her keys down onto the hall table with a vehemence that caused a resounding clatter. There were agonising minutes, maybe even hours still to wait.

She pressed play on the answering machine, hoping that he'd called, but the first message was from Jacob to Rachel reminding her to pick up the kids from soccer practice that afternoon and the second and last was a brief blast of: 'Hello, hello, anyone there?' It was the deep, excited voice of Willem Swanepoel. He must have tried the house before getting hold of her at work.

Anna looked around, unsure of what to do. The house felt hugely silent and hot. She went into the kitchen to pour herself a glass of water and as she stood at the sink gulping cool mouthfuls a movement in the street caught her eye.

A pale blue Opel Kadett was pulling up onto the kerb outside. The passenger was obscured, but the driver was all too visible. Frans Nel. Security Police Captain, John Vorster Square. Captain Frans Nel. The bastard who'd woken their house before dawn on so many occasions Anna had lost count, but the last time it'd been to take her and Paul into detention.

Captain Nel was a vain man who wore a permanent smirk beneath the stiff brush of his moustache. A squat sadist who prided himself on his light touch and his terrifying success rate. He was a master of 'tubing', a torture technique that involved near-suffocation of the prisoner. The tube happened to be his personal favourite, but he wasn't averse to variety and was also known for dangling his victims by their feet from the tenth-storey window of his headquarters, or sticking probes up their anuses, even from time to time shocking their genitalia with a surprisingly clarifying little current.

Anna put the glass down and turned off the tap.

Nel climbed out of the car like a snake uncoiling, smooth and confident and deadly. He hadn't changed much since his last visit; his mullet haircut seemed a bit longer, his sideburns were just as excessive. Those long burns were a Security Police trademark, like the patchwork leather jacket he wore with his ironed jeans and silver grey slip-ons. He scanned the front of the house with scaly precision and when his eyes lit on her his mouth tightened, it was the briefest flicker of recognition.

Anna moved through the house to the front door, her heart jumping. She walked out onto the front stoep and his cold eyes were waiting for her. Not once did he shift his gaze, not even when the passenger door opened and Paul emerged.

It was all she could do to control the breath that shot from her when she caught sight of him, as if she'd been kicked in the stomach. This wasn't the man they'd taken away in February. This wasn't Paul. This was a frail man, so thin his clothes hung off his large frame. His thick curls were limp and flat against his gaunt face, his blond hair dirtied to dull brown. His skin was the colour of porridge, except for the purple smears of exhaustion under his eyes. When he smiled at her there was nothing in his eyes.

In his hand was a yellow plastic Checkers bag, which Anna knew contained the few possessions he'd been allowed in detention. She knew that because she'd dropped it off with a spare change of clothes months ago, not knowing where he was or if he'd ever get it.

Nel slouched back against the car and continued to stare as Paul moved towards Anna. He towered over her as she curled her arms around the unfamiliarly bony frame. Tears burned in her eyes and crumpled her mouth as she pressed her face into his chest, and a powerful new scent washed over her. It was the smell of institutions, of Jik bleach and Cobra floor polish, not the familiar, sweet sweat scent of him.

Paul let go of her and turned numbly towards the cop who had brought him home. She felt a chill in her gut as Nel jerked his head up in a kind of salute. When he smiled it was the smallest twitch of the muscles at the sides of his mouth, almost a grimace.

It was only once the Opel Kadett had disappeared from view that Anna looked deeply into those much-loved eyes, moist now with a film of tears. There was something desperate in his look that frightened her, something she didn't want to see, so she turned and led him inside.

He stopped in the doorway of their room, gazing slowly

around as if he were seeing the space for the first time. Then at last he smiled and so did she, her heart pounding, breath coming too fast.

She emptied the Checkers bag onto the trestle table against the wall. A meagre collection of possessions tumbled out onto the scrubbed pine surface: the shoelaces the police had taken from him on his arrest, the tattered blue nylon strap of his watch, a purple toothbrush and an almost empty tube of toothpaste, a green plastic comb and an aerosol deodorant. On top of that fell a change of underwear: grey Woolies pants and a vest, followed by the navy tracksuit bottom he used for pyjamas. The last item to unfurl was the shirt he'd been wearing when they pulled him in. Anna noticed that all the buttons had been ripped off. A small thing, but it signified to her the violence that had been done to him. She swung round to ask and found him watching her. His brown eyes gleamed darkly, his expression warning her off; he didn't want to say. She put the buttonless shirt down and went to him.

She helped him to take off his clothes, her fingers fluttering across his skin, searching for bruises or cuts, for signs of the beatings and torture he might have endured, but she found none. And yet he was so unlike himself. So thin and awfully pale, his skin so milky white it was almost translucent. The weariness of his posture emphasised how skeletal he had become – his shoulders slumped forward, his hips jutting out.

'You hungry?' she murmured, her hand caressing the inward curve of his stomach. 'Can I bring you food?'

He shook his head and slumped back down onto the bed, eyes closing in relief as he sank into the pillows. Anna wanted to cry, seeing him changed like this, but she mustn't cry, she told herself. Not now, after he had endured so much, not when he'd at last arrived in the sanctuary of their home.

She lay down beside him and pulled the covers over them and put her arms around his tired body. He held on more tightly than she could ever remember him doing.

'I'm scared,' he whispered hoarsely. The first words he'd uttered. She saw at once that he'd felt her draw back so she tightened her embrace, hooking her chin over his shoulder so he couldn't look into her frightened eyes. Her fingers stroked the tiny lick of curls at the top of his neck.

Fear freezes the soul and paralyses the spirit. Anna had heard Paul say that so often, not just to her, but to other comrades as well. He never showed fear. His courage was incredible, sometimes terrifying because of the risks it led him to take. Paul emboldened her, strengthened her with his example. She had never seen fear in him, let alone heard him express it. This wasn't how things were between them. *She* was the frightened one. Anna stared up at the ceiling feeling hollow and thin.

What had Nel done to him in there? She wanted to ask him, but Paul was not one to be pried open and if she tried he'd close tighter than a lock.

'It's okay. It's okay,' she breathed. 'It'll be all right. Just go to sleep now. It'll be all right. And I'm here. I'm here, my love.' She stroked the words into his hair, softly, like a song, her lips brushing the feathery softness of the tips of his ears. Gradually his breathing changed, became shallower, louder and soon she knew he was sleeping.

Shadows danced across the ceiling, the projected curves of the burglar bars billowing out as the curtains did in the breeze. This shadow person who slept in her arms would disappear. Paul would come back. Her love would coax him to life again.

And – as if he could hear her – his face softened and relaxed, his mouth loosened gradually into its familiar sweet shape. Watching him, Anna's heart filled with simple gratitude. He was safe. No matter what had happened, he was home now, everything would be all right.

She was aware of the comforting sounds of people arriving and moving about the house, the clatter of footsteps on wooden floorboards. She was dimly conscious too of the telephone ringing repeatedly, of the tinny sound of the answering machine picking up and the ecstatic tones of friends leaving messages. She may have slept, she wasn't sure, but Rachel's impulsive shouts of 'Where is he? Is he here?' startled Anna out of the daze or dream she'd drifted into. Seconds later Rachel's face appeared around the door, her eyes shining. Anna dipped her chin to indicate the sleeper in her arms. Rachel's hand flew up to her lips to shush herself as she withdrew. The house seemed quieter after that and Anna's breathing fell once again into a rhythm with Paul's.

Evening was a silvery light at the edges of the curtains. Anna shifted her hips against Paul's frame. His eyelids fluttered, his eyes opened and he smiled suddenly with all the luminosity and mischief of the man she loved.

She smiled back and felt the caress of his hand across her thigh then moving upwards under her shirt. She breathed in sharply at the delightful shock of his warm fingers on her belly. Desire lurched in her mouth and rippled between her legs. Then he was kissing her and she was lost in the velvet familiarity of his body, the heady pleasure and heat of his intense, certain love-making. Knowing him with his body inside and enfolding hers, knowing that sudden coolness inside his mouth just before he came, made her cry. Then Paul cried too, as she'd never seen him do before.

She ran a bath, but Paul wanted to shower, wanted to rinse the detention off him, let its dust and poison drain away, not soak deeper. So Anna climbed into the warm water while Paul watched her from where he sat, cross-legged on the blue bathmat.

Anna reached out and ran a soapy finger down the line of his jaw. He grinned, those tiger's eyes alight again: 'Have I ever told you just how much I love you?' His voice burned with feeling, so much so that tears lurched in her throat again.

'What happened?' She asked it directly, not expecting an answer, but hoping for one. She had to give him the opening, even if he was unlikely to take it.

He held her gaze for a long while, his eyes narrowing and mouth tightening. Then, on the pretence of trawling for the soap near her feet, he freed himself from her hand.

'It was bad.' That was all he said amidst the splashing and frothing of water he created in the search for the soap. His face was severe, unreadable for a moment, and then it changed suddenly as he pulled the cake of Lux from the bath, like a magician pulling a rabbit from a hat. Anna smiled, a little wearily, as he moved around behind her and began to wash her back. That was that then.

But he surprised her.

'Yussus!' he began. 'I tell you, those bastards are getting

heavy.' He said it with all the lightness and bravado of a man commenting on the performance of his team after a winning match. But he wasn't talking about soccer. He was talking about Captain Nel. His lightness was a front, a way of masking the harshness of it all, probably even from himself. 'There was one night when I really thought they had me. I really thought my time had come.'

Anna felt her throat tighten.

'I think it was night, but I wasn't sure.' He sighed. 'There was something not right about them, something just too bladdy cheerful about them when they came for me. I could smell the booze on Nel's breath and I knew they were up for a big jol, a big party night.' He sighed heavily. The sound of water trickling through the pipes nearby seemed to Anna to be full of foreboding. 'They took me to the interrogation room. White room. Small. No windows.' Paul took his hand from her back and sat back on his heels. She tried to imagine the cold horror of that room. 'There was a table in the middle. Like a school desk, like the ones you write exams on. They sat me down there. Big smiles going down all round.' He sighed again.

'I thought about you and that made me calm, just pictured your face.' She turned to smile at him and he smiled back, but his eyes were tunnels of darkness.

'Then I check Nel taking this thing out of his pocket. He dumps it on the table in front of me.' Paul dropped the soap into the dish beside her, his arm brushing against her shoulder. 'It's a limpet mine detonator.'

Anna felt cold.

'He's watching me all the time and I'm fuckin' cold as ice. I know that when that thing goes off it's not going to be pretty. He knows it too and that's what he wants me to think. He asks me if I know what it is and I shake my head; tell him I've never seen anything like it before. He laughs, and then he sets the detonator and leaves the room. And that's it. I'm alone with that thing counting down in front of me. I think I better start counting too. I know I've got a full fifteen minutes of counting before that thing goes off and that if I touch it I'm dead. They've got me. And if I don't, I'm dead anyway – in a small space like that I'm mincemeat.'

Anna sank deeper into the water, seeking warmth. Paul shook his head then actually chuckled at the memory, like a hunter might chuckle wistfully about the one that almost got away. This bravado wasn't Paul, she thought, it wasn't him, it was a mask. And yet he was becoming it.

'Shew! I tell you. I am sweating in there. I'm counting as hard as I can, wondering if it's too fast or too slow, thinking those fuckers don't care anyway, they're just gonna let me die.'

His hand swirled the bathwater. His eyes were far, far away. She wasn't sure that he saw anything at all.

'Then I get to twelve and a half minutes and the door bursts open. It was Nel. Sweating. Purple face. Man! He comes up to the table, picks up the detonator and defuses the thing in seconds. It's all I can do to stop myself jumping up to put my arms around him. Then he looks at me, angry-like, and he tells me to get out. Get out!'

Paul shoved out his chest as he impersonated Nel's thickly accented English. Anna flung her wet arms around him. 'Yussus, you should have seen me that night! I've never sweated like that in my life, I'm telling you!' Anna squeezed him with all her strength. Then Paul took her face in his hands and kissed her. Anna felt herself swept away by his love, her limbs liquifying from the heat of it. 'I thought about you all the time,' he whispered. 'Every minute of every single day. It was like you were with me the whole time. You gave me the strength to get through it.' Anna shuddered with the intensity of the feeling that flowed between them.

Then Paul stood up, his tone light and laughing again. 'We'll tell the kids all about it one day. And they probably won't give a damn! Little fuckers.' He stepped into the shower, drawing the curtains behind him with a theatrical flourish. 'When they're sitting by their pool in Sandton, counting the cars in their driveway and wondering what the hell all that struggle fuss was about, hey? We'll have beautiful children, you and me. Beautiful.'

Anna liked that thought. Liked its plainness and its connotations of school lift clubs and packed lunches and the idea that it carried of a simple future. Hope. That was his endless gift to her. He encircled her with so much hope she couldn't recall now the anxiety and weariness and dread that had risen with her that morning.

Anna lay back feeling happy. She knew this was merely a respite, a moment between, and that events would soon be racing at them again, but she would enjoy it for as long as she could make it last.

They emerged from the bathroom into the whooping shouts and wide-flung arms of Jacob and Rachel and their boys. And when the family welcome subsided, the crane-like figure of Willem Swanepoel stepped forward, his long fingers wrapped around a bottle of beer, his eyes bright with triumph. He'd pressed every lever the law had to offer and whether or not Paul's presence at home was a result of those efforts his sense of victory was deserved.

Willem was a wise old head on young shoulders, a crazy, brilliant attorney in his early thirties who acted for the Trade Union. An Afrikaner who'd burst into their English-speaking lives years before, fired up with indignation and an unswerving sense of justice. His commitment was all-consuming. No doubt as a consequence of that, the lovely Mrs Swanepoel always had the resigned look of one who could never compete for time with his quest for justice, nor all the lithe young waitresses and predatory women journalists Willem encountered on the way.

Rika was there too, smiling wanly in the background, an ethereally beautiful, quiet presence. There was an aura of discomfort around her; she didn't fit in with the Left wing, but Willem did, so the Left was the place she had to be. Generally that meant you could find her in the kitchen or looking after the kids in the garden.

A meal was being prepared, meat was marinaded and the barbeque lit for a celebratory braai. Beers were cracked open and the group drifted outside as the sun sank towards the jagged city skyline. They stood at the edge of the lawn where the koppie dropped away dramatically and the city rose to meet the distant horizon. Rika and Rachel were bathing the children and getting them into pyjamas. Anna stood with the men, staring into the fire. Joe would come by soon and then her family would be complete. Contentment settled in her, like a curled-up cat.

She listened vaguely as Willem and Jacob ran through a familiar checklist of questions with Paul, noting the names of his interrogators, what issues and whose names they had circled back to, their shifting moods and emphases over the weeks. Paul's account gave a useful snapshot of what the Security Police concerns and targets were at that point. It was interesting background for Willem and straightforward intelligence for Jacob. He would feed it to Joe, who would feed it to the broader network of the movement.

The movement was located underground, in cells. Rachel, Jacob, Anna and Paul together formed a political cell. Their work was mostly education, propaganda and liaison. It was possible they formed a link in military operations from time to time, though they might not know if they had. Like their enemy, they worked on a need-to-know basis.

Jacob brought information and ideas, Paul strategy, Rachel was the political commissar, kept them together, made sure that they were emotionally and politically fit. Anna's strength was organisation and logistics and even administration, if you could have such a thing in a unit where nothing was recorded, where details were kept even from some of its members.

As a result of their involvement their lives had a heightened quality, an urgency that had become everyday as their participation in the movement had deepened and the struggle in the country had intensified. They lived every day in the heady anxiety of preparedness to pay the price, whether it was harassment, arrest, detention, trial, imprisonment or even death.

As far as Anna knew Willem had never been told of their cell, but he asked no questions and they took that as a sign of his trust.

Jacob was particularly puzzled about why Paul had been held in detention for so long. Paul had heard and seen little to shed any light on that mystery. He put it down to poor information or someone's deliberate misinformation. By that he meant that someone must have given the cops to believe that he, Paul, and the cell were up to something they weren't. None of them said it, but the implication was clear. It was possible they'd been close to a spy.

Rachel was convinced of this, that Paul had been picked up on the information of someone near to them who had grassed to the

Security Police. She raged suspiciously about making lists of friends and comrades who might have been in a position to do this. Anna had heard it all before. She put down her beer and went inside on the pretext of organising food. She hated this kind of talk.

Smear campaigns were a much-used weapon of counter-intelligence. The cops loved to sow suspicion by spreading information that might lead you to suspect there was an informer in your midst, thereby destabilising a unit. It was an old and effective tactic, used by both sides. Anna knew also that there *were* spies around, generally people who'd been captured by the cops and tortured so badly that they turned on their own. There were also the plain greedy ones who would do anything for the money, broken people with no principles or family or community to guide them. But Anna was sure there had been no spy close to them when Paul was arrested. Rachel's talk was destructive. Anna hated the poison it released into their world, so she escaped, unnoticed, into the house.

She found Rika in the kitchen, smoking a cigarette at the table. She smiled as Anna entered. She really was ridiculously beautiful, with her long straight hair like raw silk over her shoulders, smoke curling elegantly from a cigarette held between her perfectly manicured fingers. 'You okay, Anna?' Anna nodded, not sure that she was. 'It must be hard,' Rika said softly, 'to see someone you love so damaged like that.' Anna felt the tears welling up in her throat. There was something in the gentleness of the woman's voice, in her simple and direct concern that contained no brave words about sacrifice and courage that melted Anna. She sat down at the table, covering her face until she'd recovered her composure. Rika smoked quietly. 'Shew. Sometimes I'm not sure. I'm just not sure . . . it's hard . . .' Rika nodded with cool compassion, then stood up. 'Shall we take the food out?'

They returned to the garden carrying salad bowls and a basket of soft Portuguese rolls. Anna was relieved to hear Jacob's fine, powerful voice putting an end to Rachel's speculation. 'We don't know *why*. So let's leave that behind, love, and move forward. Cautiously, as you say. But without the poison of all these accusations and suspicions. Okay?' He slipped his arm around her shoulder as he finished speaking.

Jacob, the articulate one. Jacob, the one whose steely, velvet tones and beautiful, simple turn of phrase could stir a crowd to action, just as magically as they could subdue an angry rabble. He made the perfect partner for Paul who was the silent, strategic one, the man of action.

Anna shot a glance at Rachel, who returned the look with a nod of understanding and acquiescence. The power of the trust that existed between them never failed to move Anna. It was what made them such an effective unit.

She slipped her arms around Paul's waist and he leaned down to kiss her hair. Then he murmured into her ear, 'No word from Joe?' Anna shook her head. Looking up at him she was surprised to see anxiety in his eyes.

'Something I should know?' she asked. He looked down, squeezing his empty beer can inside his fist, crumpling it into a ball of scrap. Then he shook his head, disentangled himself from her embrace and went inside. 'Gonna fetch a couple more beers,' he said quietly.

The Oliphant boys and Swanepoel girls raced each other around the garden, whooping and shrieking in a complex game of catch and wrestle. Paul cracked a Castle with the relish of one who had really earned it and took a long drink. The sun sank behind the city and set the sky on fire. Long, livid licks of gold, orange and the bloodiest red streaked the smoky sky. The smell of the meat cooking on the fire was intoxicating.

How benign the city seemed at night. All the dirt and violence concealed by the glittering lights. Anna's face shone as she looked around at the small gathering, at these friends who had become her family. She felt the hope pulsing through each one of them and she saw it humming in Paul's eyes as he looked to the horizon, waiting for the appearance of the Southern Cross, for that magical moment when the first tiny, dazzling diamonds of light would pop through the seemingly infinite velvet blue of the sky.

'There it is!' he cried. And there they were, the four stars that long ago had pointed the way south to the Europeans navigating their way across the seas in search of spices and the east.

'Do you see the dust cloud inside it?' Willem asked, pointing into the darkness. Paul nodded, not taking his eyes off the brilliant constellation. 'They call it the Coal Sack,' Willem continued. 'It's a dust cloud so thick it obscures a part of the galaxy beyond.' Paul sighed and tightened his arm around Anna's shoulder, murmuring to no one in particular, 'Makes me feel so small.'

Much later – after the Swanepoels were gone and Rachel and Jacob were putting their boys to bed, while Paul and Anna clattered through the washing up in the kitchen – there was a knock on the back door. Anna knew it was Joe from the quiet, urgent, single rap of his knuckle against the wood.

She smiled up at Paul, who pulled her to him and bit playfully into her neck. 'No peace for the wicked,' he whispered, and then went to open the door. He seemed relieved, as if a part of him had been waiting all night for this.

Joe stepped inside, dressed in workman's clothes – blue pants and jacket over an old grey T-shirt. On his feet he wore heavy, paint-splashed boots and he'd pulled a knitted beanie hat down low over his eyes. Anna grinned. 'Like the look,' she teased. There was elegance in the way he moved, an authority that breathed off him and shone through those dark eyes, which no disguise could hide. Joe stepped past her into the kitchen, briefly squeezing her shoulder by way of greeting.

Anna was flushed with happiness that night and she expected Joe to be too. Expected his eyes to be alive with the fire that mesmerised people around him. But they weren't. Tonight they were cold, blank, black holes. The eyes of the damaged, like so many others she'd seen, like Paul's that afternoon.

Anna watched as he enveloped Paul in those huge arms. Joe was thin, a little too thin for those broad shoulders of his. It occurred to her that he was built broad like that to hide all the shock absorbers, all the ballast that kept him so calmly afloat. Joe had an inner stillness that she envied. It made him unreadable, unlike Paul whose face was so mobile, so instantly responsive you could read him like the surface of the sea.

Joe was more than usually eager to get down to business that night. He declined her offer of a beer and indicated with a

16

backwards jerk of his thumb that Paul should follow him into the garden. Which he did, disappearing into the darkness outside where they would be safe from prying eyes and ears hooked up to listening devices, an old favourite of the Branch.

Anna turned back towards the sink and the pleasingly simple task of washing up. She wondered what was on Joe's mind and whether this meeting might be more than the routine debriefing she assumed it would be.

Joe was their Commander, their link to the wider movement, a member of the joint political and military management committee that covered their region, and who knew what other rank and responsibility he carried. It was Joe who brought their instructions and dealt with execution of missions and operations.

Anna left the dishes on the draining board to dry and then got herself ready for bed. It was less than an hour before Paul came in, alone.

Paul climbed into bed beside her, curled his arms around her waist, his hands stroking her belly. Anna leaned her head back against his, basking in the sense and the scent of him. I wonder, she addressed him silently, if there will ever come a day when I'm not grateful for you? She closed her eyes, smiling. No, there would never be such a day.

two

Carlos, the surly Portuguese owner of the corner café cracked an uncharacteristic, wolfish smile at the sight of Paul in his shop next morning. 'Hey, china. Long time no see,' he mumbled. Paul grinned broadly. 'Howzit, bru? Never thought I'd be so happy to see *your* ugly face again.' Paul raised his hand in a clenched fist, a mock salute. He was positively jiggling with energy and the excitement of coming back to the world. His world, the world of hot rolls on a Saturday morning, freshly baked by the café owner who slipped you beer and wine from a special cupboard late at night when the booze at home had run out. The man you exchanged rugby and soccer scores with, bemoaned the latest choices of the coach or the manager and sometimes, darkly, discussed events in the country.

'Ja, I heard you been inside,' Carlos growled, his eyes on Paul while his hands worked through a tray of avocados, sorting them, testing each one for ripeness.

'Ja,' Paul sighed, looking down at the green fruit in Carlos's hands.

Carlos shook his sad head slowly from side to side. 'You okay now, ay?'

Paul nodded, still not looking up, his eyes focused vaguely somewhere over the boxes, arms bent at the elbows, fingers hooked into the back pockets of his jeans. 'It was no picnic, I'm telling you.'

Carlos nodded his long sad face sympathetically. 'More power to you, ay china?'

Paul smiled gratefully and ambled to the back for hot cross

buns. Anna trawled the aisles for a pot of fig jam and some mild, hard cheese and the bright morning felt wonderful.

They strolled home, hand in hand in the sunshine. Greeting neighbours, patting dogs on leashes, chucking balls back at kids. A neighbour called out to them and they wandered over, chatting to her over her wall. Maggie's sister had been detained three weeks before, she wondered if Paul'd seen or heard of her while he was inside. He shook his head, nope, sorry. They could have been talking about the price of eggs. 'Okay, well, it's good to see you out!' Maggie chirped and went back to her gardening.

The day was Good Friday. The city had emptied out leaving behind an uncharacteristic calm, heightening the holiday mood.

They made a huge breakfast, which they ate in the kitchen with Rachel, Jacob and the boys. Quiet descended as they finished, food and newspapers spread out on every surface in homely chaos.

Rachel and Jacob sat side by side on the bench at the kitchen table, Rachel's hand resting carelessly on her husband's thigh as she leafed through the weekly *Mail*. Their sons, Bram and Delarey, were sprawled out with the comics on the floor.

Paul was bent over the newspaper in front of him, lost in that obliterating concentration of his. Anna could see the intensity of his absorption in the movement of a muscle in his cheek, jaw clenching and unclenching.

She smiled to herself as she poured coffee into a mug, then settled down to some work in the dining room and around her the house settled back into its routine.

Paul took her out for lunch at the Yard of Ale in town. Willem was there, a pretty young woman in tow. He introduced her as a colleague. Anna frowned at him with mild disapproval, which amused him no end. Also there were the usual host of politicos and journalists, friends and comrades.

Paul looked so happy as he laughed, telling stories of his detention. He was so beautiful; sometimes it took her breath away.

In the afternoon he went into the garden with Jacob. Anna sat at the dining table with Rachel and Delarey, helping with a school project. The subject was Jan van Riebeek and Delarey spent much time rejecting their input on the grounds that his teacher wouldn't want to know about how Bushmen had been living in the Cape for centuries before Van Riebeek claimed to have discovered it. Glancing up occasionally Anna observed Paul and Jacob with their heads close, expressions grave, caught up in discussion.

That night Paul seemed preoccupied. He brought Rooibos tea with a teaspoon of honey stirred in, just as he knew she liked it. When he climbed under the covers next to her he told her the news that explained the long conference with Jacob. He put his arms around her, holding her close and whispering the unwelcome words into her hair. 'Little one, I have to go away. I'm taking Jacob. We leave early tomorrow.'

Anna said nothing. She knew he felt her flinch, but he held her tighter. It was pointless, but she felt angry and disappointed. Not so much with him as with their situation. She knew there was nothing she could do, that that was how things were, yet she burned with frustration. Couldn't she have him to herself just for a little while?

'Baby?' he murmured, wanting her approval, but she wouldn't give it.

'It's not what I expected,' she answered dryly. 'I thought we'd have some time ... Ag, just forget it.' She tried to shrug him away, but he pulled her closer and suddenly the injustice of it exploded in her. She sat up, pushing him away. 'Fuck!' She shook her head, tendrils of long hair across her face. She moved to climb out of bed, but he caught her wrist in his fingers, lightly looping it. She didn't resist, but wouldn't look at him. He stroked the back of her neck.

'I'm sorry, liefie. I know it's been hard.'

'But why so soon? You've only been out two days, not even that. I mean you've been away for months. Why can't someone else do it?'

She slammed her hands down on the bedcovers, feeling petulant and childish. She hated to use the power of disapproval, hated to make him work for her blessing, which she knew she'd have to give in the end, but she felt she deserved more. She was tired of being so bloody self-effacing, of bravely making all these sacrifices, wasn't she allowed some things just for herself sometimes?

Paul sighed heavily, took his hand from her hair and curled up into a ball, arms around his legs, knees up to his chin. She looked at him accusingly. 'I've never asked you before, but I'm asking you now. Please make another plan?'

He shook his head. 'No one else can do this.'

'Bullshit!'

He looked up at her. There was pain in his eyes. And pleading. 'You've got to trust me on this.'

She stared back uncertainly, searching his face for some reason not to trust him, but it wasn't there. She fell back against the pillows, tears streaming down her face.

'I know. I know,' he murmured, leaning close to her cheek. 'I promise you, things are going to be different after this. I promise you we'll have more time, you and me. And it won't be a long trip. Seventy-two hours max. We'll be back Sunday night.'

Anna could feel herself relenting. She turned towards him, burying her face in his neck. He stroked her hair and she wept bitterly. 'Next weekend I'm taking you to Durban,' he whispered. 'We'll walk on the beach, eat bunny chow in the sand at sunset . . .'

And as he spoke she pictured the beachfront and the sunset over the city and the bunny chow, remembering the first time she'd bought one for him and how he laughed with relief when he saw the half loaf with its centre scooped out and filled with mutton curry. He'd thought they were going to eat rabbits.

Gradually her tears subsided and she began to feel better. She drank her tea and smiled back at him when he made a funny, sorry face. Then he took her cup from her hand, put it down on the floor and straddled her, pressing her shoulders back against the soft pillows, pushing her hair from her face.

'We'll check out the matinée at the Avalon Albert. I swear.' She grinned, helplessly. He'd got her. She loved the Avalon. It was one of the only movie theatres in the country where they could legally sit together as a 'mixed' couple, breaking the laws that disallowed even the slightest caress between the races. 'And I'll snog you in the back row. Just like any couple crazy in love and can't take their hands off each other.' His hand slid up her leg past her knee, underneath her nightdress. The thick cotton slid from her shoulders and she felt again the delicious shock of her skin against his. 'Oh God. I love you, Paul.' A lifetime with him wouldn't be long enough.

He fell asleep before she did, his legs tangled in hers, his chest and neck moist from the heat of the love they'd made. Anna lay awake, listening to the disjointed sounds of the argument next door. She'd heard it before and it rose and fell with more force than she and Paul could muster. For Jacob there was more guilt about going and for Rachel less remorse about wanting him to stay. In the end the mission would take precedence. It was the same for all of them. The same for Anna who'd missed her mother's sixtieth birthday when a last-minute instruction had sent her alone to the Karoo with a message she didn't understand for someone she wasn't sure she ever met. Orders were orders. That was always how it was and would be.

Anna closed her eyes, letting sleep take her under.

They made love again the next morning, before Paul left. He woke her gently, his tongue tweaking her nipples, his thumb soft against the inside of her thigh. He entered her with a sweet urgency. Anna was hazy with a sleep she'd barely surfaced from and into which she quickly returned once he'd gone. She wasn't sure if she remembered or imagined her last sight of him, a blur of denim and bright madras cotton in the doorway, hand to his mouth as he blew her a kiss.

Hours later she found a note from him in the bathroom, sticky taped to the shower curtain. 'There is no fear in love; but perfect love casteth out fear.' She smiled as she read it, loving him not just for the message, but also for his knowing her. Knowing that she was always first up and first to use the bathroom and that her first act of every day was to stand in the rush of water, rinsing off the shadows of the night. Knowing too the reassurance in those words, for she was often afraid and he was never anything but fearless.

Yet she could not wash away the uneasiness that settled around her when he was away.

Delarey's Van Riebeek project was spread out all over the kitchen table, so Anna ate her breakfast standing up. He and Rachel were going to the library to see if there was anything they could find there that would convince the boy of a different view of this flouncy, powder-puff Hollander who'd arrived in the Cape in 1652, its first inhabitant according to Delarey's teacher.

Anna decided to go and see her family.

Her mother lived in a long narrow apartment on the second floor of a building in Fordsburg, near the centre of town, with two of her three sisters – Nadia, Sonya and Natasha. Anna's father, a tailor, had had a passion for Russian novels. He'd died years before, killed instantly when the delivery van he was driving collided head on with a sports car. The other driver was drunk. Neither man knew what had hit them.

Anna's father was Indian and her mother Coloured. She'd grown up a half-cast in a half-caste, with the mix of her mother's Protestantism and her father's Islam. Her Ma, Yasmin Kriel, was a schoolteacher, still working, still struggling to get the best for her students. Anna found her out on the balcony, working quietly at her sewing machine, while the street seethed and rocked with life just two storeys below. Her sisters were busy with homework and boyfriends inside.

Yasmin Kriel was a diminutive woman, dressed typically that day in bright green nylon slacks and a loose, shiny floral shirt. She was a bundle of energy and industry. She stood in the kitchen preparing a meal while she caught up with Anna's news and kept half an eye on the TV in the corner of the living room. 'Ag, I'm sorry not to see Paul. You'll bring him over Thursday night?' Anna nodded, feeling strangely bereft. It was good to be in her mother's kitchen, surrounded by all the noise and colour of home. Her mother was wonderful about her odd choice of boyfriend. Her Muslim father would not have been so understanding about a white atheist, not for his lovely oldest girl. But as far as Yasmin was concerned Paul was already part of the family, as long as he loved Anna and didn't interfere with her work. Anna stayed for a late lunch, helped her sister with some homework, and then headed back to Kensington, her spirits restored.

By nightfall there had been no word from Paul or Jacob. Anna was restless for contact. She could feel the disquiet in Rachel too. Neither mentioned it, but they were both straining for the phone as they went about their household chores, fed the children and put them to bed.

Anna didn't sleep much that night, but insomnia was an old friend. She took a novel from the stack by her bed, propped herself up against the pillows and read, waiting for sleep or day, whichever came first.

She was still reading, a faint dawn light creeping in at the edges of the curtains when at last the telephone rang. She leapt out of bed, almost crying out with relief as she ran out into the hallway.

But the caller wasn't Paul.

The voice that slithered down the line was that of a journalist Anna knew mostly through reputation and only slightly by acquaintance. There could be only one reason for such a call at such an hour. Panic exploded in her, trapping her voice in her throat. 'Do you have someone there with you?' asked the woman at the end of the line. Anna didn't say anything at all. Then the woman spoke with eviscerating bluntness.

'Paul and Jacob have been shot. They're dead.'

Nothing in her sweet, short life could have prepared Anna for this. It was as if she were standing in a hail of machine gun fire. Each word ripped through her like a bullet. The solid elements of the world seemed to separate, like a slow motion shattering of glass, like the shards of a broken mirror cascading outwards, splintering into tiny fragments everything they met.

She said nothing. The silence of the dying night howled in her ears.

Rachel found her in the hallway, Paul's T-shirt fluttering around her thighs. 'Hello? Anna? Are you still there?' The panicky journalist called out repeatedly from the other end of the line. Anna tried to say something, but not a sound came out of her mouth. Rachel grabbed the phone. The eerie, awful cry that flew from her, was all the pain and disbelief that Anna could not express.

The bodies had been found less than an hour earlier, on the road between Mafikeng and Vryburg, a couple of hours north-west of Johannesburg. Jacob had been shot just once, in the back of his head. Paul had taken at least three bullets, as if he'd gone down with a struggle. Both their bodies had been doused with petrol and set alight.

These cold facts were repeated over and over, first by the

journalist, then by Anna herself as she set about telephoning the news to her family and friends, but no amount of repetition could make them real. Nothing felt real.

Woken by their mother's terrible cry Bram and Delarey scrambled from their room, eyes puffy with sleep and wide with fear. Bram still clutching the frayed bunny rabbit that was his constant companion and sleep mate. They rushed to their mother, all of four and seven years old, putting their arms around her, comforting her confusedly as she slid to the floor.

Anna looked at them clinging to one another in shock and had no idea of how she was going to get through this, though somehow she had to. Somehow they all had to.

It was Anna who explained what had happened, though she'd barely understood it herself. She put her arms around the boys and took them into the living room, up to the window that looked out over the waking city. Phrases flew into her mind as fast as she discarded them. There was nothing that could soften such a blow. The only words that would do were the ones the journalist had used just minutes earlier. 'Your daddy's been shot. He's dead,' she said at last.

And Jacob's sons looked up at Anna with their father's bright eyes, burning with the courage of innocence. Somehow they were calm, while she was not. 'Was it the police?' Delarey seemed to grow older before her eyes. Anna looked away, at the city with its night lights still glittering and the blue dawn sky illuminating the buildings. She nodded. 'Yes, it was the police,' she said numbly. Then she pulled the boys to her, holding them as tight as she could while the heat of rage surged through her, a tornado of anger swirled in. And that was when the decision came, the key to the door that would take her beyond this night. 'But we're gonna catch them. We're not gonna let those bastards get away with it.'

The Swanepoels arrived not long after, both bleary with sleep and shock, Willem with a child in his arms and another clinging to his legs.

Rachel wept. She wailed and thrashed and railed against the injustice, the pain and the horror of it. Grief jerked out of her in spasms of tears and sobs. Rika took her to her room and gave her pills from a little box she carried and held Rachel while she rocked and cried.

Anna couldn't bear the sound of Rachel's grief. She feared the pure and uncensored expression of feeling. And Rachel was unhinged in her sorrow. So Anna closed herself up in the kitchen with Willem, trying to concentrate on things that would defer the onset of sadness. Delarey padded through in his pyjamas and made a pot of tea. He brought two cups to the table, his face so serious that Willem had to look away. It was that child, coping, that undid him. Anna saw him jerk against the pain, saw the tears slide down his cheeks, but still she didn't cry. She couldn't. Anna was cushioned in deep shock. On the one hand the reality was stark, but on the other she couldn't pin together the pieces of what was happening.

Willem lit one of Rika's cigarettes, then pulled a yellow legal pad from his bag, uncapped a pen and began to write. 'I want to go up there. Before they sew the investigation up. The sooner we go, the better. Will you come?' Anna nodded, then together they got to work. Willem sat by her, smoking steadily as he made call after call, trying to get as clear a picture as possible of what had happened. In between they fielded calls from friends and journalists and began to put together the funeral arrangements.

And more and more people came. The house and garden filled up around them. Like a strange, muted party. Bring your own tears and memories and pots of food.

Anna sent word to Joe via an emergency contact they'd arranged long ago but never used. Never had to use, till now. It was less than an hour before a message came back, in the hands of a neighbour's domestic worker.

The note was handwritten, a scrawl she didn't recognise. On it was an address in Parkview. That was all. She understood immediately that this was where she would find him. It wouldn't be safe for Joe to come to the house now, not with so many people around and who knew how many watching.

Anna was surprised when Rika Swanepoel offered to drive her, but she accepted and they set off immediately. 'Mind if I smoke?' Rika asked mildly. Anna shook her head. Rika lit up and Anna sank back into the comfortable leather seat. Exhausted and wired, she felt like the victim of a wildfire. Alone in the wasteland, the taste of ash in her mouth, the cinders of hope in her hair and all around her the blackened stalks of a once lush life.

Rika drove them to the Parkview address, said she'd wait in the car and that Anna should simply shout if she needed anything. Joe was sitting on a bench in the garden of the house, deep in the leafy suburbs. He looked broken. Anna had never before seen him cry and it shook her profoundly. The tears rolled silently down his cheeks.

Anna reached out to put her arms around him, but he waved her away, as if ashamed. 'It's okay to cry,' she whispered, her throat burning, swollen with unshed tears of her own. For a long time he said nothing at all. Anna waited numbly, arms wrapped around her knees.

When at last he did speak it was not to give her the words of comfort, nor the plan of action that she expected. Joe wiped his sleeve noisily across his face, his sorrow turning suddenly to fury. And his rage was murderous. 'What the hell happened?' he spat suddenly. 'What the fuck were they doing there, Anna?'

'What?' Anna felt her grip on reality slipping even further.

'Where were they going?' Joe repeated angrily, as if she must know.

Anna shook her head frantically. 'What do you mean? *You* sent them.'

Joe stared at her incredulously as they realised simultaneously that something had gone very wrong. Anna felt herself break, exhaustion crumpling her body. She slumped down against the bench, but still no tears came. They got stuck in an acid swirl in her throat. She looked at the manicured garden of the neat suburban house and suddenly had no idea where she was or what she was doing. She felt as if she were floating in a strange, green dream. As if her anchor had slipped and the world had drifted away.

'I knew nothing of this mission,' Joe repeated.

Anna's mind felt like lead. 'Maybe they got their orders from another section?'

Joe shrugged. 'Possible. Irregular, but possible. I'll ask.'

'Please.' She put her hand on his arm and he seemed to shudder at the pressure. 'We can't let them get away with this.'

He nodded sadly, tears escaping from his eyes, coursing down his cheeks. She'd never seen him so defeated. They sat in awful silence for some time, slumped side by side on the bench. There was nothing more to say.

Rika drove her back to the house. They spoke little. Nevertheless Rika's presence was a reassuring one. Anna looked over at the coolly beautiful woman in her expensive clothes and wondered if she'd underestimated her. Perhaps this was Rika's strength, bringing comfort, and sweet tea and calm, practical help. Perhaps it was because she'd had a more than glancing acquaintance with sadness herself.

Someone had put candles in paper bags all along the path up to the house. Anna put her arm through Rika's as they walked in silence past the solemn groups gathered on the lawn, up the steps and into the house.

It was Easter Sunday, 19 April nineteen eighty-seven. The day of rest on which the architects and executioners of apartheid donned their hats and set off for church, where they knelt in fervent gratitude for God's recognition of their sacred mission on earth.

Anna would never move through any 19 April in all the years of her life to come without tasting all day the terrible sweetness of their parting and the nauseating savagery of Paul's murder.

three

The next day Anna set off for Vryburg with Willem Swanepoel, travelling the same route Paul and Jacob would have taken just forty-eight hours earlier. Willem drove in a fury. 'It's too easy,' he raged. 'This time they've gone too far. This time they must pay.' And Anna was sure they would.

Their plan was loose and simple. They would collect as much evidence as possible; make certain the police felt their presence, let Murder and Robbery know that they were watching. Murder and Robbery often worked hand in hand with the Security Police so they were not to be trusted.

As the hours rolled by Willem fell silent and the pressure of the silence pulled Anna's nerves taut. Her sense of foreboding mounted in intensity. She tried to turn her mind to other things. To Paul. Living, not dead.

Their story began, as it would end, with a funeral. It was at the beginning of the time when funerals became the focus and the forum for all opposition against apartheid, when any other kind of organisation was banned and the leadership was jailed or in exile.

Anna was among the thousands who'd come to bury six young activists mown down in the dead of night at a police road-block as they travelled home from a meeting in town. The day was hot, the air choked with dust and clouds of tear gas fired by police attempting to disperse the angry mourners. In the chaos Anna was separated from the contingent of students she'd travelled to the cemetery with. Suddenly police came from all directions, armed with guns and loudhailers and straining on the leashes of murderous dogs.

A helicopter's blades chopped the sky terrifyingly close, the crash of each rotation like the air-cutting cracks of gunfire. People were running in all directions. Anna fled towards the graveyard.

Then she was trapped in a net created by cops who'd pressed a part of the crowd up against a long, high fence surrounding the cemetery. The pressure of people was terrifying. She couldn't move her feet, her arms were pinned against her sides, and she felt her chest squeezed so hard she could only take the shallowest of breaths. To make it worse the people around her were screaming in panic. Anna lifted her chin and sucked for air, over and over, like a fish out of water, desperate for breath. As the swaying crush intensified, so that at times her feet were lifted from the ground, Anna noticed movement at the fence, about fifteen people away from her. Someone had broken through, she couldn't see how, but as he stood up to push the first person through to safety a tall white guy turned to look out across the sea of faces. Later he called it fate. Later he would say that there was no other reason for him to have looked up, at that moment and quite so directly at her. In that moment Anna's panic-stricken eyes had met Paul's and he'd grinned. In all that mayhem, with her gasping for air like a half-dead guppy, Paul had grinned at her.

Paul was beautiful. He shone with youth, with ardour, with ideals. Not just for Anna, for everyone. He'd dragged her through that hole in the fence and held her as she shook and sagged with relief. Paul had saved her life that day and so she'd given it to him. It was that simple.

In the car on the way to Vryburg, Anna felt the grief convulsing through her, spreading over her with a weight that was smothering. It burned in her eyes and choked in her throat. But no tears came. Willem glanced over at her, his eyes dark with purpose. 'You okay?' She couldn't speak, simply nodded, her knuckles white with holding on, just, to her self-control.

They arrived at the scene of the murder almost forty hours after the discovery of the bodies. 'Forty hours in which the sweepers have had all the time they need to make the necessary rearrangements,' Willem muttered disconsolately as they stared down at the black scar of burnt grass and the ghastly shell of the car. It was deathly quiet there. Anna gazed up and down the long, narrow ribbon of road reaching two horizons, empty. Heat haze danced on the tar.

Willem took photographs from every angle as Anna paced the scene, up and down, over and over again. There was little left to tell the story of what had happened. Just a few traces of petrol leading from the road, and the awful indentations on the burnt earth where the bodies must have lain. No spent cartridges, no bullets, no tyre marks.

Setting off again for Vryburg they tried to piece together a rough chronology of events. They realised very quickly that what they knew was almost nothing. Paul and Jacob must have set off around three or four, some hours before the dawn. The nature of their mission was unknown. Joe was working on that and Anna would make contact with the local underground in Vryburg to see if they could shed any light on the matter. As to the rest, it was anybody's guess. There was no doubt that Paul and Jacob were targets for the Security Police, whose diligence in crushing opposition to the government had grown more and more bloody. And there was no doubt that Captain Nel would have had something to do with it; he treated Paul and Jacob and their partners as his own personal projects. Beyond that there was nothing even vaguely solid to be dredged up from the swamp of speculation that surrounded the killings.

In Vryburg they checked in to a roadside motel where they were met by a small posse of journalists and photographers who'd come up to cover the story. Some of them Anna knew from Joburg, others she'd heard of. Willem went out drinking with them, while Anna retreated to her room, a nest of wood veneer and nylon. She climbed into bed with two of Rika's pills for company and they quickly jerked her under. She swam through the night in a soup of sleep and chemical unconsciousness.

Next morning her face was all over the papers, alongside old pictures of Jacob and Paul. She was up early so she took a wad of them to Willem's cabin along with a cup of coffee for him. One of the reporters from the night before, a voluptuous brunette wrapped in a crimplene sheet opened the door. Willem was in the shower, she said. Anna retreated to the dining room, not wanting to know.

He appeared less than half an hour later, looking frisky and determined. There was no sign of his guest, he offered no explanation and Anna didn't ask. Together they scanned the newspapers and as she read Anna felt once again the smothering sorrow that seemed to come and go like contractions of pain. Willem saw her pale and he reached out and put his hand over hers.

Their first objective was to meet with the police, but the cops were playing hard to get. At Murder and Robbery they were told by a pug-faced young woman wearing violet eye-shadow that the officers in charge of the case would not be available until the following day. So they made an appointment.

Anna's anger quickly dissipated as she faced a task she both dreaded and longed for, that of identifying the bodies. It was a job Willem could have done, and indeed offered to do, alone. But Anna had to see Paul.

With them was an independent pathologist Willem had flown up from Cape Town. A white-haired old man with a soft face and a streaming nose. 'Hay fever,' he explained, though it wasn't the season. Nevertheless he kept a handkerchief to his nose for much of the time he was with them. He was to conduct his own autopsy and provide a second post-mortem report.

They entered the morgue in silence. The stench of chemicals crinkled in her nostrils. Anna could literally taste the smell of the cold, sterilised metal. The attendant led them past rows and rows of drawers, behind which the corpses were stacked floor to ceiling. 'We're very full at the moment. What with the unrest,' he informed them, 'gots to truck the overspill to Mafikeng.'

He led them to the far end of the refrigeration room where two chrome trolleys were parked, side by side. On top of the gurneys were two shapeless lumps, draped in white. Anna braced for the impact.

Standing perfectly still beside Willem, the pathologist and the coated attendant, she stared at the attendant's pink little hand as it took up the edge of the first sheet. 'Theys not been cleaned up yet,' he warned, hesitating. 'We can't do that till after the autopsy.' The pathologist nodded matter of factly, and then the attendant lifted the sheet to reveal Paul's body.

His eyes were open. The shock of meeting his wild stare rippled through the four of them like dominoes falling as the sheet slipped back. The attendant reached forward to pull down the lids of the corpse, but Anna stopped him. 'Wait. Not yet,' she said quietly. The young man took an obedient step backwards.

The corpse before her bore only a slight resemblance to the man she loved. His hair was singed to nothing and though his face was contorted by pain, it was otherwise unharmed. The bullets had ripped through his left thigh, gouged a hole near his right hip and taken him clean through the chest. A purple rose had bloomed there over his heart, the entry point of the slug that killed him.

Strange, it wasn't in the brown depths of his eyes that she saw the horror of his dying moments; it was the terrible snarl, the awful sideways set of his jaw that most upset Anna. And stayed with her, jumping into her thoughts unbidden, like a bloodied jack-in-the-box, for years to come. Somehow that was worse than the blackened arms sticking up and outwards, beseeching. Or attacking. She wondered which.

His clothes had been burned off him and his watch had melted into the flesh around his wrist. The smell was indescribable, but Anna made no move to protect herself from it. She stared at the body with a mixture of terror and fascination, her hands twisting, twisting, twisting the gold ring she wore on her wedding finger, the ring Paul had given her.

She remembered the note he'd stuck to the shower curtain the morning he left. 'Perfect love casteth out fear.' And thought she understood it differently now. It was Paul who was scared. But what of? Who of? What fear had her love for him helped cast out only to return so monstrously – materialising as death?

Rage swirled around her like a hurricane. She made a silent promise to him and to herself that night. If she did nothing else she would find the person who did this and bring him to justice.

Her fingers shook as she reached for Paul, but she didn't fumble or falter as she pulled the waxy, cold skin of his eyelids over his eyes and closed them for ever. Then she bent down and kissed him. Her lips touching the strange coolness of his forehead for the very last time. 'There will never be a day when I'm not grateful for you and for your love,' she whispered. 'I will always love you, Paul.'

No one spoke as they walked out to the car, the stench of the morgue still clinging to their clothes and their hair.

Fear was Anna's enemy now. Fear of being alone, of moving through life without him. And the fear that right didn't always defeat wrong; that in the real world injustice wins out after all. But most of all Anna feared feeling. And so, piece by piece she began to erect the carapace of action and anger that would protect her for years to come.

Next day they met with the police. Lieutenant 'Balletjies' (little balls) Badenhorst and Warrant Officer Jeff Curry of Vryburg Murder and Robbery introduced themselves as the investigating officers. They made the usual noises of condolence, for which Anna was grateful, but they couldn't stop themselves checking her out, their pop-eyes grazing her from head to toe.

They invited Willem and Anna to the Officers' Bar at the station. It was a windowless salmon and burgundy imitation of an English pub, with original smell. Willem accepted a whisky, Anna had a Coke and the cops drank brandy and Sprite in serious measures.

Badenhorst was a large, hirsute man who sat calmly on a stool next to Anna, his pants tight around massive lock-forward's thighs. He was wearing a safari suit – that strange sartorial statement of Afrikanerdom, soon to be consigned to the dustbin of fashion history, along with sideburns and knee-length socks. Curry was a mousy creature with a whining voice and a palpable fear of his superior.

The police investigation, unsurprisingly, had so far yielded only one thing, an obvious and often used theory about internal feuding in the 'terrorist' ranks. Their evidence was unsurprising. A Makarov pistol found at the scene. Badenhorst declared this conclusively. Willem laughed out loud. He knew that the Makarov, in the legend of apartheid, was an Eastern Bloc weapon handed out to the 'terrorists' by their communist backers, the hand-gun counterpart of the AK47 automatic rifle.

Willem's youth and intensity and perfect Afrikaans clearly

rattled Badenhorst, who took a long slug of brandy before he shrugged, raised his thick-fingered hand and then let it fall with a dull thud onto the bar. 'There's no doubt about it in my mind. It's execution-style killings. The bullets and cartridges found on the scene come from the Makarov. Case closed as far as we're concerned. The evidence is upstairs on my desk, I'm more than happy for you to take a look.' He glanced over at Curry, who nodded gravely, as if that was all the proof they needed. 'I'm sorry, Miss Kriel,' Badenhorst mumbled gruffly, not seeming sorry at all.

They did go up to look and sure enough, there it was, a Makarov pistol, spent cartridges and bullets mangled by their passage through Paul's body. To Willem and Anna this was the first, high, bright flag of a cover-up. The cops had hundreds of Makarovs, AKs and other weapons which they used to make their dirty work look like the work of the other side.

And that was how the state-supporting newspapers reported the story, front pages screaming out the lurid details, further proof of how savage these terrorists were. They would stop at nothing; they even killed their own. The minority opposition press, and even the middle-ground English papers, reported it differently. They called the Mafikeng murders assassinations, and the culprits in their view, like in Anna's, were the police.

A week later Paul and Jacob were buried with full honours. Their coffins draped defiantly in the black, green and gold flag, the colours of the banned African National Congress. Anna led the illegal throng of marchers, taunted by the heat and police dogs snarling and snapping and straining at their leashes. The street shimmered and shook with the toyi-toying mourners, a dancing ocean of resistance. It was as if Freedom Day itself had come, with the Communist Party and ANC flags everywhere and the police just standing sullenly by, watching, intimidating people, but making no move to break the demonstration up. Anna imagined Paul there beside her, borne up on the surge of energy and defiance.

The thousands of mourners flung their fists into the air, punching the clear Highveld winter sky – 'Amandla!' Power. 'Awethu!' To the people! And on that day the crowd had cried out for answers, for killers, for justice and an end to the system that created these murderers.

At the graveside Anna took up the spade offered her and attacked the dirt with all the rage and incomprehension of her loss, plunging the blade into the red earth, flinging load after load of soil onto the coffin. The grave-diggers watched as she worked, her face etched with grief, while the crowd sang and took turns to help her. Sweat ran down her arms and trickled over her belly, her dress was splattered with dirt and dust, but she didn't stop until the coffin was covered over and the grave was full.

four

fter the funeral Anna's life was more than ever charged with activism and her energy was infinite. She cut down on her extra commitments to the Union and began to spend her evenings and weekends working with Willem on preparations for the inquest.

For the State, such hearings were essentially a formality, a brief statement of arguments – mostly speculative – and a handing in of documents from both sides. More questions than answers generally remained.

For the Left, inquests were useful. Not just for the publicity they brought to a case, but even more importantly as fishing expeditions that sometimes delivered up unexpected sprats of truth. Sometimes they backfired with macabre comedy, like the inquest into the death of a student leader found hanged in his cell. The judge laid the blame squarely at the feet of a fellow detainee, another student, who police said had failed to notify the authorities that his comrade was suicidal.

Nevertheless Willem and Anna set about a strategy that would get Nel and Badenhorst into the box and at the very least pin them, under oath, to a version of events. At worst they would emerge with the all too common verdict of 'no one to blame'. But Anna intended to persist until she got to the truth, no matter how long that took.

So she lived in a state of hopeful purpose. She kept Paul's clothes and books as he had left them, as if he might one day return to use them. And she grew back into the habits of his last detention, summoning his presence when she needed him, living close to his memory.

Rachel was upset by Anna's refusal to accept the finality of Paul's absence. She'd felt to the very ends, the darkest extremes of her loss. After the funeral she'd packed up Jacob's clothes and given them away. She tried to do the same with Paul's things, which caused a rare argument. 'But he's dead!' Rachel snapped. The colour drained from Anna's face. She found it suddenly difficult to breathe and the sense of suffocation was made worse by spasms of dry sobbing that jerked through her for what seemed like hours. Rachel was terrified and sorry, but nothing she did could shake Anna out of her upset state. As if she were having a fit. In the end Rika Swanepoel was summoned and she took the pain away with a little coloured capsule from her pill-box.

Anna grew thin, too thin for her sturdy frame. When Rachel remarked on it one morning Anna merely frowned and looked down at her body with vague surprise, as if it were a thing she'd forgotten she was carrying around.

Joe was a more frequent visitor to Valley View Road in those difficult months. His investigations yielded nothing to shed light on the mystery of the nature of Paul and Jacob's mission and Anna soon learned to stop pressing him about it, lest he withdraw into silence. Nevertheless, it irked her that Joe seemed to think that Paul and Jacob had taken off on their own plak. With it came a suggestion of disorderly, ill-disciplined conduct, some private mission. Joe shook his head when she raised this. 'It's not like that. They died heroically in the course of the struggle. No one can ever question that.'

It was spring when Willem and Anna returned to Vryburg for the inquest, this time accompanied by Rachel and the boys and a box of papers that amounted to disappointingly little.

Circumstantially there was a great deal linking Captain Frans Nel not just to Jacob and Paul, but also to Officers Badenhorst and Curry and their so-called murder investigation. But that was all it was, circumstantial. Nevertheless, Nel, Badenhorst and Curry had been called as witnesses. That would afford Willem the opportunity to take a few shots.

They were met at the entrance to the courthouse by a small, but vocal crowd of supporters. The comrades swarmed around

Anna, Rachel and the boys, forming a toyi-toying guard of honour as they processed into the Chamber. The chanting and stomping echoed off the polished floor and the high ceiling, drumming in on Anna's ears. It was a relief when they fell back and took their places on the long wooden benches and the court echoed instead with the hush of anticipation.

Captain Nel shot Anna a brief nod by way of greeting as he walked in. His presence electrified her, pumped her full of adrenalin. Here was the man who'd killed them, she was sure of it and she wanted to fly at him, to tear off strips of his skin, gouge at his flesh. She wanted to make him pay with pain, with infinite, unending physical and mental torture. Instead Anna could only stare back at him, her eyes beaming disgust.

The other two cops shuffled past without a glance. Rachel stood with her head high, looking neither to the right nor the left. She wouldn't dignify those bastards with acknowledgement of their presence.

The morning was a stream of irritating legal formalities. Schalk van Straaten represented the State. Fresh from Stellenbosch University and glowing with a passion so fervent he would defend the Nationalist Party government wherever its opponents clamoured at the walls, even in far-flung Vryburg.

Van Straaten argued the internal ANC feud line. Lieutenant Badenhorst was his key witness. Badenhorst sat in the box and answered the Prosecutor's questions with the thoroughness of a robot. His thick fingers lay clasped in his lap, tufts of dark coarse hair sprang loose from under his collar.

Then it was Swanepoel's turn. He rattled Badenhorst's composure, but could not shake his story. It was the same with Curry, who held adamantly to the line. When at last the Captain took the stand Anna was hoping for some inconsistency, some sign in his face or his story that would amount to a confession of some sort, but he gave nothing away.

Nel admitted that he'd had dealings with both Paul and Jacob on more than a dozen occasions, but claimed to have had nothing to do with their deaths. He'd been playing golf with colleagues on the afternoon of the murders and they'd gone drinking in Joburg on Saturday night. A fistful of affidavits from cops he worked with supported the alibi.

The cover page of the folder in Nel's hands carried a simple title – 'Verslag oor 'n resgeneeskundige lykskouing'. 'Report on a Medicolegal post-mortem examination'. It was stamped with the insignia of the South African Police medical laboratories. Anna knew it almost inside out. It was on the 'lys warneemings', the schedule of observations, that she'd found herself fixating helplessly. 'Stomach and contents: contains partially digested food.' The phrasing stripped Paul of his personhood, reduced him to lists of decomposing matter and dissected body parts. 'Cause of death: bullet wound to the chest.'

Anna's own post-morten was clearer and simpler and more precise than the one offered by the South African Police medical laboratories. Cause of death: conscience.

Nel stepped down with barely a dent in his confidence. The smirk on his lips and the swagger in his step spoke of the smug certainty he felt about getting away with it, getting away with murder.

By afternoon and the tea adjournment Anna had had enough. Willem had warned her over and over of the disappointment she was likely to feel at the end of this process, nevertheless she was unprepared for the despair that had settled like lead in her gut.

The sign on the door of the gingham- and ribbon-curtained Tannie Hester Se Café opposite the courthouse read 'Europeans Only'. Rachel had walked in regardless, sweeping her sons in front of her. Willem Swanepoel followed without question, too tired to care. But Anna was in no mood to fight for her right to be served toasted chicken mayonnaise sandwiches next to the whites only Annual Crochet Club Committee tea, so she'd left Rachel and Willem to make their stand and wandered further up the street where she found a Steers and a few minutes of solitude.

Anna raked her fingers back through the thick black hair that she habitually wore in a wild cascade that fell to beneath her shoulderblades. Today it was scraped back and tied up in a band. Unframed, her beautiful face seemed unusually severe. Her milk-chocolate skin had drained to a muddy grey. There was also an unusual severity in her dress. Anna had chosen a conventional tailored blouse in sombre blue worn over a loose dark cotton print skirt that fell almost to her ankles. Smart as she was, she looked nothing like the mostly white people she'd passed on the street. The good citizens of Vryburg glared openly, narrowed eyes in hard faces, at the slick city crowd of lawyers and policemen and journalists who'd invaded their town for the terrorism inquest. Anna watched them watching her, chased by their long shadows in the late afternoon sun.

By the time she stood up to return to the court she'd begun to steel herself against a disappointing verdict. This was only the first round; it was going to be a long, long fight. But persistence and endurance were in her corner.

Out on the street the air was hot and dry and still. Anna found Rachel and her sons at a partially obscured corner table in the Tannie Se Café. They were sitting in quiet triumph over the remains of tea and Knickerbocker Glories. Willem sat amongst the debris, frowning at the open file in front of him. He closed the folder with a snap and stood up sharply. 'Let's do it!'

He put his arm around her as they walked. 'You know what's coming, don't you?' he murmured.

Anna gazed up at him, grateful for his presence and his candour. Then she nodded, 'Yep, I know what's coming.'

Willem looked amazing that day; concentration had burned lines into the skin at the corners of his eyes, somehow enhancing his boyish features. She was sure he hadn't failed to notice the brunette journalist among his admirers in the court, though she'd seen no sign of communication between them. Nevertheless Anna suspected that the woman's presence added fire to his argument. No wonder Rika had such a sadness about her.

They walked close together, Anna, Rachel, Willem and the boys. Pushing a path into the crowd that jostled at the entrance to the magistrate's court. The journalists and supporters and the idle curious gave way, opening out into a funnel of flashing cameras and grave faces through which they slowly made their way inside. The pressure of bodies was uncomfortable, a tug at Anna's elbow irritated her and she jerked her arm away, not wanting to face yet another hail of comforting words or unanswerable questions. Another slight squeeze on her upper arm and she wheeled around crossly, only to find herself face to face with Joe.

He'd shaved off all his hair and his scalp glistened like smooth, wet clay. His huge, hooded eyes glittered as he swayed and chanted with the crowd. Anna felt a shudder of happiness, a surge of strength at the sight of him, even though he showed not a flicker of recognition.

The clerk of the court called for all to rise. Anna stood very still, very composed. Inside her pocket she fingered the folded square of paper. 'Perfect love casteth out fear.' She was oblivious to the hustle around her, the shoving and bumping of the press and their photographers, the hushed speculation of journalists, the excited, urgent chatter of the comrades who had come to bear witness and to show the white judge and the policemen and the other liars that they were watching and waiting. That they *knew* the time would come when the tables were turned.

Anna watched the inquest magistrate trudge heavily across the polished wood floor. She searched his face for some sign of what was to come, some glimmer of the possibility of truth. Rachel stood next to her, her body melting against Anna's straight back and defiantly squared shoulders. Bram and Delarey stood in front of their mother, their faces sullen with confusion, crushed with grief.

A hush fell on the crowd as the magistrate began to speak in his now familiar gruff, ungrammatical English.

'In the case of Paul Alfred Lewis and Jacob Oliphant. Whether the deaths was brought about by any act or omission involving or amounting to an offence on the part of any person.'

The magistrate paused to clear his throat, watery eyes glancing up briefly from the paper in front of him.

'I find that Mr Lewis and Mr Oliphant was killed by person or persons unknown.'

It was over. The tiny gavel slammed hollowly into the carved wood of the bench, squashing speculation, truth and all that a just world might offer.

Anna stood very still amidst the pandemonium that erupted around her. Her fingers locked tightly in Rachel's, her eyes lost in the distance, ears deaf to the assault of questions, body braced against the shove of supporters. The tiny, empty phrase echoing through her head. 'Killed by person or persons unknown.'

There was no one to blame.

part two

If it were not for hope, the heart would break

THOMAS FULLER M.D.

1997

five

James leaned his temple against the cool metal windowframe of the black cab as it chugged through Hatton Cross. He was travelling into London from Heathrow and it felt odd that morning, seeing England again, but through the eyes of one returning after a long absence, almost the eyes of a stranger.

It was a cool spring morning. The trees so delicately sprinkled with buds, like a dusting of snow or icing sugar, fragile and lovely. You never saw that fragility, that prettiness in Johannesburg, where everything was brittle as matches and as beautiful as fire. Here the air tasted cool and wet and the green was intense. Huge white pom-poms of blossom encrusted the cherry trees, there was blossom in some of the hedgerows too. The colours were so *sombre* and fresh – greys and blues in tissuey layers, the colours of water. James smiled. Mist doesn't hold the mystery of a heat haze, he mused.

He thought of how, thirty years before, they had arrived – his frightened family – on a rain-slick, April morning. Vulnerable as babies. Tender with the pain of leaving home, still smarting from the shock of it. They were exiles, immigrants. Strangers in a cold land which gave little comfort when they needed so much. And yet this country took us in, he reflected, and we made it home and slowly it opened itself to us. Until South Africa felt like a distant dream and Britain became home.

His family was settled now. James even passed as a Brit – with his flattened-out London accent and his sharp, self-deprecating humour. But he wasn't comfortable here this morning. Something to do with the absence of light. Something to do with Alison.

Alison and Alan. How cosy their names sounded together. Cosy as snakes.

James winced at the mere thought of Alan Richter, his boss at the paper, the pudding-faced king of the foreign desk. Alison worked there too, editing the lifestyle magazine. She'd moved fast. When James first fell for her Alison was making tea and answering the phones, bursting with potential and tight button-down tops bunching around unbelievable breasts.

And now Alan, the man she left him for – it made James laugh, the sheer banality of it – was none other than the one destined for the top. The craven bastard. The loathsome, lumpy, tub-shaped, pasty-faced fuck.

When James left for his posting to South Africa it was Alan and Fiona, his wife, who'd thrown the farewell party, Alan who'd toasted James's future with the awesome Alison, who'd be following him to Africa shortly. It wasn't so long after that Richter had walked out on his wife and kids and their perfect Islington terrace and boldly crossed the river to live in sensational sin with none other than the supposedly Joburg and James-bound Alison.

It was months since that bombshell had dropped. James was thousands of miles away when it did. Nevertheless its obliterating, eviscerating effect was undiminished by distance. For several days he'd lain in the rubble of his life, paralysed by shock. Then he'd somehow lurched to his feet and into the bars and bathrooms of Joburg's singles scene, numbing himself with booze and cocaine and edgy, delinquent fucking. It seemed the glamorous, heartbroken thing to do. But the truth was it was mostly grubby and tedious and expensive, so it wasn't long before he staggered into the light again and back to work – his spine, his sanity.

That spring morning, as he travelled into London for the first time since Alison and he ended, James felt cut off and cold.

First stop was his parents' house in Battersea where he dropped off his bag and checked in briefly with his father. His mother was at work. They sat together in the comfortable basement kitchen. His father wasn't good at the emotional stuff, didn't really know what to say. 'I never liked Alison's writing,' he declared abruptly, shifting his head slightly to one side. 'Did I

48

ever mention that?' James chuckled. For his father there were few greater evils in the world than poor writing. 'No, Dad, you never did. But thanks. It's good to know.'

He took his father's car and set off for the house around lunchtime. His house. But no longer. He'd sold it to her, at a profit of course. Not quite as fat a profit as he'd have made if he'd put it on the market, but a decent one. At least he'd made one good investment in his life. Though Alan must have given her the cash. Alison couldn't afford it. He'd sold her a lot of the furniture too. All Habitat stuff, nothing old or sentimental.

Maybe he'd buy himself a place in central London when his posting was up. Maybe he'd never come back. Maybe he'd resign. Didn't know that he wanted to stay on at the paper, working with the smug Richter. Maybe he'd disappear. He had the money now, didn't need to work for a while.

The drive to Brixton was tortured with thoughts of all those Sunday afternoons they'd spent lounging around the Richters' dining table, discussing the paper, politics, the world with Alan and Fiona – the skinny, nervous creature who was a devoted mother to his two over-educated sons. All those times Richter had complimented Alison on her wonderful cooking, her *unusual* articles – in truth he was coveting her long neck, her wide, inviting hips, the breasts bobbing luxuriously beneath her clingy knit tops. The thought of Alan's fat fingers kneading her dark nipples, of his dirty fingernails tracing the edge of her always silky knickers, of Alison lifting her skirt, opening her legs for him on his desk – the place, she'd had the kindness to inform James, where she and Alan first 'made love' – made him sick.

Once he admitted them, thoughts of those two entwined in a torrid swirl of ambition and self-importance tormented James like a virus, endlessly mutating. His head swam with nauseating jealousy at all those afternoons and evenings and weekends when he'd called and called and there was no one home and she'd laughed it off, telling him she was in a meeting, or away on business, or with girlfriends, or working late, or out on a shoot. And all that time she was wriggling her hot hips astride the sweaty, putty-coloured, blob-like form of the Foreign Editor. Her lie. Her new life. Her so-called true lover. Now they slept together in the bed James had made.

And there was nothing left now but the desultory task of dividing possessions. James was in London to collect his things. The other way round, the upside-down version of how it was supposed to have been; Alison packing their place up to come out to an exciting new chapter of their life.

One-thirty on that overcast Saturday found James steering his way through the narrow streets of sturdy old terraces on Brixton Hill. He parked his father's ancient Volvo on Helix Road, in a residents' bay right outside the postbox-red front door.

Looking up at the little window in the peak of the roof, the window that looked onto the street from what was once the bedroom he shared with her, he wondered if she had changed anything. He hoped she had; he had no desire to re-enter a landscape that had once held such happiness and was now walled in pain.

At first James had refused to accept that she could do this to him. The disbelief subsided rapidly, after a ridiculous man-to-man call from none other than Richter himself. He was contrite and repulsively supercilious. 'You're the best man we've got,' he burbled. 'We can't let something like this come between us professionally.' What kind of psycho could imagine thinking such a thing, let alone actually uttering it? James had thanked him tersely, and then smashed the phone against the wall, sending shards of plastic into every corner of the office.

He couldn't believe the irony of it. The first time he'd committed to a place and to a person. The deliberate, step-by-step changes he'd made in his life to get to where he was with her – on the brink of something like a family, an ordinary life. He'd tried hard for her, made changes, narrowing things down in order to broaden himself as a person. To focus on just one other, instead of drifting from lover to lover, encounter to encounter, everything fitting in around his work. He'd been faithful to Alison too, in his way. There'd been the odd one-night thing – Bangkok, Kabul, far-away people and places, discreetly else-where, private and sealed off and disposable. How bitterly ironic that she was the one who'd wanted all this commitment and convention and that she was the one who broke it. He didn't hesitate to let her know.

Alison's response to his rage was – at best – childish

peevishness. At worst it was the mean-spirited cruelty of not sparing any of the unnecessary detail. Mostly she stuck to the love defence. Love conquers all, love cuts through all. You don't really know it until you know it, though you think you know it and all those people you thought you were in love with should willingly see that you weren't. All it had taken was for Alan to show her. All it had taken was a 'real' man to show her 'real' love. Her cruelty was so blinding it was almost innocent.

At least this trip had given him a pretext to hook up with a source he'd been tracking for a while. And the paper paid. Small mercies, he thought, as he sighed heavily and climbed out of the car.

Brace! Brace! Brace! The warning signal clanged through his head, barked in of all things an Australian accent, a bizarre flashback into a dizzying flight from Sydney to Gladstone on a long-ago assignment.

And suddenly there she was, standing in the doorway before him, drawing him in with that familiar look of sincere concern in her eyes. The self-assurance was still there too, that confidence she had in her sexiness, her ability to turn heads, to arouse hard-ons as she passed. She did it so knowingly.

She'd cropped her hair super short, a cute pixie cut for the comely bride-to-be. For she and Alan were planning to marry.

James didn't smile. He couldn't. 'Heeey!' she breathed, as if they were long-lost friends. 'Hello,' he growled. She put her hand on his shoulder, stared meaningfully into his eyes. He assumed she was satisfying herself that he'd not come looking for a fight. Alison hated a fight. She stood back to let him in. Patted him on the bum as he passed. 'You look great, Jim.' Giggled breathlessly as she closed the front door behind him. 'I'd almost forgotten how deadly that combination of blue eyes and black hair is.' James said nothing. He stalked down the all-too-familiar hallway, his head down, his hands shoved deep into his pockets.

The place was exactly the same.

In the kitchen she showed him where she'd prepared the boxes and a stack of lists that she wanted him to look over before they started. He sat down on the stool at the counter, sickened by her politeness. Inwardly gagging on memories that didn't fit with this new tone, he found her callous cheerfulness awful. At least she could have wrung her hands a bit, tugged at her hair, rent her clothes, something to show some remorse, or loss. But she didn't appear to notice his feelings at all, her face all smiles, her busy, let's do this like adults tone seemed numbingly insistent – let's not pretend that we never loved one another, that we were never friends.

It should have been a welcome change from her sullenness on the end of the phone, the tone that told him there was no tenderness left, just sulky acknowledgement and a desire to move on. But it wasn't. Somehow this was worse.

He got straight down to the packing. She trailed brightly after him, ducking close to make eye contact, chuckling with a self-conscious largesse when any book or CD or once-shared ornament, memento of a shared time, was disputed and she so generously wanted *him* to have it.

And then, when evening was closing in and the worst of the task – the division of the spoils – was almost over, she suckered him. It didn't take much, a glass of wine and the glow of a fire in the grate, sweet words and a sudden show of sadness. 'I will always love you, James,' she said, tears slipping out from beneath her long lashes, sliding silently down the lovely curve of her cheek.

'Bullshit,' he snarled.

She looked genuinely hurt. 'How can you say that?'

'It's over, Alison. In the rear-view mirror,' he snapped, the words grating against his throat nevertheless.

A quiet sob sprang from her, and somehow she managed to make the sound knowing and soulful and tragic all at once. And all at once he was helpless.

'Ali—' His voice caught and she knew he was cracking and that was when she came to him, wrapping her slender arms around him. And for a mad moment he let her, and leaned towards her. Then her face was close and her lips were on his and her leg curled around him and pulled him hard towards her. Her pelvis pressed against his, her tongue slid hotly across his lips. And James almost gave in.

Then something deep inside him recoiled. He pulled away like a spring opening, like a jumping jack. She staggered a moment, but quickly recovered, her lips wet and wide, her eyes hot with surprise and indignation. 'What are you doing?'

James felt his mouth crinkle with disgust and hurt. 'Leave me alone, Ali. Please, just leave me alone.' His eyes shimmered with contempt. She saw it. She breathed in sharply, eyes darkening, but she was tough, she took it. She could take anything. She could even take him.

The next day Alison wasn't there. She'd arranged with a neighbour for James and the shippers to be let in, so they could take the boxes away. Part of him was glad, but there was another part of him that still ached for a different ending.

Once all his things were gone James was itching to follow them, to get away from the thoughts of Alison that followed him through the city, lying in wait for him in the dark corners of restaurants, ready to ambush him at every turn.

He avoided the office, though he knew he'd have to stop by there at some point. He spent time with his family, visited galleries with his dad, snatched lunches with his mum in between her busy schedule of classes. He saw a couple of movies and he managed to track down this guy who might prove a valuable source in a story he thought he'd do back in South Africa. He had no idea if there was anything in it, but he might as well check it out, give it a try.

It was thoughts of Alison that preoccupied him as he swayed with the lurching motion of the tube on his journey to meet the potential source, staring vaguely out at the rushing darkness of the tunnel on the way to Earl's Court. She had telephoned that morning, sounding hurt. She wanted to talk. Could they meet? Just one last time. Make it a proper ending, a dignified one. He didn't see why not, he'd grumbled. He'd sounded more indifferent than he felt, but once it was said there was no taking it back. She said it was difficult for her to take the time, Alan didn't like her seeing him, but she could get away for a quick lunch. 'Can't,' he'd said. 'I'm meeting a source.' There was a long silence on the end of the line. 'You always are, James,' she breathed quietly. It stung. That old accusation – his work always took precedence over her and their life together. 'I'm sorry I hurt you in the way that I did,' she went on calmly, without malice or self-pity. 'But it's not good enough to believe that I'm the only one who's responsible for the way things have worked out. I never came first for you, baby. No woman ever has. Some day you'll see it. I just hope it's not too late when you do.' He was stunned into silence. She'd waited a while and then hung up, without a goodbye.

James was left with an unpleasant sense of disquiet. Perhaps she had gone as far as an affair with Richter, he mused, to get a rise out of him at last. If that was her plan it had certainly worked, but surely not even she could have been so calculating.

It was true that he took an uncompromising view of his work, that he never let anything get in the way of a story, that nothing would stand between him and the relentlessness of his assignments and deadlines.

Was it possible he'd made a mistake? That he'd asked too much of her? He always believed that he'd met his match in Alison, that she was as driven, if not tougher than he was. And he'd given up a lot for her, a whole rootless way of life for the cosiness of coupledom and a neat little semi in South London. Why didn't she understand that? Surely she saw that. This was her rationalisation, her own refusal to take responsibility for what she had done, passing the buck onto him. Bitch.

He found himself bent double on the bench of the tube train, his head between his knees, his fists clenched against his gut. The oddness of his position struck him in a rush and he sat up. He felt a little dazed, hadn't realised how deeply he'd been lost in thought. He studied his hands, lying open on his lap, the palms streaked with red where he'd dug his fingernails too hard into the skin.

Then the tube lurched to a stop. He stood up to get out, but the station was an unfamiliar one. Dammit! He'd missed his stop. He'd come to in the wastes of Ravenscourt Park, and stood on the platform in a light drizzle, cursing his stupidity. Cursing Alison who, on top of everything else, was about to make him late. And he couldn't be. He could not lose Groenewald.

He broke into a run, racing desperately out of the tube station, down unfamiliar, empty streets. One or two cars passed, but no taxi. James stopped, catching his breath on the corner, his gaze swinging wildly from one empty end of the road to the other. Shit! Then, from the street behind him, the familiar thrum of a diesel engine. Incredibly, the cab was free! He almost threw himself into its path.

He arrived on Earl's Court Road with not even a minute to spare, shoved a handful of bills through the taxi driver's window and dashed into the road, tacking dangerously through the traffic to cross the street. He strolled breathlessly into Nando's at precisely the appointed time.

The place was busy, but not packed. He had some idea of who he was looking for. The man who called himself Mr Groenewald must have been in his late forties, maybe early fifties. From their conversations on the phone James pegged him as a beefy guy, Lowveld farming stock, bred big and hard. From the descriptions of others, James had gathered that Mr Groenewald was also no oil painting and that he was notable for his unusually large and exceptionally slender ears.

So far there was no sign of such a man.

James bought himself a coffee and slid onto a bench at the side of the shop, from where he commanded a good enough view of the comings and goings of the place and would easily be seen. Their meeting point struck James as faintly silly. This source had laid such an elaborate smokescreen, believing his life to be in serious danger, only to end up choosing the London outlet of a South African fast-food chain. Something familiar to Groenewald, he assumed, as he sipped at his coffee.

The minutes ticked by; he watched people come and go. No one approached or even glanced in his direction.

This story James was chasing might or might not turn into a good one. More interesting for the local press in South Africa than for the international, but a big one nevertheless, if it led where he thought it would. It had started as a follow-up on a series of cash-in-transit robberies that had left a grisly trail of corpses. The three security guards shot dead in the most recent heist were killed with tracer bullets, the kind used by marksmen; this was not the ammo of trigger-happy amateurs. They'd walked away with a cool twelve million in that operation. There was nothing slapdash about the robberies; they were planned with military precision.

James believed the thieves were not only highly trained, but also highly connected. It was possible they were cops, or military, or former cops joined up with former soldiers.

Mr Groenewald had promised to provide information that would show just how high up their connections went. Groenewald was a former Security Policeman. Before he'd fled the country, fearing who knew what, his beat was the Right wing and his speciality bomb disposal. He'd been assigned to an undercover job infiltrating a car-theft syndicate run by a group of uniform cops. Several months later it became clear to both sides that he was riding a fine line, that he no longer knew which side he was on. The gangsters bust him first and he ran, skipping the border into Zimbabwe, and ending up in England where he lived on the run, always in fear of his life. James felt his paranoia was exaggerated. It seemed more than unlikely that anyone would come this far to silence some dried-up ex-cop, but then who was he to say? There were some strange and frightening people in the world.

When half an hour had gone by James began to assume the meeting had fallen through, that Groenewald was a hoax. The only other customer who'd been sitting in there as long as he had was a painfully thin woman, probably in her fifties, positioned with her back against the far wall, keeping what seemed to James to be an unnecessarily vigilant eye on the door and onto the street beyond. But no Mr Groenewald.

James stood up to leave. Oh well, there were other Groenewalds, he thought to himself as he pulled open the door and walked out into the rain. Not three steps on he felt a hand grip his arm and turned to find himself facing the anxious woman. 'You Mr Kay?' she asked hoarsely. He stared down at her bony fingers on his sleeve, then into her weary eyes. He nodded. 'Come with me,' she said.

James followed her into a bookshop a short way down the road. She skittered along and across aisles until she found a quiet corner. She had chosen, to James's amusement, the self-help section.

At last she faced him. Pale and nervous, her fingers played on the strap of her bag. She kept looking around, but there was no one showing any unusual interest. 'My husband sends his apologies,' she murmured, fingers flicking the spines of a row of paperbacks in front of her. 'Aah,' James said, rubbing his chin. Wondering if this meant that there was more or less information than he'd been promised. Thinking that he wanted to get in a movie that afternoon, maybe even go into the office at last. However James sensed the proximity of Mr Groenewald. A prickling sensation between his shoulders told him the ex-cop was watching from somewhere close by. He turned to scan the bookshop, but no one caught his eye. He turned back to the woman. It didn't matter where the guy had concealed himself; it was so pointless, so absurd amongst the indifferent bustle of Earl's Court Road on a spring morning.

'Who's your husband scared of?' he asked quietly.

'He's not' – her voice quivered, so she paused – '*scared*, so much as careful.'

James shrugged, wanting to get this over with.

'He's not a violent man, my husband, not by nature,' she stammered.

She wouldn't need to say it if it were true, he thought. As far as James was concerned bloodlust was hardwired into every human being. That and greed – the desire for power, sex, adulation – whatever got you high.

'Did he give you anything for me?'

She nodded slightly and reached down into the shapeless sack of the bag that she wore close against her body. From it she produced a thick folder, dog-eared with handling, bound with frayed pink rubber bands. She held onto it for a moment. James slid his hands into his pockets, non-committal.

Her eyes flicked down and she took note of his action, aware that he might walk away, that nothing would stop him doing so. She didn't want to have come here for nothing. This wasn't about the good of the world and the good of the country. This transaction was about money.

'Where did you get that, Mrs Groenewald?'

She glanced up at him, a slight smile at the edges of her mouth. Perhaps it was the relief that he hadn't completely lost interest.

'My husband took it when he left the police. Insurance.'

'And now it's time to cash in?'

She nodded, her fingers fiddling with the rubber bands around the file, eyes flicking anxiously all over the place. 'He said you'd bring something too.'

James nodded. Not sure if he was being given a dud, and happy to let her sweat while he sized her up.

He pulled an envelope from his pocket and handed it to her. She almost snatched it from him. He took the folder and began to open it, but she stopped him, clutching at his arm. 'You have to go Mr Kay. We mustn't stand around here. It's not safe.'

James frowned, unconvinced. 'How do I know that this is what he promised?'

'He just said to trust him. What you need is in there.'

James sighed and shrugged as he tucked the folder under his arm.

He left quickly marching out to gulp the spring air, to leave the claustrophobic, pathetic encounter behind him. There'd been a time when he would have waited and followed her; curious to know what happened next but those games no longer interested him. He got his adrenalin rushes elsewhere.

James went directly from Earl's Court Road to the office. There wasn't much to pack up; his place was only there for times like this, trips to London, home to touch base. He took a box from Janet, the receptionist who had the tact and kindness to greet him sharply, as she had always done and not to cast the sympathetic, embarrassed look other colleagues he encountered had. He'd emptied the last drawer of stationery ends and other junk into the bin when he looked up to see Richter. The man's sweaty little hands tapping nervously on the desktop.

'Alan,' James sighed, relieved that the encounter was occurring at last, eager to get it over with and move on.

Richter looked both sheepish and panic-stricken. A ridiculous grin stretched across his lips. 'I'm sorry, mate. About how things have worked out.'

James couldn't suppress a smile. He shook his head. 'Forget about it. I'm gone anyway.'

Richter's smile faded. His fat face looked puzzled.

'Here. My resignation.'

James presented him with the brimming dustbin. Richter took it and held onto it like a life buoy. Then James slung his jacket over his shoulder and marched for the door. The Foreign Editor followed him, clasping the dustbin in his paws, trailing paper clips and balled-up post-its. 'James! You can't do this. I mean you mustn't. For a *woman*—'

James turned turned to face him. 'This is for me, Richter. I'm done here. Enjoy Alison.' Then he spun on his heels and left the building, feeling a crazy kind of freedom. The freedom that comes with shattered certainties.

Hours later, as the damp evening closed in, James sat brooding at the desk in his old attic room at his parents' house, his laptop open in front of him, the screensaver bouncing and swirling off the edges of the monitor.

Scattered on every surface were pages from the folder he'd purchased earlier. Its contents were stunningly uninteresting. Mr Groenewald turned out to be a sleazy chancer who'd discovered he could make a few bucks out of some useless papers he'd picked up.

The information, what little there was, had nothing whatsoever to do with the cash-in-transit heists. There were one or two intriguing scraps, but nothing truly significant. Ah, you win some, you lose some, James thought. The encounter with the source had been eclipsed anyway by his visit to the office and the elation he'd felt as he strode out of the building.

James stared out at the rooftops, at chimney after chimney after chimneystack and in the dim distance the gloomy peaks and towers of the city. The night was dark and wet. He missed Johannesburg, the gritty, glittering heart of South Africa, the city of gold. The day he left was a gorgeous, sunny, winter's one. It was always sunny there, relentlessly, glaringly sunny in the Highveld, even when it was cold. He longed for the light he'd become accustomed to.

A knock on the door brought him back to Battersea. James turned to see his mother leaning against the frame, her eyes narrow with concern. 'Have some supper with us?' She smiled a quizzical smile, searching his face, knowing that no matter how much pain her son felt, he wouldn't share a stitch of it. 'Dad's cooking,' she added reassuringly. James gazed back at her fondly, and the tiny lines at the corners of his eyes creased into the slightest smile. They always teased her about her food, yet the truth was she was a perfectly decent cook. His dad had flair though, because he enjoyed taking the time. To his mum it was just a chore.

'I've resigned from the paper.'

Her eyebrows shot up in surprise, but she showed no signs of disapproval.

'What're you going to do?'

'Go back to Joburg. Pick up some work there. Hang out. I've got enough cash to drift for a while.'

'You won't have to do that, you'll be snapped up in a second.' Then she smiled, her eyes glittering with what might have been tears.

'What?'

She folded her arms across her chest. 'It's funny, that's all. It was me who wanted to go home all those years. And now it's you who's going back.'

He nodded, smiling too. 'For a while . . .'

'I'm glad. It feels right,' she said, and then she turned in the doorway and slipped out. 'See you in a sec.'

As James gathered up the papers a group of names scrawled on the back of a typed page next to a list of numbers caught his eye. There were five of them, four he didn't recognise. But the last one he did. Paul Lewis. He frowned, his attention caught. Paul Lewis? What could his name be doing here? Maybe it was another Paul Lewis, nothing to do with the martyred hero of the South African struggle. Maybe it was one and the same. Curious, James thought. That was one of the famous and still unsolved murders of the apartheid era. He'd check it out when he got back. He shuffled the documents back into their folder, closed it and went downstairs to join his family for supper.

six

Anna slipped gradually out of the feathery embrace of a dream, slowly becoming aware of light filtering softly through the curtains and the busy ticking of the clock at her bedside. Her eyes shivered beneath the delicate skin of her eyelids. She was vaguely conscious of wishing she could remain for ever caught in that delicious, all too brief, in between moment of floating up from slumber towards the starkness of day. She was dimly aware too of some still formless anticipation at the coming of this particular day. It had been a night of restless dreaming and sweet remembering and she carried that sweetness with her as she ascended drowsily towards waking.

Strange, she thought, how life spirals. How you spool out and away from an event for so long and then, without warning, life has you spinning tightly back towards it, so that you are for ever circling it. Anna stood up and padded across the carpet. Reflected in the long mirrors of the cupboard doors was a striking woman, not conventionally beautiful, but attractive. Ten years hadn't changed her much. Her once wild hair was tamed into an elegant, loose wave that curled in against her collarbone. Her large eyes had the same curious and deceptive tranquillity about them; her nose was small and unremarkable while her mouth was full and sweetly curved. Hers was a face made lovelier by age. But there was something about Anna that was wounded, something in the dark depths of her eyes that spoke of her scars, but dimly, like the shapes of stones glimpsed on a riverbed beneath the froth and flow of water.

Anna went into the bathroom, turned on the shower taps and stepped under the jet of hot water. She tilted her face upward into the stream, closed her eyes and succumbed to the sensation of heat and liquid coursing down her skin.

She stood there for some time and as she did so the scent and sense of a dream she'd had of Paul came back to her. It was a dream she'd had before, but not in a long while. It was as if he'd visited deliberately that night, perhaps to bring her courage on a day when she would need it. The dream came to her with vivid clarity now, as if the scent of him clung to her still.

They'd found each other at sea, in a storm so violent Anna could barely distinguish between water and air. At one point, on her way to him, she was in a life raft which was mostly below the surface of the waves, and she'd had to breathe through a tube sticking out of the plastic sheeting that enclosed her. She wasn't scared – she was too focused on her destination to be panicked by the journey. Paul was waiting on a larger craft, which Anna boarded easily, despite the heaving sea. He was sitting in a chair wrapped in what looked like a sleeping bag, but he shed that as he stood up to greet her. Underneath he was wearing a bulky red sweater. Anna noticed that his hair was thinner and finer than the last time, but still curly blond. He held her to him and she pressed her face into his sweater, hard against his chest. His body felt firm and strong – it was not the body of a dead man. He had laughed when she remarked on that. And then they sat and talked, with all the ease of old, good friends.

As the conversation wore on and the time passed he seemed to grow more frail and Anna noticed there were bones sticking out of him. When Paul gesticulated broadly to emphasise a point, a piece of his skeleton snapped off. His eyes flicked down to where the bone had fallen and he tutted irritably, but didn't pick it up. It distracted him only momentarily, as a broken pen nib would the flow of writing. He didn't seem to see it as consequential, though it worried Anna terribly and she reached down for the piece of skeleton. Tied to it was a tag with a label, but she didn't know what it said because she couldn't read the writing.

Water thudded against Anna's forehead, drummed on her skull. She stepped out of the jet of the shower and leaned against the cool, slippery tiles. She couldn't remember any of what they had said to one another, just remembered the sense of his company. It was bittersweet, because she knew their time was limited and pieces of him were breaking off.

In the bedroom Anna stood before her mirror, slowly pressing and sliding a towel along the length of her hair. Thinking about him calmed her. It brought him close again, where he belonged.

Anna pulled the towel off her head. She was standing alone in the bedroom of her new home in Johannesburg, a decade away from Paul's death, but she saw him as clearly as if he were standing before her now and she smiled, recalling words from a speech he'd made to their imaginary children after the first time they had made love: 'Our eyes met across a crowded funeral. And the rest . . . is as they say.' The rest is as they say, she thought, repeating the phrase to herself.

Sadness mixed suddenly with a curl of lust. Like sand with sugar. Anna wanted very much to cry, but she couldn't. The tears got stuck, as they always did, somewhere in the lower part of her throat. She turned away from the mirror, flinging the towel onto the bed as she crossed the room. She opened a door of the cupboard and slid her hand inside, amongst the tailored suits and elegant blouses of her new life.

Anna pulled out a light brown trousersuit and a cream shirt. She dressed quickly, then glanced over the tray of make-up on her dressing table and picked out a lipstick that she stashed, along with a hairbrush, inside a small bag. Finally she turned, as she did every morning, to the long shelf beneath the window, to Paul. She scanned the frozen moments of him collected inside all those frames and she smiled back at him, at once both grateful and sad. He still gave her strength, even from all that time ago. The past was all she had now that her future with him was dead. The home they would have made together, the work they would have done, the children they'd joked about and wanted, all those hopes and possibilities were murdered with him.

Anna knew that to be trapped in the past was to be choked by shadows. She knew that to live there was to dwell in a chamber of echoes ringing with lost voices, hollow with loneliness, dark with the howling of the moment when time stopped, when life became too bewildering to allow for motion towards any kind of future. For those who never wake from the past, life is a coma in which the present is ever receding, as the past should be, and the past is a painful, present haunting. For some, for just a few, surfacing does come at last, and with it the incredible joy of light after a long, suffocating swim through darkness.

Anna strolled into the kitchen, flipped on the radio to SAFM's morning news round-up and filled the kettle at the sink. It soothed her to look around her house and out onto her garden. Beyond it the suburbs shimmered in the winter sun and the city rose like a concrete ant-heap. She'd bought the place for the view and had slowly turned the ugly little cottage into a pleasant, light space. The rooms were furnished simply, with few pieces and neutral colours revealing a certain ascetism in her taste. What she did own in abundance was books, which lined the walls from floor to ceiling.

She took her coffee into the living room and sat down into the deep sofa to gather herself for the coming day. She was due to testify that morning before the long-awaited and much-vaunted and criticised Truth and Reconciliation Commission.

Anna was all too aware that the Truth Commission was more about acknowledgement, about jogging the collective conscience than it was about thorough investigation. However, it just might inspire someone to come forward, might jerk an amnesty application out of one of the killers, or at least someone who knew them. The Truth Commission's Investigative Unit simply didn't have the capacity to initiate the kind of thorough checking out that Paul and Jacob's case required. So it was not a new investigation she expected from this, but rather the publicity and the recognition for Paul and Jacob that might awaken consciousness or memory in someone who could shed light on the mystery.

It was hard to explain, this need of hers to know, to put a face to Paul's killer. It wasn't about revenge; she had no desire to enter the killer's life as intimately as he had entered hers. It was about a promise she'd made to Paul. And it was about understanding, explaining the seemingly inexplicable, about imposing an order on the chaos and madness of what had happened. The need to know was overwhelming, had been all consuming, had even alienated friends and family who wanted to leave the past behind and move on into the present. But Anna couldn't let it go, even now, ten years down the line.

In spite of her fixation and in spite of friends' concerns and criticism Anna herself knew she *had*, slowly, emerged into the present. It was a place where she lived precariously, but with a greater measure of contentment than she'd known in a long, long while.

Rachel arrived a predictable quarter of an hour late and in an equally predictable hurry. She entered Anna's house as she always did, swamping the place in a rush of laughter and scattered energy. 'Lekker suit, babes. You look gorgeous!'

'You sound surprised,' Anna teased.

Rachel planted her heavily ringed hands on Anna's shoulders and looked into her eyes. 'You ready for this?' she asked sternly. Anna blinked, tried for a light tone. 'You're late. Drink your coffee.' Rachel's eyes narrowed regarding her friend with inescapable concern.

Anna looked away, aware that her evasiveness was noted and might well be challenged. 'Where's Joe?' Her voice failed to hit the careless note she wanted.

'He sent his car and a driver, said to tell you he was sorry, but he'd meet us there. I said I'd believe that when I saw it.' Rachel snapped out her response in the matter-of-fact tone of the headmistress character she'd become.

Anna frowned, unexpectedly disappointed. 'Where is he?'

Rachel shrugged. 'You're asking *me*?'

Anna sighed, pushing her hair behind her ears. Joe and Paul were so alike in some ways, always one step ahead on the road to the shining future. It was impossible to keep up. But he'd show up, he always did. In his own time.

There was a simplicity to Rachel's life that Anna admired, coveted even. Unlike Anna, Rachel lived overwhelmed by the big things, by the hugeness of the internet, of information and technology and globalisation and all the problems of her people and her country, so focused down and walked her path, not sure any more of all the old ideologies that had sustained her beliefs, certain only of some simple, core values of fairness and openness and service. Otherwise it was all too big. And Rachel had the comfort of Temba. There was solidity in that, in her family and her plans to marry and have more children, that Anna couldn't help wanting.

Rachel took the mugs into the kitchen, rinsed them under the tap and put them neatly on the draining board. Droplets of water flew from her fingers as she shook her hands dry and then she smiled her beautiful, gap-toothed smile. 'I'm scared too,' she said and with that Rachel grabbed her bag, planted a reassuring kiss on Anna's cheek and swept her out towards the car.

Driving out of the city that morning the sky was the dirty colour of industrial pollution that often hangs over Johannesburg, the smog that makes for such spectacular sunsets. How things had changed for them, Anna reflected as Rachel barked directions at their nervous driver, a pimply white kid, straight out of school, who'd never been to Soweto before. Here they were, being driven in a government car to attend a hearing of a Presidential Commission where their sacrifices would be honoured. It was a far cry from their lives as pariahs, enemies of the state, terrorists even. Lord, they'd become veritable pillars of the establishment. How Paul would have laughed – Anna a senior civil servant in government and Rachel, working for the Trade Unions, but heading up a training college. And Joe a policeman, Assistant Commissioner on top of that.

Anna had moved to the Department of Safety and Security straight from the Union, brought in by the new Minister who was a long-time comrade. She'd arrived at Wachthuis, the SAPS headquarters in Pretoria, hating the police. Wachthuis itself positively reeked of the all too recent past, when the cops were the boot boys of apartheid. Anna, like many of the former underground people who were moved into the top echelons of management there, saw the entire force as corrupt, incompetent and politically dubious. Four years later nothing was so clear. Now she was defensive of the Service, sometimes even of the formerly bad guys who'd survived the transition. Now Anna felt impeded by the public and media perception of the police as corrupt and evil and was angered at the way the press overlooked and sometimes even undermined some of the good work that *was* being done. The task of transforming this creature was enormous and Anna was frustrated, like so many others, at the miserable help and support given to public servants.

She had arrived with the noblest of concerns – the establishment of a human rights culture, increased transparency in government, improved community services and all that. But the inertia of the beast that she was now a part of had gradually eroded her high hopes. Nevertheless Anna refused to let frustration and disillusionment get her down. She was determined to see every problem as a challenge, every setback as a lesson. This tireless enthusiasm of hers attracted, inevitably, a great deal of extra responsibility.

She ran Human Resources, but beyond her essential duties of recruitment and people management, it also fell to Anna to keep an eye on operations for the Minister, brief him, write speeches for him and deal with management issues around him. She was stretched to her limits. Her personal life had narrowed to virtually nothing, perhaps two or three hours a week of meditative oblivion at the gym and one night a week, if she was lucky, with Rachel. Time with Joe was more intermittent. They often saw one another in the course of the working day as they had offices in the same building, but time alone and for themselves was rare. Truth was, that suited her. Anna's life was too full to allow for much reflection on it.

Staring out at the implacable ordinariness of Johannesburg's suburbs she was struck afresh by how little the city itself had changed. People still lived on quiet streets behind high walls in houses with names like 'Aloe Brae' and 'Jacaranda Haven'. Soon they'd be gliding into the township from the no man's land that apartheid's town planners had created as a buffer between what had been the white and black zones of the city.

Anna leaned back against the seat. Shadows strobed across the interior of the car like the reflections of waves underwater. Sunlight caught on the chrome knob of the door lock and spun around, like a tiny disco ball; it mesmerised and drew her down into the tunnel of remembering. How she longed to be uncoupled from her past, to slip loose of all the burdens of memory. Yet memory was her lifeline. Letting go of the past meant letting go of Paul and she couldn't do that. So Anna kept the pain in a pocket of her mind, somewhere she could touch it whenever she needed to, just to know he was still there.

seven

It was nearly nine as their car approached Regina Mundi Cathedral in Rockville, Soweto. The fog of wood and coal smoke that clings to the rooftops at night still clouded the sky over the township. They bounced along the rutted, muddy road on the final stretch, skirting a group of children playing on an old BMX bicycle, discarded no doubt by the children of a white family one of their mothers worked for in the suburbs. The corner they turned resembled every other major intersection in the township, where men and women sat by stalls selling everything from second-hand exhaust pipes to haircuts, drugs, guns, CD players and dental treatment.

Stepping out of the car, Anna breathed in the familiar smell of fires and winter. It was warm in the sun, but she pulled her coat around her as she looked up at the peaked façade of the Cathedral spiking the dirty sky. Regina Mundi lacks the proportions or grandeur of a great cathedral. It is not an old building and its simplicity and lack of finish reveals the poverty of the community it was built by. Yet in its short life the Cathedral has witnessed the most terrible and the most transcendent acts of the human spirit – at least as much, if not more so, than its grander and older European counterparts. It has been a place of sanctuary, of mourning and of celebration. On this particular day the Truth and Reconciliation Commission banners flapping at the entrance announced that Regina Mundi was also a place of remembering.

This was a Human Rights Violations hearing, where victims or their survivors came to tell their stories and to ask the Commission for truth and reparation. The Commissioners had become a travelling circus, moving week by week, sometimes day by day, setting up in town halls and churches and school gymnasiums in every corner of the country. Every day the Commission sat, collecting the stories of the victims of gross human rights violations committed in the name of the struggle both for and against that terrible, racist regime called apartheid. There were no confrontations between victims and perpetrators at such events; those would come later during the amnesty proceedings.

So far no one had applied for amnesty for the Mafikeng Road Murders.

Anna's heart lifted when she caught sight of Joe. He was standing in the massive doorway, deep in conversation with a young woman Anna didn't recognise. As always he was restless with energy, shifting back and forth from one foot to the other as he talked, hands stuffed into the pockets of his long, tailored charcoal grey coat. He seemed larger than life, though he wasn't particularly tall, just a half-inch or so less than six feet. It was his broad shoulders, like a quarterback's, atop those narrow hips and slender legs that gave him the look of restrained power that held people in such awe. He could carry the world on those shoulders, hold anything in that wide embrace.

He looked younger than his thirty-seven years, with his beautiful Tswana features and shining, shaven head. Sometimes Anna watched him in the early mornings, unfolding a newspaper on the floor while he talked to her, head bent, shaving his scalp in careful, easy circles, the tiny ends of his hairs falling like iron filings onto the paper.

'Heita!' Rachel called out to him. Joe turned towards them, the coat swung elegantly and his eyes lit up as he saw them. Anna, grinning now, walked into his warm embrace.

The familiar pressure of his hand against the curve of her back and his arm beneath her jacket, encircling her waist, was unexpectedly powerful. She looked away, swallowing emotion and trying to hide the shock of sudden, welling tears. 'You crying, baby?' He sounded as surprised as she felt as he slipped his thumb under her chin, tilting her face towards his. Anna shook her head. 'Dunno. But I'm glad you're here.'

'Of course I'm here.' He stroked the tears away with his fingertips and she pressed her face into his coat.

Anna knew herself well enough to know her defences were so strong she could conceal her vulnerability even from herself, but she hated it when any emotion burst through and she felt like she was losing control. She breathed into the soft wool, breathing in the calming scent of him.

Joe was the third corner of the triangle that was Anna's life after Paul. And now the three of them held one another, remembering the two who *should* have been with them. Knotted into that tight embrace on the steps of Regina Mundi Cathedral was a decade of pain and loss and triumph. They were the three who'd survived.

Somewhere nearby a camera whirred and the pop of a flash startled Anna out of the embrace. A couple of press photographers and a TV cameraman had materialised all too close to them in the chilly shade. Anna pulled away from Joe, covering her feelings with a wan smile. 'Sharp suit. Not bad for a policeman,' she teased quietly, patting Joe's coat, smoothing down the soft collar. 'Don't ever accuse me of letting the side down!' Joe boomed. He was already smiling for the cameras. 'Morning, gentlemen!'

The journalists pounced. The camera and radio microphones nudged closer and flashes flared in Joe's eyes.

'Joe! The N1 cash-in-transit heist yesterday. Any comment?'

Anna and Rachel stepped away, back into the darkened doorway.

They caught sight of Temba jogging across from the parking lot, cameras and lenses jiggling across his torso, towards the impromptu press conference gathering around Joe. Rachel waved and Temba grinned briefly back at her, then cocked his camera and went to work. Anna shivered at the electricity she saw in that moment between them. Temba was tall and skinny, the opposite of small and comfortably padded Rachel. He wore his hair short, tight against his head and framed his sweet mouth in a small, neat goatee. His front teeth were crossed slightly, but there was always a smile on his lips and a gargantuan laugh waiting to bubble out of him.

Anna looked at her friend who was shining with love and she

found she had to look away. The intimacy was too sharp, too excluding, too redolent – for Anna – of another intimacy long lost. She turned her gaze instead towards the crowd around Joe.

'Is it true that armour-piercing rounds were fired?'

'Does the use of AK47s not suggest that there's a possible link to former MK soldiers?'

'Is it true that Army and Police issue R4 and R5 assault rifles were also used?'

Joe put up his hands, waiting for silence. He smiled as the questions died and there was quiet. It was at moments like this that he came alive, his eyes flashing with a powerful mixture of humour and gravity, his voice pitched perfectly to captivate. He was the consummate politician and Anna, like everyone else, had no doubt that his destiny was the highest. She felt a surge of pride and love for him.

So different to the kind of love she saw between Rachel and Temba and to the kind of love she'd had with Paul. Her love for Joe was the love of a sister for a brother, with a sexual twist. A different category, another universe entirely. It had to do with comfort and connection in an otherwise lonely world.

'I simply wish to say this. We *deeply* regret the deaths of the two security guards in yesterday's cash-in-transit heist. We would like to extend our sympathy to the families of the victims, of the slain guards – and to assure them that we are doing everything we can to catch the perpetrators of this ghastly deed. Of course I cannot disclose the details or present status of our enquiries, but I would like to state—'

At this he paused dramatically, his eyes focusing on the distance, his hands slipping back into the pockets of his elegant coat. He chose his words deliberately, speaking in a quiet, measured tone.

'We *do* have *information* that a disgruntled group of former Defence Force members, men whose special units have been disbanded now that they are no longer required to do apartheid's dirty work – and I refer here to those from the 121 and 32 Battalions as well as Koevoet and even the CCB – are involved and—'

The print journalists scribbled furiously, barely keeping up.

'—these are people who were promised impossible things by

their paymasters in the previous regime and who now feel badly done by, so we believe that they are bringing weapons into the country on supply lines established during the border wars, from Mozambique and Angola where these former soldiers have access to vast arms caches.'

Then he waved at a journalist, a scruffy youngish white guy who had just arrived and was scrambling for his notebook.

The thing about the cash-in-transit heists, as Anna knew all too well, was that the police were out-manned, out-gunned and outwitted by the gangsters. While Joe talked the talk with the press, Anna knew that arrests were nowhere near. The freeway heists that were the subject of Operation King-Size had been carried out with military precision; the shooting was exact, the planning immaculate and the robberies were accomplished in less than five minutes. That didn't mean, however, that the thieves were former SADF. Those disgruntled former soldiers were simply Joe's theory, his invention, just as the statement at the impromptu press conference was political point-scoring to make the police look good. Anna knew that it was important to give the journalists something to run with and it wasn't exactly a lie. None of it was a lie. In fact Joe's theory was perfectly plausible. But that was all it was, a plausible theory.

Nevertheless, if anyone was a match for these gangs, it was Joe.

Joe was the country's youngest Assistant Police Commissioner. In the old days he would have been called General, it was the same rank. Unlike most former ANC and MK operatives who had been absorbed into the National Intelligence Agency or Secret Service, Joe had requested deployment into Police Intelligence. That group was divided into two – Crime Intelligence and Internal Security. Crime Intelligence was where Joe had been sent. He ran a special unit tasked with cracking organised crime – the car syndicates, gun smugglers and drug gangs amongst others. It was rough, nasty work, but full of the complex webs Joe loved to disentangle.

'So the guns supplied by the previous regime to their surrogate armies during the destabilisation of the region are now turned inwards, on us. More than that I cannot say at this stage, but I can assure you that the police will not be outdone. Arrests are imminent.'

With a weary smile Joe was finished. Reporters gabbled, showering more questions on him, cameras flashed, but Joe was already moving away from the jostle, his arms raised, palms open, eyes shining.

The journalists hung back respectfully as Joe turned towards Anna and Rachel with a determination that said, *here* are my priorities, right now. 'You all right?' he asked quietly. They nodded, their pride in him evident. Then he opened his arms wide to gather them to him and together the three of them walked into the Cathedral.

eight

James stood at his front door, immobilised by the stuff in his hands – coffee cup and notepad in one, house and car keys in the other. Okay. Get it together now. He slugged back the cool dregs of the coffee, put the mug down on the ironing board, then slipped the notebook into the deep side pocket of his pants and was at last free to unlock the door. Walking across the stoep he tripped on a broken slat in the floor and cursed himself for the carelessness with which he treated his home, a crumbling semi on a jacaranda-lined avenue of otherwise bright and beautifully renovated Melville cottages.

There was always something that kept him too busy to attend to the work needed to make it liveable in and meanwhile the place was disintegrating around him. Shit, I'm gonna have to do something about this, he told himself as he skirted the hole in the path. As if to drive home the point the front gate simply would not shift when he pulled at it. The lock dangled mournfully from a single screw, as it had done for months now, so that couldn't be the problem. Looking down James realised the obstacle was a wad of post and papers which had fallen through the mail slot and never been picked up. He scooped up the mess and could see at a glance it was mostly junk.

He was heavily targeted by the burgeoning security and armed-response industry. Apparently fired up by the shocking lack of razor wire or high walls around his home they'd showered him with fliers exhorting him not to become a statistic, urging him to invest in the latest gadget to protect himself against the muggings, car hijackings, rapes, burglaries that were simply part of life in Johannesburg. 'It's a dangerous world.

Everyone is constantly susceptible to attack,' the pamphlet screeched and went on to offer a catalogue of electric shock devices, flamethrowers attached to the undersides of cars, electric fences and laser beams. James chucked the lot onto the floor under the passenger seat of his car, a battered but much loved nineteen sixty-four Mercedes roadster.

His baby was the colour of vanilla ice-cream, with grey leather seats and a gorgeous walnut-wood dashboard. Piles of discarded newspapers, Aqua D'or bottles and other assorted junk lay everywhere but on the driver's seat. James loved the fact that in winter he could leave the hood off for days and traverse this crazy city with the wind whipping around his face and the hot sun on his head.

It was a perfect winter morning, the sun glinting off the glass and steel skyscrapers of downtown, air vents pumping clouds of condensation into the clear sky. Flying over Newtown on the freeway he glanced left and saw a line of women, no more than five of them, brightly coloured water buckets balanced on their heads, walking slowly across the no man's land near the Market Theatre. Beautiful! The anarchy and order of this city never ceased to delight him. Smiling, he turned south and slipped onto the Soweto Highway.

He found the media centre at the back of Regina Mundi Cathedral, a pair of cold rooms divided from the main hall by a layer of soundproof glass. The press room buzzed mildly as James entered. People turned and looked up to greet him, some with a smile, some with quizzical frowns. And he returned their greetings with a sly grin, knowing that they would all want to know what he was doing here, the *Sunday Chronicle*'s brand-new Chief Investigative Reporter at a run-of-the-mill Truth Commission hearing.

He was interested to note that a couple of the international papers were back. They'd lately been represented by a minimal contingent of just one or two journos filing only the occasional, truly sensational horror story. Perhaps they were after the same story, though he doubted it. Probably just a slow week for news.

The local press, on the other hand, was there in force as usual. They were a motley crew, ranging from weary old hacks to bright-eyed and bushy-tailed young reporters. They had sat together in more stompie-strewn, smoke-filled hearing rooms than any of them cared to remember.

James flung glances and greetings and pats on backs to right and left as he slid between the rows of tables where the print reporters sat, fingers poised on keyboards, pens hovering over notepads, eyes locked on the monitor hooked up in front of the glass that divided them from the hall. Proceedings were about to begin.

He waved to a radio reporter friend who was slouched against a long trestle table at the back of the room, half hidden by a mass of computer and recording equipment and cabling. 'Hey, Darren!' he called out.

'Howzit, bru!' the guy shouted back, smiling wanly between the headphones glued to his ears, ready to pounce on the right bite for the hourly bulletins.

Proceedings inside the hall would be fed to the media from a makeshift TV control centre set up in the front corner, a jerry-rigged Outside Broadcast Unit. The only signs of life coming from behind that tower of silver equipment boxes were an endless, slim stream of cigarette smoke and the muttered commands and colourful commentary of the Switcher.

The television teams, like the radio one, rotated their journalists. James was delighted to see that the TV reporter on duty that day was Ilse McLean, a curvy, lovely redhead with a spiky haircut and an equally brittle sense of humour. Ilse wasn't exactly a friend, but they hung out in the same crowd and therefore knew each other well enough. They were part of a loose posse of Melville residents, crazy singles, junkies and journos whose lives consisted of working, drinking, drugging and crashing somewhere comfortable if it wasn't home – which it often wasn't – before getting up to start the next round.

Ilse was holding a cigarette in the fingers of one hand and with the other she switched between the two cameras positioned on either side of the stage inside the hall, checking her shots. Her eyes flicked between the monitors before her and she spoke almost continuously to the cameramen through a microphone hanging from the headset she wore.

Ilse looked up to see James plonking a chair down into the small space next to her.

'All right?' he mumbled.

She raised her sharply pared down eyebrows for a moment then her eyes flicked back to the monitors as she responded archly. 'Surprise, suurrprise,' she purred, her voice gravelly and moist. 'Look who's descended from his ivory tower to stroll amongst the minions. There must be *something* happening here today. And I thought it was going to be just another tedious round of murder and mayhem.'

James shrugged, tipping the chair back as he dug into his pocket for the notebook and a chewed biro. 'Ag, slow week at the office. Ya know. Haven't seen you in a while. Thought I'd check you out on the beat.'

Ilse raised a single eyebrow as she stubbed out one cigarette and perched a fresh one between her brightly painted lips. It wobbled as she spoke. 'Yeah right, James Kay.'

Being near to Ilse was like walking into a particle storm of pheromones. Her sexiness was so close to the surface it was impossible not to respond. James sighed and looked away, his finger moving back and forth across his bottom lip. He'd fallen back into his old habits, pre-Alison. Lots of encounters, lots of potential, never any follow-through. But he didn't want to think about that right now.

'Truth is the news desk was getting a little too cosy for me. Needed a sharp dose of cynicism.' James winked as he held out a light for her.

Ilse's eyes shone up at him as she leaned forward and took it. 'Shew! Wrong way round my friend,' she murmured tartly, breathing smoke into his face. 'What *you* need is a good dose of *sweetness.*'

James grinned back at her, his eyes flashing with unmistakable arousal. 'Looks like I've come to the right place after all then.'

Ilse grinned impishly and turned back to her monitors.

The hearing began with a song. The singing seemed to breathe from the crowd: 'Senzenina, senzenina, senzeni-na, senzeni-naa. Senzeehhni-naaaa . . .' What have we done, what have we done, what have we done to deserve this? It was the most heartbreaking and stirring of all the struggle songs and brought a lump even to James's throat.

As the lament swelled, the Truth Commissioners filed in, led by their Chairman, the solemn Archbishop in his flowing purple robes. He lit a single, plain, tall candle halfway up the altar steps and stood with his eyes closed as the hymn came to an end. Then he put his hands together and bowed by way of greeting the congregation. The weariness in his eyes and the sadness etched into the corners of his mouth showed that no one, not even this invincible messenger of God, was inured against the pain recounted freshly, day in and day out before this Commission.

'Okay, boys, here we go, stand by with the Twinsavers,' Ilse crooned.

James ran his eyes over the list he'd been handed by Mdu, the Commission's irrepressible Media Officer. A dozen or so witnesses, mostly women, were due to testify that day. The widows of Paul Lewis and Jacob Oliphant were scheduled to appear before lunch. Several hours and many sad stories from now. James settled in for a long wait.

As the first witness came to the end of her story one of the Commissioners asked how she felt. Sophie Thema replied that her wounds had never healed.

'They've always been open. I've told the story a hundred times. I do feel good about sharing it today, but the wounds are always open.' James looked down at his hands, at his fingers twisting and untwisting a strand of woollen thread unravelling from a seam on his jacket. He sighed. Took a cigarette from the pack on the monitor in front of him and lit it with Ilse's bic.

A Commissioner's voice crackled through the speakers. 'In practical terms – what does being paralysed mean to you?'

Ilse groaned louder than all the others in the press room. She'd attended too many of these hearings for her patience and compassion to be left unscathed. 'For Christ's sake!' she squawked. 'What the hell do you think it means? Or can't you tell through all that fuckin' hair?' Ilse cut away from the woman Commissioner on One to Camera Two and a slow pan under the table, across the feet of the rest of the Commissioners, fidgeting in comfy low heels or tight ecclesiastical boots and soft suede slip-ons.

The morning wore on and the voices bore down relentlessly.

James used every mind game he knew, but not even he was immune. You couldn't avoid the pain, there was too much of it.

There was the story of a man shot by police and left blinded; of an ANC cadre tortured by his comrades in the camps while in exile; of a white farmer whose last memory of his wife was of pulling her out of a bombed car and seeing that he'd carelessly left her leg behind on the front seat.

James was balancing on the two back legs of his chair, hands at ease on his head and elbows fanned out at his sides. Every time Ilse cut away to shots of the audience he searched the faces for Anna Kriel, but he hadn't seen her yet. The photographs he had of her were ten years old, mostly from the time of the inquest where she looked gaunt and grey and intense. He hadn't seen anyone resembling her, not so far anyway.

James found himself sagging under the weight of the terrible murmur of testimony escaping from beneath the flat staccato of the translators' voices.

A Mrs Nkosi testified about her only son who went into exile in Botswana after the students' uprising of nineteen seventy-six. He was killed in a bombing there in the eighties. 'I last saw him in Gaborone in nineteen eighty-three,' she said calmly, then suddenly she lost control, the pain of her loss ripped into her afresh and she let out a cry that seemed to come from a pit of grief so deep that it pierced the hearts of everyone in that room. Even Ilse fell silent and stared hard, hoping no one had noticed the tears that welled up in her eyes. James's throat burned and a hot tear slipped down his cheek, but he quickly brushed the evidence away and lit another cigarette.

When Mrs Nkosi had recovered a Commissioner asked her what she wanted from them. 'I could be happy,' she said simply, 'if I could get my son's body back. Bring me my son's bones. According to our custom. I want his bones so I can bring them home and bury them here, so I can put his soul to rest.'

nine

Inside the Cathedral hall Joe sat between Anna and Rachel, his arms spread out over the backs of their chairs like a guardian angel. Next to Anna were Rika and Willem Swanepoel. Rika was elegant and aloof as ever, but lighter and sexier too, with her gorgeous pale silk tresses cut off and her wedding band missing. Since their divorce they seemed to go out together a lot, though Rika was militantly single. Nothing would make her go back to the life she and Willem shared when they were married.

He had been shaken to the core by her leaving him. Stunned and diminished by her 'out of the blue' departure, he'd shrunk while she blossomed. Anna and Rachel found it incredible that he hadn't seen it coming, but Joe sympathised with Willem, calling Rika's exit a 'bombshell'. The difference between men and women, Anna guessed. However, it seemed to have been good for both of them in the end. Willem had been doing some long overdue growing up and Rika having some much-deserved fun. Anna was delighted for her.

Anna's mind meandered from her friends' relationship to observations on the Truth Commission machine in action, anything to take her attention away from the nerve-jangling expressions of grief booming through the loudspeakers. She watched the statement takers who moved quietly through the crowd, bringing tissues here, a glass of water, or words of comfort there. Then the translators inside their grey and glass booths at the side of the stage, their mouths moving soundlessly, their words bleeding out of the headphones given to those who needed them. The voices spoke in English and Afrikaans and Xhosa and Sotho and all the other languages of the South

Africans listening inside that church and on their radios and in their cars and homes and schools across the country.

It moved Anna in a manner she found hard to bear. It touched chords so raw and painful that she was terrified she'd snap. The strange yellow and blue light cast by the high stained-glass windows swam over the faces of the audience.

It was hard to remember clearly now how terrible those times had been and just how arrogant and evil and insanely ambitious the enforcers of apartheid were. Anna was glad of that mechanism in her mind, the one that sorted the bad memories from the good and edited accordingly. In her new and comfortable life it was easier to lose the memory of the daily humiliations. The petty stuff. The segregated train carriages, buses, park benches, and the beaches that were demarcated for 'Europeans' or 'Asiatics' or 'non-whites' only. Blacks weren't even black. They were a negative, a minus, a 'non-European'. It was harder still to take oneself back into the hellfire of the worst of it. It was what Anna had dreaded about today, the splitting of scars and the gouging open of wounds.

She sat pinned to her seat now by the lilting and sweet voice of a woman who talked about how she found her neighbours dead in their house on the morning after a police raid: 'There was blood on the floor and splashed on the furniture and squirted across the walls. I'd sat there on the sofa only the night before, talking and laughing with him. And the next morning there he lay with his feet on that rug, his arms spread out on the floor behind him and all his blood drained out all over the floor. He was wearing his underpants. I'll never forget it. They were blue, the plain ones you get from Woolworths.'

Anna twisted the bracelets on her arm, her eyes locked vacantly onto their silvery curls of sprung wire, but she was unable to block out the testimony of the witness. 'He was such a shy man in life and there he lay, so exposed. The place looked like an abattoir . . .' Suddenly the woman smashed her open palm against the tabletop, then looked down at it as if it were not a part of her.

And the jack-in-the-box sprang open in Anna's mind. The memory of Paul's body in the mortuary, of his singed hair and his wax-like skin spattered with garnet beads of blood. 'You can't imagine that this is the person that you love,' said the witness. 'This wonderful person lying there, broken. Dead. I went to touch him, but I think I collapsed, the next thing I remember I was sitting in the car and couldn't remember how I got there.' Anna covered her face with her hands, screwing her fists tight against her eyes. Nausea constricted her throat. Her mouth was dry and there was a bitter, bile taste on her tongue. She couldn't get the image of Paul out of her mind.

At last the woman looked up at the audience and smiled strangely, finishing her testimony with the words: 'That morning I never imagined there would be a day like today. I never imagined I'd be saying – I'm free.'

Anna stood up, her hand over her mouth, knowing she was going to vomit. Blood rushed towards her feet as she rose, as if the world was pulling away below her, and her head was light and swaying far above her. Joe caught her as she wobbled, taking her weight before she fell. Anna felt hands supporting her, voices calming her as people helped Joe carry her out of the Cathedral and into the sun.

The warmth hit her at once, like a salve, and she began to cry. She couldn't stop herself and the more she tried the more sobbing burst from her throat. She covered her face in shame. 'You see, this is what happens when you try to keep it all in,' Rachel scolded. Rika said nothing, she no longer had her pill-box to offer, but she took Anna's hand and squeezed it comfortingly.

'Keep what in?' Anna asked faintly.

Rachel shook her head. Joe put his fingers to his lips. 'Shhh,' he said. 'It's just the heat inside. I was starting to feel a bit weird myself.'

'What? It's *freezing* in there,' Rachel gasped.

'Did you eat breakfast?' Joe spoke directly to Anna, ignoring Rachel. Anna shook her head; she hadn't eaten a thing in almost twenty-four hours.

'That's what it is then, I'll get you something to eat.' He turned towards one of the Truth Commission's Briefers hovering nearby. 'Chief! Bring her something to eat – a biscuit or something sweet, okay?' The guy nodded and ran off. Joe held onto Anna and all the while her tears kept coming, the sadness emptying out of her, surging up even when she thought there couldn't be any more left.

For Anna this eruption of feeling was terrifying. She tried to talk herself down, rationalise and explain to herself what was going on. Paul's murder was an event so savage, so momentous, and she'd somehow accommodated it, but no more. She could never accept or overcome it, or ever put it entirely behind her. She knew the theory all too well. She knew that most of the time, once such an accommodation has been made you *can* discuss the event, describe it, and remember it even, without it arousing this kind of seismic emotional activity. But sometimes the strangest, smallest, most unexpected things can trigger a true, feeling response. That's all this was. Feeling.

The Briefer came back with a cup of Oros and a biscuit, which she took, but couldn't keep down. She retched until her throat was raw and at last the crying had stopped.

She felt like hell and she was sure she looked it too. Rachel and Rika were staring at her with expressions of frightened concern. 'Sorry,' Anna mumbled. Then she started to giggle hysterically. 'Fuck, look at me! I'm pathetic.' Rachel and Rika caught the infection and laughed too. Joe smiled thinly, unamused.

Rachel handed her a wedge of tissues that she pulled from her bottomless handbag. Anna took them and dabbed at her mouth. 'Trust you to bring tissues,' she murmured.

'Ja. And trust you not to,' Rachel responded softly, with the kind of quiet, caring rebuke that was her way.

Anna blinked hard and pushed the soggy tissues into her pocket. And when she looked out at the street and the life that was continuing, oblivious, around them she felt better.

'I'll wait out here till it's time for us to testify.'

'We'll stay with you,' Rachel retorted bossily. And so they waited in the winter sun and the sound from inside pressed in still. The litany of pain resounded from the Cathedral and rang out into the world.

ten

Inside the press room the picture on the monitor swung sickeningly as the cameraman swept his lens across the audience. 'Shit!' Ilse swore as she switched back to Camera One, fixed steadily on a shot of three listening Commissioners. 'What the fuck are you doing, Simon? At least give me warning,' she snapped. Simon's camera came to rest. 'Oh, okay, thanks.' Ilse's tone shifted as Camera Two settled on Anna Kriel and Rachel Oliphant walking down the aisle towards their seats. 'Stand by. I'm back on Two. Thanks, Simon.'

James sat up, the front legs of his chair hitting the floor with a clunk. Ilse's eyes flicked between the three monitors in front of her, the two feeds and the edit. She was concentrating hard now. Camera Two tilted down as Anna sat, and the picture zoomed into a close-up of her face.

'Anna Kriel. This week's story.' Ilse fumbled for another cigarette in the pack on top of the monitor and lit it without taking her eyes off the screen.

James raised his eyebrows. 'Hmm.' He looked down at the notepad balanced on his knee, flipped the pages to a clean place and began to write for the first time that morning. Ilse glanced sharply at him, cupping her hand over the mike as she did so. 'Hmm?' She positively fizzed with playful jealousy.

James winked at her then turned back to the picture on the monitor. Anna's hair fell across her face as she looked towards Joe Dladla, seated next to her. The Assistant Commissioner spoke something into her ear, which made her smile. The shining black curtain of hair swished back revealing her face again. With her eyes lit up like that she didn't look much like the woman in those press photographs from ten years back. James had a wedge of them in a file on his desk. In those she looked severe, but the woman he saw on the monitor had something gentle about her, vulnerable even. She's beautiful, he thought.

More than that, she struck him as powerful. Someone you couldn't help but be drawn to. And he suspected she was unaware of the extent of her own magnetism.

'It's a nice story,' Ilse babbled. 'Lekker high-profile, big, soft love story, you know? Paul and Anna, the Romeo and Juliet of the struggle. The rainbow tragedy. Easy too. Everyone knows the killer was Frans Nel – it's a matter of time before the poes applies for amnesty.'

James took another cigarette from Ilse's pack and fired up her lighter. Smoke puffed around his face and he squinted through it. 'I've heard he was very jealous.'

'Who?'

'Paul.'

Ilse turned towards him, making a face. James shrugged.

'That's what people say. He used to go into these jealous rages at parties. Freak people out.'

Ilse turned back towards her screens, eyebrows arched. 'Shew, I never knew that.'

'Unpleasant for her,' James added.

'Ag, you can see why. She's kind of drop-dead.'

James nodded in agreement as he sucked deeply on his cigarette.

'She's taken, honey,' Ilse put in acidly.

James laughed softly. 'They always are, babe. They always are . . .'

There was movement in the hall. 'Okay, guys, stand by for the up and in. Camera Two, go to the Archbishop. One, I'm on you, can you give me a three-shot of Joe Dladla and the two widows? Ja, that's nice, just ease it out. Cool.'

James tapped his pen against his teeth, eyes flicking between monitors, watching the scene unfold. The Archbishop rose, smiling to greet the witnesses as they approached the stand. It was clear from the warmth with which he embraced the women that they were old acquaintances. Cameramen inside the hall rushed forward to capture the moment. News photographers obscured the picture on the monitor, their cameras flashing as the cleric enveloped Rachel and Anna in his arms. Ilse switched to Camera Two as it zoomed in to a tight close-up of Joe Dladla, beaming presidentially and vigorously shaking the hands of the Commissioners who all beamed back, positively lit up by his presence.

'So who's the boyfriend?' James asked.

Ilse raised her finely-plucked eyebrows. She evidently enjoyed being in possession of knowledge James didn't have. She pointed to Joe with her cigarette and watched James for a reaction. He didn't attempt to conceal his surprise.

'Well, well, well. Doesn't he just have it all?' James imitated the sharp, fast patter of a football commentator. 'Commissioner Joe Dladla. Not content with his meteoric rise in the police force, this young and *extremely* ambitious man has publicly declared his intention to move into politics and here he is pressing the flesh at the Truth Commission at the side of his luscious partner, struggle widow Anna Kriel.' James leaned forward, addressing the screen, which was just inches from his face now. 'Groomed for power at his activist mother's nipple, Dladla has his sights set on the Ministry and – no doubt – after that he'll shoot for nothing less than President. Charming but ruthless, there is every reason to believe that the charismatic "People's Joe" will get *exactly* what he wants.'

Ilse scowled as she cut away from Joe to a shot of Anna and Rachel. 'I'll have you know that's a hero of my people you're talking about.'

'You think I'm not your people?' James sat back thoughtfully.
She shook her head. 'You're nobody's people, James Kay.'

James glanced briefly towards Ilse, momentarily distracted from his intense scrutiny of the proceedings inside the hall. Her green eyes flashed away, triumphant. She'd seen the ripple of hurt in his eyes and she seemed pleased to have needled him.

Why do I bring that out in women? he wondered. Then she reached over to give his knee a reassuring and reconciliatory squeeze. He looked down at her bright orange fingernails against the dark grey twill of his cargo pants. And that too, he mused darkly.

Then he returned to his thoughts of Joe Dladla. He knew from all he'd read and heard about the young Assistant Commissioner that he enjoyed a bit of glory, though he didn't seek it. He was a loner. In the man's eyes there was that intensity, that blank depth he'd seen in many former operatives, from both sides. They were hooked on adrenalin those guys, always seeking the edge. Yet there was something smooth about Joe Dladla that marked him out as different. The dude was devastatingly comfortable inside his own skin. You can do anything if you believe you can and Joe *believed*. That was what drew people to him. That and his looks, not to mention his flash clothes. Where did a kid from Meadowlands acquire such taste? James wondered. On the other hand, he reminded himself, why *shouldn't* a kid from Meadowlands acquire such taste?

James had been trying unsuccessfully to get an interview with the Assistant Commissioner for weeks now. Joe's unit was directly responsible for investigations into the very cash-in-transit heists James was fascinated by. And trying to do a story on, though so far he had little to go on.

The camera followed Joe back to his seat. Then Ilse cut to a shot of the Archbishop. 'What've you got against Dladla?' she asked.

James shrugged, teasing. 'He's got the girl, he's got the gear . . . He's the man. What's to like about that?'

Ilse positively glowered back; her purple and green eye-shadow glittered menacingly.

'You should have heard him at the press conference this morning. Then you might not be so bladdy dismissive.'

'What press conference?' He shot her a suspicious look.

Ilse smirked and jiggled her shoulders in a triumphant little motion. 'Wow, you're slipping, bok. That's the second time this morning I know something you don't.'

'*What* press conference, Ilse?'

'On the steps outside, this morning. He was responding to the criticism of the police handling of that freeway robbery the other day.'

James slammed his notebook down against his thigh. 'Shit! You're not serious?'

'That'll teach you to arrive late,' she trilled.

James shook his head disconsolately.

'Ag, don't sweat it, sweetie. I've got it all on tape. If you're very, very nice to me I'll play it back for you in the lunch break.'

James's eyes narrowed and his mouth smoothed out into a smile. 'When have I *ever* not been very, very nice to you?'

Ilse glared playfully back at him.

'Okay, I owe you one,' he grumbled.

'Dead right you do, china.'

Then she was silent as Anna Kriel and Rachel Oliphant took the stand. James leaned forward to concentrate.

eleven

'You are amongst many friends,' the Archbishop declared warmly. Rachel squeezed Anna's hand and Anna tried to smile, but her head hurt with tension.

'Your name?' The soft, deliberate voice of a Commissioner echoed through the speakers.

'Anna Kriel.'

A clutch of photographers in front of her cocked their cameras.

'Do you swear to tell the truth, the whole truth and nothing but the truth?'

The moment was taut, it shivered, then exploded as Anna raised her right hand and a battery of flashes burst in her face. She blinked, 'I do.'

'Thank you, Anna.'

She dipped her chin very slightly in acknowledgement.

'I understand you are resident in Johannesburg?' The Commissioner's tone was level and calming.

'That's correct. I work in Pretoria. I am a Deputy Director in the Ministry of Safety and Security.'

'I understand you have prepared a statement?'

'Yes. Thank you,' she murmured, pressing her fingers down over the folds of her statement, flattening the creases in the paper. She didn't need to read; she knew exactly what she'd come to say. Nevertheless it was there in print before her. In case.

She closed her eyes and began to speak into the waiting silence. Facts first. 'In the early hours of Easter Sunday, nineteen eighty-seven, my partner, Paul Lewis, was travelling in his car with our comrade, Jacob Oliphant. Their destination was unknown to us, Rachel Oliphant and myself, that is. They had left Johannesburg the night before. We had no idea of where they were going or what they intended to do. The four of us made up an underground cell, a political and propaganda unit of the banned African National Congress. Secrecy was paramount in our work. All we knew was to expect them back within seventy-two hours. That was all we needed to know.'

Her voice came back to her through the speakers, sounding strong and clear.

'Paul and Jacob never reached their destination. On the morning of April nineteenth, nineteen eighty-seven, a local priest found their charred bodies by their burnt-out car on the road between Mafikeng and Vryburg. Precisely what transpired on that long stretch of tar that night, we still do not know. They had been shot. Jacob just once, through the back of his head. Paul three times. The bullet that killed him pierced his heart. Their killers have never been found.'

Anna paused, reaching for the glass of water that one of the Briefers had placed in front of her. She took a long, cool sip before resuming.

'That was ten years ago. I don't need to remind the Commissioners of the State of Emergency then in place, of the townships that were ablaze, of the violence that was our everyday experience. Not to mention the harassment, detention and possibility of death faced by those who fought against the regime.'

Anna looked out across the audience, beyond it to the windows at the back and the faces of the journalists watching her through their monitors.

'I have been haunted ever since by the question – why? And that leads inevitably to – who? Who killed Paul and Jacob? Ten years later, I still know nothing of the mission that took Paul and Jacob on that fatal journey. I have long been convinced that the killer, or at least the man who gave the order to kill, is Frans Nel.

'In those days we called him the Captain. He was then an officer in the Security Police. Nowadays he is a Brigadier in charge of a Community-Policing Unit in Pietermaritzburg.'

A murmur of disapproval rattled around the hall. Rachel

squeezed her leg, to let her know she was doing well. The Commissioners made notes.

'Frans Nel is not unusual in that respect – many former Security Policemen have stayed on in the force. It's hard to swallow, but an important gesture towards reconciliation. A gesture that I hope will be returned, though up to now the Brigadier has remained as tight-lipped as ever on the subject of the Mafikeng Road Murders.'

Anna cleared her throat, turning the pages of her statement. 'I have met with the Brigadier to discuss the matter, but in spite of a stated eagerness to sit down with me he remained as evasive as ever. He's not budged from his story in ten years.

'Balletjies Badenhorst and Warrant Officer Curry of the Vryburg Murder and Robbery Squad have proved harder to track down. Curry was killed in a single-vehicle motor accident near Cape Town in nineteen ninety-three. Badenhorst has simply disappeared.

'In the course of my investigation I have applied to the Police and Military Archives for all documentation relating to Paul and Jacob and the surveillance and periods of detention they endured. The Police yielded up a slim file of details already known to me. Paul's date of birth, address, Security Police File Number and his date of death, attached to some press clippings from the time of the inquest. The Military are still processing my claim three years down the line.

'Up to now, all investigations have led to the wall of silence surrounding the Security Police. The Truth Commission offers the first and last hope that Paul and Jacob's assassination will be fully, officially investigated. We want to know who killed Paul Lewis and Jacob Oliphant – and why?'

In the wake of the question came an unexpected wave of emotion. Anna trembled in the way that an acrobat will pause on a high wire in the breathless seconds after an almost fatal wobble. She mustered all her strength towards balance. When she found it she spoke again.

'I ask the Truth Commission to subpoena Brigadier Nel and Balletjies Badenhorst and to question them about their knowledge of the Mafikeng Road Murders. I appeal to them – on behalf of Rachel, Bram, Delarey and myself – and indeed to anyone who has *any* information, to come forward and to tell the truth about what happened to Paul and Jacob. To put our minds to rest at last.'

Mumbled agreement skittled through the audience.

'It's been said so often, that death is part of life, that life is part of death. And I do believe, if you have fought all your life for something right and good and just, then death is easier to accept. And you will live on, in and through the people who survive and take the fight forward. It is so that Paul and Jacob's lives continue in me, in Rachel, in Jacob's sons Bram and Delarey and in our comrades.

'But – and I speak for myself now – I will never come to terms with the brutality of the cutting off – too soon – of Paul's life. That April day in nineteen eighty-seven I lost not only my love, but also the future we would have shared together. I have learned since that you cannot lose your grief. It travels with you. It becomes a part of you. The trick is learning to carry it.'

Anna's voice cracked, betraying her. She stopped. Cleared her throat, staring down at the words she'd so carefully composed the night before. Then she closed her eyes, a shiver in her shoulders revealing an inner battle to quell the surge of emotion. Her voice rose up on it.

'But South Africa lost too. South Africa lost a vital force for good, a brilliant strategist, a man of action who would have contributed so much today to our new struggle, that of making the new South Africa into the country we promised our people it would be.

'Worst of all it was Paul who lost.' Anna's voice dipped now. She paused and then raised her eyes up again to the audience. 'There is so much he's missed.' Anna felt her throat tightening and tears prickling in her eyes. 'But he was denied that. Denied the pleasure of watching Madiba walk free from prison, of laughing and singing with his friends as we queued for hours to vote in a free South Africa, of dancing at the inauguration of our President, Nelson Mandela. Paul was denied his own victory. He was denied *life*.

'Long ago, I made him a promise. That I would find his killers and bring them to justice. Not out of a sense of hatred, or revenge. Those motives belong to the repertoire of the killer. But out of a sense of righteousness.' Anna's voice soared now.

'It is up to me and to all of us to fulfil our obligation to Paul and Jacob and the hundreds of others who died fighting against apartheid. It is our obligation to uncover the truth of what happened, to identify the perpetrators and the people who armed and exhorted them to killing. Not so we can avenge our loved ones with more blood. But so that we can ensure such bloodshed is *never* repeated.'

Her voice shivered with the intensity of her feelings.

'I close with the words of Maya Angelou who wrote that, "history, despite its wrenching pain, cannot be unlived. But if faced with courage, need not be lived again".'

Anna stood still for a moment, her fingers balancing on the edge of the table in front of her. The hall was utterly silent. Then she looked over to the grave, hushed faces of the Commissioners. 'Thank you. That is all I have to say.'

Applause exploded like a thundercloud and rained down inside the hall. And the Archbishop rose, asking the audience to stand and join hands. 'Let us be silent now to remember all those who have been spoken of this morning.'

And as the silence came to an end a song swelled up in the hall, the women's voices first, then the men's joining them. 'Hamba-aa gahle m'khonto.' Anna closed her eyes as the beautiful, solemn hymn rose up around her. Hamba gahle. Farewell, they sang, fare well our fallen soldier.

twelve

James rose to his feet, moved by the singing, but most of all by Anna Kriel's words. The other journalists stood too as the lament surged from the hall. Ilse leaned forward, straining on the end of the taut lead to her comms. 'Coming to you, Simon,' she whispered. Then cut to a shot of Rachel, head held high and tears coursing brightly down her cheeks. Then a close-up of Anna, dry eyes, pale and eerily beautiful.

James was fascinated. She evidently drew strength from her love for this guy. It positively glowed in her. It couldn't be healthy.

He was still thankful for his timely reprieve from a life sentence with Alison. It was dull not to be in love. The days never lit up like they used to. But at least they were calm.

The lunch adjournment was announced as the song ended and the press room erupted in a hubbub of scraping chairs and excited chatter. 'Fuckin' amazing!' Ilse declared, wiping the tears from her face and rubbing the damp tip of her nose.

'You've been crying,' James remarked dryly.

Ilse shot him an irritable, well-done-Einstein glance.

'Do you think that calm exterior reflects inner composure, or do you reckon she's all at sea like the rest of us?' he wondered aloud, more than a sliver of irony in his tone.

'I dunno, James. That's a question often asked about you,' Ilse replied tartly as she pulled out the last tape and slapped a label on it.

James raised his eyebrows, about to quip back with equal acidity, but Ilse was too caught up in the emotion of the morning to want to play. Anyway he wasn't quite sure if they were

94

sparring or serious. So he sloped off without another word towards the hall to find Anna Kriel.

Truth was he found the prospect of meeting her intimidating. It wasn't just this morning's performance that had impressed him. Anna, by reputation, was tirelessly committed to her work. She transcended the current cynicism and fatigue with her infinite energy and hope, determined to build the just society her lover had died for. Not one of the people James had asked about her had a bad word to say. He'd begun to admire her for the way she was said to handle herself and nothing in her bearing that morning contradicted reports.

Beneath the podium Joe Dladla was fielding questions from reporters who had pressed in around the widows, bristling with pens and microphones. James saw Anna turn, her eyes scanning the room above the heads of the journalists as if she was looking for a gap, an exit. Her eyes met his and held his gaze for a moment. He felt it like a sharp buzz of electricity. What she thought of what she saw he couldn't tell; her face was expressionless. She began pushing her way through the crowd in a direction that happened to be towards him. She would have made it past and out through the side door had he not reached for and caught her arm.

Anna recoiled from the contact, and though it was only the slightest movement away from him, he felt the flinch. And found himself once again impaled by those fathomless brown eyes. He smiled sheepishly, feeling clumsy and gauche.

'Can I talk to you? Please? James Kay. *Sunday Chronicle.*'

Her eyes widened. With recognition? Irritation? Hard to tell. She said nothing. But at least she held his gaze. James repeated his request and after a beat she nodded, though her eyes seemed vacant, a fact that failed to reassure him that she'd understood. 'Ms Kriel?'

Then she spoke, her chin upwards, though her voice was smooth as ice-cream. 'Fine. It's just . . . not right now. Okay?' Her long hair shivered and swung across her face as she looked around for a way out.

James suddenly realised, with the sharpness of a slap to the face, that the woman was in a state of some confusion and bewilderment. Her eyes begged for a reprieve, for an escape from the questions and the crush of bodies. James stepped closer, slipping his hand onto the curve of her back and steering her gently towards the door.

Once outside she smiled gratefully up at him as she stepped away to a distance of at least two comfortable arms' lengths from him.

'Thanks,' she breathed.

'Um, I was saying, can I talk to you? About Paul?'

She looked uncertainly around the little courtyard they found themselves in, like she was looking for help.

'We don't have to do it now,' he raced on, determined not to lose this chance. 'I could come to your office, take you to lunch, whatever suits . . .'

Anna hesitated again, then said quietly: 'Can you call my office? Set something up with my assistant?'

'Cool. Will do.' James grinned. 'Thanks.'

Anna nodded then turned and walked away, out of the shade and into the arms of a cool blonde who seemed pleased to have found her.

James strolled thoughtfully back into the press room.

'Oh my God, it's the cat who got the cream,' Ilse squealed.

'You got that presser on tape for me?' He was distractedly severe.

Ilse saluted, then pressed the play button on the recorder. She slipped her feet out of her shoes and planted them on James's lap as he watched Joe Dladla's impromptu performance on the steps of the Cathedral hours earlier.

From what James had pieced together of it, Dladla's had been an interesting life, but not remarkably different from other high-profile activists. Raised by his mother and grandmother in Meadowlands, Zone 9, Soweto. Conscientised by his environment and fired into activism by the death of his mother, a domestic worker in the white suburbs. The story went that the husband of the white housewife she worked for had raped her repeatedly. When the madam found out, she chased Mrs Dladla out of the house and ran her down in a fit of rage. The BMW came out of the collision unscathed, Mrs Dladla was dead. The madam got a warning from the judge and young Joe got a thousand rands' compensation.

Dladla left South Africa at thirteen or so, in the stream of other young men and women who were fleeing the country to join the liberation movement. He hooked up with the ANC in Tanzania where he endured the hellish conditions in the camps for three or four years, before being sent back to operate internally. Not much was known of his underground period. Dladla resurfaced during negotiations in the early nineties. From that point onwards his rise was meteoric. And there was no doubting he was still on the up.

James's interest in him was simply because of the special unit investigating cash-in-transit heists that Dladla ran and James was also looking into. From what James knew so far Dladla was dead right about the composition of the gangs. They were mostly former combatants, highly trained, well equipped and tough to beat. He'd also discovered that these gangs had close connections to the police. What he'd been struggling to find out was how high that connection went and what precisely was their nature and function? Were the cops infiltrating the gangs to bust them, or were they running them for their own gain?

James took a couple of quotes from the interview, but there was nothing much in it for him. When it was over he stood up and Ilse's feet dropped elegantly to the floor. 'Thanks. I'll see you around,' he said, gathering up his things.

'Don't forget you owe me one,' Ilse chipped in flirtatiously.

'Yeah.' James's mind was elsewhere.

'Buy me a drink at the Ant tonight,' she shouted after him. He didn't even turn around.

'Sure. That'd be great. I'll see you there.'

He slipped his notebook into the side pocket of his trousers and was gone.

Ilse shook her head in sheer lustful amazement. As she did so she caught the eye of a fellow journo who was in a similar state of attraction.

'I don't think the guy has *any* idea how totally fucking drop-dead gorgeous he is,' Ilse sighed.

thirteen

Joe's new passion was for restaurants and 'dining out'. Rachel teased him mercilessly for his buppy tendencies, but was always delighted to join him. His current favourite haunt was a place in Melville called Sam's Café, which combined the crucial elements of great food, good wine, pleasant surroundings and a clientele of people Joe either knew or wanted to know. It wasn't wholly Anna's scene, but she did enjoy the elegant simplicity of the room, and the food – though expensive in her austere book – was excellent.

It was to Sam's that they went for dinner after the hearing, along with Rachel and Temba and the separated Swanepoels. It had been a long day. Draining, but also exhilarating. Anna was surprised at how light she felt.

'It was a good day, bokkie. You did well,' Rachel said, delivering a sloppy kiss on Anna's cheek before reaching for a menu. 'But I'm *helluva* glad that it's over!'

'I'll drink to that,' Joe growled, opening the wine list.

'Ja,' Anna sighed. 'Things can go back to normal.'

'Not quite normal, my girlie,' Rachel reminded her. 'You've still got to help me get married.'

'Hey, isn't that really soon?'

Rachel made a face, eyes wide and mouth tiny, nodding vigorously as Temba put a napkin over his head.

The conversation meandered through plans for the wedding to matters more everyday, before wheeling back round to plans for a party on the big day. Anna listened, joining in when called upon to, but mostly sitting back and enjoying their familiar voices and their comfortable company.

It was perhaps halfway through the meal when Anna noticed the owner of those ice-blue eyes that had so unsettled her earlier in the day. He was at a table by the window, on his own. Reading what looked like a police file that he held up in his left hand and seemed to be devouring more hungrily than the food in front of him. Anna sipped her wine, observing him over the rim of her glass.

He was a striking man. Medium tall with coarse, curly black hair. If he'd looked after himself better he would be really good-looking, but that would have been too much. There was something soft and careless about him that Anna found appealing. She was curious. Joburg was such a small town; how come she'd never met him before?

Temba noticed the direction of her stare. 'Know him?' he asked.

Anna shook her head. 'No. I don't. He spoke to me at the hearing, but I was too out of it.' She waved her wine glass about as she spoke, feeling all of a sudden self-conscious.

Temba leaned forward to explain. 'Name's James Kay. He's the new Investigative Reporter on the *Chronicle*. Amazing guy. Used to be the London *Times* correspondent down here. Jumped ship a couple of weeks ago, came back looking for a local job.'

'Who's this?' Joe butted in and Rachel indicated James with a swing of her glass. 'James Kay,' she said, smiling sweetly at her man. 'Temba's new hero.'

'He is seriously cute,' Rika purred. Willem glanced over furtively, his lip curling with distaste. 'Looks like a moffie to me.' They all burst out laughing and after a moment even Willem managed a smile.

'I think he spent a couple of years in Russia,' Temba went on, 'ran the bureau there. His big coup was a Russian mafia story, won some awards for that, made a big noise. Then he went back to London and did a stint on the desk, Assistant Foreign Editor or something.'

'So what's he doing here?' Anna wondered.

'This is home. He's South African. His mother is Diane Kay?' Temba's voice rose at the end of the sentence, so it sounded like a question.

'Who?' Anna had never heard of her.

'Don't you remember? Part of that group of whitey students in the late sixties – those African Resistance people?'

Anna nodded, remembering, but only dimly.

'She was tried for sabotage in sixty-nine, I think. You must have heard about the whole dramatic escape thing? She slipped the cops while they were taking her to court, skipped to the UK. It was a huge story. She was public enemy number one for a while. Don't you remember?'

Anna nodded with more conviction now. She *did* remember. A photograph floated up into her mind, of a rather beautiful, dark-haired woman in an elegantly tailored shirt and ultra cool sunglasses, her arms wrapped around two little boys. One of them must have been James.

'He's the hottest, I'm telling you,' Temba went on effusively. 'James Kay is the *man*. Yussus, I love that guy. But he's seriously hardcore. There's a joke around how he once killed his own mother to get a story – faked her death certificate just to get on some military flight out of Iran or somewhere.' Temba's shoulders shook with amusement.

Anna glanced in James Kay's direction. He'd turned towards the sound of their laughter and was staring right at her. The shock of the eye contact made her blush. James smiled and raised his hand in greeting. Anna's gaze darted around the circle of her companions, but none of them seemed to have noticed. She looked back at Kay and tipped the base of her glass towards him, the smallest of gestures. Then she looked away.

The next time Anna looked over at James Kay's table it was empty.

They left the restaurant late and in a happy mood. 'Come stay with me,' Joe whispered. She giggled, holding onto him. 'Ag, you know how I hate having to wear the same clothes in the morning.' It was a half-hearted plea. His hand brushed the curve of her back under her coat. 'C'mon, baby. It's been too long.' Then he kissed her and Anna knew she needed him as much as he wanted her that night.

'He would have been so proud of you today,' Joe murmured as they drove, his fingers stroking the back of her hand. She looked down at their hands interlocking and unlocking. It was a rare expression of feeling from Joe and she was grateful, and squeezed hard on his hand.

Theirs was a strange relationship, seldom discussed, but tacitly understood. It suited Anna, because Joe could never come between her and Paul. He would never want to.

There had been other men, but not very many for ten years. Anna could count them on the fingers of one hand. A radio journalist on a trip to America, a Dutch travel writer she'd met in the foyer of a Cape Town hotel, and the Austrian airline pilot. She'd encountered them on business trips; she never would have allowed it in the course of her day-to-day life. And they'd all had the furtiveness of affairs. She'd felt she was cheating on Paul and that was undoubtedly why she'd chosen men who were foreign and unavailable. None of them was a one-night stand, but they were never much more than that.

The first time Anna went to bed with Joe was on the night of the day the election results were announced. And that was exactly what it was – going to bed and sleeping side by side. They were both so happy and so very sad that day. Freedom Day itself. And they'd turned to look around and see what was left of their lives after so many years of sacrifice and work and what they had was each other. Since then there'd been only Joe.

His home was now a fourth-floor apartment in Killarney. The place was sparsely furnished and sterile for Anna's taste. It was a place he used for sleeping and very little else.

Anna yawned as she sank into the sofa. Joe sat down next to her and flipped on the television with the remote. Then he reached across and put his hand on her knee. His fingers travelled up between her legs, cupping her crotch as he leaned forward to kiss her. His kiss was brief but warm. Then he put his hand under her shirt, his fingers moving across her back, reaching up to unclip her bra while she unfastened his belt. Slowly they took off each other's clothes, piece by piece. Joe with his eyes closed, peppering her face with kisses all the while.

Their love-making always began that way. They never made love in his bed; it was always on that sofa with the TV fizzing in the background. Anna called the sofa his love seat. It was one of the things she found odd about him, like the way he didn't make love to all of her, only to certain parts of her body. Then there was the way he turned from her in bed, never held her while she slept. And in the morning he would have nothing to offer her to drink because he never kept coffee in the house, though he knew she needed it first thing. It had become a joke between them, but that never moved him to change.

And yet he loved her, in spite of her not needing him at all. Knowing that she loved him in her way, but that she would always be with Paul.

Anna lay on her side watching Joe sleep, watching the rise and fall of his shoulder as he breathed. The skin between his shoulders was scarred with the long, harsh marks of a sjambok, a whipping strap. She found the scars beautiful, but hated the sight of the natural crease at the base of his skull, that slug of folded skin at the back of his head. There was something almost sullen about it, as if it were scowling at her.

Anna rolled over onto her other side and fell asleep listening to the gentle rasp of his breathing on the pillow behind her.

part three

Truth is not hard to kill and a lie told well is immortal
MARK TWAIN

fourteen

Anna woke sometime before dawn, dimly aware of a phone ringing and then of Joe's voice drifting in from another room. A while later there was movement in the room, cupboard doors opening and closing. She was lying face down into the pillow, not wanting to surface, but for some reason Joe was up. Anna rolled over onto her back, flung her arms above her head and opened her eyes.

He was sitting on the end of the bed, half dressed. She smiled sleepily. 'What you doing?'

He leaned down to put on his shoes, his arm jerking up as he tied the lace. 'Have to meet someone.'

As Anna's eyes adjusted to the light she saw that he was wearing smart, dark pants and a dark T-shirt. The weight of something on her feet was a shoulder holster. He picked it up and began to strap himself in. 'You coming?'

Anna didn't know what was going on, but with Joe there was no point in asking. 'You want me to?'

'Up to you,' he shrugged as he slipped the cold weight of his gun into the leather slot underneath his arm.

Joe carried a police issue Beretta, 9mm pistol. Dull metal with a wooden grip on the handle. A large, inelegant piece, hard to conceal, but intimidating up close. It could do some serious damage.

'Where's yours?' he asked matter of factly.

Anna giggled. Shook her head. He was incorrigible. 'It's in the safe at home, where it always is.'

'Why don't you keep it on you?'

Anna said nothing. Had he just snapped at her? If so, she

wouldn't accept it. He turned to fix her with a look of serious concern. 'I told you to keep it on you.'

'And I told you I *hate* guns,' she shot back, mimicking his overly patient tone. He turned away, shaking his head as if at a naughty child.

Joe had given her the gun when she moved into her place in Melville. The first time she'd ever lived alone. He'd taught her to use it at a shooting range in Wonderboom, near Pretoria. To both their surprise Anna was an excellent shot. Hers was not the little .22 that was a favourite 'ladies gun'. It was a .38 Special, a Browning revolver. An ugly but effective weapon. She had to use two hands when firing it, the kick was so powerful.

Joe stood up, ready to go. 'You've got three minutes.'

'You think I can't resist you?' She grinned.

'I *know* you can't,' he retorted.

Anna looked at her watch. It was almost five. She might as well. Didn't feel like loafing around in Joe's bed, waiting for sleep that was unlikely to return.

'They got breakfast there?' she asked.

He nodded. 'Yep.'

Anna peeled the cover off a little way and immediately jerked it back. 'Oh, it's too coooold,' she moaned, rolling herself up in the duvet like a sausage. Joe grinned, then yanked the cover right off her and Anna gasped as the cold air struck her skin. 'Okay, okay!' she cried as she skittered out of bed, pulling on warm clothes as quickly as her sleep-fuzzed brain and fuddled limbs could manage.

It was a brisk winter morning. The street was empty as they pulled out into the half-light, Anna at the wheel of her car, Joe in the passenger seat. That was how he wanted it.

'Where we going?' she asked, rather enjoying the mystery and the early hour.

'Airport,' he answered.

'Well, that explains everything,' Anna murmured cheerfully and turned onto the freeway.

His cellphone rang several times. The exchanges were brief and oblique. 'They should install the SIM card in your head,' Anna teased.

'I've got my people working on it,' he countered. There was an air of excitement about him now.

The moon was a massive pearl directly ahead of them, hanging close to the concrete spike of the Auckland Park Tower. They left it behind as the freeway curved southwards and they slipped past the city, glittering with glass and steel, unseen vents breathing columns of steam into the cold air. The streetlights popped off just as they came up alongside the Top Star Drive-In. The mine dumps flashed gashes of gold, brilliant ochre peeping through the green grasses on their slopes.

Anna loved the early morning. Loved the clean raggedness of it. That morning even the freeway was clear, making a change from the tedious bumper-to-bumper grind of her daily commute to Pretoria.

The sun rose directly ahead of them. It shimmered and swam – an enormous, blood-red orb – as it soared above the cluttered Edenvale skyline. Joe's silence mounted in intensity. He positively emanated tension. The pressure in the car built until the air almost crackled. Like the hours before a mission, Anna thought, wondering what she'd got herself into, but to ask would be pointless now. She knew Joe too well to make a mistake like that.

She pulled into the parking lot of the airport Holiday Inn just before six. The place was empty but for a white panelled van parked near the entrance to the lobby. Anna took it for one of their tracking vehicles. Joe strode past it and into the hotel without a glance. Anna skipped and jogged to keep up.

'Who we meeting here, Joe?' she asked, trying not to sound concerned, as she struggled to keep pace with him.

'Willie Mkhize,' Joe answered distractedly as he scanned the lobby.

Anna's heart was racing now. 'This got something to do with Bazooka Rabopane?'

Joe nodded.

'Great,' Anna growled darkly. 'What the hell am *I* doing here?' It was a statement more than a question. Joe didn't answer.

Bazooka Rabopane was the prime suspect in the cash-in-transit heist investigation. He led a gang known as the Mozambicans.

Something to do with Bazooka's place of exile. He'd been a member of MK, like Joe. But somewhere along the line he'd gone off the rails. He was sharp, highly trained, armed to the teeth and extremely dangerous.

On the other hand, the man Joe had come to meet, Willie Mkhize, was small fry. A scaly creature, inhabiting the no man's land between cops and criminals, he scraped together a living from trading information. Trusted by neither, used by both. Anna always felt soiled by contact with such characters.

But there was no sign of Willie in the lobby of the airport Holiday Inn. He was about to be late, or a no-show. Joe dialled his room from the reception desk, but got no answer. He tried several times more, but the phone simply rang. Joe stood listening with his hands in his pockets, jiggling keys.

Five minutes passed, then ten. Anna's stomach growled in response to the nutty aroma of coffee drifting out of the restaurant. Abruptly Joe was in motion, striding towards the lifts, metal heel tips clicking on the marble floor. Anna scrambled after him, just making it into the lift, which took them up to the fourth floor.

They found Willie's room empty. The door was open and a tired chambermaid was already stripping the bed.

'Dammit!' Joe slammed the side of his fist against the door. Anna leaned back against the wall, as Joe swung his angry gaze from one empty end of the long corridor to the other.

'What's the deal here?' she asked quietly.

Joe dragged his fingers across his scalp. 'We think he can take us to Bazooka. That's if we can get our hands on the bastard.' He strode back to the lifts and banged on the call button.

A moment later the lift doors opened to reveal the sly and very surprised face of a tall, thin black man with a sculpted, razored haircut. Joe relaxed instantly, a menacing smile spreading across his face. 'Leave something behind, my friend?' he crooned.

Willie looked terrified, though he didn't move a muscle and kept his hands in his pockets as Joe stepped forward, hand against the lift door. 'Heita! Howzit, Willie my bru?' Willie shrank back against the mirrored wall as Joe and Anna stepped in on either side of him. Joe pressed the button for the lift to take them down.

'Hey, you people! Can't you just leave me alone? What do you want with me, ay? I would just leave me alone,' he bleated. Joe didn't even look at him as they descended.

'Willie, I'm longing to leave you alone. You give us what we need and we'll be gone.' Joe sounded so reasonable through that ominous smile. The situation suddenly felt dangerous.

The lift hit Ground and the doors slid open. Willie followed Anna with Joe close on his heels. Willie Mkhize was a bigger man than Joe, but he was no match for the Assistant Commissioner's tenacity and he knew it.

Joe's grip on Willie's arm tightened as he escorted him back across the lobby and outside into a courtyard. 'Listen, boy,' Joe snarled. 'Don't waste my time. All I want is Bazooka. We do it here, or you come back to my place. What do you say, Willie?' They came to a halt on the wide stoep outside. Pretty white Impatiens flowers bursting from the borders.

The courtyard around the swimming pool was all textured cream walls and red roof tiles, in keeping with the Spanish hacienda theme of the establishment. 'Nice place,' Joe said mildly, unbuttoning his coat.

Mkhize's eyes narrowed, flicking nervously from Joe to Anna. Anna smiled. Truth was, she didn't like this at all. Joe was dangerously calm as they faced off.

'Where is he, Willie?'

Willie shook his head, like a kid who's been caught out. 'I can't say in front of the lady,' he sniggered, leering at her.

'Of course you can't,' Joe sighed. His eyes were black.

'I'm no lady, Willie,' Anna laughed.

'I can see that,' he tittered.

Joe's hand flew from nowhere and slapped Willie hard across the cheek. He staggered backwards, but only briefly, barely losing his balance. And his hands remained in his pockets. He looked at Joe with fear and disbelief. Joe smiled back, terrifyingly calm.

'He's at the Clit Club,' Willie snarled breathlessly. 'Rosebank. I'm sure you know it.' His eyes flicked insinuatingly from Joe to Anna and then back.

'I know it,' Joe retorted sharply. 'Now give me the cellphone number.'

Anna kept her eyes on those hands as they slowly came out of their pockets. Joe looked up into the clear winter sky, unconcerned, as if he had all the time in the world. All Willie drew out were some screwed-up chewing-gum wrappers and an empty cigarette box. He gave the box to Joe; a number was scribbled on the lip. Then he shrugged and looked out over the pool, as if nothing much at all had happened.

Joe pulled out his phone, pressed in a number and after a wait of only a second or two, gave a command that was inaudible to Anna. Willie lit a cigarette and looked up at the sky too, a picture of studied nonchalance.

Anna felt the winter wind, cold in her hair and against her cheek. Willie spoke again in his quiet drone, to no one in particular. 'Wish I'd taken Bazooka out last night. Wish I'd shot that bastard, then I'd have shot myself. At least then I would have done something worthwhile.'

Joe slipped the phone back into his pocket and then turned the full blast of his broadest smile on Willie.

'Thanks, china. See you around.' He blew Willie a kiss and walked away.

Anna ran to catch up with him. 'What about the informant?' she asked breathlessly when she came up alongside him in the lobby.

'What about him?' Joe clearly didn't give a damn.

Anna shook her head. This was police work, Joe Dladla style. Sleeves rolled up, wading into the thick of it, leading from the front, making it happen regardless of the rules. Anna tolerated it, like his superiors did, because he got the job done, but it made her anxious to observe it up close.

'He's got no protection. They'll kill him, Joe.'

'Couldn't happen to a nicer person far as I'm concerned.' He grinned, striding past the doorman out into the forecourt. She knew he intended to get to Bazooka first and that would keep Willie safe for now, but what if he didn't?

Anna didn't have time to pursue it with him.

The screeching tyres of the tracker van interrupted her as it slammed to a halt by the lobby entrance directly in front of them. The van's side door slid open. Inside were the surveillance team, four uniformed, flak-jacketed cops. Joe handed over the cigarette box with the number on it and they got to work, even as the door was sliding closed and the van was pulling away.

Things were happening so fast and so unexpectedly that Anna didn't have time to compute it all. A roaring sound pulled her attention up towards a chopper swaggering into view over the freeway before touching down in the parking lot. Joe squeezed her hand, shouting something she didn't hear, then jogged to the waiting helicopter.

Anna stared after him, her hair whipping around her face in the storm of beating blades. Seconds later they were airborne and disappearing into the brilliantly blue sky.

Anna found herself alone on the steps of the hotel, dressed in her clothes from the day before, stomach growling with hunger and mind reeling from the events of the still early morning.

The trackers in the van were using a piece of equipment that was relatively new to the service. The South African cellular network being digital, Anna knew phone calls could not be overheard, but they could be located to the cell that the phone was being used from or even merely passing through. If Bazooka's phone was switched on and if it was he who was using it, they'd find him in a matter of minutes. Whether or not he'd submit to arrest was another thing, but if Joe did manage to capture him it would be a huge coup for his department and a massive blow against crime.

Having no God Anna wasn't sure if her prayers would be successfully transmitted. Nevertheless she prayed for him to be careful and to be safe as she picked up a take-away coffee from the restaurant, got into her car and drove back towards Johannesburg.

She switched on the radio and the traffic news gave her an idea of how things were going. *There's congestion on Oxford Road. Drivers should avoid Rosebank, parts of which have been cordoned off by police. And in Sandton the William Nichol has slowed down to just a single lane due to an accident at the intersection* . . . Anna turned the radio off and headed for Rosebank, too curious and excited now to miss out on the action.

When she got to Rosebank, to the edge of the giant mall, one of Joburg's main shopping areas, it was swarming with cops and emergency vehicles. Anna's heart was pounding as she pulled up by the cordon. A young uniform with an acne infestation on his face stopped her. Anna flashed her Secretariat pass, knowing it didn't give her clearance to be there, but hoping he was too young to know the difference between a cop and a bureaucrat. He waved her through and she pulled over into a space between an ambulance and a squad car which was more abandoned than parked, its open doors a sign of the haste with which it had been evacuated. There was no sign of the chopper, but that might have come and gone.

Anna jogged towards the thickest concentration of policemen beyond the initial cordon. The Clit Club was at the end of a narrow service lane, which was now completely blocked off by a wall of blue. As she approached a shot went off, its report cracking the air, fear rippling through the line of cops like a rumour. There was a moment of stillness, then nervous motion as radios crackled and orders were barked.

She couldn't see Joe anywhere, he must be in the alleyway, at the club. Near to the shooting.

Fired up on adrenalin and given cover by the confusion around her, Anna pushed her way through the flak-jacketed uniforms and into the alley in the wake of two marksmen who'd been called in. By the time she was seen it was too late, she ignored the shouts and ran, keeping close against the wall, dodging the oily puddles and putrid trash along the lane. Please be okay, Joe. Please be okay. She said it over and over to herself, like a mantra.

Then another shot rang out. Anna hit the tar. Her knees scraped against the gravel as she took the weight of the fall in her wrists. 'Fuck!' The pain was sharp, but quickly dissipated by shock. The silence that followed was total. She looked up at the white rectangle of sky between the windowless buildings that rose around her. Her heart thudded against her chest. Then she heard a long, sharp intake of breath and realised dimly that it was her own.

After what seemed like minutes, the officers ahead of her stood up and Anna followed on jelly legs. Then came the sickening report of a third shot. And this time she didn't stop running.

Swinging round the sharp corner at the end of the alleyway she found herself in a crowded cul-de-sac before a short flight of steps leading up to a heavy fire door. In front of the door stood the infamous Bazooka, his eyes blazing, his feet planted defiantly apart and a 9mm clasped in both hands. Who the hell was doing the shooting? Was it him, or the cops?

Anna scanned the backs of the men lined up facing him and saw that the gun was levelled at Joe. And Anna saw that he'd been hit. Blood seeped from his left shoulder. He'd clamped his free hand over the wound and the gore trickled through his fingers. In his other hand was his Beretta, pointing straight at Bazooka.

It was a crazy stand-off. The man was completely surrounded, covered from every angle. What was he doing?

The air swam with fear.

'Gee my die twa Bazooka.' Give me the gun, Joe ordered coolly. The gangster's eyes scanned the alleyway and the firepower facing him. Anna followed his gaze up to the rooftops surrounding them, where police snipers stood at the ready. Then his gaze flicked back to Joe.

'So, comrade, we meet again,' he murmured and his voice resounded off the dirty walls of that dead-end street. Joe nodded. Anna's blood positively boiled. How *dare* he use that term, comrade, he who was betraying the very people he'd fought for, robbing them to line his own pockets?

At that moment Joe lunged for the pistol, but Bazooka was faster than him. He dropped the gun before Joe could get to it and flung his hands high in the air. It skitter-clattered to the ground. Then Joe was on him. Bazooka went down face first into the dirt and Joe's boot made contact with his face. Anna looked away.

That was Joe, unorthodox but effective. Bazooka certainly deserved to have his face kicked in, but that didn't make it right. It was the kind of behaviour cops were always being hauled up for, the kind of issue she dealt with in disciplinaries almost every week. Then again, none of those guys had pulled a criminal of this stature.

Bazooka was handcuffed, pulled off the ground and taken away, his face a mess of blood and pulp from the kick he'd sustained. Joe watched him go, squinting into the morning sun, his eyes devoid of any emotion. It terrified her when she saw him like this, like so many others who'd been damaged by violence. An affliction of my generation she thought, or of those of us who struggled.

Then he caught sight of Anna and smiled, raising his bloody hand in salute. Cameras whirred and shutters clattered. Anna waved back, not smiling at all, as paramedics swarmed around him.

Next morning that picture was on the front page of every South African newspaper and Assistant Commissioner Joe Dladla was everybody's hero.

fifteen

J ames was looking forward to this appointment. It had been
easy enough to arrange. He'd called up Anna Kriel's office,
been politely and efficiently put on hold by a bright-sounding
young woman, presumably her assistant, and then given a choice
of dates and times. He'd selected Saturday lunchtime, hoping
that'd mean she wouldn't be rushing back to work or to some
other meeting on the dot of two, so he could take his time.

James walked to the restaurant. It was a perfect morning.
Pavements were overflowing with coffee tables of chatter and
shop awnings shone brightly. Winter in Johannesburg never
ceased to delight James. With the light so bright and the sun so
hot during the day, it was easy to forget about the cold that
lurked in the shade and seeped up from the frozen earth at night.

The distance from James's house to Nuno's restaurant was
negligible, a half block along Third Avenue, dodging the
pavement protectors who clean and watch over cars for a
handful of change. Left on Seventh, past the esoteric gift shop,
the Full Stop Café and the pharmacy that never had any stock in
it, then across the street to his favourite haunt.

He intended to arrive early. An old habit that gave him time to
observe his subject during those unguarded moments as they
arrived. So James strolled into Nuno's at ten to one and glanced
around the room looking for the table with the best vantage
point. Then a pair of steady brown eyes caught his. She was
already there.

He grinned. She got me. One step ahead already. Uh-oh, this is
not going to be a picnic.

He skirted the tables, crossing to the corner she'd commandeered by the window. Anna stood up to greet him, took his hand
and shook it firmly. That forwardness and ease in her was
somehow both collegial and sexy. Feminine, but in a robust way,
like a rose in full bloom. She was wearing cargo pants and a
fashionable close-fitting T-shirt. Stripped of her sombre work
wear she looked younger and lighter. Looked good.

'Thanks for coming.'

She shrugged, smiling, and then folded her arms underneath
her breasts. 'Sorry about the other week, I was a bit ...
overwhelmed.'

He shook his head too vehemently. 'No, no! Should be me
apologising. Can't imagine what it must have felt like. I certainly
wouldn't have wanted a bunch of journos in my face!'

She nodded, then sat down, indicating for him to do the same.

James reached for a cigarette and lit up and a waitress brought
them menus. 'Will you have a glass of wine?' he asked.

Anna dipped her chin by way of acceptance. 'Thanks.'

He ordered two glasses of Sauvignon Blanc, and the waitress
departed.

Anna kicked off.

'You know, I'm surprised we've never met before, this is such
a small town. But you haven't been here long?'

It was a question, not an observation. Christ, now *she's* doing
the interviewing. James flicked his cigarette against the edge of
the ashtray. 'Nope. Not long at all. Was posted here for a British
paper, but resigned. Now I'm with the *Sunday Chronicle*.'

She nodded as if she was mentally ticking something off. 'So
what are you – Brit or South African?'

'I guess I'm a bit of both,' he said thoughtfully.

'Where's home?'

'Oh, I dunno. Everywhere?' James laughed throatily.

She seemed puzzled by his answer and perhaps a little
judgemental too. He wasn't sure, but he felt as if he sounded
rootless, irresponsible, bit of a dilettante. He stubbed his
cigarette out, feeling uncomfortable under such intense scrutiny.
She shifted in her seat, cupping her hands beneath her chin,
waiting for him to go on.

'Guess I've lived in a lot of places. No doubt I'll live in a lot more. But you know what I *love* about this country?' James reached for another cigarette and searched in his pocket for matches while he spoke. 'It's like a huge puzzle. And I love that. I love mystery, all mysteries. People are a mystery. It's like meeting someone new and exciting, a whole new adventure, *every* day. Do you know what I mean?'

Anna glanced at the scrape and flare of James's match as he lit up. 'Uh-huh, I know,' she answered mildly, 'but it's never long before their mysteries are unwrapped and the disappointing ordinariness underneath is revealed.'

'That doesn't always happen,' James said flatly.

'Always,' she asserted.

He cocked his head to one side, drawing on his cigarette while he watched her.

'Do I disappoint you already?' he asked, with more than a hint of flirtation dancing in his eyes.

'Not yet,' she smiled back. The directness of her gaze electrified him, unsettled him in the most delicious way. Was she doing it on purpose? He couldn't tell. James wasn't interested in understanding the alchemy of attraction. He loved to feel it though, as if his skin, indeed the very air around him, was humming.

She was a tough one to read. He couldn't be sure he'd got a handle on what was in her mind. Anna Kriel didn't look at people in the glancing way that most people do, her scrutiny felt penetrating, disquietingly so.

'But you're quite sure I will? Disappoint you, that is,' he said finally.

Anna laughed, beautifully. James sucked on his cigarette as he waited for her answer, but she said nothing. He frowned, feigning disappointment, but his eyes remained curious.

'Poor Anna. A life with no mystery. How very communist of you.'

'Oh, but I was *never* a communist,' she bridled playfully.

'That's not what I've heard, though by all accounts your transformation from Bolshevik into bureaucrat didn't take so long.'

'Well, I'm not the best of bureaucrats unfortunately. I have trouble with that phrase – "Yes, Minister".'

'So I've heard.'

She looked surprised, but not displeased to learn that he'd been enquiring about her. 'And what else have you heard?' she asked, raising her wine glass to her lips.

'Oh, general damning evidence of an independence of mind and spirit, which no doubt makes you inherently unreliable in the eyes of our great leader.'

'No comment,' she said, with a wry smile.

They were interrupted by the waitress, who returned to take their lunch orders. Anna hadn't even glanced at the menu. James ordered in the time she took to open it.

'You eat here often?'

He nodded, feeling a prickle of embarrassment. Yet more evidence to support a profile of him as free-floating, rootless, undomesticated.

'Here or Sam's,' she smiled, looking down at the list of choices.

'Yep, you've noticed. No time to cook.'

Anna raised an eyebrow as she handed her menu back to the waitress. 'Give me what he's having.'

'No problem.' The waitress took their menus and departed.

James sat back, tilting his chair onto two legs so he could look at her with more distance.

James belonged as entirely, snugly and elegantly as a bespoke suit, inside himself. His environment and community mattered only peripherally. He was his writing and he was utterly self-contained in that. So distinctly individual he sometimes felt he was in danger of becoming isolated by it. Whereas Anna was the opposite, so assimilated, so much a part of the world around her that she was in danger of disappearing in the opposite direction. And that wasn't the only difference between them, James reflected. She was all angles and lines and coordinates. He was a meanderer, all spirals and backtracks and haphazard inter-sections.

'So, about Paul,' he began at last.

'Yes, about Paul,' she sighed. Took another sip of wine and looked out across the restaurant. There was such longing and distance in her gaze; he wondered what she saw that he didn't.

The restaurant was almost full now, with Saturday shoppers taking a break and lingering lovers and girlfriends gossiping.

'I often wish I could be like them,' she murmured. 'Ordinary. Out for lunch to hang out and catch up. Instead I'm always circling murder.' She looked back at him and smiled disconcertingly.

'But you don't have to, do you?' he asked bluntly. She seemed to flinch inwardly.

'I suppose that's a matter of opinion,' she answered with a brittle edge to her voice.

'Yes, I suppose so,' he mumbled apologetically. 'But back to Paul.'

Anna dipped her chin again in a gesture that was becoming familiar.

'I gather he had a number of drug convictions before he went to Wits University.'

Her eyes narrowed, assessing him before she nodded curtly.

'Did he talk much about that?'

Anna's steady eyes were locked on him; she appeared not even to blink as she launched dryly into the story. 'Paul was always very honest about his mistakes, but very ashamed too. He had a tough time as a child. Apparently his mother ran off with the neighbour and either by choice or out of fear of her ex, disappeared for nine years. For nine whole years there was no contact between mother and son.'

She took a sip of her wine, still not breaking eye contact. 'Paul's father was a difficult, cruel man who beat his sons. At sixteen, Paul dropped out of school and into dagga smoking. He got expelled from school, his dad threw him out and he slid into an underworld of dealing and dossing. At seventeen he was arrested for marijuana possession and served a couple of months. At eighteen he was done for dealing and sent down for longer. It was during the second prison term that he pulled himself together. Finished school by correspondence course and began to see things around him that he knew were wrong.'

James smoked as he listened to her. Her voice was clear, unwavering. 'It was one of the very first things Paul told me. He didn't speak about it much. How did you find out?'

James shrugged. 'I'm a journalist. It's my job.' It hadn't been hard either. A quick trawl through police records and he'd got a fat folder of information. Nothing of the scale of importance as the page that had floated to the surface in London, but a lot of interesting details that were left out of the hero's standard print profile.

'So he enrolled part time at Wits, got involved in student politics and was recruited into the underground. Any idea who by?'

'Oh ja, that's easy. It was Joe who identified him. He was liaising with the Joburg campuses at that stage. It was Joe who recruited me as well.'

'And military training?'

She shook her head, her hair shimmering darkly. 'Not for me, though Paul did get some basics. He enjoyed all that stuff. You know? Those games they play – dismantling and reassembling AKs blindfolded, messing around with limpet mines. But Paul wasn't military.'

'What about Joe Dladla?'

'Joe?' Anna played with the stem of her empty wine glass, gazing thoughtfully past James and into the busy street. She shrugged and then her eyes met his again. 'He had some military links, was somehow connected to the Transvaal Urban Machinery, but I don't know much about that. We don't really talk about that time, especially not Joe.' She sat up, leaning forward onto her elbows. 'The present is too demanding and exciting, he's not interested in the past.'

'Where would he have trained?'

'Angola and the Soviet Union.' She signalled to the waitress for more wine. 'I know at some point he was based in the camps in Angola, but he chose to operate internally. Exile was like death to so many of our comrades. Maybe you know more about that than me.'

James shifted in his seat, tilting his head to one side thinking about exile. For his mother perhaps. Not for him. The waitress brought a bottle and James waited for her to fill their glasses before carrying on.

'And the night Paul and Jacob were killed ... what do you remember?'

Anna's hand flicked through the air dismissively. 'Ag, that

stuff's all been written about ad nauseam, can't you find it in the clippings?'

'Yes, I *could*,' he challenged. But Anna was not prepared to be drawn. She sipped at her wine, then put the glass down very definitely.

'You know, the things I remember are strange, as if my mind very deliberately veers from the horror of what it was presented with. Like in the mortuary, when we went to identify the bodies. What I recall most vividly is being struck by the change in the quality of the air. It wasn't the smell as much as the texture of it – sharp and metallic.'

James looked back at her quizzically. Anna went on: 'Like now, when you want me to tell you about his death, my mind goes blank. And I'm not going to try and dig deeper just to give you a few tears to report first hand.'

James raised his eyebrows and made a face, nodding as he did so. There was no way round such candour.

'You know,' she said, leaning forward as if she was warming to him again, 'the thing that gets me is – how can it still be so obscure? The wall of silence – around the police at least – has mostly crumbled since the Truth Commission, but on this case, Paul and Jacob's, there's *nothing*.'

'Maybe it's so muddy because no one wants it to be clear. Because it's just not as simple as a Security Police hit on a target from the other side.'

'Listen. Anything's possible.' Anna picked up her glass and took another drink. 'For a long time I believed it would come out, then for a long time I believed I had to come to terms with the possibility I would never know. Now I feel hopeful again. Certain even. The mystery will be solved.'

'And if it isn't?'

Anna frowned, then half smiled and shook her head.

'What?' James looked puzzled.

'How long have you been a journalist?'

'What. . . . What do you mean?'

'I mean that's a stupid question.'

'I'm sorry, I'm trying . . .' He found himself momentarily lost for words. 'I'm trying to understand your . . . to understand *you*. That's all.'

Anna's face was close to his now, her arms resting on the table, hands closed around one another just inches from his. 'I *have* to know.' She almost whispered it. 'I want to know more badly than you've ever wanted to know anything in your life. With every inch of my being, with every moment of every day. It's like needing to know your genetic map, where you come from. Why you are who you are.'

He was locked in the intensity of what she was saying, couldn't move, couldn't react, could only listen.

'I sometimes imagine the release of it. The pure letting go I could feel if at last someone were to illuminate for me the one shadowy part of my life. *If only* someone would name it, explain the inexplicable,' her voice had dropped to almost nothing, 'I think then I'd be free.'

James felt breathless by the time she finished. He leaned back, regarding her with open fascination.

It was her control, and the passion that pulsed so close to the surface, which compelled him. It was like a throbbing vein beneath a silky smooth skin.

'And if that explanation turned out to be unpalatable, to be something you didn't want to hear?' he asked quietly.

'At least I would *know*!' she declared. Her voice had returned to a level pitch again.

'But *could* you handle it?'

Anna was thoughtful for a moment. 'Well, I've handled everything else,' she said, and then she smiled, her eyes glittering.

James smiled back. 'So you have. So you have.'

At that point their lunch arrived and the practical matter of making room for the plates and setting everything down provided a welcome pause. There was a brief silence after the waitress departed and Anna tucked into her food.

'So, do you think all this makes you a fucked-up person?' James wondered, teasingly. Anna laughed out loud.

'No, I don't. In fact I think I'm a lot less fucked up than most, probably even than you.'

'Well then, *my* sources were wrong about you,' he countered playfully.

'How's that?'

'They say you're a workaholic, that you don't go out, don't talk much, that you certainly don't give interviews.'

'Is this an interview?' She was playing along.

James smiled mildly. 'Oh no. This is a conversation.'

'Well, most conversation is pointless,' she said, her tone shifting back to serious. 'I mean it's just noises that indicate pleasure or dissatisfaction, distaste or dislike, or threat, or dominance, or submissiveness.' Her hands weighed up and tipped out each word as she spoke.

'Or attraction,' he added.

She looked at him sharply. 'Or attraction,' she concurred.

'And you think you're less fucked-up than me,' he chuckled.

'Yep. And there's a lot less noise in my life too.'

They finished eating in a companionable silence. James pulled another cigarette from the dwindling packet in front of him. She smiled and he watched the passers by as he lit up.

'So, you're a quiet one,' he said, breathing out smoke. 'No, not quiet, just economical. But this is all pointless conversation.' She leaned forward, her eyes shining with mild amusement, or maybe it was just the wine. '*You* were going to tell me something about Paul,' she said.

'Yes. Yes. I was.'

James felt himself come back to earth with a thud. He had no idea of how to broach this and wasn't sure if he wanted to any more. Who the hell was he to do this to her?

'So. Let's hear it.'

'Okay.' He took a deep breath and jumped. 'Were *you* ever a spy?' he asked, pointing at her with his cigarette, an exaggerated gesture of intimidation that he was hoping might soften the blow.

But the second he'd uttered those words he regretted them. The shutters came down in her eyes. The clang was almost audible. Their verbal dance had come to an end, the music screeched to a halt like the needle sliding and bouncing off a record, leaving a horrible dissonance in the air.

'What?'

James shifted, opened his mouth to speak, then closed it again. He leaned forward, stubbed out his cigarette. Looked up at her. The cold in her eyes was awful; it was hard to hold her gaze.

Riptide, then tsunami. He'd been pulled from the beach into the glittering sea and then yanked upwards on a tidal wave and flung back onto grating sand.

'Anna, this is not a story you're going to like.'

'Well, we won't know until I've heard it.' She spoke calmly, but her tone was serrated.

'Look . . .' He spoke reluctantly, his voice softer and heavier. 'Were you aware that Paul Lewis was assigned a Security Police Source Number?'

Anna frowned. 'You mean a File Number?'

'No, I mean a *Source* Number. I have documentation that shows his Security Police *Source* Number.' He repeated this slowly. 'It suggests that Paul,' James paused, delicately clearing his throat before he continued, 'was working for the other side.'

And he saw, as he said it, that he may as well have stubbed his cigarette out on her hand, or shoved the table into her solar plexus.

'You mean that he was a spy?' Anna flung this back at him incredulously.

'Yes. That's what I mean.'

'But who would talk such kak?' She struggled for words, her outrage increasing with every second that passed. 'I mean, the fact that they were murdered – and in the *way* that they were – is enough to refute that. I mean why would the cops kill one of their own?'

'It wouldn't have been the first time,' James countered.

She nodded. 'That's true. That *is* true. But it doesn't answer the question, why Paul and Jacob?' The initial sharpness of her tone had subsided. She took a deep breath. 'So you've got this story. Where's the proof?' she demanded, as if this would sort the thing out once and for all.

'Okay,' he sighed. 'What I have is a scrap of an old file and a couple of Source Reports that I matched to the numbers in the file.' James reached into the breast pocket of his shirt and pulled out the single useful piece of paper he'd salvaged from the file he'd bought in London. Folded up with that were three pages of typed-up source report forms. He unfolded them and spread them out on the table in front of her. She didn't touch them.

'I came across these by accident,' he went on. 'Was working on a completely different story.'

James felt terrible watching her. She was breathing fast and shallow, her chest heaving with emotion. He looked down at the first page, wishing he'd never met Mrs Groenewald or followed up on this unlikely lead, but it was too late now.

'It's a list of four names and numbers. I didn't notice it at first, but looking closer I realised it's a key code of some sort. Three of them were names I'd never seen before. I checked them out and they were small fry, not worth following up, but they were all men who informed for the police. The fourth name is Paul's.' James lowered his voice. 'The number written next to his corresponds with the number of a source who was reporting to Captain Frans Nel of the Security Police.' He turned over the top page to reveal the one beneath it. 'This is one of his reports. This is the original, in Afrikaans.' Anna scanned the page with the thoroughness of a pro. James had had it translated so he knew it contained only mundane stuff and made no mention of anything or anyone that would connect it conclusively to Paul Lewis. He knew she'd see that in an instant.

'Are there any more?'

He nodded and showed her the other two. Same deal though, nothing to show either way that it definitely was or definitely wasn't Paul who'd typed these reports.

Anna kneaded her forehead with her fingertips as she read, the pressure leaving reddish marks on her skin. James wanted to reach across and touch her, to comfort her, but when he did, she moved her arm away. Finished with the papers, she looked up at him, eyes shimmering with contempt.

'Do you understand who we are dealing with here? Do you know who Paul is?'

James came back at her calmly. 'That's precisely why I wanted to see you about it first.'

She didn't seem to hear him.

'Paul's commitment was absolute, his integrity was impeccable. He gave his *life* to the struggle.'

'Then what are these documents?'

She shook her head wearily. 'I have no idea. But I do know

that Paul was no spy. I *know* Paul,' she declared finally, her voice husky with feeling.

James wondered if she'd used the present tense deliberately. It was the second time she'd done it.

'*How* can you be so sure, Anna? How can you be sure that you know anybody?'

She glared back at him with incomprehension. It was blindingly simple to her. 'You just do. You *know* when someone is lying to you.'

James looked down at the white tablecloth. That was it, he realised. That was Anna Kriel. A true believer, a person who took others at face value, who trusted because she was undoubtedly trustworthy herself and could not imagine another way.

Alison reared up in his mind. Had he known about her and Alan? The truth was that he both had and hadn't. In retrospect it all fitted, but at the time he had trusted her and therefore had seen only what he wanted to see.

'How do you know you aren't being set up?' Anna asked more calmly, though he could feel the pressure of her anger. 'Those reports and the key code you found, how do you know they aren't a plant?'

'It's possible. Anything's possible,' James said quietly. 'But I don't think so.'

Anna shook her head, her face contorting bitterly. 'And that's all you have? Nothing else to check it against?'

James looked down at the tablecloth again, at his fingers making invisible circles. 'As I told you – the other three names *do* check out as registered informers. That gives us evidence that's strong enough to publish.'

Anna swung her head away and then back towards him, as if she were about to spit, or scream, or strike him.

'And you're going to publish?' She could barely get the words out.

James bit down on his lip, finding it hard to look her in the eye.

'Yes.' He was going to publish. It was a great story. And it looked like it was true. What else could he do? She looked at him with such outrage and bewilderment that he wanted desperately to explain, but he knew there was no point. Besides, she wasn't going to stick around to listen. Anna stood up, took her bag and walked out and James could do nothing but watch her leave.

sixteen

Anna did not think, for even a moment, that there was any truth in James Kay's allegations. His 'evidence' was too slender, too out of the blue, too off the wall to dent a reputation like Paul's. It was mud-slinging, sheer vandalism of the kind that only journalists are capable of in their insatiable quest for bad news and sensation.

Nevertheless the encounter with Kay had rattled her to her core. She realised, as she tossed and turned sleeplessly, that this awful disquiet stemmed from recognition. She'd had the distinct sense that she *knew* James Kay. It was the same shiver of familiarity she'd experienced when she first met Paul, a kind of excitement that lit her up. The symptoms were identical – that jump in her stomach, the self-consciousness that made it hard to look directly into his eyes, the terrifying, exhilarating, unbidden charge of merely being close to him.

She was furious with herself and felt guilty too, as if somehow she'd deserved the blow because she'd felt attracted to him. She wanted to kick herself for the way she had spoken so freely. Kay was a reporter; it was his job to create an instant intimacy. If that involved a bit of flirting and the smoothing on of a bit of charm, then so what? The means always justified the end.

And she'd opened up to him like a willing fool. Let him look right in at all her loneliness and her longing.

This was not the life she'd wanted, not the life Paul had promised. Her grief had frozen her so she couldn't move forward, couldn't unlock herself from the tragedy, and couldn't start afresh because that would be like abandoning him. It should have been him and her and their kids and their life together in the new South Africa. Instead, here she was in her little spinster cottage, living with ghosts. Childless and spectral. A sad, workaholic bureaucrat with no future, only a past.

James had ripped off the veil and revealed the true Anna behind it. She felt violated and exposed and desperately alone.

By the following morning the anxiety seemed to have settled in, like a background hum, like air-conditioning. Anna pulled on some clothes and set out to pick up breakfast and the Sunday papers on Fourth Avenue. A pleasant weekend routine of hers transformed today by dread.

It was early. The Melville streets were empty and spattered, as always on a Sunday, with the flotsam of the previous night's partying. She marched up Seventh, head down, hands balled up into fists, hoping with all her might that James Kay had dropped his story.

But he hadn't.

Anna saw the headline from across the street. She felt it as a dull thud to the back of the head, as if someone had coshed her with incredulity. Disbelief nailed her feet to the pavement. There it was on the newsstand, between the fragrant boxes of coriander and mangoes, the blunt black type glowering at her: STRUGGLE HERO WAS SECURITY POLICE SPY. Somehow Anna dragged the dead weight of her body across the street.

Below the bold type was a sub-heading: *Paul Lewis murder riddle deepens – Sunday Chronicle exclusive*. Staring up at her was a photograph of Paul from his Union days, fist raised in defiance, eyes shining with determination. Next to that was a blow-up of the handwritten key code of sources – a fancy graphic that damned his heroism to hell.

James Kay's tone made Anna want to scream. He wrote as if it were true. And that was how people would read it, or too many people at any rate.

It seems likely that Jacob Oliphant died unaware of the true nature of his and Lewis's mission that night. For Paul Lewis was the traitor in their midst.

Anna scanned the page frantically, trying to take it all in at once, her eyes catching phrases here and there.

When was Lewis recruited as a police informant and by whom? Who was Lewis's Security Police Handler? Was it Frans Nel, the Captain he reported to? Or are there others lurking in the recesses of this mystery? And perhaps not least, who else in Lewis's circle and in his cell knew of his spying? His partner, Anna Kriel, vehemently denies allegations that Lewis was a spy.

Anna dropped the newspaper back onto the stack and stumbled away, her mind reeling.

The bastard! How could someone do such a thing? *Why* would someone do such a thing?

At home Anna switched on her cellphone. There were a couple of messages in her voicemail box, but only one from that morning. Incredibly it was from James Kay, speaking in a voice that was halting and tentative. 'Anna, hi. You're very much on my mind. Call me when you can.' Fuck you, she muttered, pressing the delete key.

There was only one thing to do. Anna climbed into her car and drove over to Fordsburg, to her ma's place.

Yasmin Kriel still lived in the same apartment, though it seemed to get smaller and smaller as the years went by and sons-in-law and furniture and grandchildren accumulated. Yasmin was in the kitchen in her dressing gown, feeding Natasha's youngest when Anna arrived.

'Hell!' her mother exclaimed as she struggled with the padlocks on the security gate. 'What on earth's happened to you!?' Anna fell into her mother's arms, a difficult feat, as Yasmin was a diminutive woman compared to her daughters. They all had their father's solid build. Anna was shaking as she slumped over her ma's tiny frame, comforting koala-bear arms holding her tight.

The baby, sensing Anna's frazzled mood, started to cry. Yasmin disentangled herself from her daughter's towering embrace and went to pick the baby up. 'What's happened?' She demanded sharply, a hint of panic in her voice, as she plugged the baby's mouth with a bottle.

Anna sank into one of the kitchen chairs, her head in her hands. 'You haven't seen the papers yet?'

Yasmin shook her head as she adjusted the child on her hip and went to put the kettle on.

Anna mumbled through her fingers. 'It's on the front page of the *Chronicle*. Paul Lewis was a spy.'

'What?' Yasmin squawked.

'That's what it says, Ma.'

Yasmin began to laugh. Anna took her hands from her face and looked up to see her mother chuckling and shaking her head over the teapot. 'Oh, but that's ridiculous,' she clucked. 'Come! I'm making you some sweet tea and putting you straight to bed.'

Anna happily submitted to her mother's attention, allowing herself to be tucked up in her big, soft bed and attended to with trays of tea and hot food. She felt better immediately. Her ma was right, it was ridiculous for anyone to accuse Paul of being a spy. James Kay and his article would be laughed out of town.

Then her phone started ringing.

Rachel was reassuringly furious. Mouthing off about libel and lawsuits and generally taking Kay and his paper to the cleaners.

Willem Swanepoel didn't seem to think that suing the *Sunday Chronicle* was necessary, that in fact it might prove counter-productive. 'No point in giving credence to their story by dragging it into court.' He was unconcerned about the damage to Paul's reputation. 'This stuff is as old as smear campaigns and counter-intelligence and they've sprayed it all over the front page because they haven't got anything else to sensationalise this week.' His deep voice and beautiful Afrikaans accent calmed her even more.

Joe too was unfazed by the allegations, though he expressed concern about the motives for the article. Anna didn't speak to him for long. Instead of resting and allowing his body to recover from the gunshot wound Bazooka had inflicted on him, Joe had spent much of the week holed up in a police station, conducting Bazooka Rabopane's interrogation. He'd been there much of the night when he called, and sounded tired. 'It's not a crisis, but we need to take this Kay character pretty seriously, find out what he's up to. I'll look into it this week.' Anna thanked him and told him to try and get some sleep. 'Plenty of time for that later,' he joked and then hung up.

But there were others who called sounding anxious and

doubtful. For them Anna was calm and reassuring, repeating over and over that the story wasn't true. She felt her certainty quieting them, but it was clear that some of the mud had stuck.

'Why don't we take a break, go down to Durban together?' her mother suggested cheerfully. 'Come back when this has blown over?'

Anna smiled. 'That was what Paul said the day before he was killed. He was gonna take me to Durban when they got back.'

Her mother smoothed back her hair and kissed her on the forehead. 'Shew, a holiday would be nice. Can't remember the last one,' she murmured.

Anna leaned into the pillows her mother had plumped up behind her. Durban was where her father had taken them every year for the mid- and end-of-year school holidays. They'd been happy times with her family, though for some reason the particular memory that floated into her mind that morning was one of disappointment.

She was all of seven years old and she and her sisters had dressed up in identical catsuits made by their mother. Their skin darkened to a shiny coffee brown by the sun. Their glistening hair plaited and tied up with bobbles and bows in matching pink. They were standing on the beachfront with their faces pressed between the slats of the fence around Newtons Amusement Arcade, staring longingly at the happy faces of the white children swinging high up on the Ski Lift, swirling around on the Octopus and speeding around in Dodgem Cars. 'Why?' she'd whined to her daddy, 'why can't we go there?'

'Because it's for whites only.'

'But WHY, Daddy?'

It was one of the few questions Daddy couldn't answer.

Anna left her mother's place feeling better, but the buzz of anxiety hadn't quite left her. Something important had changed. She could feel it, but she didn't know what it was.

An inkling of it came through to her late that night in the form of a phone call from the Minister's PA. He wanted to see her in his office, first thing the following morning. It didn't bode well. Why didn't he call her himself for a start? He was an old friend, Anna knew his wife, sometimes even babysat his kids. It was all too clear what was going on. The accusation against Paul, if true, immediately cast doubt on her. It was how he would think. How could two people be so close and not know one another's deepest, darkest secrets?

Anna didn't sleep much that night either. She felt jumpy, unsafe. She took her gun from the safe, loaded it and set it down in the drawer of her bedside table.

seventeen

James was struggling to concentrate. It wasn't just Bara, a hospital which had the capacity to jangle even the steeliest of nerves. He'd visited the place often, but its capacity to shock seemed to increase, rather than diminish, each time. The place was one huge, haemorrhaging Emergency Room, where the overstretched doctors barely kept up. They no longer bothered to record if a patient was HIV Positive. Positive was the norm, not the exception and it was only Negative patients whose status was noted, and they were an ever-decreasing number.

James found the stench and the vastness of the place too much. He had to wind up this interview fast.

Refiloe, the woman who sat before him perched on a hospital gurney, was thirty-one years old, a domestic worker who commuted by taxi between her home in Meadowlands and her job in Sandton. Four months earlier she'd been raped. 'I had pain in my womb,' she explained softly, 'so I came to look for a doctor to help me. The doctor took some of my bloods and told me I've got this thing. This HIV.' She didn't look James in the eye as she spoke, just sat very still on the edge of her bed, her hands folded into her lap. 'At least I know he's dying too,' she murmured. 'That's the only consolation.'

James couldn't get out fast enough. He rushed through the corridors, dodging nurses and wheelchairs and distraught relatives in his flight towards the exit. Welcome to South Africa, he thought angrily. Welcome to the hell of being black and poor and living in a township. Welcome to torches and voices and invaders in the dead of night. This young woman dragged into the street, screaming her lungs out but to no avail. No one came to help – her neighbours cowered behind their closed windows and barred doors, listening to the cries of just another woman going down.

He lit a cigarette before he reached the door. No one stopped him.

Rape nauseated him. It was the crime he simply couldn't grasp. He could imagine himself stealing or murdering or breaking the law in thousands of other ways, if pushed, but rape was unimaginable. And now that young woman was dying for some bastard who'd given her no choice. He would get the story down and out of his mind as quickly as possible.

He jumped into his car, fired up the engine and the sound system and took off.

The freeway glittered with cars, like steel bugs. The mid-afternoon sun hammered against his head as he drove. He slipped a cigarette from the pack on the seat next to him and lit it. All things considered, he should have been fine. The work was great, the stories incredible. His cash-in-transit investigation was bubbling nicely on the backburner. No ties, no complications. But the truth was he couldn't stop thinking about Anna Kriel.

She was so strangely remote from herself, so dreadfully, defiantly alone. He wondered if it was fear that kept her apart, it couldn't simply be grief, could it? Surely not after such a long time? Or could it be? If a person is too frightened or too aloof to risk herself and her heart then her life must empty out, it must narrow to almost nothing. Undoubtedly it would feel safer that way – never being reached for, never reaching out, but surely it didn't have to be so?

Thoughts of her spun back to him against his will all too frequently since their disastrous lunch. Earnest, beautiful Anna, who had lost the great love of her life, but kept him alive in her mind so that she could get through the present. Who had taken Joe as her lover because he wasn't interested in a committed relationship and perhaps also because he was the closest to Paul?

James kicked himself over and over for having been so crass, for blundering so cynically into her life thinking that she'd be interested in his little discovery. He hadn't broken any code of journalism, but something really irked him about how he'd behaved. Maybe it's just that he'd fancied his subject. Mustn't let that happen again, he told himself sternly.

He'd talked the situation over several times with his editor, Chris, who was delighted with the scoop and the reaction it had caused. The daily papers had exploded with it. The *Star* carried pictures of Anna leaving her office the next day, her hand up to fend off photographers. There was talk of an investigation into her past, of her being 'suspended pending further enquiries', which James felt was not just ludicrous, but completely unjust.

What a button he'd pressed. He'd simply had no idea. And it was pretty clear that she wasn't interested in any apology. None of his calls had been returned. He'd have to give up on trying to repair that damage. Pity, he thought, as he sailed along the freeway towards home.

The phone rang. A welcome distraction. Even more welcome was the singsong tone of the caller. It was Ilse, demanding that he pick her up immediately. She's just finished filming an interview at the Parktonian in Braamfontein and she needed a drink.

'Your command is my wish!' he declared happily and slung a left, slipping off the freeway at Smit Street.

He saw her from halfway down the hill. Ilse looked amazing – her hair was aflame with fresh henna and she was wearing a short lime-green dress with a sexy zip down the front. In one hand she carried a bright pink PVC handbag, in the other a burning cigarette. She grinned like a kid, jumping up and down the second she caught sight of him in his vanilla convertible.

She jumped in over the door, flashing a triangle of lacy lilac panties as she bounced into the seat next to him. 'Nice wheels,' she breathed huskily as she settled back against the soft leather. James grinned, pleased to see her and pleased to be driving such a cool machine. The afternoon angst was instantly erased by Ilse's wicked lipstick smile and the city seemed magical in the golden light. 'Bar, James,' she ordered, like a punk Lady Penelope on acid. And he obeyed.

He cruised to a stop in front of a red traffic light at the intersection of Empire and Jan Smuts and turned to look at her, smiling helplessly as he took in the full effect. She smiled coyly back, curling the pink tip of her tongue upwards to wet her lip.

He was reaching over to take the cigarette from between her fingers when a movement behind her caught his eye. Out of nowhere a man dashed in between the cars, past Ilse, straight up to the passenger window of the mustard-coloured VW Beetle in front of them. The sound as his wrapped hands broke through the window was a terrible splintering crash. The man grabbed and was gone, a brown handbag swinging from his shoulder as he raced across the intersection and down onto the freeway, disappearing from sight in seconds. It happened so fast that James was briefly uncertain of whether or not it had happened at all.

'Did you see that?' he asked dazedly, his eyes fixed on the gap in the bushes into which the thief had disappeared.

Ilse shrugged nonchalantly, apparently unimpressed. 'Ja.'

The female driver of the car in front was frozen in surprise, her hands glued to the steering wheel, her mouth agape as she stared at the lethal shards of glass sticking up out of her window-frame. James opened his door to go and help her.

'What are you doing?' Ilse shrieked.

It was a sound of such dismay that he stopped dead, one foot inside the car and one on the road.

'I'm going to see if that woman's all right.'

'Of course she's all right. Get back in the car!'

Ilse was laughing and yelling all at once. James stared at her, appalled. In the meantime the traffic had started rolling forward, drivers behind were tooting and parping angrily and the woman who'd just lost her handbag was already driving shakily away.

'Welcome to Gauteng Province,' Ilse giggled as James put his car into gear.

They drove on in silence for a while. It wasn't the incident that shook him as much as Ilse and the other drivers' reactions, as if the robbery were so minor and commonplace it barely deserved a moment's reflection, and even worse how it was a given that the victim would just have to look after herself.

'I can never say that word without difficulty,' James said at last. 'Gauteng. It sounds like you're spitting. You roll the mucus around on the "Gau" and then gob out the "teng".'

'Sis!' Ilse exclaimed, relishing her disgust.

James slowed down as he pulled into Melville, past the busy

restaurants and bars, checking out the people enjoying the street in the soft glow of evening. He parked outside the Ant Bar, a candle-lit hidey-hole of a place on Seventh Street where the other members of Ilse's Special Report team had been dug in since lunchtime.

The talk was of the Truth Commission and violence and crime. Flip and hard and fast, there were no bleeding hearts or sensitive souls at that table – they were tough enough to take anything life chose to slap them with. And they carried off this impression with great success; there were no chinks visible in the armour that night.

Ilse sat beside James and sparks flew from her, more and more as the evening turned to night and the empty glasses stacked up in front of them. James warmed to the game, enjoying the attention and the carelessness of it, though he wasn't yet committed to seeing it through.

And somehow, in the naked way that it often does when the fizz of pheromones is in the air, the conversation turned to sex.

Squinting through a haze of cigarette smoke Ilse indicated a tall, bearded man who'd just come into the room with someone young enough to be his daughter on his arm. 'My ex,' she declared.

James wasn't all that interested. 'Bad scene?' he asked.

Ilse nodded. 'Bastard.'

James didn't know what to say. Took another sip of his drink. He was feeling distinctly woozy.

'But I'm way over that,' Ilse declared. 'As my mother always said – the only way to get over a man is to get under one.'

'So who'd you get under?'

Ilse laughed, her mouth open, lips wet and close to his.

'Oh, everyone dahling,' she drawled, 'everyone.'

James shrugged and drained his glass. 'So love really is dead then,' he muttered darkly, doing his best brooding poet impersonation.

Ilse's eyes glimmered as she quoted grandly, slurring some of the words. 'Oh yes, dahling. "What we call love is the desire to awaken and to keep awake in another's body, heart and mind, the responsibility of flattering, in our place, the self of which we are not very sure.'" She finished with a twirl of the wine in her glass, then lifted it to her mouth and drained the lot.

'Bet you don't know where that comes from Mister Oxford-andCambridge education.' She set the empty glass down with a triumphant flourish.

James watched her, smiling. 'You're damn right I don't.'

Ilse cocked her head to one side, regarding him for a moment before she replied. 'Paul Gerardy, *L'homme et l'amour.*' She looked immensely pleased with herself.

'Impressive,' he declared. 'I must reread my *Dictionary of Quotations*. You never know when one will come in handy.'

Ilse didn't like that. 'She really got to you, didn't she?' she said sharply.

'Who?' James shook a cigarette out of the box they were sharing and tapped the end on the rough wooden tabletop. He was smoking too much, would hate himself in the morning, but what the hell. Another day, another hangover.

'That one you left behind in London,' Ilse said, wiping the tips of her fingers across her mouth. 'The one you never talk about.'

'Ah yes,' he said slowly, 'the one I never talk about.'

Ilse raised her overly arched eyebrows. Her hand was on his leg now, her rings spiking through his jeans. He felt drunk and high. The warm room and the easy laughter carried him away.

'And what about you and the Ice Queen.' Ilse spoke the word ice with an emphasis that made it seem colder and sharper than it already was.

'Now who might that be?'

'Anna. Kriel,' she said, reaching up to run her fingers through his hair.

'Well, *there's* a story,' he breathed, not looking at her.

Ilse stood up abruptly, put her hand out towards him. James took it and followed her. She led him towards the bathroom, her hand small and hot in his. She hustled him ahead of her, into the cubicle marked Ladies, smiling at the girl who came out of the Men's next door. The girl didn't bat an eyelid. The sight of people bundling in and out of the loos was commonplace here. The toilet lids of Melville are covered in the trace lines of thousands of cocaine nights.

Ilse crouched down and her dress rode up. She scooped a

quarter gram or so from the little origami envelope she'd fished from her bag. Pulled out the frequent chopper card and cut the powder into two long rocket launchers. James leaned against the door, looking up at the ceiling fan and the flies grouped around the lamp. He felt drunk. Not sure what he was doing here. Not like he hadn't been here before, but the thrill of it was paler now.

He looked at Ilse crouched down by the loo, her head bent as she concentrated on rolling the note. Her skirt had ridden up so he could once again see the flash of her lilac knickers. The whole picture depressed him. He bent down to snort up the line anyway. It was there.

The hit was immediate. Ice in the face, storm in the brain, pump, pump, pumping heart. He felt great. She reached her hand behind his neck and pulled his face towards hers. Her mouth was hot and wet, she bit his lower lip, slid her tongue into his mouth and it was fan fucking tastic. 'Let's go,' she whispered.

James drove recklessly, one hand on the steering wheel, wiping his lipstick-smeared mouth with the back of the other. The street was a blur of lights and music.

At the house he pulled an almost empty bottle of Jack Daniels and two mugs from a kitchen cupboard. He handed her the whisky as she prowled from room to empty room. He switched on the only new thing in the house, the sound system, and played music. She sat down on the only piece of furniture that allowed for such comfort, his bed. She cut another line on a little mirror out of her bag. Held it up to him like the girl with the tray in the Martini ads. He smiled and snarfed it up in a second.

The phone rang. James ignored it, wanting to kiss her, but Ilse stood up distractedly and stalked over to the window, appearing to make a study of the garden. James watched her. There was something wild and animal about Ilse. And there was something secretive in the smile that spread across her lips as she turned from the window and looked at him across the room.

'You know, I always get the feeling with you that you're not quite here.'

James lay back on the bed, resting on his elbows, and waited. He wasn't sure if he wanted this. Yet he didn't *not* want it. The telephone rang again. He couldn't pick it up now without confirming what she'd just said, so he ignored it.

'Like you're distracted. Or there's someone else on your mind.'

Her look was a teasing one, half reproachful, half come-hither.

'Oh?' He hated this kind of fishing expedition. Didn't really know where it was going, what it was for, how he could say anything that would be the right thing. 'You fishing?'

'Maybe?'

'Don't,' he said bluntly.

The phone stopped ringing. Ilse ran her tongue over her lips. Then she put her mug down onto the windowsill and kicked off her shoes. She unzipped her dress.

'One day you're gonna tell me what made you so *hardegat*.'

'What's that?'

'Hardegat is Afrikaans for you, James Kay.'

She grinned and pulled her dress up over her head in a single, confident action, letting it fall slowly from her fingers to the floor and pausing a moment before she crossed the room, allowing for the full impact of her milky skin and lacy lilac underwear to hit.

'I'm not sure I like the sound of that,' he answered weakly.

'I can't blame you, but for now, Mister Kay, this interview is over.'

She climbed onto the bed astride him, one knee planted either side of him. He lay back, watching her as she leaned down to kiss him. He closed his eyes. Ilse tasted of cigarettes and chewing gum and she smelled of sweat and sickly, cinnamony perfume. He reached up, sliding his hands around her soft hips and over her back, pulling her towards him.

Then the telephone rang again.

Ilse giggled playfully as she pulled away and lunged for the handset. She was beautiful in that moment, her cheeks flushed and her mouth wet from kissing. She picked up the phone and was about to speak, when James grabbed it from her, not quite playfully.

'Kay,' he barked as Ilse unbuttoned his shirt.

It was Chris, his editor. James groaned inwardly, knowing this meant an emergency and that he would be called back to the office. At the same time a shudder of delight shivered through him as Ilse's mouth made contact with his left nipple, her silky hair skimming his chest as she moved down, sinking her tongue into his belly button.

'Sorry, Chris, can you repeat that?'

James turned onto his side, cupping his hand over the receiver to hear more clearly. Ilse's exploration of his body grew more insistent.

'I *said* – Bazooka Rabopane has escaped from police custody,' Chris shouted back.

'Fuck!'

James sat up, almost knocking Ilse out of the way. She looked startled for a moment and then hurt, but only fleetingly.

'I'll be there in ten minutes,' he said, a different kind of fire in his eyes now as he clicked off the phone.

Ilse sat very still, looking at him through narrowed eyes, a kind of haughtiness thinly masking disappointment.

'Listen, Ilse, I'm really—'

She shook her head. 'Told you. Your head's always somewhere else.'

He felt terrible, but only for a moment. It was true, his head was already somewhere else.

Ilse shrugged, pulling her dress over her bra and wriggling it down her hips. She planted a cigarette in her mouth and lit it with the rhinestone lighter that hung on a pink plastic cord around her neck. 'One of those things, baby,' she murmured, and then scooped her shoes up from the floor.

eighteen

Anna heard the news of Bazooka's escape on the radio as she was driving to work, flying along the Ben Schoeman Highway in the wintry glare. She couldn't believe it. Couldn't believe the sudden adversity of the universe. Why was everything going so wrong? Joe was even less accustomed to failure than she was and Bazooka's escape so soon after the very public victory of his arrest was catastrophic not only for Joe's unit, but for the Police Service in its entirety.

Even the landscape was hostile that morning. The Highveld was dry and sickly yellow. Black scorch marks snaked across the hills where fires had crackled through the tinder-dry grass. A huge blaze was burning in Midrand, lines of flame slicing across the veld; the smoke glowed orange above it, drifting in a lambent fog across the freeway. Traffic had slowed down to a crawl passing through it. Anna clenched her teeth as she tailgated the car in front of her and followed it through, her eyes stinging, hands tight on the wheel.

The traffic failed to clear with the smoke and minutes later Anna saw why as she inched passed the wreckage of a recent accident. She looked away from the mangled cars at the roadside, but her eyes landed on a body stretched out along the white line. A slender pair of feet in snappy snakeskin high heels jutted out from one end of the blanket covering the corpse. Anna's hand flew to her mouth as she recoiled from the sight. It had been the merest of glances, but the unwelcome image was vividly imprinted. She shook her head in an attempt to shake it from her mind.

Welcome to South Africa. Welcome to carnage on the roads and crime gone crazy.

Oh no. Mustn't start. Don't want to sound like those people, Anna told herself sharply. But a gloomy mood had settled around her. The Voortrekker Monument loomed on the horizon like a massive brick shit-house. Then there was the prison to greet you as the highway curved between koppies and you entered the city proper. Somewhere in the depths of that hideous sick-yellow building resided the infamous Colonel Ig Du Preez. Anna couldn't imagine a better home for him. A grim place for the grim reaper, she thought as she drove on into Pretoria.

But thinking of Ig Du Preez gave her an idea.

The Colonel was South Africa's most notorious prisoner, apartheid's most ruthless and effective assassin. Currently serving four life sentences plus a hundred and eighty years for committing some of the most vicious murders in the country's history. He had killed with anything that came to hand, guns, grenades, a garden fork; he once beat a man to death with a snooker cue.

He was the hero of the back-room boys of coercion. His was far from straightforward thuggery, done for individual enrichment or aggrandisement. Leaders utterly intent on power and maintaining it at all costs whipped up men like Du Preez into a patriotic fervour, armed them to the teeth and set them upon the enemy like dogs. Set up on a farm outside Pretoria, given the most ruthless men available and as much cash and weaponry as he wanted, Du Preez's death squad became legendary.

When negotiations started he was cut loose. Suddenly the politicians had nothing to do with the torture and assassination of their former opponents and the Colonel and his unit were shut down. What they'd done out of the Farm was, according to their former political masters, at best – a misinterpretation of policy, at worst – a private mission of murder and mayhem.

The Colonel had lacked the political shrewdness to change sides with the changing tide as many other operatives did. Instead he was arrested, tried, found massively, multiply guilty and locked up for several lifetimes. So Du Preez's legendary career, his decorations, his achievements amounted in the end to nothing more than the pile of ash.

It was rumoured that he had undergone some kind of change of heart in the months since his incarceration. After years of lying and covering up, he was said to be willing to talk now, to spill his guts to anyone who would listen. Amazing what the prospect of life in a dungeon can do for a man's morals.

At one time the very mention of his name was enough to send a chill through Anna. The thought of meeting him was another thing entirely. Anna had long ago established that Du Preez and his unit could not have had anything to do with Paul and Jacob's murders. And yet it was entirely possible he'd be able to fill in some important gaps in the story. Perhaps even come up with a something that would, damningly refute the allegation that Paul was a spy. Perhaps he could restore Paul's good name.

The Truth Commission Investigations Unit had proved useless. They'd read the *Chronicle* article, but were swamped with other cases, it was unlikely they'd get to the case before the end of the year, they'd told her. She would have to do some investigating of her own.

She decided to arrange a visit to the Colonel.

Anna was very much taken up with this idea and how to proceed with it as she strolled into the Secretariat Headquarters at Wachthuis and found herself abruptly face to face with her Minister. The man almost doubled up with embarrassment. It was the first time they'd set eyes on one another since he'd ordered the investigation into her background. He'd been refusing to meet with her and failing to return calls. But there was no avoiding her now.

'Anna!' he squirmed.

Anna smiled broadly, not because she was pleased to see him, rather because she was delighted to take up the opportunity this coincidence offered.

She got straight to the point. 'You owe me an explanation.'

He blushed, as deeply as a black man can, putting a nervous hand on her shoulder. 'Listen, you know how it is,' he said lamely.

'I'm afraid I don't.'

'We have to at least be seen to be going through the motions. The Service can't be perceived as a haven for, for, for –' He stumbled, lost for words. She watched him flounder. 'To be um, full of holes. You understand?' He was positively wriggling with discomfort.

'You're telling me this the morning after a suspect escaped from a maximum-security holding cell? You're gonna have to do better than that, sir.'

He was stumped. His face contorted painfully. Caught out. He couldn't do better and they both knew it, but that wasn't going to change a thing. He patted her shoulder repeatedly, an odd nervous gesture that Anna found intensely irritating. Weariness and anger and unpleasant, unfamiliar insecurity welled up in her, swirling around as one dreadful, tumultuous mood.

'But you *know* it isn't true. You *knew* Paul!' she blurted out furiously. He didn't like that, didn't like it at all. Somehow it snapped him back into ministerial mode and the script.

'I'm more concerned about the doubt this casts on you. Given your position, Anna, it doesn't look good.'

He couldn't look her in the eye, but he said it. Her old comrade, her *friend*, speaking to her in a voice of doubt and delicate detachment.

'This is *me* you're talking to, Chief.' Anna slapped both hands against her chest. 'Me! How dare you insinuate, accuse—'

But the Minister cut her dead with a final, brusque declaration. 'No one is above suspicion, Anna. Not ever,' he snapped. And then he was gone.

There was no point in her putting up a fight, it would only snarl up and protract the process, but it was humiliating in the extreme to be put through it. Worse, the profound trust that had existed between Anna and her Minister, not to mention the rest of her colleagues at the Secretariat, was broken. It was impossible not to see how cautious people had become around her, how they shrank from her in the corridors and the cafeterias. It was impossible not to be upset by it.

Anna found herself alone in her office, pacing the length of the carpet in front of her desk, adrenalin pumping out pointlessly like a burst mains, her stride lengthening with each rush of it, so it felt like the room was contracting.

There had been moments during the past week, like this one, when she felt as if Paul had deserted her and she was alone. It was her greatest fear, facing the world without him. Death had not taken him away from her, but lately, from time to time, she couldn't feel him near and it made her dizzy. It was a sensation like vertigo, where she was aware only of her frailty, her ant-like insignificance in the world.

There was no way out of this murk but through. Do something, she told herself. Just start somewhere.

She was reaching for the phone when it rang. She picked it up. 'Anna Kriel,' she announced calmly.

'Anna? Hi. It's Prudence Hopa.'

Anna didn't recognise the name at first.

'I know. It's been a while,' the caller said faintly and began to explain. But it didn't take long for Anna to remember; it came back to her with garish clarity.

Prudence spoke in a thin, high voice that faded at times almost to a whisper. She was a former student activist who'd experienced a long and appalling detention during which she'd suffered torture and sexual abuse at the hands of her interrogators.

'I'm calling because I want to know if you're aware of any involvement Paul might have had in my arrest?'

Oh God. Anna leaned back against her chair. This was not the first such query she'd had to deal with since the article.

Prudence had been detained all of fifteen, maybe more, years ago. Anna hadn't seen her in years. Not since the day before her arrest in fact. Not since a wild party she and Paul had attended at Prudence's place in Yeoville.

It was a drunken, dagga-dazed, lefty bash. Anna remembered it because of the argument she'd had with Paul afterwards. He had disappeared for more than an hour, sometime around midnight. He'd done it in spite of knowing how she hated to be abandoned, how little she enjoyed such gatherings. He was the joller, the gregarious and chatty one who loved to drink and dance. Anna had always been quiet and nervous of talk that wasn't serious enough for her to forget herself in the issues.

The party was heating up and Anna wanted to go home. Their car was parked outside, yet Paul was nowhere to be found. When at last he reappeared, around two a.m., she was distraught, relieved and furious all at once. Bickering escalated rapidly into an all-out screaming fight on the drive back to Valley View Road. Anna was incensed by his secretiveness and he was enraged by her doubt. He'd told her to get out of the car if she didn't trust him and she'd tried to, but as she opened the door he accelerated away, petrifying her into silence. He'd climbed into bed in a black mood, but they quickly made up making love and afterwards, watching him sleep, Anna resolved never to mistrust him again.

Prudence was arrested at her house, plucked from the debris of the party, the very next morning.

Thinking back to that hazy, horrible night, Anna realised that she could not vouch for Paul's whereabouts with any certainty at all. He could have been anywhere. Though he'd most likely been doing the work of the movement. This was Paul they were talking about after all.

Anna swerved away from doubt as suddenly as she had careered towards it. 'Let's not forget, Prudence, who we're talking about. The same Paul who talked the cops down and stood up for you, for all of us, countless times. If you think back, if you really search your heart you'll know. He *couldn't* have betrayed you, or any of us.'

Prudence was quiet during most of the rest of the conversation, but she apologised before she hung up. 'It's so weird when something makes no sense. You know? Sometimes I think that's the cruellest thing they did, planting the questions and the confusion that will sit there for the rest of your life. You can end up suspecting everyone.'

'Ja. I know.'

That evening Anna made supper for Joe at her house. He'd called in the late afternoon, sounding shattered. He needed to eat, needed some company that wasn't angry or disappointed or accusing, he said.

Anna didn't cook often, so she always made an event of it for herself when she did. She put the TV on in the living room, poured herself a glass of wine, laid everything out across the kitchen and got down to the pleasant, methodical tasks of preparing a meal.

The seven o'clock bulletin carried the story of Bazooka's sensational escape. With speculative comment from a furious Joe at the scene of the break-out. There were no signs of forced entry or exit; he explained it looked very much like Bazooka had made an easy getaway. Yet this was a maximum-security cell and Bazooka was at the height of his fifteen minutes of fame. It had to have been an inside job.

There were any number of ways to pay people off and any number of people willing to take a bribe, Anna reflected. South African prisons and police stations are among the most porous in the world. But this was bad. It really didn't reflect well on Joe's unit, on any of them.

Joe arrived late but she didn't mind. At times like this he would simply retreat into himself. There was no point in trying to coax him back out. As he stepped into the light cast from the open doorway she saw suddenly how haggard and sick he looked. He gave her a brief squeeze, then went to the table and poured himself a drink. 'Cheers,' he said grimly, before raising his glass and taking a long slug of wine. Anna switched off the TV and put a plate of food in front of him. She'd already eaten, but she sat down at the table to keep him company. He attacked his food hungrily.

Anna poured herself another glass of wine.

'Saw you on the news,' she said. 'You were great.'

He let out a kind of grunt of acknowledgement.

'Any idea who he paid off?' she asked mildly.

Joe sighed, shook his head and then laughed harshly, bitterly.

Anna slumped back into her chair. 'Aish! I don't know what to say.'

'Ja, well, it's a disaster. There's no other name for it.'

'You look terrible.'

'I've had better days,' he growled. 'But what about you? How're you doing?'

She shrugged, ran her hand through her hair. 'Weird. People are avoiding me, Joe.'

He was silent.

'What am I going to do?'

'Paul's name is impeccable, incorruptible,' Joe said calmly. 'You don't have to do a damn thing.'

'No,' she contradicted him sharply, 'the mud is sticking. It's not going to go away until I get to the truth about the murders.'

Joe looked at her wearily. His eyes were bloodshot with fatigue.

'Don't do it to yourself, Anna. Just lose it, everyone else will have forgotten it within a week, believe me.'

'I wish I could.'

'But what's the point in turning over all these old stones?' Joe lowered his head and stabbed at his food. Anna leaned back in her chair, folding her arms over her chest.

'All I'm saying is, why go there, baby? The past is over.'

'Not for me,' she said angrily.

He dropped his fork onto his plate with a clatter.

'Listen, we all know who killed them. It was the system. It was the Nats, the Security Police, and the whites who sat behind their high walls in their huge houses and voted for a government that employed assassins to protect their privilege. It was all of them – they're all fucking guilty as Nazis. Now why do you have to put a face to the finger that pulled the trigger?'

Anna shook her head, she didn't know how to explain it, didn't feel she had to any more, but he ought to know that.

'And what if you do find them. Then what?' he snapped.

'I don't know.' She felt close to tears, but was far too proud and too angry to let them fall. 'Listen to him explain? Put a bullet through his head? Make him a cup of tea? I have no idea.'

Joe shook his head despairingly.

'I have to do something, Joe. I can't just let these people drag his name through the shit.'

'Okay, so what are you going to do?'

'I'm seeing Ig Du Preez tomorrow for a start.'

'What?' It was as if she'd thrown her plate against the wall. Joe's chin jerked upwards. 'Why?'

'Wanna hear what he has to say about the killings.'

Joe tilted his head to one side, narrowing his eyes as he looked at her. He didn't say anything and she had no idea what he was thinking, though he looked like he might blow at any moment. Then he reached across the table and put his hand on hers. 'It's unhealthy,' he said gently. 'This obsession with the past. You need to do something about it. Get out of Joburg for a while, get away from the police and from all the violence. I think you've become addicted to it.'

His tenderness moved her, broke the dam, and the tears slipped hotly down her cheek. 'I'm sorry,' she said. 'I know this is hard, I know it takes its toll on you. But you and Rachel, you're the only ones who understand . . . I'm sorry.' She picked up a corner of the tablecloth and wiped her eyes, feeling sad and small.

Joe squeezed her hand harder. 'I do understand, baby. I just wish I could help you move on. You know?'

Anna was silent. Joe finished eating, and the click-click of cutlery against china rang in the air as he put his knife and fork down. He went home alone that night.

part four

The truth must dazzle gradually, or every man be blind
EMILY DICKINSON

nineteen

Anna pulled into the visitors' parking lot at Pretoria Central Prison just minutes before two. The place was completely deserted. She felt tense, eager to get it over with. There had been a time when she'd got strange kicks out of the weird people and worlds she encountered in the course of the search for Paul and Jacob's killers. Now she felt contaminated by them.

She had second thoughts as she sat in her car, waiting for the arrival of the attorney who would take her in. Was Joe right? *Could* the Colonel help her? Would he *want* to? She had no idea of what to expect from the meeting.

Her first encounter with Du Preez had been in nineteen eighty-eight, when he and his men blew up the headquarters of the Union. That was a year after Paul's murder. The bomb went off at night. Nobody was injured, but the toll it took on work and morale was massive. Her office had been completely destroyed in the blast. She remembered stepping over the crunching glass, hoping to salvage her things, but there was nothing intact enough to walk away with.

The first and only time she'd seen the Colonel in the flesh was when she paid a visit to the court-room during his trial. All she recalled was the abhorrence with which she'd stared at the huge, cold-eyed, very still man who'd sat glowering in the defendant's box. He looked like the grown-up version of the geek at the back of the science class. The kid with the thick glasses and no friends who got noticed only because he excelled in dissection.

Rage and disgust and pure hatred had burned in her eyes when her glance fleetingly met his as he scanned the public benches.

When at last he was sentenced and thrown into prison she'd felt only triumph. Justice had prevailed. Now she would face him at point-blank range.

A gunmetal-grey Mercedes saloon car cruised into the lot and bounced to a halt beside her. The man who stepped out of it was not at all the moustachioed, beer-bellied, right-wing apologist and proselytiser that she expected. Henk Steyn didn't fit the profile of the average former Security Policeman's lawyer. He was a tall, slim man, in his mid-forties she guessed, perhaps a little older. He wore an elegant oyster-coloured silk tie over a perfectly matching shirt. His suit was dark and well cut, rather warm for Pretoria, Anna thought, which was always a couple of degrees hotter than Johannesburg. Yet he seemed nothing but cool.

He shook her hand with cordial indifference, anxious to get on to their meeting. 'It's better if we drive through to Maximum together,' he said, as he opened the passenger door of his car for her. Anna smiled uncertainly, unused to such unaffected, gentlemanly gestures. She climbed in. The interior smelt of leather.

They drove past security checkpoints bristling with khaki flak jackets and guns, into the grim complex that is Pretoria Central. It was only a short distance to the massive fortress of the Maximum-Security Section.

As they drove Anna's mind scrolled through lists of Du Preez's achievements. He was famously bold in contacts, had always led from the front, always taken the initiative that other, lesser men would have been too scared or too drunk to take. He'd once beaten an informer to death with a jammed rifle. He'd used abandoned mines for the disposal of bodies – blowing them to pieces with hand grenades. Latterly this was a service he'd frequently performed for the Branch, when they bungled an interrogation and ended up with another dead detainee. The President hadn't wanted any more Steve Bikos becoming martyrs for the cause, so Du Preez and his men would be brought in to clean up the mess.

Prison was the right place for such a man, she reflected.

Once they'd parked it took some time to clear additional security for the Section. Anna's cellphone was taken, to be held for her return, and her bag checked for firearms while Steyn was body-searched. It was evidently routine for him. He took it all calmly, chatting to the guards as they patted him down. Then they were ushered out of the gatehouse into a broad, concrete dry moat where goats and a flock of geese roamed freely, lending an incongruous pastoral tranquillity to the scene.

'Goats?' she asked, surprised.

'Belong to the prisoners,' Henk Steyn smiled, the irony of it not lost on him either.

Before them was Maximum-Security, an ominous, squat building with narrow windows, too thin for anybody to slip through, but barred for good measure.

They stepped into a caged lobby, divided off from a huge and echoing entrance hall by massive steel bars. What struck her immediately and with force were the sounds of the place, of disembodied voices, metal gates clanging open and shut, of jangling keys. She followed Steyn through the first of many gates, into the visitors' reception.

She handed over her ID book at Steyn's request and sat down on the bench to wait while he signed the relevant requisition forms. The warders made no effort at speed. They seemed as bored as flies.

On the dusty window-ledge stood a tall glass bowl. Sunlight streamed through the water and illuminated the brilliant colours of the two fish swimming inside. Anna was transfixed by this loveliness amidst such severity. A man with a baby-face and a sly smile approached her, smirking. 'Oskars,' he said. 'They're hunting fish. If you put another fish in there the Oskars would kill them in a minute. They're very aggressive.' He looked from Anna to the bowl, smiling beatifically all the while. '*Very* aggressive.'

Steyn sat down beside her on the narrow visitors' bench. He was silent, legs crossed confidently, chin resting in his hand between his thumb and forefinger. Anna found it curious that he'd asked so little about her and her reasons for wanting to see his client.

'How do you get on with him?' she asked.

He looked at her for a moment, seeming surprised – as if the answer was obvious. 'I like him,' he said simply. Anna couldn't conceal the disgust that flashed in her eyes. Steyn looked away. 'You'll like him too.'

Anna bit her lip. *Yeah, right! I don't think so.*

She was queasy with dread. How does one greet a man so drenched in blood that no amount of remorse or absolution will ever cleanse him? Was it right at all to seek help from such a monster, elevating him to some kind of oracle?

In one interview with him she'd read recently he'd described himself as a 'veteran of lost ideologies'. His war was over, he insisted. 'When they start negotiating they have to get rid of the cupboard full of dirty tricks, so instead of being the blue-eyed boy who would be the next General, I'm the leper they must dispose of.'

Steyn touched her arm as he stood up. 'There's my boy,' he murmured.

'Where?' Anna asked, swinging her gaze from one end of the hall of cages to the other.

'There,' Steyn pointed.

He was a massive presence, dwarfing the warders who stood either side of him. He was dressed in prison-green pants, shirt and sweater with green twill epaulettes. A manila folder was tucked under his arm and he stood as stiff and inscrutable as a presidential guard.

The gates creaked open and clanged shut. One, two, three of them. The Colonel's gaze was on them all the time. Anna walked behind Steyn and somehow her feet carried her across the battered linoleum towards the killer who stood waiting.

Then she found herself extending her hand towards him. 'Hi, I'm Anna Kriel,' she said, firmly.

He mumbled a response, as if he were shy. But the Colonel's handshake was powerful; Anna could feel his strength in the fleeting pressure on her hand as he shook it.

'I recognise you from the newspapers,' he said, his voice gravelly, his accent thickly Afrikaans.

'Oh. You get the papers here?' Anna winced inwardly. The words had jumped out of her mouth before she'd had a chance to think.

'Not always. At the moment I'm a bit short of reading

material. You can't believe how boring the Bible gets by the fifth reading.'

Anna smiled anxiously, not knowing what to say, but the words seemed to spill out of their own accord. 'I dunno, I never made it all the way to the end the first time.'

'Well, I won't tell you what happens then. Don't want to spoil it for you.' The corners of his mouth turned upwards in an uncertain smile. Anna found herself disarmed by it, wrong-footed already.

The warders ushered them into a consulting room off a long, putty-coloured corridor. The room was putty too, with mismatching chairs chained to the table legs, which in turn were bolted to the floor. The Colonel asked one of his guards for some coffee to be brought for the lady, then indicated for Anna to sit down.

'If we could just get some business out of the way first . . .' Henk Steyn murmured as he set a number of documents down on the table.

'Oh no, please. Go ahead,' Anna chimed, shifting on the hard wooden chair.

Steyn began to guide his client through a series of applications he was making to the Truth Commission's Amnesty Committee. He must have hundreds, she thought. It was his only chance of ever walking out of this place and he listened with earnest concentration. It was curious to observe him and the childlike way he deferred to Steyn, nodding in agreement to everything the lawyer said. He signed each document with a fluid, strong hand.

Once the papers were signed and cleared away, snapped back into Steyn's copious briefcase, the warder brought a tray of coffees and set it down before the Colonel. He seemed in awe of his prisoner, behaving like the man's servant, not his jailer. Du Preez glanced bashfully in Anna's direction as he passed her a cup and fussed over whether she had sugar and how much milk.

She looked down at his hands as he stirred four sugars into his coffee and the description of a detainee sprang into her mind, of those very same hands around his throat, pulling the tube down over his face – the plastic sack that would stop his breathing.

'If I'd known you were coming I would have shaved,' he said. Anna didn't know what to say.

'I'm going to have to answer a lot of questions from the people around here. I don't often get attractive women coming to visit.'

It was an artless, childlike compliment. She'd assumed he'd be cold, bitter, even crazed perhaps; the last thing she'd imagined was this disarming politeness and effusive courteousness.

'Mr Du Preez, I came to talk to you about the Mafikeng Road Murders.'

At this he smiled. 'You don't have to call me Mr Du Preez, call me Ignatius, or Ig.' Then he stopped self-consciously as if embarrassed at being so forward. 'Ag, you can call me whatever you like.' He reddened as he bent his head down and stared into the cup in front of him, which he stirred again with unnecessary vigour.

Anna cleared her throat. 'You know the story?'

'Of course.' The Colonel looked up, the spoon still suspended in his fingers. 'I was quite surprised when I saw that article in the Sunday papers. Is that why you're here?'

'Yes.'

Henk Steyn sat back in his corner chair, his long legs crossed, hands folded together in his lap, eyes fixed on the floor.

'And you still don't know who killed them?' the Colonel continued.

She shook her head. It seemed to Anna this was both a statement and a question. She looked into his eyes, eyes buried deep behind layers and layers of optical lenses, like lights gleaming murkily in a pool, indistinct, yet compelling.

'From what I've seen of the Truth Commission boys, you're not gonna get very far by relying on them.'

'I'm afraid I can't disagree with you,' she said.

'Look, I can tell you,' Du Preez began, 'that – if Lewis *wasn't* a spy – he was *definitely* a target for the Security Police. Your cell was known and monitored, more than you'd like to know, believe me. You guys were effective and that made you all hot property. But the story in the *Chronicle*, well, that was news to me. Of course that doesn't mean it isn't true,' he added hastily. Then he sat back, stretching his legs to one side. 'No, but the Oliphant–Lewis murders, I tell you, I've often wondered. That was a strange business that. A strange business.'

Anna shivered, tension snaking through her body.

'You understand the principle under which we operated, of need to know?'

'Oh yes.'

Need to know. The phrase that stuck like a piece of gristle in the throat. It was the cover-all suspects always used to explain their supposed ignorance. It was what they told the daughters of Ruth First and Rick Turner and so many others. It was the first retort on the road to 'no one to blame'.

'So you understand that we dealt with a lot of rumour?'

Anna nodded again. 'But that talk was pretty reliable, wasn't it?'

'Ja. The things men said round the fire or propping up the bar, there was a lot of truth in it.' The Colonel brought his hands up onto the table, leaning forward on his elbows, resting on the round patches of dark olive twill. 'And the late-night loose lips always said it was Nel who took those two out. Lewis and Oliphant.' He sighed. Anna had no idea what it signified, but it was a heavy, weary sound. 'But what I've always wondered is – why it's only *his* name that comes up? And why has there never been any detail? You know, usually with this kind of stuff there's nods and winks and a bit of elbow nudging in the corridors and you've got a pretty good idea of what went on. But with this case it was different. I've always wondered why it's so . . .' He searched for the English word, 'Vague.' He folded his hands. 'There's no way it was just one guy who carried out that hit, doesn't take a rocket scientist to work that out.'

'But Colonel,' Anna jumped in clumsily, 'you *do* believe, don't you, that Frans Nel was involved?'

Du Preez looked directly at her, smiling very slightly. 'Oh ja. And old Frans is not known for his compassion,' he said dryly. 'A person isn't cut out for that kind of work if he thinks too much about suffering and the Ten Commandments.' A snort of sour laughter escaped him.

'Nel denies it of course.'

'Well, you know where old Frans is now, don't you?'

Anna nodded. 'Ja. I've met him on a couple of occasions, but he's sticking to his story. I've got to come at it from another angle.'

Du Preez rubbed his hands together thoughtfully, narrowed

his eyes. 'Ja, you see in nineteen eighty-seven we were just getting going on the Farm and at that point we were still mostly dealing with cross-border stuff, it was a year or two more before we got involved in internal matters. When we started working with people like Nel from Joburg . . .' The Colonel trailed off, shaking his head.

'Colonel, there are a number of other policemen who might—' He leaned forward, interrupting her. 'Pardon me?'

'Sorry,' she said louder, 'there are other cops who might have been involved, most of whom I've been able to trace through the regular files. Some, like Jeff Curry, are no longer with us, but there's one man in particular I've been unable to locate. Badenhorst. Balletjies Badenhorst from Vryburg Murder and Robbery. Did you ever come across him?'

The Colonel frowned. 'Bit guy, heavy set. Quite a hairy oke if I remember correctly?'

Anna nodded.

'Ja, I know the guy, had contact with him a coupla times. We didn't hit it off. He was a quiet one. Bit of a cold fish, I thought.'

Laughter escaped from Anna's throat, and she picked up, still grinning at his observation, 'He retired from the force in nineteen ninety-two, shortly after Mandela's release. Then he disappeared, wife and family too. After ninety-two the files come up with nothing at all, like he doesn't exist.'

'You want me to put some feelers out?' he asked quietly, almost conspiratorially.

'If you can. Yes,' she answered.

'I can't do much, but I'll try!' he declared, apparently pleased to be of assistance. 'But, I think I know,' he went on deliberately, 'someone else who might be able to help you in the meantime. Guy by the name of Shane Fourie.' The Colonel pronounced the name slowly. Anna shook her head, this was the first she'd heard of that name.

'If anyone knows about this spying thing it's him. He's a strange chappie, Shane. Left the force in eighty-six, went off on stress, went a bit crazy with all the . . . *pressure.*'

Anna swallowed, trying to contain her excitement. 'Where is he now?'

'Northern Cape. Think he lives on a farm, Bulletrap, or

something like that. Funny name. It's far, about as far as you can go and still be in the Republic.'

Anna fished a notebook from her bag and scribbled down the names. 'Thanks.'

'Whether he'll talk to you is another matter, but these days – who knows?' He smiled ironically. 'All kinds of people are talking to one another.' He laughed then, reached forward and patted the back of her hand.

Anna felt that sensation again, of swimming through darkness, as if the air was thick and viscous and too warm. She looked down, trying to slow her breathing and regain her composure. She could feel the imprint of his fingers on her skin as if he'd burned it into her.

'Thank you, Colonel,' she mumbled.

His hand flicked through the air, waving her thanks away. 'Ag, it's nothing. The least I can do. Anytime. Just let me know what happens.'

Sunlight streamed in through the narrow windows. Anna looked over at Henk Steyn who nodded. The interview was over. It was time to leave.

Du Preez stood up first, awkwardly pulling his sweater down over the waistband of his pants and instead of a hulking beast Anna saw an eager little boy in front of her. 'Let me know what happens with Shane. And if there's anything else I can do – you know where to find me.' The Colonel laughed again and Henk Steyn chuckled mildly behind him.

At the door Du Preez put his hand on her arm. She tried not to flinch. 'One other thing,' he said suddenly, as if he'd just remembered it. 'That cash-in-transit arrest. Did you have anything to do with that?' He loomed a little too close and Anna stepped backwards. 'Yes, yes I did,' she answered. 'I mean, not me personally, but—'

'That guy who escaped,' the Colonel said excitedly, 'Bazooka. He was one of ours from the Farm. He was a cop. Did you know that?'

Anna was completely thrown. 'No. No, I didn't. How strange. Is there any record of that?'

The Colonel shrugged. 'Probably. Don't know where you'd

find it nowadays, but he was on the payroll for a good few years. Must be some paperwork lying around.'

'And would you be prepared to testify to that effect? That is, if we needed you to.'

He raised his hands up at his sides and let them drop, slapping against his trousers. 'No problem,' he answered.

She looked up at him quizzically, wondering if she could trust this information. Wondering if this wasn't a spanner deliberately dropped into the works. If true, it was serious, not for the police investigation, but it would mean that the movement had been infiltrated at a high level. She'd check it out with Joe.

'Ja. Funny old world, hey?' the Colonel quipped, as he clicked his heels and fell into step behind the warders who had come to escort them out.

In the entrance to Maximum, Anna turned to look back into the caged halls of the prison and was startled to find the Colonel watching her. He smiled and raised his arm in a salute. Anna waved briefly back, then turned and followed Henk Steyn out into the concrete moat where the geese and goats roamed freely and wardens were playing cards at a table they'd set up in the sun.

'Thank you,' she said simply when they were back in the car park. 'If I may – could I come again?'

Steyn nodded. 'Ja. Call me. He likes you.'

Anna didn't say anything. Steyn laughed softly. She walked to her car, disturbed by the whole encounter. She could not say that she *dis*liked Du Preez.

Then Anna thought of Leila, a gangly twelve-year-old she knew, bright and funny and pretty. Du Preez murdered her mother and father, felled them in a hail of fire from a semi-automatic. Leila wasn't yet two. Hours after, when the massacre was discovered, the baby was found crawling through her parents' blood.

Evil comes dressed in the plainest of clothes, she thought.

twenty

The sky was growing light as Anna slipped out of the waking city onto the open freeway. She left early on a Friday morning, with the weekend ahead and no one to answer to for her absence.

So far her background check on Shane Fourie had not differed from the story the Colonel told her. Fourie had been in the South African Police and had indeed worked for Frans Nel in the seventies. He'd left the force voluntarily in nineteen eighty-six. From what Anna could gather he'd been caught dealing confiscated narcotics and got off with a warning, but had decided to take a retirement, or 'pressure' package.

Anna wondered how Fourie would react to her arrival and what he might have to say. She found herself driving in a state of excited anticipation. It was her first real lead in years.

The journey to the Northern Cape was long, but relaxing. Anna flew past tiny towns, tattered ribbons of buildings along the road – a butcher, general dealer, petrol station and panel-beater, and the obligatory off-licence. Gradually the towns began to dwindle and the landscape grew flatter, the vegetation more and more sparse. By mid-morning she was in dry, empty country passing a cattle station every fifty kilometres or so.

The solitude grew as the hours and the telegraph poles flew by. In the early afternoon Anna pulled into Kuruman, a small town at the eastern edge of the Kalahari. She was hot and thirsty so she stopped at the Eye, famed for being the largest natural fountain in the Southern Hemisphere. It was a dreary place, with very few visitors that day, desultory lovers occupying the benches and a scattering of litter around a small take-away hut called the Burger Box. The cafeteria had outside tables looking onto the brackish water. It didn't appeal.

So she drove on to the nearest service station where she filled the car with petrol and strolled into the adjoining fast-food outlet to find some fuel for herself. She sat a while sipping hot, muddy coffee and staring out at the petrol plaza. In the booth next to hers an old crimplene-clad auntie was harping on to a younger woman with a greasy ponytail and pasty self-loathing in her eyes. The auntie was piping shrilly about a murder that she'd either read or heard about. From what Anna could gather a man had been axed to death in his bed. His wife lying next to him had taken a few blows, but survived. 'It wasn't a kaffir who did it,' the auntie declared, stretching her bird-like neck, 'there was no *smell*, you see?' The young woman registered no reaction at all so the auntie was forced to lower her voice confidentially to explain. 'There would have been a smell if it had been a black. Né?'

Resuming the drive, Anna rested her elbow on the window-frame, one hand on the wheel, the other in her hair. And she thought about Paul. She had been visited lately by a number of disquieting recollections, the rough edges of her time with him that had been smoothed over by memory.

She wrapped her arms around the steering wheel as she drove, rested her chin on her hands and stared at the endlessness of the straight, straight road and the flat, flat veld. The radio played a song with the words: *and I miss you, like the deserts miss the rain*. The sadness and longing in it struck a deep chord in Anna and hot tears tumbled out, rolling down her cheeks. The road and the song reminded her of a long journey she'd once made with Paul.

They were in his old beaten-up, student car, driving across the beautiful, endless Karoo. The road cut straight through the landscape, stretching ahead for miles and miles and miles, like the road Anna was driving today. Immense, barren, clear. No places to hide. A car would pass going the other way once an hour at most. Then their car gave out. Without warning it clanked and shuddered to a halt. Paul opened the bonnet and steam poured out, a filthy rust-coloured cloud hissing from the radiator cap.

It was late afternoon and no cars came into view for what seemed like an age. Then at last they saw a vehicle hurtling out of the heat-haze. They watched its long approach, wondering if it would stop. When it did, screeching abruptly to a halt, they climbed into the kombi-van with all their bags and were whisked away.

The driver was a lanky white guy, pale with jet-black hair that hung very thick and straight to his shoulders. He wasn't going anywhere near Joburg, but he said he'd take them to the train and he drove them for nearly an hour over dirt roads to Merriman, a deserted railway station in the middle of nowhere.

They found themselves completely alone. Along the track they saw a herd of springbok grazing. No trains passed. They sat in the shelter of an ancient waiting room and watched the sky darken. Night fell and then they couldn't see beyond the train tracks and the sets of three bright red signal lights to the north and the south. The electric striplight in the waiting room buzzed loudly, but Anna was happy. Together she and Paul would meet whatever fate delivered. Just being with him made her feel high and invincible.

Sometime in the night, long before midnight, with very little warning, a freight train came screaming through the station. The engine shot through out of the darkness, wild and terrifying, and flew on into the blackness, leaving them windswept and stunned. Paul put his arm round her and they went back to the waiting room and looked around at the bare, dusty room that was to be their home for the night.

Incredibly, at the stroke of midnight, a second train chugged slowly into the station and came to a creaking halt. Anna and Paul stared at the lights and the passengers leaning out of windows as if at an apparition. Then people started shouting and gesticulating at them. 'Maak gou! Maak gou!' Hurry, hurry! Anna leapt on board and Paul threw their bags on and jumped in behind her and they stood in the clammy corridor, panting as the train pulled off and rattled on across the semi-desert of the Karoo. It wasn't long before the drunken conductor found them and told them slurringly that they were in luck. There was a couchette they could have all to themselves.

Paul made love to her on that train that night, sweetly and carefully, balanced on the narrow top bunk.

Sex with Paul had been a revelation to Anna. There was something so achingly beautiful about it, the way he began with the tenderest of kisses them moved slowly down her neck, caressing the skin at the base of her throat while he undressed her, stroking her so gently and exquisitely before he entered her that she felt she would explode.

Making love with Paul was what Anna believed sex was supposed to be. It was the harmony of two souls and two bodies, charged with mystery. Even in that narrow bunk on a train rattling through the hot night, theirs was a borderless world.

And there was an added sweetness that came from the defiance of the act. In those days it was illegal for a white and a black person to travel in the same compartment and the Immorality Act made it illegal for them to caress, let alone make love to one another.

Tears came with the memory. And doubt departed.

Anna drove through Upington as the sun was sinking and everything was bathed in golden light, nevertheless she felt the whine of depression that was her reaction to ugliness and pollution. The town is something of an oasis, situated on the lush banks of the Orange River and yet it was covered in shredded plastic and discarded cans and all the disposable junk of life. Our national disease, she thought. The plastic bag has become our national flower.

She drove on as the sky turned to brilliant, blood red and night fell softly around her. The guesthouse where she'd booked a room was a simple old homestead with deep verandas and cool stone walls. It was run by a quiet but wonderfully hospitable Afrikaans family – the Van Dyks – mother, father and a grown-up son.

Anna arrived at dinner just as the other guests, a large, jolly English family, were preparing to pray. The father greeted her heartily and took hold of her hand.

'Will you join us in saying Grace?' Anna must have looked taken aback because he went on to explain, 'We *always* say Grace as a family.' A kind of embarrassed gurgle emerged from Anna's throat, but it was quickly overlapped by the Englishman's booming voice. 'For what we are about to receive may the Lord make us truly thankful.' The family sat with their eyes closed, holding hands as they spoke the words in unison. Anna stood by her chair, her hand locked in the father's grip, staring at the sunflower-print plastic-coated cloth that covered the long table.

Anna ate little, though the food was ample. Dinner began with a floury vegetable soup served with surprisingly good bread rolls. Then there was steak slathered in brown sauce with yellow rice and squash and something that looked like cauliflower cheese, but tasted more like cabbage in white sauce. Anna had no choice but to listen as the jolly Englishman chatted to Mr Van Dyk.

'We're visiting Africa from Sussex,' he boomed. 'Twenty-five years ago my wife and I were married and we came here on honeymoon. Now we've come back – with our four children *and* my mother-in-law.'

He was plain and dishevelled, with wire-rimmed spectacles and uncombed straight black hair, but his wife was really quite beautiful. She had long dark hair only lightly streaked with silver. She wore a denim pinafore over a white T-shirt and almost no make-up – just enough to define her large brown eyes. She chipped in with a much slower, deeper voice, explaining that she was South African and her husband English. 'I've lived in England all these years, but South Africa is still where my heart is.'

When they asked Anna about her journey she was momentarily thrown. She wouldn't tell them the real reason for her overnighting here. Her reasons were not of their world. 'I work for the government,' she said at last. 'I have to conduct an interview with a farmer nearby.'

'Oh how *interesting*,' the woman declared. 'I'm always so *fascinated* by women who go out into the world, I think it's so brave.'

Anna smiled weakly.

'Doesn't your husband mind you being away?'

Anna looked at her uncertainly, then realised the woman was looking at her hand. Anna glanced down at the ring she still wore on her wedding finger.

'Oh, no!' she spluttered. 'No, I'm not married. This was given to me by an old, old friend.'

The woman's smile seemed to freeze, as if she were disappointed, then she turned to Mrs Van Dyk and Anna was relieved to contemplate her meal and her ring alone.

Thinking back to the night Paul had given it to her lifted her mood. He'd been away in Swaziland for almost a fortnight, on a mission he'd undertaken with members of another cell. The plan was they'd be gone for seven days, but that had changed and he hadn't been able to get word to her. So Anna had waited, not knowing where he was or what might have happened to him. Then one night she woke to find him climbing into the bed next to her, his skin cold, his breath sour with the familiar smell of cigarettes and booze, his eyes puffy with fatigue. And she'd warmed him and welcomed him home with her body and afterwards he'd taken her hand and slipped the ring onto her finger and she'd wept with joy and relief at him being home and safe and loving her.

Anna got up from the dinner table, fetched a cup of coffee and slipped outside to sit on the stoep. The sky was clear and brilliant with stars. Inside the English family could be heard settling down to a game of cards together, their happy voices drifting out on the warm night air. Anna often forgot that she shared the world with people whose lives were harmonious and uncomplicated.

She found herself thinking cynically that these were English and nothing about the English was as uncomplicated as it seemed. On the surface they're so fresh and interested and quick and witty. And it's a front, you can see from the speed with which their eyes lose focus and their concentration wanders. It's an attractive front, but it conceals nevertheless. Perhaps she *should* have told them the reason for her being here; perhaps she ought to have shaken up the lives in that room.

Then she felt bad. Why was she so cross with those nice people? It was envy at their innocence and the completeness of their satisfaction with life. Let it be so, she told herself, let the world be nice for them.

Anna sipped at her coffee and tried to clear her mind as she sat in the darkness and listened to the night. She remembered what James Kay had said to her at their abortive lunch. And there was a moment, before the vast blackness of that landscape, beneath the infinity of a star-encrusted sky, when she wondered if she might be wrong about Paul. *I can't be*, she whispered into the darkness. *My life has not been a lie.*

Anna cast the words up to the stars, like a prayer spoken into the wide arch of the Milky Way. And the Van Dyks and their English guests laughed and slapped their playing cards down on the table inside and the crickets sang beneath the moon and the earth turned. *I can't be wrong.*

twenty-one

The next morning Anna was up early. Outside, the light was filmy and the grounds of the guesthouse were alive with shadows. She fetched a cup of coffee from the dining room, avoiding eye contact with the English crew, who were also up early and were eating and chattering excitedly about the day ahead. She took the coffee outside and sat down on the terrace to watch the sun come up.

It rose fast, an eerie, shimmering, orange ball behind the black tangle of thorn trees. In the dawn light she saw that she was on the lip of a hill overlooking a vast, flat plain. In the far distance were the bluish shapes of sandy, bush-speckled hills.

The air was sultry and moist and it was already hot by seven. By midday it would be unbearable. But by midday she would be miles away in her air-conditioned car on the road back to Johannesburg. The interview would be over and – she was sure of it – she'd have something that would take the investigation forward at last.

A sprinkler spluttered and jerked water across the grass. A rooster with a brilliant red comb strutted out from the bushes, followed by a black hen and her scurrying band of tiny black and yellow chicks. The high-pitched sawing sound of Sonbesie Beetles seemed to thicken the air.

Anna set off for Bulletrap around seven-thirty. The distance wasn't great, but the roads were mostly dirt and they slowed her progress. An hour or so later she came to a halt outside the tiny rural police station where a Constable Jan Koekemoor was expecting her. Stepping out of the climate-controlled car into the heat was like walking into fire. The air danced and glittered.

Koekemoor was alarmingly over-excited by her appearance, practising his English with an accent thick as stywepap. 'We don't get many strangers out here, but a visitor from Head-quarters, well that's *unprecedented*. We are deeply honoured, Miss Kriel, and I hope you will find everything in order and to your satisfaction.'

Anna had explained on the telephone that she worked for the Ministry of Safety and Security and that she needed to conduct a routine interview with a Mr Shane Fourie regarding an old murder investigation. Anna realised now that for Koekemoor her visit was attached with far greater significance than it merited. She was embarrassed into making a show of looking around the immaculate little station and taking an interest in his work by scanning the Charge Books and other records.

This was a different world, where the pace of life was unhurried and attempting to speed things up would most likely slow them down. So Anna drank the tea Koekemoor presented her with and listened attentively to the list of concerns he hoped she would take back with her to Pretoria. His thoroughness and dedication touched her; it would have felt rude to rush him. So Anna waited until the Constable got to the point in his own good time.

'I must say I never heard of people visiting there at Fourie's,' he said adding hurriedly, 'I'm not suggesting there's anything suspicious out there. They just not the visiting type. No one goes in. No one comes out. Myself, I haven't seen Shane since New Year's Eve last.'

Anna grimaced, not much liking the sound of the place. Koekemoor sensed her concern and drew the wrong conclusion. 'I'll be coming with you, of course.' Anna hesitated. Instinct told her the presence of a uniformed policeman alongside her might be intimidating. Alone she would undoubtedly provoke suspicion and surprise, but she did not want to seem threatening in any way. Anna sat up very straight, hoping that her perceived rank would prevail.

'Actually, I'd rather you didn't come. But I tell you what, I'll come past here on my way back. Let's say if I'm not back in four hours you come looking for me?'

Koekemoor seemed disappointed. He bolted down the last of

his sweet tea and then shook his head resolutely as he wiped the moisture from his moustache. 'No. I'm afraid I'm going to have to disobey orders here, Miss Kriel. I'll take you to the gate and I'll wait for you there.'

'Great!' Anna was happy with the compromise. 'Just make sure they don't see you,' she said as they stood up to leave. Koekemoor laughed raucously, the gleeful laughter of the country bumpkin at the city slicker's ignorance. 'The gate is three ks from the house, at least. There's *no* chance they see me!'

It was another half-hour's bone-rattling drive on dirt roads before they reached the farm entrance. A small square of tin nailed to a wooden post with the name 'Fourie' painted sloppily on it in red enamel announced they'd arrived. Koekemoor parked his patrol van in the lacy shade of an acacia tree. 'If you not back in two hours, *precisely*, I'm coming in.'

Anna had the distinct impression that the Constable was looking forward to rushing to her rescue. She wanted to avoid that at all costs, so she promised to return within two hours. Nevertheless she missed his fussy presence as soon as his bakkie was out of sight and she found herself alone on the bumpy single-track road.

This silence was oppressive and the heat didn't help. It was a few minutes before she saw the farm buildings, standing in a sandy clearing amidst drooping gum trees. The place was a dreary tableau of poverty. The house itself was a crumbling box of a building, an old tin-roofed dwelling with a stoep all the way round it. The walls showed traces of pretty, powder-blue paint that had long ago crumbled away and faded. Washing flapped on a line strung between the rusty gutter piping above the stoep and a brick water tower. The clothes were grey with age and the grass beneath was yellow and brittle, long dead like the blue gum tree in the centre of the yard. Its wiry, blackened branches reached upwards, as if pleading with the relentless sun. Anna switched off her engine and the utter stillness of the place flooded in, like despair.

She was suddenly startled to see a woman staring at her from a corner of the stoep.

The woman's face was deeply lined, her eyes narrowed to slits against the sun. Though her hair was caught up into a knot at the back of her head, neglect had given her a halo of wisps of peppery blonde hair. She stood with her arms folded over sagging breasts, dressed in a loose beige cotton dress, blue flip-flops on her dirty feet. Her legs were marked with purple bruises. She gave no sign of greeting, nor did she move towards Anna. She simply stared.

Anna reached for the doorhandle and had one foot out of the car when three huge dogs exploded from the house, streaking across the stoep and down into the dirt yard, tongues flapping and spit flying from their fang-studded jaws. Anna flinched, pulling as far away from the door as possible as the dogs flung themselves at the car, rocking it back and forth with their weight as they snarled and slobbered and scratched at the windows.

Then the woman moved, trudging down the steps and across the yard towards the car. A single, quiet word from her subdued the dogs. They shivered and panted and slunk back to wait in the meagre shade cast by the roof of the house. The woman looked incuriously down at Anna, as if life held no surprises.

Anna wound down her window an inch or two. 'Morning. How are you?' she smiled, speaking in Afrikaans and delivering her Joburg greeting with as much warmth as she could muster. The woman nodded wearily by way of response, but said not a word.

'I'm looking for Shane Fourie,' Anna went on gamely. This time she got a reaction.

The woman dipped her head sideways, indicating over her shoulder towards the house. 'Shane's in the back.'

'Can I speak to him?'

The woman shrugged as if it made no difference to her. 'He's in the back,' she repeated deliberately.

Then, with the smallest flick of her hand she indicated for Anna to follow her. Anna hesitated, reluctant to leave the safety of her car.

'Don't worry about the dogs, they won't touch you.'

Not quite convinced, Anna opened the door cautiously and tentatively stepped out into the yard, her gaze fixed on the huge mongrels lest they make the slightest move towards her. But they hung back, as the ghost-woman had said they would.

Anna followed her across the stoep and into the dark house.

The first thing that hit Anna was the smell. It was the sharp stench of must and mould and human decay. As her eyes became accustomed to the light she saw that the interior was a mess of peeling paint, broken furniture and cracked windowpanes. What little the Fouries owned they were careless of, with a single, telling exception. A pair of well-oiled shotguns and a lethal-looking crossbow hung tidily on a rack in the hallway next to the kitchen.

It was in the kitchen that Anna found Shane Fourie. He was sitting with his back to her as she entered. The blinding light of the day outside streamed in and illuminated his face and his bare chest. There were two others with him, a man and a woman – they were grouped around the plastic table by the door. Anna saw at a glance that on it were the remains of a meal of fried eggs, bully beef and baked beans.

'Shane. Lady to see you,' the ghost-woman said placidly as she placed a hand on the shoulder of the hulking man at the head of the table. Shane turned disinterestedly and stared at Anna. There was not a flicker of response on his face. No surprise, or pleasure, not even disquiet. He was big and muscular yet lean with long straggly brown hair in a mullet haircut, and had piercing green eyes. He stubbed his cigarette out into the tomato gravy on his plate and stood up without fuss or hurry. He extended his hand and Anna stepped forward, shook it and said firmly, 'Hi, I'm Anna Kriel. Pleased to meet you.'

She spoke in Afrikaans, hoping to put them at ease. Knowing they would be suspicious of this well-heeled Coloured woman who'd arrived in a fancy car for reasons they were yet to be made aware of. And yet they had the look of people who were so far beyond wonder that nothing could startle them out of their state.

The atmosphere reeked of suppressed violence. Scanning the room in the silence that greeted her entrance, she almost retched at the sight of three bloody carcasses hanging from the ceiling. There was a wart-hog and two impala and they looked to Anna's novice eye like they had only recently been killed. The puddles of blood on the floor below them were smeared and skidded with the paw marks of the dogs that had no doubt fed on the entrails and gore that dripped from the slit necks of the three animals.

Anna swallowed hard, trying to quell the spasm of retching in her throat. Her instinct was to flee the abattoir stink, the airlessness of the house and the torpor of these people. What on earth could they have to tell her?

Then Shane pointed to the woman who'd shown her in. 'My wife Shawna. Her sister Nerice and her husband Dillon.' They all looked older than Anna knew they must be, their skin frazzled by the harsh sun. Nerice was a wide woman wearing a button-through flower-print dress. Her flabby arms were bare. She had wavy salt and pepper hair and wore thick-lensed glasses that were too large for her face. Anna noticed that instead of hands Dillon had a pair of steel pincers. Nerice saw Anna's shock. 'Not pretty, hey?' Her tone was angry and defensive. 'That's what you get for hard work and having a bladdy boss. An eleven-thousand-volt electric shock burned those hands away. Accident, they said. The mine gave him calipers for compensation. Nothing else.' Anna stuttered an apology.

Shane grabbed a chair from a corner near the hanging carcasses and put it in front of Anna. She sat down and so did he, then he stook a cigarette from a pack of Chesterfields on the table and lit it.

'So, Anna Kriel. What can I do for you?'

She took a deep breath. 'I was hoping you could provide some information about a friend of mine. His name was Paul Lewis.'

Shane smoked on impassively.

'You may not be familiar with the case.' She paused again, but still he didn't blink. 'Well, Paul was killed on the night of April eighteenth, nineteen eighty-seven. He and a comrade, Jacob Oliphant, were shot dead on the road between Mafikeng and Vryburg. We believe the killers were Security Policemen, from a Captain Frans Nel's unit.'

Fourie reacted with only the slightest of nods, blowing a long stream of smoke from between his lips. Yet it was still not clear to Anna whether he had any idea of what she was talking about. A sudden eruption from Nerice interrupted her.

'It wasn't just your people who lost loved ones, you know,' Nerice spat bitterly, tears gushing from her eyes. 'That's what they try to say now,' she bleated. 'That it was only *our* people who were murderers, but *your* people were worse.'

Her face crumpled with grief. Anna looked to Shane and

Shawna for help, or explanation, but they both looked away, Shane's lip curled into a contemptuous sneer. Then Dillon spoke, the only words Anna heard him utter.

'Her kid was killed in a terrorist attack on a disco in Vryburg. Valentine's party in ninety-three.'

His voice was like gravel. Nerice sobbed violently. Anna sat very still, not knowing what to do, but trying desperately to transmit sympathy.

Shane Fourie had had enough. He banged his fist down on the table.

'Ag, come *off* it, Nerice! She didn't come here to listen, to *your* fucked-up life story!'

Shawna moved forward to help, pulling her weeping sister from her chair and supporting her out of the room. Dillon took another cigarette with his caliper hands and lit up. Nerice's sobbing faded into another room. It wasn't long before the numbing silence of the house reasserted itself.

'The reason I'm here,' Anna continued cautiously, 'is that I was told by Colonel Ignatius Du Preez that you might have known Paul.' For some reason Anna's voice trembled as she spoke his name.

Shane Fourie studied the bulging veins on his forearm. 'You a journalist?' His tone bordered on hostile. Anna shook her head. 'No, I work from the Ministry of Safety and Security in Pretoria.' She dug into her bag for her Secretariat ID and handed it to him.

He looked it over, then passed it to Dillon, who frowned importantly, checking the photograph against the woman who sat before them. 'You not bugged?' Fourie challenged.

Anna shook her head and lifted up her arms. She was wearing a plain cotton T-shirt over thin twill pants; there was clearly no space between her clothes and her skin for a wire. Fourie reached over and patted Anna's bag, which was gaping open on the table inviting inspection, but he seemed satisfied with her answer.

Fourie lit another cigarette, leaned back in his chair and seemed to study Anna for a while before he shook his head, sighed wearily and began at last to talk.

'Ja. I remember Paul Lewis.'

At last. Anna's heart seemed to stop, waiting for what he had to say.

'It made me sick what they did to him. I mean it could have been me.' He spoke with disgust. His mouth set, his eyes a piercing, wild green.

'You?'

'Ja. I said that could have been me,' Shane repeated.

'Who?' Anna asked, confused.

'That young guy. *Paul*. He was one of *ours*. And they killed him.'

The words hit Anna like bullets, ripping through her flesh. She felt the blood drain out of her face, her tongue felt dry as ground glass and the air tasted like ash.

The rest of what he said came to her in a shimmer of lips moving around words, his mouth closing around the dirty yellow filter of his cigarette, sucking in the fire, exhaling the ash. The stabbing glances of those green eyes, flicking expressionlessly towards her and then away.

'Whatever you think you know with those people, you know shit. That's why I got out. Paul didn't see it. Maybe not till too late.'

Anna gripped the sides of her chair. Somehow a voice came from inside her, spilling words into the hot air, words she heard as if from an echoey distance.

'Paul was one of *yours*.'

Shane scratched his chin. 'Ja, he was a cop.'

Here was a poisonous truth, seeping from this filthy, blood-spattered, white-trash room. Shane Fourie's words dismantling the house of her spirit, cornerstone after cornerstone crumbling to dust until there was nothing left.

'I'm telling you,' Fourie went on, 'Paul Lewis was a policeman. Sure as God made little kaffirs.' He laughed coarsely. Anna breathed out as far as she could, then slowly back in again. She concentrated deliberately on her breathing as a way of calming herself.

The men smoked. The dogs licked at the puddles of blood beneath the animal carcasses. Words formed like small stones in her dry mouth.

'But why *kill* him?'

Fourie looked at Anna and shook his head as he rolled the

burning tip of his cigarette against the rim of the plate in front of him. 'I don't know,' he shrugged. 'Maybe, because of his wife.'

Anna didn't follow.

'Ja.' Shane's eyes met hers, as if he were sizing her up now, as if he was just beginning to understand the impact on her of the violence of what he had to say. She wondered if he was getting any kind of sadistic pleasure out of this.

'Whose wife?' Anna breathed.

'Paul was knocking off Nel's wife, Sherry.'

Anna swallowed drily.

'Ag, a lot of the guys were, she couldn't get enough of it. But our Fransie didn't know that. When he caught her with Paul he just lost it.'

Anna's heart pounded against her chest.

Shane flicked ash onto the floor. 'Ja, he was fucking the Captain's missus. Got caught with her on the bonnet of the car, in the goddam garage.' He chuckled moistly at the idea, but his eyes didn't laugh at all, his eyes were dead. 'Up against Nel's car. Cheeky, ay? I think that's what made the old man flip, because they were doing it up against his fuckin' sacred Merc.' At this, Shane erupted with throaty laughter and even the taciturn Dillon smiled.

Disbelief washed in and then receded again. Like the tides of a fever.

'It doesn't sound like . . . I just find it very difficult to believe,' was all she could manage.

'You don't have to believe it, lady.'

He shrugged, scattering ash over the remains of his meal as he stabbed out his cigarette. 'It's what happened. Makes no difference what *you* think.' The coarse golden hairs on his arms caught the light as he opened his palms in a take-it or leave-it gesture.

Anna squirmed in her chair, sweat gathering in the creases of her knees, a prickling sensation like stinging all over her skin.

'Ag, it was a strange business.'

Fourie was warming to his subject and from the ease and the ardour with which he told his story it was clear that it was no fiction.

'I got mixed up in it too. I was called over to the Nels' house one night. They had this huge fuckin' house in Brooklyn, Pretoria. Our Nel had smacked his wife up badly and was threatening to shoot her. She phoned in and I happened to be on duty, so I was the one who was sent out. I got there and found the kids in the garden, completely hysterical. Sherry and Frans in the garage screaming and threatening and slapping each other. Jissus, I've never seen anything like it. She'd already smashed the windscreen of that precious car of his, kicked a moerse dent in one of the doors and he was firing shots all over the place. But he wasn't going to kill her. Just wanted to put the fear of God into her. And he did. She left him coupla months after that.'

He paused to light another Chesterfield. Anna watched the orange glow at the end of the cigarette expand and shrink.

'Where was Paul?'

'No, he was long gone by then.' Shane waved his hand over his shoulder, trailing a curve of smoke through the air.

Anna nodded limply.

'Sherry Nel,' Fourie repeated, staring out at the bright day. 'What a piece of work. Sexy little poppie, always hot for it, used to wear these tight, tight dresses with only a G-string underneath, so tight you could see the line of the panties going into her crack.' Shane's hands curved the air, cupping the shapes he had seen through the Captain's wife's dress, the smoke from his cigarette lingering as curves in the air.

Anna couldn't breathe. She stood up, her head spinning, the air spangled with stars. Running her fingers through her hair she was startled to find it wet with sweat.

All she could see outside was empty, endless, hellish desert. It was so soundless Anna thought she could hear the moisture and the life being sucked from the earth. She turned back towards the room and the sun burned into her back.

'Heat getting to you?' Shane growled.

Anna nodded and sat down hard, and fanned herself with flaps of her hand. 'Could I have a glass of water?' she said, her voice tremulous. Dillon got up and went to fetch the water for her. She took it gingerly from between his caliper hands and took a long sip of the lukewarm, muddy liquid. All she wanted to do was flee this place. She wanted to be in the sanctuary of her home, in the safe cocoon of her bed, unconscious.

But there was more she had to know before she could leave. She finished the water and put the glass on the plastic tabletop.

'Do you have any proof that Paul was in the police?' She didn't doubt his story, but she wanted something solid as evidence. Fourie seemed to understand. He jerked his head towards the door and shouted to his wife. 'Shawna, fetch my box!'

Anna stared down at the floor while they waited, her body limp, her mind wrung out. A rat-like scrabbling and scratching came from the next room, then Shawna appeared. In her hands was an old biscuit tin, with a painting on its lid of an English village, the sort that never existed except perhaps in Surrey, in a modern recreation of some idyll of past times.

Fourie pulled it open. It was stuffed with envelopes and papers and old pictures and postcards. He flipped through it with his yellowed fingertips. A grunt signalled that he'd found what he was looking for. He pulled out an old colour snap, one of those ones printed on a card with zig-zag edges.

The picture shook in her hand. It was of Paul and Shane on a fishing boat, one of those big pleasure crafts that were used for catching marlin and kingfish on the Northern Natal coast. Drinking. Frans Nel was there too, with a bikini-clad Sherry draped over him. Paul was smiling, saluting the camera with a beer.

It was unmistakably him. She knew those terrible tartan swimming trunks. And that body, so slim and white and young.

She stared at the picture for a long time, wanting to say something to Paul's picture, but words were useless, there weren't any big or vicious or damning enough to convey to him what she felt.

'What about Jacob Oliphant?' she asked at last.

Shane's eyes narrowed against the smoke that streamed upwards from his nostrils. 'What about him?'

'Was he spying too?' It felt like another person saying these words, a person with no past and no bitter taste of brackish water on her tongue.

Shane shook his head. 'I don't know, never knew the guy. Only knew Paul Lewis for a short while, lost touch when he was sent to varsity.'

'So how did you come to know Paul?'

Shane explained how he had been part of the team that had identified Paul when he was in prison. Fourie couldn't conceal the pride he felt at this insight, at the role he'd played in helping to pick Paul out as a potential spy.

'I was in the police, working for Captain Nel. Nel never liked *me*,' he said bitterly, 'so I never got past Warrant Officer. Most probably still be at that rank today if he had anything to do with it. I worked mostly on narcotics. Not the big stuff, mostly dagga and buttons.'

'You mean Mandrax?' Anna clarified. Fourie nodded. Mandrax was a prescription sleeping pill, a powerful barbiturate much favoured by drug takers.

'Paul was a buttonhead when he started doing time; he was big into that stuff. People like that are useful. We kept him vrot for a while, then we took him off it. Did it *our way*. Made him grateful.' A glimpse of the sadist in Shane emerged in the way he uttered those words. 'We cleaned him up, taught him the rules and then gave him an early release. Conditional. *We* paid for him to study at the university. We needed people there. Easy work if you ask me. But you had to be the right person for it.'

Dillon smoked and Shane talked. Anna was hot and cold, her bones brittle and her flesh crinkly-thin covering them. Every hair on her head was a needle sticking into her scalp.

'He was a real amateur at first, we had to train him, but he turned into a good operator. I don't know what they did with him after he left the university. I was out by then. I got out when things got ugly.' The way he exchanged glances with Dillon suggested there was more to the story of why he'd left the police, but Shane didn't take that further and Anna wasn't interested in pursuing it. 'And I'm glad I did, when I saw what they did to Paul,' was all he said.

Fourie knew nothing about the murder.

He was only aware of what he'd read in the papers.

'Would you be prepared to testify to all this in a court?' Anna asked, her voice thin with exhaustion.

He shrugged, taking no time to think about it. 'Long as you pay for me to get there. I got no problem with that.'

Anna nodded. She'd had enough. It was time to go. 'May I keep the picture?'

Fourie shrugged. 'If it means so much to you.'

She mumbled a thank you as she slipped the damning image into her bag.

'You come from Pretoria?'

She shook her head. Her response was rasping; the words felt like sandpaper in her throat. 'Joburg.'

He seemed impressed. 'It's lucky you found us here. We were out in the bush till this morning. Hunting. Wasn't coming back till next week, but we had some problems with the bakkie.' He gestured vaguely in the direction of the rusty pick-up truck parked in the narrow shade cast by the dead blue gum.

At her car Shane Fourie put his dry, rough hand on her arm. The contact was unpleasant. Anna looked up at him almost fearfully, willing him to let go. He spoke in a tone that was new, low and urgent and pleading. 'You got any brandy on you?' The look of craving in his eyes was pathetic.

Anna shook her head and he withdrew his hand, stuffing it into the frayed pocket of his jeans. 'Just wondered. Just in case,' he sniggered. It was a strange expression. Cruelty and thwarted desire both at once in that ravaged faced. Anna looked away as she said a brief thank you and goodbye and climbed into her car.

She fumbled with the keys, her heart racing, hands shaking. Then at last she was driving in a blast of cool air-conditioning and the two men were receding into the distance. On the radio, the weatherman was also speaking in Afrikaans. *Last year was the hottest on this planet since measurement began.*

Koekemoor was leaning against the bonnet of his car, cool as a cucumber despite the heat, in full uniform. He grinned as she drove up alongside him, but took fright when he saw her face.

'Oh no, lady. You look like you've seen a ghost!'

Anna said numbly, 'No, I'll be okay. It's just the heat.'

'Ja, ja. It can get to a person if theys not used to it.'

More than anything Anna wanted to be alone, but out of courtesy and perhaps because she was too dazed to do otherwise, Anna gave in to the Constable's insistence and followed him back to the little police station. He poured her an ice-cold Coca-Cola and the sweetness of it helped to quell the dizzy, nauseating sense of unreality.

Koekemoor poured her another and sat down opposite her, his

expresison grave. There was evidently something on his mind. 'I don't want to seem like a trouble-maker, Miss Kriel, but there is a small matter that I must raise with you. I mean, a person of your position and influence coming here … it doesn't happen every day, you know? And I would just kick myself if I didn't take this opportunity.'

Anna's head felt as if it was going to burst, but she nodded attentively.

'Well, ma'm. It's our *uniforms*.'

He was most upset, he explained, that the new SAPS uniform, which had been announced and publicised so much, had not yet been dispatched to his station. 'It makes me ashamed, especially when a lady of your high rank arrives for an inspection and I don't even have the right uniform.'

'I'm not here—' she began.

'No, no, don't tell me,' he interrupted, waving his hands before his face. 'I know. I *am* speaking out of turn and I *am* prepared to take the consequences. But I *have* to protest. I cannot dutifully and proudly call myself a member of the South African Police Service while I'm wearing this out-of-date uniform.'

Anna leaned forward across the desk and put her hand reassuringly on his.

'Constable. You can depend upon me. The first thing I will do when I get back to Pretoria will be to issue a clear reprimand to those responsible and to ensure that your new uniforms are delivered at the first possible instance.'

Her certainty and her promise delighted him. Koekemoor was almost bursting out of his old uniform as he walked her to her car. There he pressed into her hands a handwritten card – it looked like it was cut from a cigarette packet – with his name and rank and phone number on it. Constable Jan Koekemoor. 'Next time, you don't have to drive all this way, you just give me a tinkle and I'll be happy to conduct any interviews on your behalf.' He grinned and waved happily as she pulled the door shut and started up the engine. 'Drive safely now and remember, we're *always* happy to help!'

Anna drove slumped forward against the wheel. The road was

a long tar ribbon hugging the curves of the landscape. It was like driving into infinity.

Her entire life was a lie and her love was a sham. In fact she had only inhabited one of the complex of compartments that was Paul's life. In fact what was love-making for her had, for him, blurred into the same category as a stolen fuck up against a car in some fume-filled garage. The lurid, smutty glow of drugs and G-strings and bribes and beaten-up adulterous wives had polluted her world at its seams. All the innocence and purity and idealism of her life and her love for Paul were destroyed by those five words uttered by Shane Fourie: 'He was one of ours.'

The road rolled away behind her. Questions leapt into her mind and looped round and round continuously. How could she have known him so little? How could her own judgement have been so flawed? If Paul was not who he seemed, then who was she? If Anna couldn't answer those questions for herself, then what would they say in the goldfish bowl of Joburg society? And what about the movement, discovering that one of its heroes was a traitor? There were already many who'd raised questions about Anna's complicity. Now self-doubt and self-pity eroded the certainty with which she had been able to rebut the questions.

Anna was crying so hard she could barely see to drive. She pulled over onto the hard shoulder and stopped the car, waiting for the grief to subside.

She imagined herself standing before him and realised she had nothing to say. Nothing to say to a man she thought she knew more intimately than any other, someone whose voice was as familiar to her as her own, whose every gesture she could anticipate, a man whose body she knew in all its detail. What on earth had happened to him that he could betray those he was supposed to be closest to? That he could betray himself to the extent that almost every minute of his life was a lie? What sort of mind could jump through such hoops?

It was some time before she was calm enough even to register where she was. When she did she looked down and found she'd twisted the ring off her wedding finger.

Without another thought Anna stepped out onto the long road that stretched emptily to the eastern and western horizons, raised her arm and flung the gold band into the air. She watched it spin and fly, catching the light before it tumbled earthwards and was lost amongst the beer cans and plastic bags and the other trash that polluted the roadside.

twenty-two

When Anna walked away from that broken house and that broken family in Bulletrap it was like walking from the centre of a bomb crater into a wrecked world. She functioned – something was working, transporting a body that looked like hers, in a manner that was recognisably her – but Anna couldn't feel anything at all.

That week she went to work as usual, moved through all her routines as usual, made no mention to anyone of her journey to Bulletrap. And in the most excruciating irony of all she sat mutely through a meeting with her Minister in which he informed her brightly that the Internal Investigations Unit had cleared her.

'I'm so sorry, Anna,' he said. 'I made a bad call. You and Paul were so close. I guess I thought that there was no way, if he was a spy, that you couldn't have known about it.'

She laughed harshly, a little hysterically, but managed to ask the important question. 'Where did you get your information?'

He shifted uncomfortably. 'Well, between you and me, it was ANC intelligence, but I'd rather that wasn't mentioned again.'

She shook her head, there was no reason for her ever to mention it. 'And what about Paul?'

The Minister shrugged. 'We weren't looking into his background.'

A formal, written apology was made for the disruption and emotional distress the enquiry had caused her and the case was closed.

But there was no normal to go back to.

She dragged herself through the days of that week, arrived late for work and left early. Deadlines were extended, eyebrows were raised, but she didn't care. It didn't matter in the way that it had. She even took a day off to help Rachel with preparations for her wedding.

The night before the wedding she was getting ready for an early night when she caught sight of the collection of silver frames in her bedroom; her gallery of pictures of him. Looking at them was like looking into a hall of mirrors. *Who are you? Who did you think you were? Who the hell do you think you are?* She picked up the wastepaper basket and with one, violent sweep of her arm she knocked the whole lot into the bin. They crashed on top of one another, wood snapping, glass cracking. Then she dumped them on the street.

Saturday, the day of the wedding, was beautiful. Anna, who had arrived a little late, took a deep breath as she climbed up onto the stoep, which was decorated with garlands of lilies, ivy and white roses.

Temba was in the hallway with his brothers and Rachel's boys. Bram was fourteen now, pimply and self-conscious, serious like his father. Delarey was a wild, gorgeous seventeen with gold hoops in his ears, long black hair tumbling around his shoulders and a huge smile like his mother's.

Delarey swamped Anna with a huge bear-hug. 'You look so fucking beautiful!' he exclaimed, making her blush. Anna was wearing a new sari of orange and gold and she did look beautiful, swathed in silk with her brown belly exposed.

'Joe not with you?' Temba looked past her down the pathway.

Anna shook her head. 'Where's the bride?'

Temba grinned and threw up his hands. 'Who knows? I'm telling you, she takes this stuff very seriously. I haven't seen her since yesterday.'

The house was humming with conversation and music. Children raced around the garden, guests clattered from room to room, women's laughter rang out from the kitchen. Moving through those familiar rooms Anna had the sense of time converging and folding in on itself. Beneath Rachel's wonderful, colourful chaos Anna could see the stark asceticism of their poorer and more serious activist days, the days she'd lived here with Paul. She could sense them in this house, but not as she'd remembered them or thought they were then. Now they were something twisted and grotesque.

The posters in the hallway, which had once punched the air with their cries for freedom and justice, were now framed artefacts, each accusing him in turn. *Victory is certain; each one teach one; get up stand up.* In the living room was their prized copy of the Freedom Charter, one of those printed and distributed by the *Sunday Post* in June ninety-eighty, twenty-five years after the Congress of the People drew it up. Her finger traced the stirring avowal. 'We the people of South Africa, declare for all our country and the world to know that South Africa belongs to all who live in it, black and white and that no government can justly claim authority unless it is based on the will of all the people.'

The words vibrated with a different meaning for her now, for those were the words Paul had betrayed. *These freedoms we will fight for, side by side, throughout our lives, until we have won our liberty*!

Anna sat down, struggling to take it in, to understand. She had given herself to Paul, entrusted him with her fragile, precious, imperfect self. All boundaries had fallen away and the feeling of knowing and being known so completely was headier than the highest high.

To learn that he'd betrayed her, that her Paul was merely her fantasy left her desolate. He'd lived in another reality, her soul mate, her single, sparking connection in the world. And she'd been alone all along, alone lying next to him, standing by him. He was supposed to have been the one, the only, who looked penetratingly and saw piercingly into her deepest self; her match, her equal, meeting her needs as much as his own, sometimes before his own. But he'd been on his own mission the whole time. He'd barely even seen her. Anna was incidental at best. At worst, she'd been the unwitting interlocutor, the key to many locks.

Had she lost herself in Paul so completely that she'd lost all judgement? Had she known that he was lying to her all along? Was there some complicity there? Some intuition she'd half listened to once that told her that the love he whispered to her, enfolded her with, was all a lie? How could she not have known?

You just know when someone is lying to you. She remembered how emphatically she'd said that to James Kay. You know because it's in the eyes, the tone of voice, in the body language and the way the liar trips themself up over the small details. And yet she hadn't known.

Real is real. Not real is not real. So how did not real *seem* so damned real? What was it about her that had preferred the sham? Was Paul just a brilliant liar? To be that good he must have been psychotic. There had been *nothing*, not a flicker in his eyes, not a scratch in his voice, not a shudder in his bearing, absolutely *nothing* she could recall that would have given him away.

She tried to imagine what it must have been like for him, living two lives or more. She knew what intelligence work was like and what it did to a person. A person living the life of a spy backs off from being forthright, from honesty, and year by year they become more devious, more damaged until they are unable to distinguish any more between their true self and all their compartments of legends and lies. She remembered that Paul was scared a lot – used to wake up in the night unable to breathe. He never screamed, never said anything, she just knew he was dreaming that he was paralysed. Now it galled her that those dreams might have been the worst he felt. He should have hurt more.

'Here you are! We've been looking for you.' Anna looked up to see Rika Swanepoel standing in the doorway. 'Shew, you look pale!' Rika floated across the room in a long sky-blue sheath dress. 'This must be hard for you,' she said sitting down next to Anna.

'No, not really. It's fine,' Anna said quickly, looking away. She felt as if the announcement of Paul's treachery must be pulsing from her eyes like neon signs. 'You look fantastic, Rika.' She managed a bigger smile now, and Rika smiled back. 'You here with your ex-husband?'

Rika nodded, taking Anna's hand. 'He's fetching champagne for us outside. Come!'

Anna followed her into the garden, which was bright with winter greenery and brilliant poinsettias and the scarlet cones of red-hot pokers. The air fizzed with happy conversation. Willem was towering over the bar, a glass of bubbly in each hand. 'Cheers!' he boomed as they each took one. Willem put his arm round Anna, pulling her against him. And she wanted to cry for him and all the others who'd loved Paul.

Anna's mother and sisters sailed across the garden in shimmering dresses of dazzling colours, nieces and nephews stuffed into suits and buttoned smocks, hair shiny and scraped into shape, just like Anna had been when she was a kid. 'Auntie Anna! Auntie Anna!' they shrieked, flinging themselves at her legs for hugs and kisses.

Yasmin giggled as Willem handed her a drink. 'Ooh, you're corrupting me again!' Then she took a long sip.

'Ma! You're not supposed to be drinking,' Anna chided her.

Her mother looked up at her with a mischievous grin. 'I drink at all my children's weddings and if you won't give me one to celebrate then Rachel's will have to do,' she countered.

Anna's sister, Natasha, asked after Joe.

'He's not here yet,' Anna said, casting an eye around the garden.

'Well he better get here in time to see you catching the bouquet!' she declared raucously. There was much laughter and teasing. Her family had clearly decided they'd waited long enough. It was Anna's turn to marry next. She excused herself from the roasting and went inside to find Rachel.

The bride was in her bedroom with her mother, Sarah, who was calmly pinning into place fine strands of her daughter's hair. Sarah was sternly intent on her task, oblivious to the clutter of discarded scarves and underwear and jewellery at her feet. Rachel grinned and waved excitably at Anna in the mirror. Her mother, Sarah, yanked her head back. 'I told you, don't move!' Rachel made a funny face and tried her best to keep still, but she was bursting with anticipation.

'Shall I come back?' Anna asked.

'No, no. I'll be done in a minute. You look lovely, Anna,' Sarah said, her fingers working furiously.

Sarah was a no-nonsense woman, a hospital cleaner who'd worked nights most of her adult life, given birth to seven children and raised the five of them that lived; she was proud of her youngest daughter's achievements but resolutely unimpressible. She moved methodically around Rachel firing off rounds of hairspray that formed a sticky cloud before settling on Rachel's head.

'Done?' Rachel asked, her hands hovering near her head, patting the air around it.

'Done,' Sarah said, looking quietly pleased as she stepped back to admire her work. Rachel kissed her mother, planting a huge set of maroon lips on her face. Sarah grimaced.

As Rachel stood up and stepped out onto the carpet her buttery yellow dress fell gorgeously to her ankles, shimmering with spirals of gold embroidery.

Anna gasped. 'Oh. Wow!'

Rachel looked away, her hand over her mouth. 'Don't make me cry now, babes.'

'Don't mess up your make-up!' snapped Sarah.

'Oh my God, Rachel. You look perfect,' Anna whispered.

Rachel blinked hard, her lips crumpling with emotion. 'I keep thinking about Jacob. I can *feel* him here in the house.'

'I know. I know.'

Sarah shot Anna a don't-get-her-started look, but they were saved by an explosive interruption from the boys, who burst in through the doorway, faces lit up, shirts untucked, hair all over the place. 'Ma. It's time!' Delarey declared while his grandmother caught him in an inescapable armlock and dragged a comb through his hair.

Rachel was flapping her hands in front of her like an agitated chicken. Anna grabbed and squeezed them while her mother wiped the smudges of mascara from underneath her eyes. 'OhmyGodthisisitherewegoboys!' she wailed.

Anna kissed her on the cheek, whispered a quick 'Good luck, angel,' in her ear and went outside to await the arrival of the bride with everyone else.

Anna found herself a place at the edge of the gathering next to her mother, who gave her a stern once-over. 'Well, at least you're not looking so pale any more.' Anna smiled and turned towards the house as the music started up, blaring from the speakers balanced on the ledges of the lounge windows.

But instead of the bride, Joe appeared in the doorway. He

smiled and waved to laughter and general applause, arms outstretched, like the winner of a race as he jogged down to join them. 'Just in time,' he whispered as he slipped into the space next to Anna.

Then Rachel and her sons walked slowly down the steps and through the centre of the gasping, delighted crowd. The boys looked so scrubbed and serious and their mother couldn't stop smiling, though there were tears streaming down her face. Temba's face lit up when he saw her. There was so much pride and trust and love beaming from his eyes as his bride came towards him it almost hurt to watch. Bram and Delarey gave their mother to him, then stood back, amongst family and friends.

As the ceremony began, Anna was conscious of herself standing apart, separated by an invisible shield of sadness. There she was, in the midst of this celebration of continuity and healing and hope for the future, locked in the past.

part five

It's a mistake to see it all in black and white
It never was and never will be
It's a thousand shades of grey

COLONEL IG DU PREEZ

twenty-three

'Okay, this is what we know so far. There are two gangs competing for the same turf in Gauteng. The Angolans and the Mozambicans. We know that the Mozambicans are mostly former freedom fighters, with a sprinkling of ex-cops thrown in for spice. Right?' James struck off each point against his fingers with a biro.

'Right.' Chris frowned, concentrating.

It was a rare overcast day, one of the few genuinely cold days that strike Johannesburg in winter. The city glowered from behind sheets of dirty rain. James was talking with his editor, Chris Rassool, a heavy-set man with rimless glasses and a shock of curly black hair that stood out in every direction. Chris always looked as if he'd just rolled out of a fight, but he was the gentlest man James had ever met.

They were sitting on the desk in Chris's office, a glass box that looked out over Johannesburg on one side and the newsroom on the other. The place was humming, the paper was twenty-four hours off deadline and there was the usual frenzy of last-minute activity. It looked like a sprawling ops room, with dirty windows at either end admitting little light. The ceiling was naked concrete; two lines of neon tubing suspended from it illuminated the chaos below. The floor was brown carpet tiles pocked with cigarette burns and trodden filth. A TV set in one corner played BBC World non-stop. At the centre of the room was a large conference table decorated with long-dead lily stalks standing in a galvanised-tin vase. The smell of cigarettes and stale coffee emanated from everything.

'Bazooka Rabopane runs the Mozambicans. He gets arrested,

somehow pays someone off, escapes and there's mayhem. Two people dead in a gunfight in a Soweto shebeen, three killed in a bungled bank robbery, the robbers escape. The *Angolans* seem to be on the ascendant.'

'Okay?'

'Is it possible,' James slowed down thoughtfully, 'that Joe Dladla's unit is working with the Angolans to wipe out Bazooka and his gang?'

Chris got up off the desk and paced the floor of his office, hands deep in his pockets. 'Well, Dladla is known for sailing close to the wind. It's not impossible that he'd infiltrate one gang to play it off against another, but it's risky.' He sat down in his chair and swung his feet up onto the desk as he finished speaking.

'You see the picture I'm getting is that the cops are trying to control these gangs by, almost ...' James opened his hands, rolling them through the air as he searched for the right word. 'Well, *licensing* them.'

'You mean like a protection racket?'

'Yeah.' He clapped his hands down against his thighs.

'Wow.' Chris Rassool seemed to be at a loss for words.

'I mean, I don't *know*. But that's the way it's looking.'

'I dunno, James, we've got to be careful here. I mean Joe Dladla is – not to put too fine a point on it – impeccable. You know, the guy's flown up the ladder, he's running a unit full of whiteys from the bad old days, guys who don't like him because he's young and black and a former fucking freedom fighter –'

Chris turned, his flow interrupted by the abrupt flinging open of his office door. Miriam, his assistant, stuck her peroxided head round. Her hair looked like sharp peaks of icing sugar on top of a face-shaped cake.

'Call for you, James. International. A *woman*.' She emphasised the last word with a meaningful wink.

'Take a message.'

'She said you'd say that and that I can't. She *must* talk to you.'

James sighed. 'Look, we're just in the middle of something. Please, Miriam?'

Miriam flounced off in a swirl of rustling skirt. James turned back to his editor, who had a sly grin on his face.

'You got a woman overseas?'

James shook his head. 'Can we get back to this story?'

Chris Rassool sat up, banging his feet down onto the floor, businesslike again. 'Okay, we need the interview with Dladla. I'll put in a call. Maybe my name'll help.'

'That'd be great. Mine seems to be mud since we ran that piece on Paul Lewis.'

'Careful with Joe, Jim-boy. Get on the right side of him and you're cool, but get on the wrong side and the guy's a meat-mincer.'

James raked his fingers back through his hair, not sure that it wasn't too late.

Miriam appeared again, this time strolling into the office with a message for James and a wedge of faxes for Rassool. She glared as she handed them over, and then stalked out. Both men glanced down at the papers she'd given them. James's heart sank as he read his. The message was from Alison. 'Please call. I really need to talk.' The number she gave was their old home number. He crumpled up the pink slip and tossed it in the bin as he marched for the door.

'Hey! Hold on. Check this out,' Chris exclaimed, leaping up from his chair and waving the fax in James's face. 'Frans Nel has applied for amnesty for the Mafikeng Murders!'

James did a double-take. 'What?'

Chris flattened the pages out on his desk. It was a Truth Commission press release, of the kind that came through several times a day. But the heading was incredible. 'Brigadier Frans Nel admits to assassinating Paul Lewis and Jacob Oliphant.'

James scanned the page furiously, taking it in paragraphs at a time. Sections of Nel's application were reproduced on the press release. In them he admitted that it was he who had ordered and carried out the killings, along with a Warrant Officer Jeff Curry 'deceased'.

'Convenient,' James muttered.

The motive for the killing, Nel claimed, was political. Well, naturally. It had to be if he was to qualify for amnesty. Nel went on to say that his unit had strong reason to believe that Paul Lewis and Jacob Oliphant were in the course of assisting terrorists with the shipment of arms into the country from

Botswana. Security Police Headquarters had been informed of their movements and had sent down a message instructing that the two men be 'eliminated'.

James glanced up at Chris. Both men shook their heads in amazement. 'Unbelievable!'

'Scuppers your story about him being a spy,' Rassool grinned.

James shrugged. 'Hey, you win some . . .'

'Take it away, Jim. And a nice interview with Anna Kriel, please, nudge, nudge, wink, wink!'

James shook his head with weary amusement and Rassool grinned back lasciviously. 'Good luck to you, my son. Braver and stupider and better-looking men than you have tried and failed with that one.'

James took a cigarette out of his pack and flipped it into his mouth.

Rassool reached over with the flame from a plastic lighter cupped in his hand. 'What about Ilse McLean?' he asked as James took his first puff. 'How was she?'

James shook his head. 'Don't know. Didn't go there.'

Chris looked amazed. 'Serious? That's not what I heard.'

James laughed. 'This town!'

'She's hot, that one,' Chris went on as he settled back down in front of his computer, fag hanging from his bottom lip. 'Hope you don't mind if I give her a try?'

'I didn't hear that. I know I didn't hear that.' James let out a disgusted snort as he strode out of the office and across the newsroom towards his desk, the press release tucked under his arm.

His office was a cubicle marked off with a sign that said 'Kay Hole'. The desk was a hamster cage of papers and post-its and little pink while-you-were-out slips sellotaped all over it. He scrabbled around in the mess for his Rolodex, found it and flipped to the card marked 'KRIEL Anna'.

This was the ending she wanted, James thought as he dialled her number. Clear cut. With good guys and bad guys and Paul's heroism intact. He was glad for her.

A secretary answered. Anna was 'in a meeting'.

'Can I leave a message?'

'Sure, but I won't be able to give it to her before Monday. She won't be back in the office this afternoon.'

'Damn!' He hadn't thought of that possibility.

'But I can give you her cell number if you like?' the secretary offered quickly.

'Oh! Great. That would be great,' he exclaimed, fishing around for a pen.

She answered almost immediately. Sounding as cool and collected as ever. James grimaced as he heard his own voice spinning down the line, all breathless, puppy-dog eagerness.

'Anna! Hi. It's James. Kay.'

'Oh. Hi.' Neutral, he thought.

'Wanted to be one of the first to congratulate you!'

'Why?' Borderline hostile or just plain puzzled.

'The amnesty application. You must be delighted. Vindicated at last, hey?'

A sigh. Not good. 'I don't know. I just don't know any more.' Definitely not good.

'But you've got the answer you've been waiting for!' He was beginning to sound like the cheerleader on some dumb game show.

'Ja.' No emotion at all. She really hates me.

'Well, hope I'm not disturbing you, just wanted to say well done . . .'

'Look, can we meet?'

James frowned, pressing the handset closer to his ear. Did I hear that correctly?

'James? Can we meet?'

Amazing. I did hear that correctly.

'Um. Sure. Anytime.'

'I mean soon.'

Sometimes my own luck amazes even me.

'Absolutely. You name the time and the place.'

'Can you be at my house in forty-five minutes?'

'What the hell's with you, boy?' Chris Rassool scowled as James swaggered into his glass cage, jacket slung over his shoulder, car keys jingling in his hand.

'She wants to see me. Now,' he grinned.

'Who, for fuck's sake? Not the one in London. You are *not* going to London!'

'Nope. I am going to see Ms A. Kriel. At her place. Right now. Seeya.' And with that he sailed out.

Anna's house was just a few blocks from his, freshly whitewashed and bristling with the standard Joburg security devices, electric fencing atop the high wall, cameras eyeing the entrances, and automated gates. She buzzed him into a neat courtyard filled with pots of lavender and geraniums, with slate-tiled steps leading up to the front door. The door opened as he reached it. James stopped dead at the sight of her.

'I know, I look terrible,' she said, smiling palely. She didn't look great. Like she'd been ill or badly shaken up. Her hair was dirty and scooped up into a big plastic clip. She was wearing a flappy shirt over old jeans and ancient flip-flops on her feet. 'Come in.'

He followed her inside. Anna Kriel's house was very much like her. Elegant, uncluttered, practical. She wandered into the kitchen, which connected with the living room through a wide hatch. 'I don't have any drink to offer you. Do you mind tea?'

'No, that's cool. Great view!' he said, strolling over to the window. The garden was small, but it opened out onto a vista of the suburbs that was spectacular. He could see all the way to Sandton.

'Thanks.'

He walked over towards her, leaning against the counter that was between them. 'You've been avoiding me.'

She frowned. 'Oh, I dunno. It's hard to avoid people in this town.' Then she looked up at him, a playful smile dancing on her lips. 'I kept expecting to run into you, you can't avoid your mistakes in Joburg.'

James balked, exaggerating a hurt look. 'So I'm a mistake, am I?'

'No, in your case *I'm* the mistake.'

'Oh, but I beg to differ.'

Anna made a face. 'Yeah right!' she answered sarcastically.

'You know, you're not the *first* person to accuse me of being a mistake,' he went on dryly. 'I find that troubling. Maybe it's because I'm not a nurturing person. People don't seem to *grow* around me.'

Anna laughed. James began to relax.

'What's up with you? You've got an edge this wide,' he said, stretching out his arms.

'Yeah well . . .' She handed him a mug of tea, took one for herself and walked through to the living room with it, perching herself on the edge of an armchair. James sat down on the sofa opposite. In the silence he reached into his pocket for his cigarettes, took them out and then thought better of it, put them back. She waved a hand towards him. 'Oh, I don't mind. Paul smoked. I'm used to it.'

Uh-huh. Paul smoked.

'That's an odd thing to say, isn't it?' she said suddenly.

He smiled slightly as he nodded. 'But on a scale of odd to stark raving mad, it doesn't rate much higher than eccentric.' He shook a cigarette out of his packet and lit up. 'I've been trying to get hold of you so I could apologise for the story. If that's—'

'No,' she interrupted, shaking her head. She was frighteningly pale. 'No. You were right.' She uttered the words with a heavy finality. 'Paul *was* a spy. You were right. As it turns out. Things I told him led to people's detention and torture and maybe even death.'

James took several drags on his cigarette as he absorbed this. She looked at him the whole time, her eyebrows knitted together, eyes black.

'Have you known all along?' he asked gently.

She shook her head again. Then she told him the story of her visits to the Colonel and Shane Fourie.

James listened in awe. Her hurt was so acute he could feel it washing out from her in waves. And she was so alone, sitting there hunched up with her mug between her hands, her body almost shivering with tension, brittle with coping. He wanted to touch her, to comfort her, but he didn't move.

'Have you told anyone about this?'

'Only you.' She took a sip of tea. 'I don't know *how* to tell anyone else.'

'Shit, I'm sorry. I'm so sorry,' James sighed.

'It's so strange,' she said, staring up at the ceiling, a frown creasing her face. 'I keep thinking of what it was like for him, how exhausting it must have been to spin those stories, to juggle all those lives, to keep the projections alive and up in the air.'

James sat with his head buried in his hands, wishing he could help, but not having the faintest idea how.

'What are you going to do about the amnesty application?'

'Contest it. We know that he's not telling the whole truth. And that's a prerequisite for amnesty. Full disclosure.'

James looked up and met her weary gaze. 'Anna, you are one of the most courageous people I've ever met.'

She closed her eyes. 'I don't think you understand how much a part of me Paul was.'

'That makes your courage all the greater.'

'I don't even know what that means.'

'Yes, you do,' James answered softly. 'Weakness is not knowing who you are, not knowing yourself, not knowing your needs. Courage is about exceeding yourself. It's about strength revealed and deployed when the current is running against you.'

'Ja, well. Who knows?' she whispered.

He watched her looking down into her mug, not at all sure what he was feeling any more. She'd scrambled his brain completely.

'I need to ask you a favour,' she said at last.

'Go ahead.'

'It's important that this information doesn't come out until the hearing. Can you make sure it doesn't?'

He smiled, glad that her request was so easy to fulfil.

'No problem. As long as I get an exclusive interview after the hearing.'

'Deal.'

She walked him to his car. 'Shew, that's some serious babe magnet!' she declared.

James laughed sheepishly. 'Yep, I guess . . .' he mumbled as he fiddled with the keys.

He wanted to hold and comfort her, but she stood there with her arms folded across her chest, looking so stiff and self-contained, like she'd flinch if he tried. So he simply touched her arm, smiled, then climbed into his car and drove away, watching her in the rear-view mirror as she turned – head down, shoulders stooped – and went inside.

twenty-four

Willem Swanepoel's offices were in Braamfontein. The Labour Law partnership he'd started almost a decade ago had grown into a large, corporate firm occupying the top three floors of one of the tower blocks that loomed over the city. He came out to meet Anna in the reception area, as cool and imposing and comforting a presence as ever.

It was immediately clear to him that something was wrong. He ushered her into his office, sat her down, then opened the drawer of a filing cabinet from which he took a bottle of Chivas Regal and two glasses. He poured one for himself and a double tot for Anna. The drink burned her throat and she grimaced as she swallowed it down, but it worked. It warmed her, loosened her up enough to explain.

All things considered, Willem took it well. It was when she handed him the photograph that his face turned ashen. He stared at the image for some time, the damning, drunken picture of Paul and his buddies on their fishing trip. After a while he put it down on the glass tabletop, then stood up and stalked over to the window, cradling the whisky in his hand as he stared out over Johannesburg. The traffic on the street below sounded like the sea.

'I feel so ashamed,' Anna murmured.

Willem turned towards her, loosening his tie, his expression grave and sad. 'It's Paul's shame you are feeling. You have none.' Then he sat down hard on the chair opposite her. 'Shew!' He shook his head, sighing heavily, the restless gestures and expressions of one too shocked to know immediately what to say or do. 'Do Joe and Rachel know about this?'

Anna shook her head. 'I don't know how to tell them.' He nodded, understanding. 'Well, I suppose we better figure out what to do,' he said finally.

Frans Nel's admission was everything Anna had wanted for all these years, but she knew it was a lie. Even if he was the killer – and it was clearer than ever before that he was at least involved – there was a glaring omission in his story. If he'd made the application just weeks before then everything would have been different. She would never have gone to Bulletrap, never have met Shane Fourie and could never have known, *truly* known, Paul.

And yet part of her still longed for him, longed to sit him down and talk to her Paul. Not to that person described by Shane Fourie, not to that liar, that fucker of Security Policemen's wives, not to that traitor, that violator, that exploder of everything who'd invaded Paul in her memory. No, she longed to talk to that friend with whom she'd sat for hours in meetings and in cafés, with whom she'd lain so happily in the warmth of a shared bed. She wanted to talk to the unguarded, honest lover who could express himself so simply and so beautifully. But the desolate knowledge that gripped her was that he had never existed.

Everything had to be revisited, everything mistrusted. A lens of weariness and cynicism fogged her vision, coloured everything she saw. Part of her wished she could reverse it all and revert to the happy certainty that he'd died a hero and that he'd be with her for all time. She wanted to smother the endlessly probing instinct in her that wouldn't let the investigation go, that had brought her to this awful truth.

Willem picked up the file on his desk and brought it over to where Anna was sitting. 'I keep going over it, over and over and over,' she said numbly, rubbing her hands together, rolling them over one another, knotting and unknotting her fingers. 'Like that day of his release. I mean, what was going on there? I just can't believe that was all an act. What was he so scared of?'

Willem shook his head, his hand covering his mouth. He knew as well as she did that the reason for Paul's death was more obscure now than ever. He sighed again. 'Okay, let's start with the amnesty application.'

'We oppose.'

'Absolutely. Full disclosure is where we hit him. There's also a question mark over political motive. Nel knew that Paul was a cop; just the photograph is sufficient to establish their connection beyond any doubt. So he can't claim this murder was the straightforward elimination of a dangerous political opponent.'

Anna found herself rocking backwards and forwards on her chair. It felt so strange, so completely unreal to be having this conversation. The atmosphere in the room was heavy as water.

'There has to be a reason Nel is telling this version right now,' she said.

Willem agreed. 'The way to flush that out is to let him tell the story his way and then we slam him with Shane Fourie and the proof that he has not disclosed.'

'What about the . . . affair?' Anna found it difficult to say the word. Willem looked at her, pain and compassion in his eyes. 'I'd rather not go into that. If we can avoid it,' she added.

'Ja, I think that's best. For now,' Willem concurred. Walking back to her car, Anna became aware of a familiar, old sensation. That of being watched. She swung round, scanning the concrete bays of the underground parking lot. The place seemed empty. Reason told her she was imagining things, but instinct said there was someone following her.

She remembered the fear they used to live with, the intense paranoia that was born of real experience. The police raids in the middle of the night, the taps that were placed on their phones and sometimes in their houses. The harassment, people waiting outside in cars that followed you sometimes for a few hours, sometimes for a week. The fire-bomb attack on the house at Valley View Road, the burning of Jacob's motorbike. The cops liked to let them know they were there, close by, watching all the time.

Pulling out into the street she noticed a car coming out of the building behind her. It turned where she turned, keeping a good two or three vehicles behind. And it stayed with her as far as Kingsway and the Melville turn-off. She felt silly making a note of the make and the registration number, it was probably just coincidence. Nevertheless it irked her. If someone had put a tail on her who could it be? The Captain's people? Someone else?

Some old network still functioning intact? All her antennae were singing. She checked for the Beretta in her glove compartment. It was still there.

twenty-five

Anna drove slowly through the city, past the long lines of men and women snaking the pavements of the main arteries, waiting for taxis to take them home. The sky was smoky pink. Buses and taxis cluttered the streets, people streamed into the railway station in the deepening blue light. Anna felt as if she was floating, like a ghost amongst the living.

Frans Nel's amnesty hearing was less than a week away. She was heading for Valley View Road and the meeting she dreaded, but could no longer avoid. What she feared was the pain of their reactions and not being able to handle them. For her the news had struck like lightning, the shock had electrified and cauterised every nerve ending, every sense impulse. Somehow she could handle that. But she wasn't sure she could handle the pain she was about to bring to the people she loved the most.

Joe was already there, holding forth at the kitchen table with Rachel and Temba and an open bottle of wine. Anna greeted them briefly before retreating to the bathroom to await Willem's arrival. She'd asked him to be there, for support and to help explain if she found she couldn't. He arrived moments later, with Rika at his side and Anna was glad of that, though their expressions were severe. They looked as exhausted as she did.

'Hey, what the hell is up with you people?' Rachel teased. 'You look like someone died.'

Joe said nothing.

Anna looked up at Willem. He looked back at her, with his hands deep in the pockets of his coat, the muscles in his cheeks clenching and unclenching.

'What's going on?' Rachel's tone was suddenly sharp, anxious.

Anna opened her bag and pulled out an envelope from which she produced the photograph. Her hands shook as she laid it down on the table in front of them. Rachel, Joe and Temba leaned forward to look.

It seemed an eternity before they registered its meaning. 'Is that the Captain?' Rachel asked at last. They still called him the Captain though Nel was now a Brigadier Anna nodded stiffly, every muscle in her body tensed. 'Jesus!' Rachel exclaimed. 'What the hell is Paul doing there with the Captain?'

Anna's throat and mouth were so dry it was hard to get the words out, but she did, recounting for a third time the story of her meeting with Ig Du Preez at Pretoria Central and how that had led her to Shane Fourie and the photograph.

Rachel sat with her brows knitted together, her hand over her mouth, shaking her head and repeating the same words over and over. 'I can't believe it. I just can't believe it.'

Joe's response was an awful silence.

When Anna finished they simply sat there, stunned, not moving, not saying a word. And then an even more awful realisation dawned on Rachel. She let out a strange cry, gagging into her hand. Anna's mouth crumpled, the dam burst and hot tears streamed from her eyes. Temba held onto his wife as she sobbed into his chest, a terrible, low wailing sound coming from her. Anna knew what it was, Rachel didn't have to say it; Paul may as well have killed Jacob. By taking him along that night he'd effectively signed the death warrant of his best friend, Rachel's love, the father of two children he lived with and loved like his own.

Anna wept silently while Rachel rocked in Temba's arms. Rika put her hand on Joe's shoulder. 'How're you doing?' she asked softly.

'I'm okay,' he said bluntly, but the disappointment was burning in his eyes as he jerked his chin upwards and stared at Anna, addressing himself to her. 'What's done is done. It's disappointing, but I'm not going to lose any sleep over it.' Then he added pointedly, 'it's in the *past*.'

Anna sighed heavily. 'I'm so sorry, Joe. And I'm sorry that I didn't see it. It must have been there, right in front of me.'

Joe shrugged. 'Maybe he was a *good* liar. Must have been.

Had us all fooled. Why beat yourself up about things he did? It was a long time ago. Doesn't matter now.'

'How can you say that?' Rachel screamed, the sound tearing the air. 'Can't you see how much it matters? It's everything. It's who we are. Or thought we were . . .'

Joe cut her off as he turned on Anna, his voice rising with fury. 'Do you see what you've done?' He gestured towards Rachel. 'Why are you doing this? I mean, at last you hear what you've been waiting to hear all these years. Confession. Confirmation. *Truth*, for God's sake.'

He shook his head violently, but somehow his eyes remained locked on hers. 'Then you have to go and throw *this* into the works.' He picked up the photograph and waved it in front of her face before flinging it down on the table. 'You can't let things be. You have to keep pushing and pushing and pushing.'

He rose to his feet, unable to contain himself, pacing angrily up and down the length of the kitchen. Anna was pinned to her chair in shock at his outburst, though some crazy, self-punishing part of her felt she deserved it. The rest of them looked away, cut off in their individual cocoons of hurt.

Then a phone rang. It was Joe's. He yanked it from his coat pocket and slammed it to his ear. 'Yes?' He turned away from them as he listened. Rachel's sobbing was the only sound in the room. Outside the night was singing.

'Hell!' Joe bellowed, kicking the cupboard door with such violence it caused the wood to split.

'Shit,' he breathed, looking down at the damage he'd done. They stared up at him standing in front of the sink with his head down. When he looked up, his eyes were black and empty. 'They got Bazooka,' he said quietly.

'Great!' Temba found a voice for all of them.

'Not so great,' Joe growled. 'He's dead.' Then he spun round on his heels and marched out of the kitchen. They heard the bang of the front door slamming and the thrum of an engine starting up and he was gone.

'He's just hurt,' Rika said comfortingly as she sat down beside Anna. 'It's such an unthinkable betrayal. He's hurt and angry and he can't take it out on Paul, so he's taking it out on you.'

Anna wiped a hand across her wet face, managing a weary nod of acknowledgement.

There was nothing left to say.

twenty-six

Anna arrived early in Pretoria on the morning of the first day of Frans Nel's amnesty hearing. The approach to City Hall was littered with cameramen and reporters with their plastic coffee cups and tripods and ladders and long lenses. The size of the crowd that had gathered was surprising, after all these years. A group of young men and women from the Trade Union surrounded Anna and Rachel in a circle of bright green T-shirts and defiant song, escorting them up the stairs as far as the security checkpoint. Anna lowered her head as she moved with the dancing, chanting crowd. It upset her to know that they were there for Paul when he'd betrayed them so brutally.

Shane Fourie was somewhere nearby, in the safe hands of the Witness Protection Unit. The long, slow dance with the ever-elusive truth would not end today, but the tempo was about to change. Anna felt a strange excitement mixed with the dread.

Inside City Hall the audience had divided like the relatives and friends of the bride and groom at a wedding. To one side of the aisle sat a small group of the Captain's followers – dumpy, ugly, white people. The men sporting moustaches and synthetic sweaters, the women dressed in lurid colours with big hair that gleamed with spray. The much larger crowd of supporters of the victims' families sat on the other side. Besides the representatives of the Union, there was a large contingent from the ANC Women's League, all dressed in black, gold and green with black berets perched on their heads. Near them was another group of workers, wearing red T-shirts emblazoned with the slogan: *socialism is the future, let's build it now*. Then there were students and old people in their Sunday suits, and families and random onlookers.

Willem Swanepoel was already up on the stage, his hands shielding his eyes from the bright television lights while he studied the documents on the table in front of him. Rachel and Anna joined him. He smiled briefly as they sat down beside him.

'Good to see you both. How are you feeling?' His voice was soft, but taut with focus.

'Ja, strong. And you?' Rachel replied.

'Always strong, my dear,' he said quietly.

The stage was all set for the peculiar theatre that would be played out over the day. Massive organ pipes framed the proscenium arch, which was fringed by heavy mustard-coloured velvet curtains. A Truth Commission banner hung above the crescent of tables. The applicant's table was opposite theirs with a larger desk set up for the Amnesty Committee in between, centre stage. The grey and glass translators' booths occupied the far corner and stacks of documentation on a further table to the right of the booths. Anna took out a notebook and pen and settled into position to wait.

Joe had called her that morning to wish her well. He wouldn't be able to make it to the hearing; he was run off his feet with the investigation into Bazooka's death. The gangster had been shot in the course of a bungled arrest, so the police and Joe's unit in particular had come in for harsh scrutiny. On the phone Joe made no mention of his outburst at Valley View Road the week before. He'd been kind on the phone and that had pleased Anna, but she was troubled by their relationship. Not the friendship, that was immutable. It was their sexual entanglement that concerned her. It seemed to have run aground. There was no passion fuelling it, no reason to continue and yet no real reason to change the arrangement other than that it irked her.

Willem slid an envelope along the table towards them and Rachel opened it. It contained a note from Rika letting them know she was thinking of them. Rachel giggled suddenly as she folded the paper and put it away. She glanced over at Willem who was too absorbed in his notes to pay any attention as she leaned forward and whispered into Anna's ear. 'From doormat to dominatrix!' she declared wickedly. 'I *love* that woman.'

Anna smiled, but sadly. For some reason the remark echoed in the deep chamber of pain that Paul's betrayal had opened up and made her wonder just how much of a doormat she'd been for him. Rachel saw at once what Anna was thinking and reached out to touch her hand. 'Oh, I didn't mean—'

Anna shook her head, looking away. 'No. It's fine. I have to get used to it. I guess they're all like that. Men.'

Rachel grimaced. 'I don't know how to explain that part, babes, but for the rest you mustn't forget that Paul was also hurt. He betrayed himself. And in a way that's worse than everything else.'

Anna sighed and squeezed Rachel's hand. It was nice of her to say it, but Anna wasn't able to find the compassion for Paul that Rachel had discovered in the past few days of thinking things over.

Frans Nel arrived moments later, creating a stir in the hall. Cameras panned with him as he strolled onto the stage, looking neither right nor left. He made straight for the place set up for him. 'The Applicant.' That was what the card in front of him said. Members of the audience stood up, craning to see him, but Anna and Rachel stayed sitting, very still, stomachs clenched like fists.

And even though Anna knew that he might *not* be the one and that his great confession was to be ruined by Shane Fourie's arrival, she felt a shuddering nausea at the sheer proximity of him.

Nel was older. Still a stocky man, but slighter than when she'd last seen him. His hair was silver now, just as coarse and thick, but cut very short. His sideburns had been pruned back too, and were not the long spoons that had once curled around his ears. He'd kept the moustache though. This morning he was dressed in a grey suit, with a sheen to it, and on his feet were white socks and grey slip-ons. His tie was the most offensive thing he wore – shiny, silver and blue with bruise-coloured blotches. He sat down and pulled a folder from his briefcase, which he began studying at once. He was distinctly ill at ease. Perhaps he felt the eyes boring into him from across the stage. Anna stared. Rachel tutted and shook her head, her upper lip curling in disgust.

Then the judges entered and everyone rose. There were three

judges making up the Amnesty Committee for Nel's hearing. Three men. They filed in, bowed quickly in unison, then took their seats, and the proceedings began.

The hearing got off to a slow start, as they generally did, with procedural objections, the introductions of representatives and the naming and re-naming and re-numbering of documents. Anna scanned the audience and noticed James Kay sitting in the front row, pen in his mouth, notebook balanced on his knee. He was arresting to look at, she thought. Yet he didn't seem to realise it, certainly didn't seem to use his looks. Curious. He was such a patchwork of qualities, he was a Wurlitzer, a lucky dip next to Anna's geometry set. He was an ocean, shifting with the tides, sudden storms and shifts in temperature. Anna was a mountain – solid, implacable, unrufflable – formed slowly and steadily in identifiable, logical layers. They were opposites. And here she was, an opposite, feeling exactly what an opposite was supposed to feel. Attracted.

And wishing she wasn't.

Forty-five minutes into the hearing, Nel rose to take the oath, blinking into the battery of flashing cameras.

'Do you, Frans Cornelius Nel, swear to tell the truth, the whole truth and nothing but the truth?'

Nel raised his right hand and mumbled into the lights, 'I do. So help me God'. Then he began at last to tell his story.

It was hard to listen to it, in spite of the fact that both Anna and Rachel knew that much of it was a lie.

'My unit had been monitoring the Kensington cell for some time. By the Saturday night we knew of Oliphant and Lewis's intention to go away, though we had no idea of the purpose of their mission, who they were to contact and other relevant details. Nevertheless it was our firm belief that they were involved in making arrangements for the shipment of arms into South Africa for the purpose of terrorising the internal population. We telexed Headquarters with the information and some hours later, I don't remember exactly how many, we got a telex back which said that Oliphant and Lewis were to be "eliminated".'

Willem pressed the red button on his microphone, interrupting. 'I don't seem to have a copy of that telex. Perhaps you could furnish us with one?' he asked, completely straight-faced, knowing full well there was no such thing.

Nel blanched. His lawyer, a large red-faced man, interjected irritably, 'I'm sure the attorney doesn't need to be told that no copies were made and that the original was destroyed.'

'I see,' Willem noted, then leaned back with his arms folded across his chest, satisfied that he'd made his point. There was only Nel's word on the matter, nothing else.

Anna held her calm, steely gaze on Nel, who even more steadfastly avoided it.

'We immediately drove to Mafikeng, ahead of Oliphant and Lewis, that is Jeff Curry and myself, checked into a motel and waited.' Nel made a big display of turning the page and clearing his throat. 'They must have stopped somewhere along the way, where I'm afraid I don't know, because it was late on Saturday night before we heard that the targets were approaching town.'

Willem interrupted again, his pen poised, eyes on the page in front of him. 'Could you tell the Committee, Brigadier, what criteria were used in selecting Jeff Curry for this assassination?'

Nel answered snidely, a smirk at the corners of his mouth, 'Well I wouldn't have sent an academic up there for such a job.'

'I see,' Willem said, scribbling on his notepad as he went on. 'And doesn't it strike you as convenient that your accomplice on that night is now deceased?'

'I don't understand,' Nel retorted.

'Oh come now, Brigadier. It should be obvious. Particularly so to an experienced policeman like yourself. There's no one here to corroborate the truth of your story.'

'Why wouldn't I tell the truth?' he smirked.

'I don't know, Brigadier, why wouldn't you tell the truth? When amnesty depends upon it. You have confessed to murder. If this Commission finds that your motives do not fit the amnesty requirements, or information that you have not disclosed is put to them you will be liable for prosecution and believe me, my clients will prosecute.'

Nel scanned the tables ranged before him and for the first time he looked directly at Anna. She stared coolly back, though her heart was pounding. His smug expression faded.

'Please continue, Brigadier,' one of the judges boomed.

'Yes.' There was a further silence as Nel found his place, then he double cleared his throat and went on. 'Jeff Curry and myself set off in a vehicle tagged with false numberplates. We picked up our targets according to plan, just outside Mafikeng on the Vryburg road. There was nothing fancy about what we intended to do. Shoot the targets dead and burn the bodies in their car. It was supposed to look like an accident.'

Nel read steadily, with as little inflection or feeling as a child might read in school. Anna watched, her mind spooling through questions. Why was he telling this version? Why now? Who else could have been involved? What the hell was going on?

'We flashed them to pull over on a quiet stretch of road, told them to get out of their car, which they did. We asked them to walk towards the bush with their hands in the air, which they did. Beyond that no words were exchanged. I remained standing by the vehicles. Curry shot them both with a confiscated Makarov. Jacob Oliphant first.'

Rachel flinched. Anna saw tears in her friend's eyes, but she felt nothing.

'Paul Lewis put up resistance. After a short struggle he was overpowered and the objective was achieved. Then it began to rain. The targets' car had very little petrol in it. This interfered with our attempts to set it on fire. We realised that we would not be able to destroy their vehicle as planned and we left the scene, returning to Mafikeng.

'As I said before,' Nel plodded on, 'the exact nature of their mission that night was unknown to us. All I knew was that they were to be eliminated.'

The Judge Chairman slammed his hand onto his microphone switch and his voice cut in sharply, distorted by the loud-speakers. 'You use these words like "target" and "eliminate" but what you are talking about here is *murder*!' he declared indignantly.

Nel looked momentarily startled, but then leaned towards his microphone and uttered his oily response – 'Yes, Mister Chairman. I'll try to get beyond the semantics.'

The judge glared at him, then switched off his microphone and leaned back.

Nel cleared his throat, now looking red and nervous. 'From

Mafikeng, Curry and myself proceeded together to Swaziland in keeping with our cover story. The legend was that we were providing support to the Nelspruit Security Police regarding a suspected terrorist arms cache.'

Then it was Willem Swanepoel's turn for a sudden and vehement interjection. 'But *you* were the terrorists!' he declared.

Nel's lawyer objected, but the Chairman allowed the comment. Nel gawped, his mouth open like a fish gulping air. His lawyer shrank back, the redness in his face deepening to purple as his client departed from his notes. 'You know, people like to harp on about government atrocities, forgetting that atrocities were committed by the ANC and the PAC. This is not conducive to reconciliation. It amounts to an attempt by people now to manipulate history.'

The audience hissed. Once again Willem Swanepoel tapped the switch at the base of his microphone. 'But the ANC has admitted to all the atrocities it committed in the name of a just war. And they have apologised. I don't hear you apologising, Mr Nel.'

Nel looked cornered. 'Are you saying that I should apologise, sir? I don't believe that's a requirement for amnesty.' His face was a blotchy pink.

'I believe you're right about that, Mr Nel,' Willem went on, not a flicker of expression in his eyes. 'Remorse is not a requirement for amnesty. At least you're right about something today.'

Nel lunged forward to retaliate, but his lawyer put his hand out to indicate that he should not rise to it. Nel sat back, rocking on his chair, trying to compose himself. But there was a high edginess in his voice when he resumed. 'On a personal note, I would like it put on record that in the years since my transfer from the Security Branch into regular policing I have put a great deal of effort into a programme of self-reform. I have been a member of Alcoholics Anonymous for almost seven years now. I am an active member of my local church and a sober, God-fearing citizen. Thank you.'

A smattering of applause rose up from the white side of the audience, which Nel acknowledged with a tight smile. Then it was Swanepoel's turn for cross-examination. This was the moment Anna and Rachel had been waiting for. Anna took a deep breath, trying to appear calm.

Willem launched straight in with little ceremony. 'On behalf of the families of Paul Lewis and Jacob Oliphant I should explain that we are prepared to accept the premise of this hearing. That the truth be exchanged for amnesty. My clients oppose Frans Nel's application on the grounds that he has not fully disclosed the truth.' Nel sat hunched in his chair, his hands folded tightly in his lap, staring down at the floor as Swanepoel's deep voice rapped out the accusations. 'You were a seasoned liar, Brigadier Nel, as you've freely told us. You lied for Volk en Vaderland. And I put to you that you are still lying, Brigadier.'

Nel's lawyer's restraining hand could not stop his client this time. 'I am telling the truth!' he yelled, pointing a stubby, accusing finger at Willem. The audience hissed again.

Willem seemed almost to smile, but not quite. 'Very good. Let us test that,' he said at length. 'If you will allow me, Mr Chairman.'

Willem shuffled the papers before him. A hush fell inside the hall. 'Tell me, sir,' he began. 'Do you recall a young Warrant Officer by the name of Shane Fourie?'

Anna bit her lip. The Brigadier paused. His eyes narrowed to slits. He sat very still as he gave his answer.

'I do. I believe Fourie left the force and was killed in a motor accident shortly after. Mid-eighties if my memory serves me correctly.'

Swanepoel looked up sharply, his hands frozen in mid-air. Anna could see that he was holding Fourie's statement.

'No, sir,' Swanepoel purred. 'Perhaps you are confusing him with Mr Curry. Mr Fourie is very much alive. Mr Chair, I beg leave to introduce a witness.'

The Brigadier squirmed visibly. His legal representative's colour shifted to an improbable shade of green. He leaned over to ask his client what was going on, but Nel said nothing. It was as if he'd turned to stone.

The judges huddled in whispered consultation for a moment. Then the Chairman switched on his mike, directing his response towards Willem. 'Your request is most unusual Counsel, however, given the unusual nature of these proceedings, we grant leave for you to introduce your witness.'

Rachel sat forward, her hands clasped in her lap.

'Thank you.' Willem smiled now. 'I call Shane Fourie.'

The audience rose to their feet to look, stirred up into a state of great confusion and excitement. Anna watched Nel, who seemed to grow stiffer and whose face grew blotchier by the second.

Fourie emerged from the darkness at the back of the stage, escorted through the heavy curtains by three burly, edgy-looking members of the Witness Protection Unit. Nel craned his neck round to look as Shane came forward blinking into the lights.

Fourie looked distinctly out of place in a shabby old corduroy jacket, faded plaid shirt and jeans. He glanced at Anna and gave her a quick nod as he took the stand. Anna's throat felt dry. This was it. The end of Paul. Rachel began to cry.

Willem Swanepoel led him slowly and deliberately. Fourie co-operated magnificently, answering questions briefly and without anecdote or embellishment.

'And is it true that you first met Paul Lewis when he was arrested for the possession of a large quantity of Mandrax in nineteen-eighty?'

'That is correct.' Shane stared straight ahead, into infinity, his hands at his sides, his body very still.

'And that Frans Nel was one of the officers who questioned Paul Lewis after that arrest?'

There was murmuring from the audience. Anna looked down at her hands on the table, at her knuckles white with tension.

'That is correct.'

'And that you identified Paul Lewis as a potential informant and took that suggestion to the then Captain Nel?'

'That is correct.'

Anna glanced down at James Kay in the front row. He was watching her, his expression grave and concerned.

'And is it true that Frans Nel did indeed recruit Paul Lewis as a police informant?'

'That is true.' Shane nodded and looked over at the Brigadier.

Sweat bubbled on Nel's forehead. Beside him his attorney had almost disappeared into his collar, like a tortoise.

Willem pulled out a blue folder from amongst the many in front of him. From it he took an enlarged copy of the photograph Shane had given Anna in Bulletrap. He passed the page to Shane Fourie. 'Can you identify the people in that photograph?'

'Yes.' Shane nodded again. Eyes flashing in that leathered face. 'That is Paul Lewis with myself and Captain Nel and his wife, Sherry Nel.'

'Thank you. Would you be so good as to put the picture before the Committee?'

Shane walked stiffly across the stage and handed the page to the Chairman, who examined it closely for some time. Inside the hall the atmosphere was now explosive. Willem was almost through.

'It would appear then, Mr Fourie, that Captain Nel, in eliminating Paul Lewis, was getting rid of one of his own? Is that not so?'

'That is correct,' Shane answered gruffly.

On the white side of the hall the aunties stopped their crocheting, blinked behind their horn-rimmed glasses and pulled their nylon cardigans tighter around them. On the other side people conferred in consternation and surprise, unsure of what to do with this great revelation. The clamour grew louder as the judges conferred and the Chair announced that the hearing would be adjourned to a later date.

'In order to take account of the new evidence that has come to light, the matter will stand down pending further investigation.' With that the judges rose and the audience shuffled to their feet to watch them file out. Shane Fourie was hustled away by his protectors, and the proceedings collapsed into chaos.

Anna saw James Kay pushing his way towards her through the crowd that was rushing towards the stage. She smiled weakly, feeling frail but glad to see him. He reached for her hand through the people clamouring around her. She reached back and for a moment he held her fingers in his. 'Well done,' he mouthed, and then he let go.

Anna linked her arms through Rachel's and Willem Swane-poel's and together they pushed their way through the crowd and out into a barrage of press.

'Anna, over here, please!'

'Anna. Were you also a spy?'

'Anna, can you forgive Frans Nel?'

Anna couldn't see the faces of the people who barked out these questions, but something about their bluntness made her angry. She blinked under the bright television lights and pushed her way through the crowd and out into the brassy afternoon light.

twenty-seven

James was ironing. He often ironed. He found it a pleasingly methodical, meditative activity with the reward of a crisp, fresh shirt at the end of it. He only ironed shirts though, everything else he wore as it came out of the Laudromat bag. That morning he was ironing a shirt for a press conference at Police Headquarters in Pretoria. He was determined to corner Joe Dladla and get an interview with the man. He had to, his story was dead-ending and it was far too hot to abandon for lack of corroboration. Rassool was keen to print what they had, but James wouldn't put his name to anything until he was sure it was true.

He was thinking through possible scenarios, how Joe might block him and what his responses would be to that, when his cellphone rang. He looked over at the screen, his hands still busy with the iron. There was no caller ID. Probably international. He rested the iron in its cradle and answered.

'James Kay.'

Silence at first, then the pinging echo of a long-distance line.

'Hellooo,' he called, shaking a cigarette from the squashed packet in his jeans.

'Hi, it's me.' He froze at the sound of her voice, the flame from his lighter flickering by his thumb. It was Alison.

'Hi,' he said coolly.

'Can you talk?' She sounded bunged up, like she had a cold. Or was crying.

James checked his watch. 'For a couple of minutes. What's up?' She didn't say anything for a while and James realised with a sinking heart that she was crying. *Oh hell, what now?*

'Jim, I'm so sorry. I can't tell you how sorry I am for all the pain I've caused you.' This was managed with several throat-jerking sobs and moist sniffles thrown in for punctuation. James lit his cigarette and sucked on it deeply, not saying anything. 'I dunno, I just lost my head. With you being away and Richter all over me. I feel like I've woken up from a nightmare. And I've lost you . . .'

Her voice trailed off into a puddle of tears. James leaned against the windowframe, looking out into his little patch of jungle. So, it's Richter now, not Alan, he thought wearily. Guess we know what that means. 'I gather the wedding's off then,' he growled. Feeling mean, but also mildly triumphant.

She burst into a frenzy of sobbing at the other end of the line. 'Oh Jim! I miss you so much. I love you, baby. Can you forgive me? Please? Jim?' James sat down on the windowsill, not sure what he was thinking or feeling. She was distraught and he took no pleasure in hearing her like this, no matter how much she'd hurt him. He sighed. 'I'm sorry, Ali. I really am. Where are you? Do you have someone there with you?'

'Nooo . . .' she wailed. 'I feel so stupid. Everyone's talking about me, everyone's secretly so bloody happy. I can't go into work. I can feel them all staring smugly at me – look at her, little tart. Didn't she just get what was coming to her?'

James felt a lurch of tenderness. Somewhere he did still have feelings for her. He couldn't just tell her to fuck off. 'What about your sister? Can't she come over?'

'I need to get away. I was thinking maybe I could come and see you. There's a flight tomo—'

James stood up, panicking. 'Ali, you can't. I mean I can't, tomorrow. I may have to go to Harare. You know, Mugabe gone mad. I'm on stand-by. I—' *Ugh. Listen to me. What a lousy, lying bastard.* James sat down again, resting his head against his hand, the cigarette burning between his fingers. He could hear Alison blowing her nose in London. 'Look. The truth is I don't know that I want you to. After everything that's happened. I don't know that's what I want.'

She seemed to pull herself together at that, and her voice came back clearer and stronger. 'I understand, Jim. I really do. But will you do me a favour? Please? Will you think about it?' James cursed inwardly. There was a part of him that still responded to her pull and to that of partnership, of being with someone in the world instead of alone. The crazy idea that had led him to her in the first place. *Oh hell!* 'Look, I'll think about it, Ali. Okay?'

'Thanks,' she breathed. 'Thanks for not telling me to fuck off.'

James let out a sigh of laughter. 'Hang in there, baby. Okay?'

'Okay,' she murmured.

James floored it all the way to Pretoria, driving as fast as his old car would take him across the dry Highveld. It was the very end of winter, the driest time. Black scorch marks from fires scarred the landscape, but it felt to James that there was a hint of spring in the air. Was it Alison's call or the prospect of an encounter with Joe Dladla that had boosted his spirits? Probably both, he thought, and then he put all thoughts of Alison from his mind.

The press conference was a surprisingly light-hearted affair, considering the gravity of the subject. Joe Dladla was as charming and vital as ever, sitting on the podium in his sharp suit, radiating calm confidence. Next to him sat Ernest Vilakazi, the member of Joe's unit who'd shot Bazooka Rabopane 'while resisting arrest'. Unlikely, James thought. The man was alone in a hotel room, asleep by the sound of things, when the cops burst in on him. It was three heavily armed detectives against one dopey gangster. They said he'd pulled a gun on them and Vilakazi reacted instantly by shooting him dead. Maybe, maybe not, James thought.

The SAPS did not, however, share this view. A spokeswoman announced that Joe Dladla's special unit had been cleared of any wrongdoing in the death of Bazooka Rabopane. Then the Assistant Commissioner took questions. Truth is, James thought, no one's upset about the death of a gangster; everyone wants the police to be winning this war. No wonder they got off so lightly.

When the conference was finished James marched straight over to Dladla, interrupting him as politely as he could. The Assistant Commissioner frowned slightly as he looked James up and down. 'Ja, I know who you are,' he said at last.

'I wonder if you could spare a few min—'

'You wanna join me for a cup of coffee?' Joe interrupted, smooth as anything.

He was good. James had to give him that. He'd wrong-footed him straight away, given him exactly what he wanted. And more, because Joe Dladla was as charming as could be.

'Your mother is an extraordinary woman,' Dladla said as they strolled out onto the street. 'Quite a heroine of ours.'

James smiled, 'Thanks.'

'She still in the UK?'

James nodded, and made small-talk about his mother's work at London University as they walked.

They sat at a corner table in the Brazilian. James ordered a double espresso. Dladla took a cappuccino, no cream. 'You've made quite a splash in our little pool, Mr Kay. It's good to meet you face to face at last,' Joe smiled. James sensed he was being sized up. Thoroughly.

'Not quite the kind of splash you've made recently, Commissioner Dladla. This case has been quite a roller-coaster ride.'

Joe nodded, but said nothing as he tore open the corner of a sugar sachet and stirred its contents slowly into his coffee. James knew they could go on like this all day, with Dladla charming and inscrutable while James circled and circled and didn't get any closer to anything. He decided to cut to the chase.

'I won't waste your time. I've been investigating these heist gangs and I have a source who claims that there's more to the Bazooka story than meets the eye.'

Joe looked up, a knowing smile on his lips.

'My source is a cop. Prepared to testify under oath that the Angolans are run by the police and that the war with the Mozambicans is a plain old turf war in which the boys in blue currently have the upper hand. Any comment?'

Joe laughed softly, and then he took a long sip from his cappuccino, his eyes positively twinkling with amusement.

'You people make me laugh,' he said. 'Really, the stories you come up with.'

James watched and waited for more.

'You know, it's hard work, police work. Most of the time it's just plain graft. Thankless. I often wonder why the hell I do it. Sometimes I think I'd like to do something completely different.'

He opened his arms as he said this, not a trace of sarcasm in his smile.

'What would that be?' James asked.

'I'd start a newspaper,' Dladla said suddenly, leaning in close. 'And I'd use it to speak the truth. You people have power. You should wield that power with care and responsibility.'

James had to hand it to him. There wasn't the slightest chink in that gleaming armour. He was assiduously and charmingly evading the point.

'And what would the responsible use of my power be in this case?' James countered. His tone was as level and low as that of his interlocutor.

'To shine the light of scrutiny into the mess of crime and gangsterism that besets this country, rather than hounding those of us who are trying to fight it. What, for instance,' he raised a questioning finger in the air, almost accusatory, 'can you say that you *know* about Bazooka Rabopane? That he died violently and in questionable circumstances? Yes. That he lived violently and in questionable circumstances? Yes. That before he betrayed his country with crime he betrayed his comrades in the struggle? No. I haven't seen any of you people dig that deep.'

Joe lowered his hand, slapping his fingers against the edge of the table for emphasis. James looked puzzled.

'Yes! I've got you,' Dladla declared triumphantly. 'You have no idea what I'm talking about.'

James scratched the back of his head with his pen, making a face. 'I have to admit that you do. Would you care to enlighten me?'

Joe laughed heartily, a big, booming sound that rocked through him. As the laughter subsided he leaned forward once again and lowered his voice. 'Bazooka Rabopane was not the loyal and disciplined freedom fighter you people call him. The man was a spy.'

James couldn't conceal his surprise. He would have to check it out later, but he was certain that it would turn out to be true. The Assistant Commissioner was enjoying this far too much to be joking. 'He worked for several years under the command of Colonel Ig Du Preez. Bazooka Rabopane has always been a liar and a crook.' Dladla's voice had dropped to a whisper.

James sat with his eyebrows in his hairline and his mouth curved into a funny grimace, and nodded over and over again.

'Well. I have to admit it. I'm at a loss for words,' he said at last, with a twitch of embarrassed laughter.

'He was clean as could be as far as we in the movement were concerned. Like so many of them. It was only after we came to power and gained access to the files that we found out the truth about people like him.'

'And Paul Lewis?'

Dladla shook his head, pain creasing his forehead. 'Paul was something else. That's a terrible thing. A terrible, terrible thing.' His voice thickened as he said this, then he leaned closer and spoke with a passion that even James found stirring. 'The crime we see now is born of the violence and betrayal of then. You see? The one gave birth to the other? That's part of why it's so important to get to the bottom of it. That's why it's so important to know.' He nodded questioningly, checking to see that James was with him. James nodded back.

And then it was over, as abruptly as it had begun. 'It's been a pleasure talking with you,' the Assistant Commissioner said quietly as he rose to his feet. 'Now, if you'll excuse me?' He smiled pleasantly and James smiled back, he couldn't help it, the man was mesmerising.

'Thanks. Thanks for your time.'

'Any time James. Any time.'

Then Joe Dladla was striding out across the street, impervious to the traffic flying past him, and moments later he'd disappeared into the lunchtime crowds.

twenty-eight

enk Steyn strolled towards her across the prison parking lot, smiling warmly, 'The Colonel will be very glad to see you again.' He shook her hand, and it all felt very congenial, very pleasant, as if he and Anna were old friends.

'I guess he doesn't get many visitors,' she replied flatly.

Steyn nodded non committally, hands in the pockets of his well-cut suit. 'You know his conditions have changed since you last saw him?'

'No. What happened?'

'He's been moved to C-Max, the super secure section. Twenty-three hours a day in his cell. No radio, no nothing. We're trying to get him put back in Maximum, but I'm not holding out much hope. Correctional Services have got it in for him.'

'I can't imagine he's their most popular guest.'

Henk Steyn seemed mildly amused by her retort. 'Shall we?' He put a hand on her elbow as they walked to his car, a gesture of courtesy often used by South African men and often pounced upon as evidence of their irretrievable sexism. Anna didn't mind, not in this instance at least.

They drove in Henk Steyn's car, following the same route they'd taken on her previous visit. C-Max was housed inside Maximum, in the section that had housed death-row prisoners until not so long ago, until hanging was banned.

Anna's reason for this second visit was much clearer than it had been for the first. She needed to identify Paul's Security Police Handler and she hoped the Colonel might prove useful again. She was hoping he'd discovered the whereabouts of the mysterious Lieutenant Badenhorst.

Every Source was run by a Handler. Just as Joe had been the link between their cell and the rest of the underground movement, Paul would have had a Security Police Handler to whom he reported regularly and who would have issued instructions as to how he should act or respond to a given situation. That Handler would have his finger on the pulse of Paul's every movement, quite possibly including his last drive to Vryburg. According to Shane Fourie, Frans Nel had not 'Handled' Paul. If Anna could get to the person who had, it would fill in a critical piece of the puzzle.

They were led deep inside the prison this time, down long corridors with narrow windows that looked out onto a concrete exercise quad. Through clanging metal gates, into longer, narrower, windowless passages. Anna found it disorientating. She stuck close to Henk Steyn, who strolled behind the warders as nonchalantly as if he were being shown to his hotel room. They turned a corner and found themselves at a dead end, facing a heavily barred door. To the right was a staircase leading up to another bolted gate. 'Those were the last stairs the death-row prisoner ever climbed. They hung them up there,' Steyn told her, as one might note with interest a cathedral spire on a European holiday.

They filed through the massive door into C-Max. The air tasted of metal and bleach. The noise was appalling. 'Legal visit for Du Preez!' The warder had to shout over the din of disembodied voices crying out in pain and jest and everything in between. They were led down a further narrow passageway, which had a series of even narrower corridors leading off it. Each finger of corridor housed a series of cells. The space was small and claustrophobic. Hands reached through bars as they marched past.

It was a relief to be shown into the tiny, soundproofed consultation room. It measured about three metres by three metres. The ceiling was oppressively low; Henk Steyn almost brushed it with his hair. A tabletop jutted from the wall. Two orange bucket seats were bolted to the floor on one side, facing a single, identical chair, also bolted down. Steyn indicated for Anna to sit beside him. 'We won't stay long,' the lawyer said. 'He gets tired very quickly these days.'

Anna sat on the edge of the secured chair, looking around uncomfortably. A moment later the door opened but Anna barely recognised the man the warders brought in. The Colonel was thinner than when she'd last seen him, by ten kilograms at least. He was eerily pale, dressed in a loose orange boiler suit with no buttons, so the dark blue band of his underpants showed through the side flaps. Anna shied away from the observation, it seemed humiliating, pathetic.

Yet he smiled brightly when he saw her and reached for her hand. The pressure she'd felt in that first handshake wasn't there; his palm felt clammy and limp. 'It's so nice to see you, Anna!' he declared. His voice as strong as ever.

She smiled vaguely. 'Yes, you too,' she heard herself saying, the sense of unreality swimming about her once again.

And once again there was the formality of paperwork to be dealt with, documents to be scanned and signed. Anna waited while Steyn and his client got on with their business. This time there was no coffee brought by willing warders.

How strange to see him like this. The once invincible Colonel looking frail and thin in his buttonless prison boiler suit. The man once needed and trusted and feared by those below and above him. The irony of it struck Anna quite forcefully this time. That Du Preez should be inside, while the men who'd constructed the policy – the politicians and generals who'd created and resourced and funded his work – were free. Living it up on the international lecture circuit and sipping sundowners on the verandas of their retirement homes. They'd gotten away with murder.

It had been easy to understand, apartheid. Easier if you didn't have much education. Like any authoritarian idea it was fervently expressed with much resort to myth and religion. Du Preez would have internalised that from a very young age. And when the time came he had the qualities that were needed for covert action, for the secret suppression of opposition. He was brave, a good leader, and he excelled at killing. You couldn't call such a man a psychopath. He killed within a context, for political masters who applauded him. For as long as it suited them. Anna had met politicians who showed more sociopathic tendencies than Du Preez. No, the Colonel was apartheid's creation, the National Party's bloody mascot. Discarded when the team plan changed. Now the only respect or attention he got was from the occasional sympathetic warder.

Steyn gathered up his files and gestured for Anna to proceed. Du Preez shifted, hands between his knees, shoulders hunched. He moved groggily, like someone on heavy medication.

She leaned forward, her hands folded on the tabletop in front of her. 'Colonel. You'll have read about the amnesty hearing.'

'Oh yes,' he chuckled. 'That was a good one. You really put the cat in with the pigeons there, didn't you? I laughed when I read about that. Yerruh, I laughed.'

Anna smiled slightly. 'You know last time we spoke and I mentioned Balletjies Badenhorst. You said you would try to find out where he is. Did you have any luck?'

It was apparent from the way he peered at her that the Colonel was having difficulty concentrating, so she repeated her question, slowly this time. He stared back at her through his thick glasses, straining to imprint meaning.

'You know,' he began slowly, 'there were *so* many people from your side working for us. The network was more extensive than anyone realises. And we'll probably never know the whole of it, because they are all quiet as church mice these days. And a lot would have depended on the level at which they were working. On whether they were a straight source, a controlled asset, a double agent . . . you get my drift?' Anna nodded, not entirely sure where he was going, but not wanting to interrupt his train of thought, no matter how circuitous a route it took.

'Badenhorst is a tough nut,' the Colonel went on. 'He might not be so friendly if he knows who you are. And he's no fool; you won't be able to trick him. Just getting to him will be a problem. Apparently he's holed himself up with his family on a farm in the Eastern Cape. My sources tell me the place is a fortress.' Du Preez seemed to expand as he said this. Even under these circumstances he still had sources he could call upon.

Anna put her hands together, forming a steeple, waiting for more.

'I can give you directions, but from there you're on your own,' he said. 'And I wouldn't mention my name, if I were you. Me and Badenhorst were never exactly, how should I put it?' The

Colonel raised his eyebrows as he stared thoughtfully at Anna. 'On *good* terms.'

'Thank you,' she breathed, experiencing a strange urge to touch him, to put a comforting hand on his. But she didn't. Couldn't.

'You mustn't go alone,' he added, with a shrug that seemed to emphasise his frailty. 'I dunno, maybe my own paranoia, but you go alone and no one will know. There'll be no one except me to explain and my word doesn't seem to hold for much. Take someone with you, okay?'

Anna nodded. 'Thanks, I'll do that.' It was odd, this inter-action, and she suddenly realised why. He trusted her. She recalled a discussion about him at a Northern Suburbs dinner party. A pair of psychologists holding forth over expensive wine, talking psycopathy. One of them, the older man, insisting that it was important not to forget the child in Du Preez, the scared little boy looking for approval in any way he could get it. The other, a younger woman, shouting, 'It's not our job to under-stand these people, it's our job to eliminate them!' It was the kind of thinking the Colonel himself had bought into. And look where that had got him.

Anna drove back to her office from Pretoria Central in the afternoon rush hour. The encounter with Du Preez had moved her in some way, she wasn't sure why. The feeling was a disquieting one.

The greatness in people, Anna believed, lay in their ability and willingness to take responsibility for the bad as well as the good that they created and that is in them. If you can claim the bad that is yours and take on its responsibilities, you are so very much the better as a person. It's a rare quality. Paul didn't have it. She wasn't sure the Colonel did either. But he had the beginnings of it, of self-recognition.

It was while she was thinking this that Anna felt again that uncomfortable prickling sensation between her shoulderblades, that feeling of being watched. And then she saw it. The same car, the little purple Corsa that had followed her from Braamfontein the other week.

As they crawled towards Church Square the car was close enough for her to see the driver's face. She made a mental note of its details, olive skin, cheap tortoiseshell glasses, slicked-back black hair. The man saw her looking at him and calmly lit a cigarette. *Who the hell are you working for?* she wondered. He turned off at the next intersection and was gone.

Anna pulled into her parking space at Wachthuis and sat for a while in her car, recovering her breath. Then she opened the glove compartment, removed the Beretta .38 Special and slipped it into her bag.

She got out of the lift on Joe's floor, hoping he might be in and available for a beer and a chat. It had been a pleasant habit of theirs to meet for a drink at the end of the day, something that had lately fallen away.

There was a light on in his office and the sound of laughter trickled out through the half-open door. Anna slipped inside. Joe was sprawled on the sofa with two of the men from his unit, their backs to the door. The TV cabinet was open and they were watching the football international that had the attention of most of the country that evening.

Anna walked softly across the carpet and put her arms around Joe's neck, taking him by surprise. 'Anna!' He jumped up and greeted her with a firm hug, then turned towards the other guys in the room. 'You know Ernest? And Peter?' Anna nodded, smiling at the guys, who raised their beer cans to her. The coffee table was littered with supplies for the night, several six-packs and three delicious-smelling boxes of Nando's chicken.

'Come. Sit.' Joe cracked open a beer and handed it to her.

Anna sat down cross-legged on the carpet and took a long cool sip. 'So what's happening?' she asked.

Joe put his hand on her hair, stroking it gently. The game had started disappointingly, he said. 'Côte d'Ivoire are all over us, but so far no one has scored.'

Ernest was dividing up the chicken, making sure there was enough for everyone. He looked drunk. 'I'm telling you, that woman in Nando's has sexy eyes,' he crooned. 'Ooooh! She was willing me with those eyes. Killing me softly.'

Joe laughed. 'No man, those are sleepy eyes. There's a big difference between sexy eyes and sleepy eyes. Don't make the mistake of confusing sexy eyes with sleepy eyes. And bedroom eyes. And lackadaisical eyes. Aish. There's a vast difference. That woman in Nando's has sleepy eyes.'

'Were you there, Dladla? I don't think I saw you there. No, God took His own sweet time to build that woman's body. Her eyes put a glow into my heart. When she moves – dammit!' Peter and Joe laughed uproariously. 'She said – please, this chap has been waiting a long time and she said to me – can I help you, brother? I said to her – please – give me three half chickens and chips please, babe. Then she said to me – hot, extra hot? And I said – very *mild*. Ay! That woman was beautiful!' He shook his head in wonder. 'Oh! I said to her – *very* mild . . . Mmmm, she was dark with a dark shiny skin. A real African woman met a ballformige butt! No. I don't want to talk any more about how I feel about that woman!'

'Good, because we don't want to hear any more,' Peter spluttered.

'Ja, maybe you should tell your wife, maybe she's interested,' Joe chimed.

'You may laugh, but today I have seen uniqueness. I tell you, it was a parable of human perfection.'

Ernest smiled blissfully and sank his teeth into a juicy chicken thigh. Peter cracked open another beer, focusing on the game. 'That Lucas Radebe, our captain, he's the most dangerous player.'

Anna looked up inquisitively. 'Why?'

'Because he gives games away,' Joe grumbled.

'Feesh! Feessh! Die Visser . . . Visserman!' Suddenly they were all shouting. Anna looked back at the TV. Mark Fish had the ball.

Ernest was screaming, 'Go! Go! I'll eat you up!'

Joe kept chanting 'Feessh! Feesh!' Anna couldn't help laughing. 'Vala! Vala! Close, close, keep it close, do it, brother!' Joe shouted.

In the stadium hooters blared and Bafana scored. Ernest jumped up from the sofa and danced a little dance. Peter sprang to his feet, mimicking the kick. 'Easy! Easy! Easy, boy – good, good, good I say, dammit!'

Joe sat back in the sofa with a beer resting on his belly, happy. The game resumed. Ernest was tense now, like a runner ready to bolt out the block; he sat down on the carpet right in front of the TV. Peter settled on the sofa again with an unlit cigarette in his fingers. In the crowd someone was playing a trumpet that rang out through the cheering and the hooters. It was almost half-time and it looked like the team would go into the break one goal up. But Côte d'Ivoire came back strong and the South African goalie was down and even Anna was on her feet screaming. Then Lucas Radebe made the save and kicked the ball away from the goal area. 'Shew!' They all sat down again.

'Lucas Radebe isn't so bad.'

'Ja, Lucas caught the loose ball.'

The half-time whistle blew. Everyone sighed with relief. Ernest stood up and danced, wriggling his hips and waving his beer. 'Ooh I'm in love with Mark Fish.'

'Now *he's* got sexy eyes!' Joe mused.

'I'm a moving lexicon myself, a perambulator,' Ernest joked as he carried on dancing. 'Moving from a dark face of life to a much brighter face. I'm moving in the perpetual struggle towards tranquillity. Tranquillity means softness, smoothness, warmth, happiness, quickness, silence . . . tranquillity.'

Anna doubled up with laughter at Ernest's nonsense. It felt good, like tension uncoiling, snaking out of her.

The second half went well. Peter explained the game to Anna while Ernest railed at her ignorance. 'Soccer isn't just a sport. It's a religion. The national religion! You should be worshipping at the altar of Jomo Sono—'

'Who's Jomo Sono?'

'Oh my Lord, forgive her. Jomo Sono is the coach – he used to play for Orlando Pirates. He used to play the most golden soccer. He is the prince of Soweto, his ball was pure magic!'

Joe waved for Ernest to get out of the way, he was blocking the view of the monitor. 'Don't try to teach her. She'll never learn, my friend. There's a vast difference between soccer being in the blood and it being in the nervous system.'

Five minutes before the end Côte d'Ivoire scored. A minute later they scored again. The room deflated. Peter put on his shoes and stood up inconsolable. 'I'll see you tomorrow guys.' Joe tried to persuade him to stay, but he wouldn't. 'I'll see you tomorrow,' he mumbled again and left, and Ernest stumbled out after him, without even a backward glance.

It was just the two of them now, Anna and Joe, side by side on the sofa. Joe switched off the TV and the room was suddenly quiet. 'At least you're looking better than when you arrived.'

'Aaaah, I dunno, Joe. I dunno,' Anna sighed, pushing her hand back through her hair. 'Isn't Ernest the one who shot Bazooka?'

Joe nodded as he bolted down the dregs of his beer and opened another one.

Anna stood up and walked over to the window. The sounds of traffic on the dark street below drifted up to her.

'I went to see the Colonel again today.'

Joe leaned forward and buried his head in his hands. Anna went on, undeterred.

'I want to know who Paul's Handler was.'

Joe shook his head into his hands. All she saw was his shiny pate.

'You remember Balletjies Badenhorst?'

Joe nodded.

'Think I've located him. Going to see if he'll talk.'

Joe rose wearily and walked over to stand next to Anna by the window. He stared down at the lights of the cars below.

'I wish you wouldn't. You can't work with those people, it's like working with snakes. Sooner or later they bite.'

Anna bristled with a mixture of hurt and defensiveness. 'Why can't you just accept that I have to do this? That I have to see it through to the end?' Her voice rose angrily as she spoke.

Joe regarded her through narrowed eyes. Then he seemed to relent. He put an arm round her shoulder. 'You've been living amongst the dead for too long. It's time to move now into the land of the living.'

She knew his intentions were good, that he said this only out of concern for her. But she also knew that he didn't really understand.

How? she thought helplessly. *I don't know how to take care of the living. I don't know how to live without my ghosts.*

Anna stared hard into Joe's unblinking eyes. Then he smiled mildly, soothingly, and gently took her face in both of his hands and she felt her skin flutter against his touch, and then he kissed her.

'You have to let the past go, baby. Someday you're going to have to let it go.'

She knew that he was right.

But the past wouldn't let go of Anna.

part six

All that is necessary for evil to flourish
is for good men to do nothing

EDMUND BURKE

twenty-nine

Anna drove round the city towards the airport. The skyline was brittle grey against an aqueous sky – pale but vivid blue, pricked with just a few diamond points of stars. The horizon was a blood-red smudge where the sun had recently set, casting a brilliant crimson light across the under-surface of the clouds. The thick prism of smog and dust that clung to Johannesburg that evening intensified the colours.

The traffic on the freeway felt dangerous. A truck veered perilously out of its lane into Anna's path. She swerved to avoid it and almost hit a huge BMW that was racing down the slow lane, taking the fastest route regardless.

Turning onto the N17 she realised there was a car on her tail again. This time it was a nondescript white saloon, like thousands of others in the city. It left her at the airport turn-off, continuing towards Witbank. In the car park she realised how much it had rattled her when she managed to scrape the bumper of her car against a metal pillar. She was glad to be getting out of town. Glad to know that she'd be met by James Kay when she landed in that sleepy seaside town so oddly named East London.

Anna checked into her flight with half an hour to spare and strode towards the firearms desk. It seemed to take for ever to get the Beretta cleared, endless forms were painstakingly filled out by tired staff. When she got to the gate a pink-jacketed stewardess was tapping her fingers impatiently on the counter. Anna was the last to board. She looked around at her fellow passengers as she shuffled to her seat. All men in suits with their evening papers open, financial pages crackling.

She settled into her seat, feeling excited. She'd not seen James

Kay in a while – they'd made the arrangement on the phone – and she was looking forward to seeing him.

He was there at the barrier as she walked through into the terminal. 'Hi,' she sang breathlessly, bags in each hand. A steward had returned the .38 to her in one of them as she exited the plane. 'I made it,' she declared brightly.

James grinned and rather obviously looked her up and down. Anna was wearing a navy-blue trouser-suit with a cream shirt, work clothes. 'Nice outfit. Very *police*,' he teased, and then he took the heavier of her two bags. 'Come, let's get you checked into the hotel.'

They drove a short way towards the sea and the Holiday Inn at the far end of the esplanade. She was in the room next to his. She unpacked hurriedly, changed into jeans and a T-shirt and went straight back down to the lobby, where she found James.

They walked along the Esplanade, which wraps around the beachfront in a neon dazzle of bars and clubs. East London is a Mecca for surfers and the nightspots were designed with them in mind. James and Anna sat out on the sea-facing terrace of a particularly tacky bar and ordered cocktails with ridiculous names.

'How're you feeling about tomorrow?' He was sitting opposite her and the low light softened his often chilly gaze.

'Okay actually,' she shrugged. 'I think I'm getting the hang of this now. And I guess whatever he says—'

'*If* he says anything at all,' James interrupted.

'Ja, *if*. But whatever he says it won't be as shocking as what Shane Fourie did.'

James nodded, looking out across the inky blackness of the sea. The truth was Anna felt anxious about the following day. She was scared of what she might learn from Badenhorst. There was no doubt in her mind that they would persuade him to talk. So many of these people were the same, and once you got them going, it simply poured out of them. James seemed calm and that was reassuring. She was glad that they were going together. She felt comfortable with him that night. Comfortable enough to talk about other things.

'You know, a couple of months after Paul died I was sorting through his things with one of my sisters. We were sitting in my room at Valley View Road. In amongst his stuff we found this Checkers bag and it was stuffed full of condoms. Every colour and shape you can imagine.' James sipped at his Long Island Iced Tea, a smile on his lips as he listened. 'I'd never seen them before and we couldn't figure out what they were doing amongst his things. So we sat there, my sister and me, on the floor, blowing condoms into balloons. There were dozens of them, it looked like New Year's Eve.' Anna was laughing now.

'The grieving widow,' he murmured, amused.

'Ja,' she repeated, more seriously, 'the grieving widow.'

He eyed her thoughtfully, and somehow she knew he understood that she'd come to some sort of an accommodation with Paul's betrayal. But she was glad he didn't say anything; it might have felt like I told you so. They were silent for a while, watching the white tips of the waves roll in through the darkness.

'I had coffee with Joe Dladla the other day,' James said suddenly. Anna's eyebrows shot up in surprise. 'After the press conference.'

'Oh really?' Anna was taken aback by her own reaction. Somehow it made her uncomfortable to think of James and Joe having a chat over coffee.

'He told me that Bazooka Rabopane was a spy.'

Anna nodded. 'I haven't seen anything about it in the papers,' she replied at length.

James shook his head. 'Haven't told anyone myself yet.'

Anna nodded again and looked back towards the sea.

'Why?' James asked. 'Why would someone like that end up as a spy?'

Anna shrugged. This was easier terrain. 'So many reasons. Some, like Paul, were suckered into it at an early age. Given a way out of a sentence for a drug conviction or whatever. The police seemed like an easy option.' She sipped on her drink. 'Others were turned by force and threat. You know the famous story, don't you, of the MK Commander who wanted a new pair of shoes?' James shook his head. He didn't.

'Well, I don't know if it's true or not, but it's certainly done the rounds. Apparently there was this unit Commander in Tanzania, in one of the camps, who picked out a young soldier for a mission. Now this kid has probably been in the camps for several years, enduring hellish conditions, eating monkeys and whatever else they can find in the bush. He's seen no action at all and he's not even sure why he's there any more. Then he's taken aside by this Commander, a man he reveres, and he's given two envelopes and a map of Johannesburg. His instructions are to find a particular shoe shop run by an Indian guy from whom he is to buy a particular pair of shoes. The size, colour etcetera of the shoes are included in the instructions.'

James had heard talk of conditions inside the camps where South African exiles were effectively interred by jumpy neighbouring states. The camps were sprawling, remote military enclosures where young men and women were trained up into a guerrilla army that was seldom deployed. So they were also places of hardship and boredom and one or two were notorious for human rights violations perpetrated within the liberation movements.

Anna paused for breath. 'Okay, one of the envelopes has money for the mission, the other he must give to the Indian guy. So off he goes, crossing borders illegally, risking his life, finally arriving at this shop in Joburg. All goes smoothly. He buys the shoes and is given a new set of instructions by the Indian man who finds them in his envelope. He's to take the shoes back to Tanzania, which he does. Once again travelling at night, skipping borders and running the risk of capture all the time. When he gets back to the camp the Commander thanks him and slips on the shoes. Mission accomplished.'

James laughed, shaking his head. 'You're kidding?'

Anna smiled. 'I don't know if it's true or not, but that's how it goes.'

'But what's that got to do with Bazooka becoming a spy?'

'Well,' Anna went on, 'what if the mission went wrong? The kid hasn't been given transport or the normal support structures and documentation for this mission. He has to take a taxi and he fucks up on his legend at the border going back. Asked an innocent set of normal questions by the Border Police he freaks out and gets mixed up. He's an incoherent mess and the Security Police are called in. The Branch guys quickly realise who he is and it's over. For three days he takes the beating and interrogation and then he thinks – what the hell am I doing this for? So my

Commander can have a new pair of shoes? To hell with that. He turns, he does a deal. The cops offer him a support system and he takes it. He goes back to exile with the shoes and reports that his mission was a success. No one's any the wiser, but now the hooks are in.' Anna finished with her hands up in the air, palms open.

James smiled, his eyes on her. Anna took a deep breath, watching him too.

Then Ilse McLean arrived with a large contingent of Truth Commission journalists and staff who swarmed around their table. They were down for a hearing and after a long day of murder and mayhem they seemed intent on oblivion. Anna sucked hard on her orange drink. Ilse's nails were midnight blue with silver tinsel in them, like a blurry, starry night. She looked great, Anna thought, envying Ilse for her carefree spirit, the wildness in her that seemed to let her do and say whatever she felt for the sheer fun of it. Anna's own trimmed, unpainted, unchewed, and unfrayed fingertips seemed so plain by comparison.

Later, after they'd drunk every cocktail on the menu and sampled all the oil-soaked, grill-charred bar snacks on offer, Ilse insisted that it was time to go dancing. She led them to a place called the Cadillac Club a few doors down the street, slipping her hand through James's arm at the head of the procession.

The place was awful, complete with disco ball and flashing lights. Almost everyone there was white and about twelve years old from the look of them. Anna couldn't believe her eyes, it was great! She went to the bar and perched on a high stool, watching the show. James ordered tequila shots for everybody and supervised the downing of them. Then he shimmied off onto the dance floor with Ilse.

Ilse was wearing a tight T-shirt and short skirt, which showed off her curvaceous body. Anna was in awe of her sexual ease, the way she swung James around, eyes locked on his all the time. He glanced over in Anna's direction several times and when the music changed he slipped free of Ilse's grip to join her. 'Another round of tequilas!' he shouted.

Anna giggled. 'Uh-oh.'

Ilse staggered over, leaning heavily on James as he passed her a shot glass. 'Cheers! Here's to Whe-e-el of Misery!' She shouted and downed the tequila. But she wasn't finished. 'Viewers don't forget to enter our weekly competition – this week's prize is an exhumation for two in picturesque Piet Retief! And just to make sure you're really fit for the event – you do your *own* digging!'

The others were laughing now with awful hysteria. One of the radio reporters joined in, swaying on his stool. 'Ladies and gentlemen! This week on Wheel of Misery we have Mrs Tshabalala – give her a big round of applause!' They all cheered and clapped over the throb of the disco beat and Ilse took up the thread again. 'That's right. Mrs Tshabalala lost all three of her sons and her house in a police raid on a night vigil where *thirty-seven* people died! Competing against her for the grand prize is Mr Mabesa! Mr Solly Mabesa was tortured and almost *killed* during five years of illegal detention by the apartheid security forces! And – you guessed it – he's traumatised! So – who will drive off with this week's grand prize of rep-ah-ration!? Stay tuned!' Ilse collapsed in a shower of giggles and even Anna laughed until she realised that Ilse wasn't laughing, but crying. Tears streamed down her face making black rivers of mascara shot with silver eye-shadow.

The others rallied round to comfort Ilse. 'Ag, come on, babes! It's okay.' Anna jumped off her stool to put her arms round the distraught girl. She realised suddenly that the carapace of hardened hack and sexy wild child was a front she put up to defend her from feeling.

Ilse sobbed into Anna's T-shirt, smearing make-up all over it. 'James likes you,' she said as Anna stroked her hair comfortingly. 'You two would be lekker together.' Then she pulled away and smiled at Anna, wiping her eyes with the back of her hand. 'I look like shit, don't I?' she laughed tearily, then she gave Anna a warm hug and stumbled back onto the dance floor. The others turned their attention to the fresh round of tequilas.

Anna watched Ilse dancing for a moment before she sensed James standing at her shoulder. 'Shame. She's taking strain,' she said, turning to look up at him.

He shrugged. 'Shit happens, you know? Come on, let's dance.' He slipped an arm round her waist and swung her onto the dance floor.

James was a wonderful dancer, he led and she simply floated where he took her. Anna loved that. She hadn't danced so wildly in years. The feeling was akin to fear, heart pounding, breath short, but her body hummed with pleasure.

They left the Cadillac Club long after midnight. The night air was sultry and alive with the sound of crickets and the rushing and sighing of the sea. Ilse and the others peeled off to bed. Anna felt a little shy in the quiet of the hotel lobby, her feet tingling from dancing, her hair wet with sweat and sticking to her face.

'Join me for a last drink?' James asked.

'Why not?' She followed him into the bar where she ordered a cup of hot milk with a teaspoon of honey in it. He had a double brandy. 'It's amazing,' Anna said, still fizzing from the fun of the disco and the intensity of the evening. 'Ilse seemed so hard. And yet she's not at all.'

James lit a cigarette. 'I guess we all have our shields, we all protect ourselves.'

'You?' She looked up at him sharply, teasing, but he looked hurt as she said it.

'How would you know?' The question was pointed, as if she'd been presumptuous, overstepped some line. Anna was too taken aback to answer him. 'You think I'm heartless.' He smiled slightly, but there was an accusatory tone to his voice that surprised her.

Anna was quiet, her fingers tracing the edge of the table, up and down, back and forth as her mind swung back and forth uncertainly. 'I think,' she looked up at him, her forehead wrinkled by a frown . . . 'I guess I never thought of your heart.'

It was a lie. Well, a half-lie. She had thought of him as heartless, hoping that he wasn't. And now she'd fluffed it. James smiled suddenly and broadly. Then just as abruptly stubbed out his cigarette, jumped out of his chair, and slung his jacket over his shoulder.

'Yeah well. G'night then.'

And with that he stalked off to his room, as inaccessible and enigmatic as she'd come to expect him to be.

thirty

They set off for the Badenhorsts' farm just after seven the next morning. It was an unsurpassable day. Dry and hot, the air sweetly scented with khakibos. Sonbesies and cicadas trilled a song of spring from all around. Anna was restless with excitement, but James was quiet, his hands gripping the steering wheel tightly as he stared hard at the road ahead.

'Why so tense?' Anna asked.

James shot a glance in her direction. He caught her gaze for just an instant and his eyes flashed that chilly, distant blue. He frowned. 'Got a funny feeling about this.'

Neither one made mention of the night before and James's abrupt departure from the bar. It seemed silly now, though Anna couldn't help wondering what his sudden exit was all about. James seemed to sense her disquiet and reached across and gently, reassuringly squeezed her thigh. She looked back at him and smiled, grateful that he'd broken the odd mood. 'You okay?' he asked quietly.

She nodded. 'Ja. Thanks. I'm cool.'

The directions were clear and simple. They took the N2 north and turned off into the R102. They drove through a lush green landscape of rounded hills dotted with traditional huts. They passed glittering lagoons and wide, mud-red estuaries. From the R102 they took a gravel road to the Kwelera River, which they crossed on a narrow, single-lane bridge. Shortly after that the road forked and they took the track to the left. From there it was a matter of counting kilometres according to the notes the Colonel had dictated to her.

It was clear why Badenhorst had chosen this place to escape

from the world to. Though it wasn't more than two hours' drive from East London, only a determined visitor would persist on these roads. Progress was slow. They came to another river and there turned right heading back towards the sea.

They bumped along the rutted track in their huge air-conditioned car, passing people living in a different era. On the hill to their right a group of men were driving a pair of oxen tethered to a wooden plough. There were women hoeing in the next field along. An old man stood on the river edge with a young boy who was helping him cast a fishing net into the water. People stopped to watch the car pass. Anna stared back at the faces, feeling like a tourist in her own country.

The river was a murky-green expanse that rippled towards the sea. On its banks were tall bulrushes and verdant tropical trees. The beach was a brilliant curving strip of cream between river and sky.

They came to a village nestled in the curve of a hill above the seasand. A group of children were playing with a stick and an old tyre, which they abandoned shrilly, to run after the car, small hands banging on the bonnet as they jogged alongside, danger-ously close. According to the Colonel's directions they would find the entrance to the farm just beyond the village.

They drove past compounds of rounded, thatched huts, dodging geese and pigs and mangy dogs, past a small jetty where the children gave up their chase and stood waving at the disappearing car.

James sighed unconsciously and Anna found herself turning from the almost painful nearness of him. She was silent, scouring the bush for an entrance, expecting to see the farm fence at any moment.

But there was no turn-off and no sign of anything like a farm. After ten kilometres or so of bone-rattling driving, James turned round and headed back to the village. The atmosphere in the car was brittle with mutual frustration. Perhaps there was no farm. Perhaps this was the Colonel's joke.

They pulled up at the jetty on the edge of the village. On the river bank below a group of women were washing clothes, beating them against the flat black rocks and hanging them out to dry on the nearby bushes. At the sight of the strangers they dropped their work and retreated down the slope of the bank. Only the children hovered close by. Anna waved and shouted a greeting to the washerwomen, but they didn't move. One of the children came forward with his hands out-stretched. 'Sweetie?' he begged. James shooed him away irritably. Anna reached into her pocket and handed over the loose change that she found there. The kids scattered, fighting over the money.

James and Anna walked out onto the narrow wooden jetty, its planks bleached grey and rippled by the sun. Across the water a small motor boat appeared, puttering towards them from the opposite bank. James waved, but the boatman did not wave back. Anna pushed her fingers back through her hair. She noticed that the boatman was sitting with a machete between his legs. He stared at them suspiciously as he came up alongside and tied up at the jetty. He was a young man with a muscular body, wearing an ancient T-shirt riddled with holes and almost equally tattered shorts, but he walked with a confident swagger, the machete slung over his shoulder.

'Do you speak English?' Anna asked slowly. The boatman nodded. 'We're looking for the Badenhorst farm.' The young man's eyes narrowed and a slight shift in the way he held himself gave him away. He knew. And yet he shook his head, as if he didn't.

James repeated the question and again the young man shook his head, standing his ground. Anna swung away, frustrated. As she squinted into the sun James took a roll of bank notes from his pocket. The boatman eyed them hungrily, trying not to as he scuffed the thick soles of his bare feet along the planks. James peeled one, then another, then a third pink note off the roll and held them up. The man's face lit up. He looked around to see if anyone was watching. Only the children stared as he reached out and snatched the money, quickly folding the notes and slipping them into a pocket inside the waistband of his shorts. Then he strode past James, clattering along the jetty towards the road. 'Come,' he said. 'I show you.'

James grinned, happy for the first time that morning and briefly slipped his arm around Anna's waist, giving her a comforting squeeze.

They jumped back into their car and followed as he led them

on foot down a sandy track that branched off the road to the right. They'd passed it on the way out earlier, but it had looked like a footpath. After a few metres their guide turned and walked back alongside the car, leaned into the driver's window and pointed with his flat hand and forearm. 'Go straight. Badenhorst is that way.'

Anna and James looked uncertainly at the winding sand track ahead which seemed to disappear into the bush, but the boatman insisted. 'Go straight. This is Badenhorst road.' So they thanked him and drove on. After a few minutes of twisting through dense brush, branches thwacking the sides of the car, the track suddenly widened to a levelled, graded two-lane road. 'Wow!' James slowed down, almost to a halt. 'We should have come by air,' he said. Five hundred metres later they came to a fence and a huge gate, at least three metres high, posted with signs that left nothing to the imagination. 'Gevaar' and 'Waarskuwing. Privaate Weg. Toegang op eie risiko'. Danger. Private road. Enter at your own risk – with a skull and crossbones painted over it just for good measure. Ironic, Anna thought, now it's them who have to hide, not us.

They exchanged the briefest of glances before they got out of the car and walked up to the gate. The fence hummed with electricity. There was no way they could climb it and there was no one around to be persuaded to let them in. 'Shit! What do we do now?' James muttered, casting his eyes around. Anna walked up to the gate and pushed against the wire mesh. It didn't give at all. She ran her fingers along it, rattling the wire as she walked up to the chain lock. She fiddled with the padlock. Incredibly, it fell open. 'James.' She turned to him with the broken lock in her hands. 'Look.' He sprinted over to her as she loosened the chain, letting it run through her fingers before it dropped with a clank onto the gravel.

They pushed the gate open and walked through. By the road was a small shelter, camouflaged with brush. Inside it were a stool and a walkie-talkie lying discarded in the dust on the floor. They looked at the two-way radio, then at one another. It could have been abandoned in a scuffle; then again perhaps the guard had left his post in a fit of bored drunkenness. Or maybe this was how it always was. Who knew?

They went back to fetch the car and drove through, leaving the gate open behind them. James took it slowly going down the road, all the time scanning the dense, low trees on either side. They swung round a deep bend and James had to hit the brakes as hard as he could, almost colliding with a jeep that was upside-down and slung across the road. Both James and Anna gasped as they came off the road and bumped and skidded to a halt in the brush. Then there was silence. 'Shew!' Anna breathed, her heart beating wildly. 'Thank God you were driving so slowly.'

'Apparently *he* wasn't.' James pointed into the trees ahead, his hand shaking. Anna was completely unprepared for what she saw.

The body of a man hung from the branches, his neck gaping open from an awful slash that had almost sheered his head off. 'He must have been thrown from the jeep,' James whispered before he climbed out of the car and walked over to the corpse. Anna got out too, but remained standing by the car, unable to take her eyes off the appalling sight. He was a white man, probably in his sixties, though it was hard to tell. His clothes were drenched in blood, but they looked military.

The realisation struck her with the force of a blow.

'That's him,' she said.

'Badenhorst?' James called out, from where he was crouching in the scrub beneath the tree.

Anna nodded, wrinkling her nose at the sickly smell of blood. 'It can't have happened all that long ago.' She felt nauseous. The air was very still, the sonbesies' song sawed oppressively. She scrabbled in her bag for her cellphone, found it and tried to make a call, but there was no signal. They would have to drive back to find one, she thought. Unless there was a phone up ahead at the farm.

James strode back to the car and grabbed a camera out of his bag on the back seat. He shot several pictures of the upturned car and the body in the trees.

Anna couldn't take much more of the smell. She climbed into the driver's seat, started up the engine and pulled the car up alongside James. He got in and she set off, continuing up the road, up the steep hill that led away from the crash.

'What are you doing?' His tone was panicky.

'Driving to the house.'

'Why?'

'There must be people there. Maybe a phone. We have to call the police.'

'Okay,' James said uncertainly, squinting into the bush ahead.

Some five kilometres or so further on they came to the house, surrounded by yet another high electrified fence. The homestead was old, built in solid ochre sandstone with a red tin roof that bristled with satellite dishes and aerials. 'Shouldn't be a problem phoning from here,' James said dryly.

Anna pulled up at the gate, startling a farm worker who was strolling across the gravelled forecourt. The man took fright, dropping the tin plate he was carrying as he raced into the house.

'Shew. This can't get any weirder.' Anna wiped the sweat from her forehead as she climbed out of the car, following James to the gate.

'Oh yes, it can,' James breathed as a pack of Rottweilers shot out from behind the building, barking viciously as they stormed across the gravel and flung themselves insanely at the wire mesh. Anna leapt backwards, terrified, but the dogs were hemmed in by the fence. James grabbed her arm and Anna glanced up at him, then over in the direction of his stare.

A woman was walking slowly down the front steps of the house. On her hip was a holstered pistol, a 9mm Beretta Anna guessed. In her arms was an R4 rifle and she had her eye on the sights. She moved forward swinging the barrel from side to side, picking out James, then Anna then James again. 'Great,' James growled as they slowly raised their hands. There was something faintly absurd about the situation, but it was also clear they could be dead in a snap. Anna kept her eyes on the rifle, knowing there'd be no neat little roses of bullet holes if that thing went off, just shredded flesh and shattered bone.

As the woman got closer Anna saw that she cut a striking figure with her pale grey eyes and intensely red hair. She wore a pretty floral shirt over khaki combat trousers and heavy boots.

'Whadyouwant?' she barked.

James looked over at Anna. The dogs cowered at the sound of the woman's voice.

'Are you Mrs Badenhorst?' Anna called out shakily.

'Whadyouwant?' she repeated.

'Nothing. We just . . . we came across an accident about five ks back along the road. We just came to tell you.'

'How did you get in?' She lowered her voice.

'The gate was open. We drove through.'

The woman was right up against the wire now, staring Anna down through the rifle sights. 'The gate is never open. How did you get in?' Anna's arms were aching, but she dared not let them fall. Suddenly she wondered if they *would* get out of this alive and she wasn't sure that she cared. Perhaps that was another difference between her and James. It was a terrible thought. How could she have reached such a place?

'Mrs Badenhorst. There's a jeep overturned on the road. The driver is dead,' Anna said wearily.

'What?'

The gun reared as the woman staggered backwards. But she recovered quickly.

'You're lying. What are you doing on my property?'

Anna opened her mouth, but no words came out. James stepped forward and Mrs Badenhorst swung the rifle towards him. 'Look, we don't want any trouble. We just came to tell you that there's been an accident. Now that you know we're quite happy to drive right out of here and pretend that none of this ever happened. Okay?'

Mrs Badenhorst's eyes narrowed as she sized him up. James stared back.

'Simphiwe!' she yelled. A moment later the farm worker they'd startled earlier appeared from the house, carrying a shotgun.

'Madam?' he called back.

'Bring the bakkie!' He nodded and disappeared again.

Mrs Badenhorst stood firm and neither James nor Anna dared move. Then the bleep of a cellphone pierced the tense silence and Mrs Badenhorst jumped, letting off a shot into the dust near their feet. 'It's my cellphone. In my pocket,' Anna said levelly. At least now she knew there was a signal, but she didn't risk reaching for the thing. James let out a long, low whistling breath.

Moments later Simphiwe reappeared, skidding around the house at the wheel of a red farm truck. He pulled to a stop next to Mrs Badenhorst, climbed out and handed her the keys. She unlocked the gate and pushed it open. Anna eyed the panting dogs warily as she and James let their hands drop and stood aside while Mrs Badenhorst conducted a quick search of the inside of their car poking amongst their jackets and bags and maps with the butt of her rifle. Anna felt her heartbeat quicken as Mrs Badenhorst looked at her handbag, then pushed it aside, more interested in James's camera bag which she picked up and slung over her shoulder. 'Open the boot!' she barked and James did as she ordered. There was nothing inside. 'Okay,' she muttered sharply. 'Drive behind me.'

They literally fell into the car. 'Shit!' James cried. 'This is either the coincidence of a lifetime or someone really didn't want you talking to that guy.' Anna nodded grimly at the wheel, following Mrs Badenhorst at a narrow distance. Simphiwe was sat on the back of the bakkie with his shotgun trained directly on them.

'James?' Anna spoke in a near whisper, her lips barely moving.

He looked over at her, his face shiny with sweat, eyebrows raised. 'Yeah?'

'Reach down inside my bag for me?'

He reached down. 'But your phone's in your pocket.'

Anna shook her head, 'No, the other thing.'

'Jesus!' James breathed as his fingers touched the metal of the revolver. He recoiled from the bag, as if something inside had bitten him. 'What the hell are you doing carrying a thing like that around?'

'Take it out and put it there, between us,' she said coolly, not taking her eyes off the road. 'Do you know how to cock it?'

'Are you nuts? I hate those things.'

'Okay, then just put it down between us.'

James did as she asked, then pulled a cigarette out of his pocket and Anna didn't complain about him lighting up in the car; if he'd given her one she would have smoked it.

She was thinking about the woman in the vehicle ahead of them and the terrible scene that lay in wait for her along the road. Mrs Badenhorst slowed down at the bend just before the crash site – seeming to hesitate – then she accelerated and took the corner. The brakes of the rental car squeaked as Anna nosed it slowly down the hill. Simphiwe stood up on the back of the bakkie, looking over the top of the cab at the upturned jeep lying across the road. James reached for Anna, putting his hand over hers on the gun. 'Be careful.'

Mrs Badenhorst sat for a moment, staring at the body in the tree. Then she climbed out of the bakkie, eerily calm as she turned away from the corpse and went over to the jeep. She knelt on the ground, searching for something beneath the wreckage. Simphiwe stood at a respectful distance watching and waiting. Anna's fingers tightened around the revolver as Mrs Badenhorst pulled an Uzi from underneath the shattered windshield. She carried the weapon by its barrel and dropped it with a horrible clatter onto the back of the truck.

Then she went to her husband and stood before him for a moment, staring into his blank eyes. Anna felt the choke of grief as she watched Mrs Badenhorst gently pulling down the lids of her husband's eyes. Anna turned away, unable to look as the woman put her face close to her dead husband's, speaking softly to him.

James got out of the car, closing the door as soundlessly as possible. Anna slipped the revolver into the back of her jeans, the cold metal pressed against her spine. Then she followed James.

Mrs Badenhorst wandered back towards the truck, looking dazed. Anna went up to her, putting a hand on her arm.

'I'm going back to the house to call the police,' Anna said calmly.

'What for?' The woman asked blankly.

'To call the police.'

The woman reached for the 9mm on her hip. 'We don't need anybody here!' she growled.

Anna raised her hands in a gesture of surrender that seemed to satisfy Mrs Badenhorst who then spoke something to Simphiwe. He leaned his shotgun against the wheel of the bakkie, pulled a hunting knife from inside his shirt and followed her to the trees. Together they began to cut Badenhorst's body down.

Anna looked at James and then they both walked forward and began to help free the body from the tangle of branches. It was no easy task. After half an hour or so they got him down. The four of them managed to carry him over to the bakkie, his neck lolling horribly open. They laid him out on the grooved metal of the back of the truck. The smell of blood was rich and sweet; Anna's hands were sticky with it. She wiped off as much as she could on her jeans, the scent washing over her like overwhelming incense. James looked grim as he followed suit.

Mrs Badenhorst gently arranged her husband's limbs so that he was lying comfortably. Then she glanced over at Anna and James. 'You better leave now,' was all she said. She walked round to the cab of the bakkie, put her hand on the doorhandle and looked once more in their direction. 'Thanks for your help,' she muttered grimly, and then she pulled open the door.

They were interrupted by shouts coming from down the road. Simphiwe picked up the shotgun and moved towards the sound. Mrs Badenhorst closed her hand around the butt of the pistol at her hip. James took a step closer to Anna; she could feel his breath on her hair and the warmth of his arm next to hers.

Then the boatman from the jetty appeared running blindly along the track, his eyes wide and white, his face glistening with sweat. He waved crazily when he saw them, his arms flailing around his head. More people came into view, a few steps behind him. There were about six of them, moving at a brisk trot and between them they were carrying what looked like a dripping log or a wet bag. As they got closer Anna realised that it was the body of a man.

He was a young white man, with carrot-red hair and freckles like Mrs Badenhorst's. His trousers were khaki fatigues, like hers. His body was sodden with water.

'Is that the security guard?' James asked above the shouting.

Mrs Badenhorst's lips crumpled, then her legs buckled and she fell onto the ground, onto her knees. 'It's my son,' she whispered. And a terrible wailing erupted from her body. She threw her hands up in the air and screamed, 'Not my son! Get your filthy kaffir hands off him! Don't you touch my son. Oh my God, that's my son.'

The villagers lurched to a stop and dropped the waterlogged body onto the gravel. All the sympathy Anna had felt for Mrs Badenhorst melted away in that moment. 'Get her into the car,' Anna said to James as she pulled the .38 Special from her waistband, gripped it in both hands and levelled it at Simphiwe.

Simphiwe stared at Anna for a surprised moment, but he was beyond caring. He dropped his shotgun into the dust and raised his hands, the boatman and villagers followed suit.

Anna kicked the gun out of reach as James helped the hysterical Mrs Badenhorst into the back of the rental car. Anna reached across James and took the 9mm from Mrs Badenhorst's hip holster. 'All yours,' James said distastefully, rubbing his still bloody hands against his even dirtier trousers. Anna dropped the 9mm onto the ground next to the shotgun, then lowered her own gun from its pointing position, clicked on the safety catch and hooked it in the back of her trousers again.

James smiled wearily at her. 'Nice work, Mrs Peel.'

Anna shook her head, smiling too. 'And who's Mrs Peel?'

James laughed shakily. 'I knew it. It could never work between us. She doesn't know who Mrs Peel is.' He leaned against the car and Anna wanted so much to go to him, to put her arms around him and sink into him. But she couldn't. There was too much to do.

She looked away, towards Simphiwe and the boatman who seemed to be waiting to be told what to do. 'Okay, let's get this guy on the back of the bakkie,' she said, stepping forward to help the villagers as they lifted the body and hoisted it up onto the truck.

thirty-one

The Auckland Park Tower loomed starkly in front of a sky boiling with leaden clouds gathering for a storm. Anna could feel it building, the air pressing in on her eardrums so that by the time the storm broke she could barely hear. Its violence was immense. The sky went suddenly black. Lightning crashed nearby and seemed to rock the house. The syringa tree across the street, not twenty metres from her, was hit. The crack was deafening. The tree split right down the middle, right before her eyes and collapsed slowly onto the power lines. The electricity went off – lights popped and her computer screen faded to black. Outside the power cables snaked across the road, shooting sparks in all directions. Then the rain came, clattering down on the tin roof so hard that the sound overwhelmed everything.

Anna watched in awe as the storm moved on, scudding across the sky. The light changed to an eerie green. The rain softened and the sound was suddenly not threatening, but beautiful, fresh and close. The lid of a drain, a heavy disc of metal, rolled down the middle of Fifth Avenue. Gutters overflowed into small streams and the trees were hung with pearls of raindrops.

Anna went to the living room and made a fire in the grate. The flames licked upwards as the fire took, brightening the room. It was almost a week since her return from the Eastern Cape and the terrible, bloody day at the Badenhorst farm. James had filed the story for the paper and it was splashed all over the front page of the *Sunday Chronicle*. Another exclusive. Another brutal farm murder. That was how he'd reported it. The real story was too strange and too full of unanswered questions.

Anna believed that what James said that day in the car was true. The coincidence was too great. There was someone out there who didn't want her talking to Badenhorst. Someone who was desperate enough to kill in order to prevent her from doing so. She assumed it must be the same person, or people, who'd put the tail on her. But who could it be?

Joe and the Colonel were the only other people who'd known about her trip. And Du Preez the only one who knew of Badenhorst's whereabouts. Could he be connected to this cover-up? It seemed so unlikely, but she would have to find out. She would have to confront him about it.

Anna wrapped herself up in a blanket on the sofa and sat staring into the fire. This sense of excitement and foreboding had been with her all week. She knew she was getting close to something. She had to be. Why else would someone be trying so hard to stop her?

thirty-two

James was lying on his back, smoking a cigarette in the dark. The storm had passed, but the rain still pattered down on the tin roof. He loved that sound. Loved the way the storms came in the spring, exploding the afternoons, unsettling the dust and leaving the air wet and cool. This evening's storm had plunged the neighbourhood into darkness, emptying the restaurants and quieting the streets.

He'd come home to get away from the noise and constant demands of the newsroom. He needed to work, but without light and his computer there wasn't much he could achieve. So he'd lain down on the bed to think things through. The power would come back on sooner or later. If only this investigation were as simple.

It was the cash-in-transit heist gangs story. James couldn't let it go, but it was proving impossible to get anyone to talk. The people he'd gotten to so far were too innocent or too involved to have anything of importance to say. Either that or they were just plain scared. The fear surrounding these gangs was like a magnet for him. Whoever ran the Angolans, currently out-muscling the Mozambicans, ruled with an iron fist. There were no cracks for a journalist to get even the tiniest toe-hold on the thing.

James was increasingly convinced that members of Joe Dladla's unit were working on a strategy that was at best unethical, at worst criminal and self-enriching. Dladla's role was unclear. James was certain the Assistant Commissioner knew exactly what was going on. He was too smart not to. He was also smart enough to want to contain and eliminate the problem before it blew up in his face.

It was possible, but seriously unlikely that Dladla was involved. What would he get out of it? No, it was more likely that he was trying to finesse the crooks, like a source of James's had said. He'd try to get inside the organisation, take it over and implode the gang from a position of absolute strength. No long court cases with uncertain outcomes. No sticky allegations of corruption in the force. It would certainly be characteristic of Dladla. The end always justifies the means. That was what the source had said of him.

James's source was the sleazebag Willie Mkhize, who was desperate and stupid enough not to be silenced by the fear that kept everyone else shtum.

A sound outside, like wood splitting, shook James from his thoughts. He sat up, listening. Silence again. He flicked ash into the saucer by him on the bed then settled back onto his pillows. It must have been the storm.

He was so close to cracking this story, but somehow it was always just beyond reach. There were connections and loose ends all over the place, threads tying knots around him. He just had to get to that one person who could put all the pieces in place. But that would mean someone risking his or her life for him.

James had thought about raising it with Anna, picking her brain to see if she knew of a way in. He had almost mentioned it many times during their insane trip to the Eastern Cape, but something had stopped him each time. She was seeing the guy after all, it seemed wrong to ask her about her boyfriend when he was unlikely to come up smelling of roses. Even worse, it might have seemed to Anna that getting close to Joe Dladla was James's only reason for wanting to be around her.

James sighed. Anna. She seemed to occupy a great deal of space in his mind lately. He didn't want to think about that, or her, or anything to do with her right now. She was so sealed off, so complex and so way beyond his reach there was no point. He turned on his side, dragging the last out of his cigarette as he leaned forward to stub it out. But a noise in the house stopped him. A thud, like a footfall.

James froze, every inch of him straining towards the sound. It was too small a noise to have been produced by one of the cats that regularly traversed his roof on their way to other cat domains. And it was too big to have been made by the fridge. Besides, it seemed to have come from the hallway and all James kept there was his iron and ironing board.

He dropped the cigarette butt into the saucer and, contrary to everything a person is supposed to do in such a situation, he went to investigate.

James's bedroom was at the back of the house, off an L-shaped hallway connecting with all the other rooms. To get to the front door he would have to turn right from his bedroom and walk a few steps along the hall before the L took him left and the front door was before him.

James advanced cautiously, keeping close to the wall. As he turned the corner he felt the cool air before he saw that the front door was open and that there was someone standing in the hallway. The dark shape of a person was clearly visible against the thin, silvery light from outside. He didn't have time to shout or gasp or even run before a shot went off. He felt the bullet slice through the air close to his face, heard the whine of it before it thwacked into the wall behind him. Jesus!

James hit the floor, managing to roll behind the corner for cover before a second shot rang out. This time it thudded into the plaster near his head, sending chips of dust and paint flying from the wall. James curled up as small as he could. The gunman took a step forward, his boot resounding through the wooden floorboards. James's heart was pounding, his mouth dry, there was no time to think. He had to get out, get away.

A scuffle, then a crashing sound, like someone else hitting the floor, then feet clattering on floorboards, receding across the stoep. Running away? Then silence. James didn't move for what felt like hours, but was probably no more than seven or eight minutes. He hardly dared breathe until he was sure the intruder was no longer in the house.

When he tried to get to his feet he found his knees uncooperative. They were shaking too much to bear his weight; he had to crouch for a minute or two more to regain some strength. Then he stood up and reached around the corner for the light switch, but there was still no power. Damn! He pulled a box of matches from his pocket and lit one. It cast a tiny pool of light, sufficient for him to get a sense of what had happened, flickering snapshots of a story. The lock on the front door was hanging from a single remaining screw. The ironing board had collapsed across the doorway and the iron was lying on the stoep.

Laughter bubbled up in James's throat. The crazy laughter of relief. The gunman had tripped over the electric lead for the iron, which had tangled round his leg and brought the ironing board down. That accounted for the crashing sounds after the shots. The match burned down, stinging his fingertips. He was in darkness again.

He began to feel his way back along the hall towards the bedroom when a voice called out from the darkness. 'Put your hands up!' It was a gruff woman's voice, coming from the garden, or maybe the front porch. James swung round, his heart beating wildly again. Which way to run? But it was too late. A torch flashed on and the beam immediately found his face. Somewhere behind that blinding light someone breathed a sigh of relief.

And fortunately it was at that moment that the power came back on.

Standing there on the stoep was James's neighbour, Mpho. Mpho was a large, grumpy black woman, a senior something or other in government, probably in her fifties though she looked older, and who was in the habit of playing Dolly Parton albums over and over at high volume. Their relations to date had been less than cordial. Tonight she was wearing a long terrycloth dressing gown and her hair was tightly rolled up in curlers. In one hand she held a neat little .22 pistol. In the other was the torch and at her feet was a larger ginger and white cat. 'Oh my goodness, Mister Kay. You gave me the fright of my life!'

James was too freaked out to come up with a decent retort. He was actually glad to see her. 'I heard the shots and I called the police,' she grumbled, 'but you know they don't come straight away, so I thought I'd better investigate.' James nodded, trying to take it all in. What the hell was going on? Had someone just tried to kill him? 'I heard car tyres screeching outside and I ran out to see tail-lights disappearing down Third Avenue towards Emmarentia.' Mpho made large gestures as she spoke, the beam of her torch swinging all over the garden. 'Mister Kay? Are you all right?'

James nodded again, more vigorously this time. 'Yeah. Thanks. You can put the gun down now.'

It was almost midnight by the time the police left. James had smoked himself hoarse, repeating the story over and over for the benefit of the sluggish local constabulary. Slow as they were they'd managed to find the bullets and cartridges in the hallway and James had watched them package up the evidence. It would be important later, he was sure of it. More sure than the weary detective who said he'd seen too many incidents like this one in the past month alone and zero arrests to match up with them. The detective cast a humoring look in his direction when James insisted that the gunman had come to kill him. 'An armed robbery, especially a failed one, can seem like that, Mister Kay, but in the end that's all it is, an attempted robbery.'

James didn't want to be alone in the house. And he wanted to talk to Anna. He called her on her cell while he threw some clothes and books and a laptop into bags. It took a while for her to answer and when she did she sounded sleepy.

'I'm sorry. It's me. Did I wake you?' James was breathless, loading his bags into his car as he spoke.

'Mmm. I'm glad you woke me actually. I seem to have fallen asleep on the sofa.' James started up the car, the engine thrumming beautifully as he pulled away from his house and danger. 'Where are you?' Anna mumbled. 'Are you okay?'

Ten minutes later she was walking towards him, picking her way through the tables at Catz Pyjamas, an all-night diner above a strip of shops on the Main Road. James had commandeered a free table on the balcony outside, with a view down onto the street. He smiled when he saw her and stood up, fag in one hand, double whisky in the other. Her expression shifted from one of sleepy pleasure to extreme concern as she took in the state of him.

'What happened?'

He told her. It didn't take long. When he was finished she didn't say anything. She looked at him for a long time and it seemed to

James that they both understood what was happening. They'd stumbled unawares into something much bigger than the Mafikeng Road Murders. 'I'm just glad that you're okay,' James said, lighting yet another cigarette. 'Someone wanted to kill me.'

Anna looked away. On the street the traffic lights changed from green to red.

'Or give you a fright,' she said at last.

'A *helluva* fright.' His retort was tinged with aggression.

Anna took a sip of his drink. 'If this was not a random incident or a robbery, then the gunman would have been a pro,' she said quietly. 'If a pro wanted you dead then you'd be dead. They fired at you to scare you off.'

James frowned, then nodded. 'I guess so. Except they hadn't figured on my high-tech security iron!' They both laughed.

Then Anna said, 'Someone's been following me.'

James's chin jerked upwards. 'Since when?'

She pushed her hair back away from her face. 'Dunno. A couple of weeks?'

'What? Why didn't you mention this before?'

She shrugged. 'I wasn't sure who it was. And anyway, it seemed like my problem. I've been getting close to something. Something someone doesn't want me getting close to. It makes sense that I'd be followed. But why shoot you?'

James realised suddenly that she'd clicked. There was something else he was up to, something she didn't know about, but that was somehow connected to her. That would account for the wariness in the way she was eyeing him. But how could he tell her it was Joe he was investigating?

'What is it that you know, James?'

He let out a low 'shew' of breath and shook his head. 'I can't say. I just can't tell you at this point.'

Doubt hung in the silence between them. But what else could he say? How was he supposed to tell her that the man he suspected of running or at least protecting these gangs was her comrade, her boyfriend for Chrissake? He was painfully torn. He could see what she was thinking, read it as if it were ticker-taping out of her brain. Here's another man with a hidden agenda. Another man I can't trust because he's not giving me the full picture. He could see the disappointment hitting her like an inrush of cold air. The frizz of animosity between them was new and unwelcome. He felt bereft, starkly alone, sensing a huge gulf where there had been a warm intimacy, a feeling of shared danger and an incredible affinity.

James smoked a cigarette and Anna slowly finished off his drink. The silence was horrible. He wished she'd scream or throw something, but she didn't, she took it calmly. She stood up calmly. She looked at him calmly. It was unbearable. He looked away, shifting in his seat. 'Just take care of yourself, okay?'

She nodded, 'You too.' Then she walked away, into the jagged Johannesburg night.

thirty-three

The following morning it was raining. Anna left home later than usual and got stuck in the long crawl along Empire Road. It took her twenty minutes just to get onto the freeway. She sat in the jam and watched the windscreen wipers hammering back and forth across the glass.

Instead of soaring beyond it Anna felt the past was drowning her. Its tentacles wrapping tighter and tighter around her, so the more she tried to break free the more powerful their lock became.

And now she was truly alone.

She didn't want to think about James and the upsetting conversation of the night before. She was worried for him, but disappointed too. Even he had a secret agenda.

Anna drove straight towards the prison. She wasn't sure what would happen if she showed up there on her own, with no appointment, no invitation and no Henk Steyn to accompany her. But she had to see the Colonel.

Pretoria Central loomed suddenly before her. Perhaps it was the greyness of the sky and the rain, but the place had a particularly sinister sickly yellow cast that morning. She pulled into the almost empty visitors' parking lot just before eight-thirty, brushed her hair, put some lipstick on and made for the visitors' entrance.

The main reception area was a dreary hall with rows of empty wooden benches. The floor had just been mopped and was dangerously slippery. A cleaning lady sat at the far end of one of the benches, staring out at the rain.

'Good morning. How are you?' Anna smiled at the guard sitting behind the desk.

'Cool as a cucumber, thanks. What can I do for you, Sisi?'

'I'm going to visit a prisoner in C-Max. Ignatius Du Preez.'

The man didn't miss a beat when she uttered Du Preez's name, he simply directed her towards a waiting minibus.

'That kombi will take you to Maximum.'

'Thank you.'

Anna picked her way across the slippery lino and out into the rain. The kombi only had one other passenger and the driver explained that he had to wait to fill up his vehicle before he could go. So Anna sat and waited and watched the rain coursing down the windows. Three uniformed guards, a plain, mousy woman and two men climbed in next to her and the driver set off.

The plain woman with hair caught up in a plastic clip under her cap, was engaged in a whispered flirtation with the heavy-set guard beside her. Something he said made her splutter with laughter. 'Ag sis! I never wanna have one of those in my mouth. Shut up, man!'

The man chuckled conspiratorially. 'You mean you *never* had one of them in your mouth?'

The girl shook her head, her expression serious with distaste. 'Uh-uh,' she said 'and I never will.' Silence settled around them again for a moment before she went on. 'I mean they're so ugly, have you ever looked at that thing?'

The other guard nodded, a grin on his wide lips. 'Ja, I look at it every day, looked at it this morning. I call it Simba – the king of snacks!' Both men shook with laughter as the girl grimaced and popped a mint between her lips.

Anna was the only person who got off at Maximum. She signed in at the first security check. The usual routine followed of handing over her cellphone and opening her bag for a search. Then a female guard arrived and took Anna across the moat under a large candy-striped umbrella. The three goats were pressed against a wall, sheltered from the slanting rain by a small ledge above them.

The warders in the visitors' reception recognised Anna and greeted her pleasantly. She filled out the prisoner requisition form, signing herself in as a member of the Secretariat and no one seemed to think there was anything irregular about it. Then she was shown straight through to the visitors' courtyard, a grim place she hadn't seen before that was like an oversized drain. The warder walked up to a metal door at the far end, banged on the grille and shouted through. 'Contact visit for Du Preez!' It seemed he'd been moved again, this time to a more spacious section, though the warder's epaulette badges were still for C-Max.

Anna stood at the edge of the sheltered park of the yard, a curtain of rain at her back as she waited. Du Preez emerged minutes later, accompanied by two more warders. He was wearing the same orange C-Max boiler suit she'd seen him in before. He was unshaven, with a few days' growth of stubble and he was visibly flustered when he saw Anna, though there was not a trace of the disorientation and depression that she'd seen in his eyes on her last visit.

They shook hands. 'I wasn't expecting you,' he stammered, indicating for her to sit down at a wire-mesh table with little picnic stools bolted to the floor around it. He seemed somewhat rattled and Anna wondered if perhaps she'd impinged on his precious and very limited visiting time. He said, 'No, it's fine if they take a couple of hours off that, no problem at all. It's always a pleasure to see you, Anna.'

'Well, you look better. I see you've put on a bit of weight,' she said lightly.

The Colonel tilted his head to one side and said, in that serious, childlike way he had, 'Ja, conditions have improved, but I don't recommend the room service.'

Anna looked down at her hands, folded on the tabletop, wondering how to begin. But she didn't have to.

'So someone wasn't so keen for you to see old Balletjies Badenhorst then.' There was a wry smile on his lips as he said this.

'That's no lie!' Anna declared breathily, relieved that he'd gone straight to the point.

'I suppose you're wondering what I might have had to do with that?' This he said quietly, looking her straight in the eye.

The rain drummed noisily on the corrugated plastic above

them and pattered down onto the cement of the courtyard floor. 'Well, ja,' Anna replied uncomfortably. 'To be frank, I was.'

'Who else knew about you going?' he shot back.

Anna looked up towards the plastic roof and the water running in rivers along the corrugations. 'Just you, James Kay – a journalist friend – and Joe Dladla.'

The Colonel sighed heavily. He looked down at the table, fiddling with a loose piece of wire as he chewed something over. Then he looked across at her again. 'Badenhorst's death had nothing to do with me. The guy I got his details from knows nothing about you or Paul Lewis or anything else. I wish I could give more, but I can only give my word on this.'

He continued to play with the wire as he watched her, waiting for her reaction. It was a matter of trust. He knew as well as she did that the evidence in favour of his trustworthiness was thin. Yet she believed him. She smiled ruefully, making a funny face. 'Thanks, Ig. I do trust you on this.'

The Colonel leaned back and grinned broadly. 'It's funny, I was just thinking about you yesterday,' he said. She leaned forward slightly, resting her elbows on the table. 'I was thinking it's nice to have you as a friend.' He said this with such simple sincerity that Anna couldn't suppress a smile. What a weird world we live in, she thought as she thanked him. Then she turned to the other question that had brought her here.

'Someone's following me, Ig. Who is it?'

He scratched his head, thinking. 'Well, depends on what else you've been up to, but if it's something to do with Paul Lewis . . .' His voice trailed off. He shifted his position restlessly, as if this was hard work. Anna nodded, encouraging him to go on. 'Simple. One of yours who was one of ours.'

Anna must have looked dubious about his logic because he answered her next question without her having to ask it. 'Paul was a spy, okay? He was playing in that grey zone. He was killed by – or at least with the involvement of – Frans Nel, a colleague of his. There must have been others out there, guys who are still here, still with the police perhaps – who thought they'd got away with murder. Till now. Till you started coming too close. That's why I say – one of yours who was one of theirs.' He opened his palms then clapped them together as he finished.

Anna sat with the back of her hand over her mouth, thinking it through. The logic was compelling she now saw. She couldn't argue with it. But who the hell could it be? Someone so deeply camouflaged she had not the slightest idea of their involvement in the equation.

'Ja,' the Colonel went on, 'it's a mistake to see it all as black and white. It never was and never will be. It's a thousand shades of grey.'

Anna looked at him for a moment, surprised, as she had been several times before, by how on the nose he could be. She nodded, thinking over all that he had said.

Du Preez glanced over at the warders. 'So what's next?' he asked. Anna sighed. 'I think it's going to have to be Sherry Nel. No one else left!' The Colonel seemed to think this was a good idea. 'It wasn't hard to find her,' Anna explained. 'Managed to track her down through her lawyer. She's living up in Northern Province, running one of these evangelical churches with her new husband, a Rob Thorpe. They run a restaurant up there as well.'

'Shew, that's gonna be a tough one.'

'Ja. 'Bout as much fun as sticking needles in my eyes,' she said feelingly.

Du Preez shook his head sadly. 'I wouldn't know what to do if my wife were unfaithful.' Anna imagined that it would be hard for her not to be, with him behind bars and her in America or wherever she was. She found herself hoping that Mrs Du Preez wouldn't say or do anything to let on if she did stray.

'Anyway, gotta do it. What do you think she's likely to know?'

Du Preez explained that Sherry Nel was likely to know a lot without knowing its value. If Paul visited her house then it was likely that people connected to the mystery did. Generally the wives of security policemen had very little idea of what their husbands were really up to. The family could be a wholesome, church-going, tennis-club joining sanctuary for a cop who spent his days and nights engaged in the business of torture and death.

'Did your wife know what you were up to all those years?' Anna asked.

He shrugged. 'I think she had an idea that I was no ordinary policeman. But I don't think she had any idea of the extent of it.' He grimaced, looking into the distance, into that out-of-focus nowhere place where people have to look sometimes. 'Ag, it took its toll you know. The strange hours, the travel. She once accused me of having an affair!' A snort of laughter escaped him. 'It was only when it was all over and I knew I was going to be arrested that I told her the truth.' He folded his arms, his eyes still elsewhere. 'We went out onto the stoep. The girls were asleep inside. And I told her everything. It was like tearing my own heart out.'

Du Preez's voice had faded to almost nothing. Anna didn't know what to say. She glanced over at the warders who were smoking and chatting on the stairs, oblivious to their conversation. The rain still clattered so loudly on the roof it was unlikely that they could hear anything anyway. The Colonel managed a smile. 'So when you going to Pietersburg?'

'Soon as possible. Maybe tomorrow,' Anna said.

'You let me know what happens,' he replied, like a concerned doctor.

Anna smiled back. Of course she'd let him know. 'Ig, I've been wanting to ask you something.' He sat up very straight, the seated equivalent of standing to attention. 'Why are you helping me?' she asked.

The Colonel looked puzzled. He thought about the question for a while and then he looked at her very seriously. 'I don't really know why I trust you. I mean, we should be enemies. We *were* enemies. But that first day you came to see me I thought – there's something good in that person. And that made me think – what would I do if I were in your shoes? If that were my wife, or my child that was murdered? And I don't know, but it troubled me. I think I'd hunt them down and bladdy hang, draw and quarter them.' He paused, looking away. 'Even if that murderer was me. I still say that's what they deserve. To be hung, drawn and quartered. So whatever I can do to help, I try, you know? I can't change what I've done. It's done. But if I can help to find out who killed your Paul and if that makes you sleep easier at night, then that's something.'

Anna listened to his mind spooling out, his voice rising with emotion, and it moved her. 'You know,' she said quietly, 'when I first saw you, at your trial, I hated you. I wished you dead.' He watched her without the merest glimmer of expression as she

275

said this. 'And here I am and here we are and we talk about being friends and you're my only ally in this investigation now.' She opened her hands in front of her, as if they might help express this difficult thing she was trying to say. 'I've wondered sometimes if I would be able to talk to you like this if you'd killed Paul. And it *could* have been you who killed him.' Du Preez nodded, assenting before she went on. 'I don't think I could. Forgive you. And I can't ever forgive you for what you did, to other people, but somehow – well, here we are. Don't you find that strange?'

The Colonel shook his head. 'No, not really. It's because we belong to each other,' he said, 'like two sides of the same coin.'

Anna smiled ruefully. The rain clattered down on the silence that followed.

But it was time to go. The warders had closed in around their picnic table, indicating with restless glances at their watches that it was time to take the prisoner back to his cell. Anna stood up, hitching her bag over her shoulder. 'It was good talking to you, Ig. Thanks,' she said. As he rose she put her hand out to shake his but then, unexpectedly, he put his arms round her and gave her an awkward hug. 'You take care now, Anna,' he said gruffly. For a moment she felt panicky, her arms flailing helplessly over his back. He'd crossed a line that a few weeks back would have been impermeable. The idea of his embracing her would have been repulsive, would have been impossible. And yet there he was, with his arms round her, and she patted his back and said he should do the same. Then they went their separate ways. He up the stairs to his cell and Anna back across the moat, through the rain.

Anna was by now so accustomed to her tail that she barely paid attention as the little purple car slipped into the lane behind her. No more black and white, Anna thought to herself as she drove away from the prison. Like the man says, it's a thousand shades of grey.

thirty-four

The flight to Pietersburg was a short one and the morning was still new as the plane descended towards the vast, sparse plain near the provincial capital. The day was hot and the air dry. Anna stripped off her jacket as she crossed the runway towards the airport building and Sherry Nel's attorney who was to meet her there. She tried not to think too much about the day to come. Paul's betrayal was more than a decade old, but the hurt was as fresh as battery acid in her face.

André Baker, the former Mrs Nel's Pietersburg lawyer, sounded like a smooth operator on the phone and was not at all fazed by her strange request. 'Fine. I'll give Sherry a tinkle and I'll get back to you in a jiffy!' he'd said brightly. True to his word, he called back within the hour to say that Mrs Thorpe would be more than happy to see her; any time later in the week was fine.

Anna guessed immediately that André Baker was the large, clumsy creature loping towards her across the arrivals hall. He looked about forty years old, but he could have been younger. His handshake was clammy and soft.

'So, Anna. I hope you don't mind me calling you Anna?' he smarmed jovially. 'It's all been arranged!' He didn't seem to have much idea of what her visit was about and he'd certainly never heard of Paul Lewis, but 'Sherry said she knew exactly'. They were to meet Sherry at her restaurant, which was a short drive away on the road from Pietersburg to Tzaneen.

Anna couldn't help noticing how often André Baker stole glances at her legs as he drove. 'Are you married, Anna?' She moved her bag from the floor to her lap and tucked her hand underneath it. There was something about the way he leered at her that made her lie. 'Yes, I am. Are you?'

'Oh yes,' he grinned. 'With four lovely girls.'

'That's nice.' Anna looked out of the window at the flat, empty plains that stretched away from the road. The way he said it, with such toothy glee, he could almost have meant that he was married to four lovely girls, but she chose to understand that he was the proud father of four unfortunate daughters. Anna felt something brush against her thigh and she looked over to see him pushing a casette into the tape player. He grinned again. Music filled the car, a silly, sweet song about a lady in red, *dancing with me-ee, cheek to cheek . . .*

'I've never been big on monogamy myself,' he chuckled, presumably referring to the song. 'I have great admiration for the French, you know,' he went on, apparently encouraged by Anna's silence. 'They have no time for monogamy. There, the mistress and lover are *institutions*! And excellent ones in my view.' Lascivious mirth bubbled out of him. 'I mean, if you're not getting breakfast at home, then why shouldn't you eat out? Hey? Ha, ha, ha . . .'

The landscape changed as they climbed out of Pietersburg, entering the hill country where Sherry Nel had made her new life. The restaurant was called The Hideaway. From the road it looked like the outbuilding of a garage. Black paint on a white board advertised a Big Screen TV. André Baker parked next to the only other vehicle in the dusty lot, a twin-cab bakkie with go-faster stripes down the sides.

Anna got out of the car and brushed down her jacket and skirt, as if that would shake out the contaminating atmosphere of the car. She looked around at the dismal buildings and the cheap sign. André Baker loped on ahead and Anna followed self-consciously, a hum of anxiety ringing in her head.

Inside, The Hideaway was surprisingly bright. It was one big room, an old shed probably, with a low ceiling made from layers of thin reed poles. The walls were painted emerald green, in shiny gloss paint. Opposite the entrance was a long bar of rough wood with a heavy, varnished pine top. Behind the bar stood a lumpy woman with scraped back dirty-blonde hair.

Anna froze in the doorway, and stared. The woman's fringe

was scooped and sprayed and shaped into a brittle-looking lick over her left eye. Her eyes were blue, with brilliant sky-blue eyeshadow painted in careful half circles over the lids. Her eyebrows were plucked thin and high and the pearly powder-blue skin beneath made her look like a startled doll. The skin on her shoulders and around the creases of her armpits was sagging and crêpe-paper crinkled. She wore a summer dress that was the same blue as her eyelids, with thin shoulder straps and a drooping ruffle above her cleavage.

'Hi, Sands!' shouted André Baker heartily. 'We're here to see Sherry.'

'She expecting you?' the woman asked sourly.

Anna almost laughed with relief.

'Of course she's expecting us, Sandy,' Baker smarmed.

'Okay,' the barwoman snapped before disappearing through a pink and yellow bead curtain into the kitchen at the back.

The bar stools were tall cut logs with a square cushion perched on the top of each one. André Baker sat himself on one of them and patted the seat next to his, inviting Anna to sit down. She stayed standing, surveying the room with a polite interest that masked her anxiety and her heightened state of mind. Anna experienced everything in that place acutely, as if she were looking for signs of Paul in everything. Not the Paul she knew, but the one who was known to Sherry.

A line of hats hung from the ceiling above the bar. They were mostly blue caps – the regalia of the Northern Transvaal rugby supporter. But there was also an air-force blue and navy plastic cap with the brass star of the old South African Police plugged into its band. Below that someone had hung a wooden sign with letters carved out and painted in black which read: 'As jy drink om te vergeet, betaal vooruit.' If you are drinking to forget, then pay up front. Just below that was another sign, made in the same style, which read: 'Die Nuwe Suid-Afrika se gat.' The New South Africa's asshole.

A small fly-spattered fan shed a rotating corona of light behind Sandy the barlady as she stalked back inside. But it was Sherry's voice that announced her arrival moments before Sherry herself appeared clip-clopping behind her blue-eyed friend. 'The Lord will provide, my baby. The Lord will provide,' she chirped in a cloying tone. Anna realised that the little blonde who swept into the room on a waft of cheap, sweet-smelling perfume was talking on her cellphone.

Anna was able to take a measure of her rival as she stood at the end of the bar, pouting and flirting into the phone. She felt both insulted and relieved. There was something slightly absurd about Sherry, but also something that Anna found a little frightening. Sherry understood the power her exaggerated femininity gave her and she used it to maximum effect. Her narrow hips were sheathed in a thin A-line miniskirt, her spindly legs balanced on high heels. She wore shiny skin-tone stockings and a silk blouse with the top button undone far enough to reveal the lacy edges of a purple satin bra. Her hair was so huge it couldn't be real. It had a red sheen to it and was carefully blow-dried into lustrous waves and bounces. 'Now don't forget, sweetie, Sherry's praying for you. With all her heart,' she chirped to her caller, then blew a little kiss into the phone and switched it off.

Sherry then squealed and jumped up into André Baker's arms, hugging him with girlish effusiveness. When at last he put her down he slapped her bum and she actually shrieked with pleasure. At last she turned towards Anna, like a goose arching its long neck, like a bird preening.

Anna's tongue seemed to swell in her throat as Sherry offered her a feather-like hand. 'André tells me you've come all the way from Joburg.' Her little body shivered with excitement. Up close her skin was haggard and there were creases at the sides of her wide mouth, lines furrowing at the top of her nose and around her eyes. But she was unquestionably a beautiful woman with beautiful dreamy eyes. They reminded Anna of Paul's eyes.

Sherry was sizing up Anna at the same time. Anna was aware of the drab shapelessness of her suit, her chapped lips and lack of make-up, her loose and dishevelled hair, and clumpy shoes. It didn't take long for Sherry to decide that Anna was no competition, and some crazy competitive streak made Anna wish she'd also dolled herself up to the max. She could out-tart this old slag any day. 'André also tells me you're very high up in the police these days?' Anna nodded. Sherry seemed to like that because she giggled. 'Well. I've often wondered when you would catch up with me.'

Anna's jaw appeared to be clamped shut, and she couldn't get it open to speak. Sherry didn't seem to mind; she was happily making enough noise for both of them. 'Why don't we sit down? I hope you don't mind if I smoke?' Anna shook her head. She didn't mind.

She swung herself up onto a stool and watched as Sherry went to fetch a packet of cigarettes and an ashtray from behind the bar. She walked as though she knew everyone could see the soft round shape of her ass through her skirt. She was wearing a purple G-string that showed through the pale floral cotton. Sherry reeked of sex, but of the satin and lace and hairspray variety. Anna pictured her in her Barbie Doll house and her Barbie Doll church, all catsuits and emerald eye-shadow. 'Vivacious,' that's what André Baker called her and she laughed vivaciously when he did.

Sherry jiggled onto a bar stool and lit up a long, slender menthol cigarette. 'Where should I start?' she trilled, looking to André Baker for help. He indicated with his hand outstretched that Anna was in charge.

'Why don't you start by telling us about your husband,' Anna suggested, amazed that she'd found her voice and even more amazed at the calm tone she achieved given the turmoil of her mind.

'Ex-husband,' Sherry corrected.

'Sorry, ja. Frans Nel.'

'Frans was a bastard, a cruel man. I was glad when he threw me out, glad that I was free to move on.' Sherry spoke about her former husband with distinctly unchristian bitterness. They had married young, he was twenty-three and Sherry a tender eighteen. At first his work was just routine police work, 'no funny business'. She emphasised this with a pointed look shared with both Anna and Baker. He was a regular policeman, who worked regular hours, but he was ambitious and good at his job and he moved quite quickly up through the ranks. Then he got promoted to the Security Police. 'We were so excited when he got that promotion. I mean, that was the *elite*. No more uniforms, no more regular hours, lots of *opportunities*.' When Sherry stressed that word, opportunities, her eyes were wide and innocent, but Anna understood her perfectly. She was referring to opportunities for personal enrichment. It was a myth in the Security Police that all of them were married to wealthy wives. In fact their affluence came from straightforward stealing and siphoning off of secret State slush funds. 'But that was when things started to go wrong between us,' Sherry continued, looking demurely at her long, gleaming fingernails.

'Frans changed, too. He grew hard and secretive and I know he was drinking a lot. They would go off all hours of the day and night, and sometimes he'd disappear for days without even phoning to tell me he was okay. Then he'd show up in the middle of the night, stinking of whisky. I didn't really know what he was doing. I mean, I knew that he was very important now and that he was helping the government to stop communism and satanism and was fighting the terrorists, but most of the time I never knew where he was or who he was with. And I was *positive* that he went with other women.' Sherry's long, mascara-encrusted eyelashes flashed innocent sincerity. She looked up at Anna who smiled tensely, but encouragingly. Sherry lowered her tone. 'I knew he was unfaithful to me and one day, when my kids were already walking and I didn't have any more babies to look after, I sat up and I said to myself – Sherry my girl, wake up and smell the roses. There's no point in you sitting on the shelf while he's out there making hay.' She threw a coquettish glance at André Baker, and then neatly stubbed out her cigarette. Anna was transfixed by the tinkerbell voice, the pert little nose and the large, fluttering eyes.

'So I started making hay of my own. In a way it was to spite him, but I also enjoyed myself.' Sherry smiled, directing this last comment at André Baker who almost drooled with excitement. Then she tossed her head, an artful movement that made her hair bounce and fall back over her shoulders. 'But Paul wasn't just one of those guys, he wasn't some one-night stand. Paul was special.' Each word stuck Anna like a knife. 'But I don't need to tell you that.' Little fingers, dry with long nails, tapped on Anna's arm. Another girlish gesture, one of complicity. We both did him and wasn't he great? Tee hee.

Anna cleared her throat. 'How did you and Paul meet?' she asked in a voice that sounded to her like gears grinding.

Sherry smiled and those dreamy eyes seemed even mistier as she remembered. 'At a party. Frans loved to throw parties and those days he had a lot of money. We had a big house, lovely for entertaining and he used to invite all the guys over, even some of the black guys. Frans always treated his blacks nicely. Anyway Paul came late, after midnight I think, when the place was really jumping. He was such a big man. I think that's what first caught my eye. I love big men, hey?' Another peel of laughter, like glass breaking. Sherry leaned closer, confiding in Anna. Anna fidgeted in her seat, the pained smile on her lips becoming more and more grotesque. 'They catch you up in their arms,' she trilled angelically, stretching her arms out and up and then pulling them in, hugging herself theatrically. 'They hold you, and make you feel so small and lovely and loved. Hey? And he had beautiful lips for a man. Such a *sweet* smile. But I think it was when I saw him dancing. That was when I knew. I *wanted* him. He could really dance. And I don't mean all this new disco stuff, I mean old-fashioned, hold you close and swing you round that room so you feel like you're floating, like you're flying around him and he's the centre of the world, making you fly. Oooh. Paul could dance. I've never known anyone who could dance like him.'

Anna was electrified. It was agony. She tried to calculate when that might have been, what excuse Paul had made, but she couldn't think clearly. She sensed this woman enjoying the story, in the way that women put one another down while seeming not to. There was a sadistic streak in her little evangelical mind. Sherry smiled, a secret, sensual smile as she looked down at the floor. 'It happened that night. In the garden. I don't think we were very careful, but my husband was so vrot, everyone was so vrot, nobody noticed. I don't think I would have cared if they did, it was *amazing*. And I think it was partly because I knew who he was, you know?' Sherry frowned at Anna, who shook her head, not following. 'I mean because he was a spy. You know what I mean?'

'How did you know he was a spy?'

'My husband told me. He said Paul was a star. I remember that was the word he used. Star. Shame . . . Only the good die young, hey Anna?'

Anna said nothing. She felt nothing. And she was grateful to whatever chemistry it was in her body and mind that could trip her out like this. So she didn't feel. She just listened.

Sherry puffed delicately on a fresh cigarette and then spoke again in a low intimate tone. 'A few years after Paul's death I was born again. When I met my third husband. Bobby changed my life. I changed my ways when I found him – and God,' she added. 'Are you a Christian, Anna?' Anna shook her head and Sherry smiled at her, with sad, but kind eyes.

The blue-eyed barlady arrived at that moment with a tray of boerewors and steak, and rolls and sauce. 'Compliments of the house,' Sherry said, smiling happily. André Baker ordered another beer and tucked right in. Anna didn't touch a thing. She watched in silence as Sherry's hand hovered over the bread rolls set out before them, but she retracted it suddenly at the sight of her husband in the kitchen doorway.

The pastor had stopped by for a bite of lunch and Sherry introduced him to Anna, clinging to him all the while, like a koala. 'This is my husband!' she crowed. He didn't seem like such a triumph to Anna. Bob Thorpe was a greasy-looking lug, big and dumb, but with an eye for skirt. Anna could tell from the way that he looked her up and down.

'You remember that boyfriend I told you about? The one who died? This is a friend of his – she's looking for the truth about what happened to him,' Sherry twittered. The pastor nodded and spoke through a mouthful of wors. 'The truth shall make you free: John, chapter eight, verse thirty-two.' Sherry rolled her eyes heavenwards. 'That's so beaurreful, Bobby.' Fortunately Bobby didn't stay long; he took another boerewors roll and a bottle of beer and went off to tend to his flock. Sherry said a long and passionate goodbye to him in the doorway. Anna stared shamelessly at the way she wriggled against him. Then at last he sauntered off with a smug look and a sausage stuffed in his mouth.

While Sherry fixed her lipstick in a tiny compact mirror she'd pulled out of her bag, Anna explained that she would have to leave shortly, that she had a plane to catch. 'Oh no! And just when we were getting to know each other!' Sherry exclaimed sweetly and snapped her compact shut. Anna was so repeatedly taken aback by the woman's utterances that she must have seemed like a stuttering half-wit.

'Sherry, what I need to know is something that's very important for the investigation.'

Sherry nodded and frowned as she listened, a study of seriousness. 'I need you to think very carefully. Do you remember if there was someone in your ex-husband's unit, or maybe in another unit, who was in charge of Paul? Someone Paul would have reported to, taken orders from?'

Sherry took another cigarette out of her pack and lit it, thinking hard all the while. 'No, you see, Anna, Paul was different. After that first night, he used to come to the house a lot. Just between us girls,' she giggled nauseatingly, 'I think it was to see me. But as far as my husband was concerned, well, at least till the last time, *he* thought Paul was there to see *him*. You follow?' Anna dipped her head, yes, she followed. 'Anyway, I used to take them drinks and food and things, any excuse just to be near Paul, and sometimes I listened to them talking business.' She paused, taking a long drag on her cigarette.

'Did you ever hear anything, a name? Someone who could have been Paul's Handler,' Anna pressed her.

Sherry shook her head, tossing her curls. 'No,' she said firmly. 'But there was a guy, a black guy, who came to the house with Paul a couple of times. In fact he was with Paul that first night, at the party. I remember him because he seemed very arrogant. He held himself very high and he was very good-looking, but a bit too arrogant for my liking.'

Anna was as taut as an uncoiled spring, willing Sherry to get to the point. 'Do you remember what his name was?'

Sherry shook her head again. 'I only met him a few times, in fact I think it was only twice and I never saw him for long, you know. They called him Steve, but I don't think that was his real name. I never knew his real name. It was like that in those days.' Sherry smiled sweetly, looking pleased with herself. She had come to the end of her story.

Anna leaned back, crossing her arms over her chest. It was something, but it wasn't enough. Steve could have been anybody, another policeman: whoever he was he was not necessarily Paul's Handler.

'Ooh!' Sherry squealed suddenly. 'I just remembered. I saw him in the newspaper not so long ago.' Anna's heart lurched. Sherry jumped off her stool with all the bounce of a cheerleader and scuttled behind the bar, chirruping all the way. 'We don't normally get the papers here, they're so full of *negativity*. But I happened to see it when I was in town. In fact I think I even kept the article, in my file!' She bent down, shuffling papers and clinking glasses on a shelf underneath the bar. 'I know I have it here somewhere. I just hope nobody's thrown it away.' She glared at the blue-eyed barlady, who turned away haughtily, *as if she would*. Anna leaned over the bar and saw Sherry pulling out a transparent folder with pink and blue Hello Kitty motifs printed on it. 'No, here it is! I knew I had it.'

Sherry skipped round the bar and brought the torn-off newsprint to Anna. 'There it is. That's him,' she sang, flattening the paper on the bar top with her long, purple nails. The picture was of Joe, moments after he first arrested Bazooka. Heroic, bleeding, *treacherous* Joe.

Anna stared at the photograph. 'Are you quite sure?' she whispered.

'Oh yes. Positive. I never forget a face. Do I, Sandy?'

'Never.' The blue-eyed barlady scowled her assent.

On the flight home Anna recalled Bobby Thorpe's platitude. 'The truth shall make you free.' *What a load of crap*, she thought. The truth had bound and gagged and paralysed her; there was nothing liberating about the truth at all.

part seven

Those to whom evil is done
Do evil in return

W. H. AUDEN

thirty-five

James stood up from his computer and stretched, extending his arms upwards until the joints cracked. He threw a couple of logs onto the fire and watched them catch. Inside the cottage the wooden floors creaked and echoed as he walked to the bathroom. He splashed water on his face, looked in the mirror and mussed up his hair. It was shot through with grey and thinning at the temples. Fuck, I'm getting old, he realised with astonishment. And it amused him.

Most things pleased him that day.

Something had happened to him out here in the wild, wide plains of the Free State, in this completely unfamiliar part of South Africa. He'd been hiding out in this tiny, whitewashed cottage for almost a week. The only contact he had with the world was through Chris Rassool, who insisted that he call in once a day. Otherwise he was alone, cocooned in a bewilderingly sudden silence. And he found himself awash with memories.

He remembered the journey from England all those months ago, the beginning of the journey that had brought him here. He remembered an English runway slick with rain, the lights out in the cabin, the hum of air-conditioning and dulled engines and the gleaming water reflecting the lights of the runways and terminal buildings. It was so vivid. He was going home. It was a moment so huge it was impossible to grasp the largeness of it, impossible to reach around it and *feel*. Instead it was almost bland, just another night, another plane journey, but he'd kept waiting for it to feel like something bigger.

There was a lot of turbulence during the flight. James had knocked himself out with half a bottle of wine and two sleeping pills. He'd slept for a long time, though it was restless sleep. He woke as the rattle of breakfast service began. Outside, far below, there was a landscape as white as ice. Namibia. It changed gradually to paprika red, to deep rust and then again to the whiteness of desert.

Twenty minutes from Johannesburg he kept grasping for a sense of the weight of the moment, wanting to feel the meaning of it. He was coming back after twenty-eight years, coming back a stranger, with a strange accent and strange ways. He felt bleary with tiredness and yet he was pumping with excitement. And there it was. Plain, ugly Johannesburg swathed in its brown blanket of air pollution, its two hypodermic-needle towers spiking the sky. He felt nothing.

James went outside to stand in the last rays of the afternoon sun. The hills were velvet brown edged with golden grasses. There was a gentle wind blowing. The sounds of the garden were the sounds of wind rustling through leaves and of turtledoves – that lovely throaty, pulsing sound.

The cottage belonged to Ilse McLean's family. She'd given him the key and hastily scribbled directions on that awful, rainy night in Johannesburg. It was a simple squat building, made from rough-hewn stone. The outside walls were whitewashed and the roof was painted brick-red with blotches of silvery tin showing through. Inside it was cold. The stone walls kept the place as cool as a fridge. James had to sit right up close to the fire to feel its warmth.

Like so many South African towns, even years after the end of apartheid, Rosendal was divided in half by the main road that ran through it. To the right-hand side was the black township, the huddle of shacks illuminated by tall, powerful street lamps. To the left was the white village, little stone cottages spread out on large plots, dominated by the spire of an enormous sandstone church. The clocks on the steeple had stopped at half past two.

The place had died almost a hundred years before when its elders, in their wisdom, refused to allow the railway line to come through, believing it would bring chaos and sin to their peaceful dorp. Nor would they allow a movie theatre years later. Now only the old and the infirm remained.

It was the perfect place to hide out.

And the strangest place for the realisation that James had woken up to that very morning. It might have come from a dream that had threaded into waking, James wasn't sure. But the feeling was a powerful one of being connected to a long history. He'd woken full of a sense of people and places he'd believed were lost to him. It was as if he was wrapped up in tissues of memory, as if he were bandaging up all the pieces of himself that were scattered all over the world, pulling them back together in a way that no longer felt fragmented and sore. And suddenly he knew. He'd come home. He'd expected epiphanies to arrive with trumpets and drum rolls, but it didn't. It was the quietest, surest thing.

And it had stayed with him all day; even now it swelled up in him on a surge of emotion as he stared out at the darkening sky. Life gets murkier and harder as you get older, he thought. He'd always thought it would be the other way round. He remembered standing in the family kitchen in England, smarting after a terrible fight with his parents, staring out at the cold and longing, just bursting for a time when he wouldn't be trapped there, when he could get out into the world, powerfully grown up and ready to make his own destiny. It seemed so clear and simple then. But there was wonder in the complexity and the mystery, a kind of wonder that excited him.

Back in Johannesburg, someone had tried to kill him. He was still shaken by the proximity of death that night, lurking in shadows, flying so close, whacking into the walls instead of into his flesh. It was a matter of randomness, of sheer chance, that he'd survived. But he had. And being alive was fantastic.

It didn't matter that he'd canned his story. There would be others. What he was thinking about now was something larger, something more important. It had to do with who he'd become and who he wanted to be in this new-found home of his in South Africa.

For years he'd had the freedom to slide on the surface of things, of places, of people, but now he couldn't. Home brought with it responsibilities; there were obligations that came hand in hand with belonging. Home required things of you. What it required of him was not yet clear and James knew that this grasping for an answer was the easy part and that the trick would be having the courage to implement it.

But there was time for that. There was time for everything now. Perhaps even for him and Anna. If she'd give him a chance. It was all too easy to deal with people, with *subjects*, at a distance. To rush in and out of people's lives and steal their pain and their triumphs for the front page when a day later you were gone and they were disappearing fast in the rear-view mirror. Anna had brought him up short; she hadn't allowed him to do that.

If there was one good thing he would do for himself, when he got out of this mess, it would be to call Anna and beg her to at least go out for dinner with him. As for Alison, that was over. He'd rather be alone than revisit the site of that train-smash.

It was dark by the time James went inside, put more logs on the fire and opened a bottle of wine. He poured himself a glass and sat down to drink it in the now warm living room. He was thinking about what to have for supper when he heard a car passing by. Then it stopped.

James stood up, listening. Someone was at the gate; he heard the creak and scratch of the bolt. He reached up and switched off the light. Now he was in darkness but for the fire. Other than the chirping of crickets and the distant barking of dogs, there was utter silence.

This is it, he thought. They've got me. An icy calm numbed his fear, narrowed everything in to the moment and escape.

He picked up the torch from the kitchen and quietly let himself out through the back door. He walked slowly into the garden, feeling his way round the side of the house until he had a clear view towards the gate and the dark shape of a car in front of it. He flipped on the torch and swung the beam across the garden.

It landed on a terrified face, eyes wide and arms up defensively. 'Anna?'

She squinted into the bright light, unable to see him. 'James?' she called out anxiously. He lowered the torch and strode over, grabbing hold of her arm to make sure it really was her.

thirty-six

Anna could hardly believe it when she found herself in a bright, warm country kitchen with James before her. He was still shaken from the surprise of her arrival, but at least he was here. And safe. 'Shew, this place is like a ghost town, there's not a light on in the entire dorp,' she said as she dumped her bags on the kitchen table. Like James, she hadn't packed much in her hurry to get out of Joburg.

'People go to bed early.' James turned the key in the inside lock and shot a huge bolt across the blue door. 'How did you find me?' He looked at her warily.

During the lonely hours of the long drive into the Free State, Anna had pictured him as her saviour, her sanctuary. But now the distance between them felt immense. Weariness overwhelmed her. She sank into one of the kitchen chairs. 'What do you think I am?' she replied sarcastically, trying to be light and not quite succeeding. 'I tracked down everyone you know. Squeezed them till they talked.'

James leaned against the door, eyes narrowing. 'Ilse,' he said. Anna nodded. Of course it was Ilse.

Anna had driven to James's office straight from the airport, too scared to go home, not knowing what to do; terrified that Joe would find her. She'd looked everywhere for James, at his office, his house, in all the Melville bars. And then she'd remembered Ilse McLean. And she found Ilse, heaven be praised, in her office at the SABC.

James folded his arms over his chest. He looked tired, but well. He had a few days' growth of stubble on his chin and his clothes looked like they'd been lived in for just as long. 'You okay?' she asked.

He smiled at last as he nodded a yes. 'I'm great, actually. What about you?'

She shivered, pulling her jacket around her. For some reason she couldn't meet his gaze. 'Not good,' she mumbled. 'Not good at all.' She felt her throat closing on tears. She hadn't cried. Hadn't told anyone at all. She'd sat with the horrible secret for hours while it churned around in her brain, spreading its poisonous questions and doubts and fears.

James came over to her and put his hand on her arm, more gently than he'd done outside just a few minutes ago. 'Why don't we go sit by the fire,' he suggested kindly. 'It's warmer there.'

She let him help her up and guide her into the next room where a fire was burning and a warm sofa awaited. James poured her a glass of wine from the bottle on the mantelpiece. She took a sip and it made her feel better. After a few more she felt warm, and calmer. James watched her, standing against the fireplace with his back to the flames.

'I found Paul's Handler,' she said at last.

James tilted his head to one side, eyebrows raised questioningly. Anna ran a hand back through her hair.

'It was Joe.'

James froze with astonishment. It seemed like an age before he reacted. 'Oh, Anna. I'm so sorry.' He sat down beside her and put his arms around her, pulling her to him. Her body felt stiff with all the grief and shock it was holding in. 'I'm so, so sorry,' he murmured.

Then she told him about the trip to Pietersburg, about meeting Sherry Nel and seeing the newspaper clipping of Joe. By the time she was finished Anna was exhausted, all her nerve endings raw.

James was quiet, staring into the flames. 'I think it was Joe who took a shot at me,' he said at length.

Anna let out a strange, breathy laugh. 'It wouldn't surprise me. Nothing can surprise me now.'

'The thing I wouldn't tell you the other night,' he said slowly. 'It was about Joe.'

Anna nodded weakly. 'I thought so,' she sighed.

'I don't know how, but he's seriously involved with the

Angolans, the rivals to Bazooka's gang. I'm sure of it. In fact now I'm beginning to think it might be Joe who's running it.'

Anna was too weary to ask him to elaborate. And after today anything was possible.

'I've got to talk to Frans Nel. Will you come with me?'

'Yeah. Tomorrow?'

Anna nodded. 'Ja. Tomorrow. Funny. He's had all the answers all along. And I knew it, but I didn't. I didn't know anything.'

James reached down and poured more wine into the glass. He took a long drink before he spoke again. 'I've been thinking a lot about you. Since I've been here.'

She looked up. 'What have you been thinking?'

'That I let you down. In the way that Paul did. And now Joe too.' He shook his head. 'I mean, not on the same scale, but there's stuff I knew that I should have told you.'

She shook her head, which was the only way she knew to say that it was fine, that it didn't matter now. Then he took her hand, laid it on his leg and ran his fingers along her palm, linked his fingers through hers. And she knew then that she was falling in love with him. The realisation was terrifying. Love was potential loss, fear of loss, inevitable loss. Love was loss. But she didn't have a choice in the matter. She let her head rest against his shoulder, melting into the warmth of his arm around her and falling into sleep.

Anna woke up around four and found herself alone on the sofa. He'd covered her with several blankets and put a cushion underneath her head. She smiled and listened to the house creaking and the crickets cricking outside and the smouldering logs still crackling in the hearth and she felt safe.

thirty-seven

They drove out of Rosendal at dawn. Anna saw the cottage and the dorp properly for the first time in the early morning light. Overgrown gardens bloomed with roses and dandelions the size of fists. It was beautiful, but that morning everything had the character of hallucination. Lines were too sharp, colours too sickly, light too bright.

A restless wind was blowing, tugging at the line of poplars along a boundary fence. The leaves were brilliant gold and they shimmered like tinsel in the warm spring sun. The colours of the earth were yellows and oranges and bloody, brown reds. In the far distance the mountains of Lesotho were lilac-tinged against a blue sky. The sky was immense, like the landscape that curved close against it.

The road was in poor condition, riddled with potholes as that expressive Afrikaans word, 'slaggaate', warned on the signs. The warning felt appropriate for the day ahead. It would take a few hours to reach Pietermaritzburg. Anna feared that Joe would get to Nel first, that they'd arrive to find yet another corpse.

She knew that if the news ever got out that Joe had been an apartheid spy the scandal would be disastrous. Not just for him either. It would ripple all around the department and cause big waves in political circles. It would cast doubt on the people around him and reinforce tension between the old and the new guard in the police. Worst of all it would cast doubt on the efficacy of the government's fight against crime, organised crime in particular. For Joe it would be the end of a dazzling career. And there was no way he would allow that.

Approaching Harrismith the landscape began to change.

They'd left the koppies and wide brown plains of the Free State behind and were skirting the top end of the Drakensburg Mountains. Enormous flat-topped mesas were majestic in the morning light.

James glanced over at Anna as they passed the sign for the N3 and Maritzburg and Durban. She smiled back at him and was once again struck by his beauty. He was unshaven, tired, dressed in the clothes she'd found him in the night before and he smelt of wood-smoke. Yet he seemed so familiar. She couldn't account for it.

They were now travelling into the lush subtropics of Kwa Zulu Natal, past rounded hills speckled with lush green vegetation, through deep valleys and winding steep passes. They could feel the moisture in the air. Kwa Zulu was a province where the British had left an indelible imprint on the architecture and culture, Anna reflected. Pietermaritzburg was a part Victorian, part modern city in a bowl in the hills. The Brits must have done something to the weather there too. It was misty and raining a little when they drove into the town at around half past nine. Anna failed to understand the fascination the place held for people who'd lived or studied there. They always fell in love with it, but Anna had never shared the attraction. It was always drizzling when she visited Maritzburg.

It was a Saturday morning, so the city centre was quiet. They drove straight to Police Headquarters on Loop Street; there was a good chance, being Saturday, that the man she still called the Captain would be at home, but they decided to try his office first. The SAPS building was an ugly modern one, several storeys high and heavily fortified. They parked at a meter. Anna looked around for signs of Joe, but there were none. So far.

'You ready?' James asked quietly. She nodded. Then she took a deep breath and jumped. Out of the car, across the street and into the building. Anna's Secretariat pass smoothed the way for them. A young warrant officer at the front desk told them they were in luck. 'Brigadier Nel has only just gone upstairs. He should be in his office. Would you like me to show you the way?'

Anna shook her head. 'No, thanks. I know where it is.'

Frans Nel was sitting behind his desk, cigarette smoke spooling out from his raised hand as he flicked through a manila-covered docket. He was a picture of comfortable composure. He could have been a nightclub owner or a minor celebrity, such was the arrogance and ease of his pose. Then he looked up and saw Anna and James. He scowled, caught off-guard, but only momentarily. He recovered very quickly. 'Anna!' He beamed, as if she was an old friend. 'Well, this is a surprise!' He stood up, knocking his chair so it rolled on its castors and crashed against the radiator. He ignored the sound as he came towards her, his hand outstretched.

Nel was dressed for leisure in a white shell-suit with purple and green stripes. He positively clanked with jewellery. There were signet rings on his fingers, chunky gold bracelets, and a thick gold chain around his neck. Anna declined to shake his hand, putting both of hers behind her back. 'How are you, Brigadier?' she said acidly. 'This is James Kay, a journalist from the *Sunday Chronicle*.'

'Oh. Pleased to meet you, Mr Kay.' He smiled toothily and reached for James's hand. James allowed the most cursory of handshakes. 'Well, what a surprise!' Nel repeated, looking anxiously from Anna to James and back again.

'We've come to talk to you about Joe,' Anna said.

Nel froze. Like a dog startled in the headlights of a car.

'We have a witness who will testify to the identity of Paul Lewis's Handler.'

Nel gave an oily little laugh. 'Oh, I doubt that, Anna.'

'I think you know Sherry?' Anna replied sharply.

And suddenly he knew the game was over. The transformation was horrible. It was like a plastic doll melting under a flame, like a mask dripping grotesquely off a face. When he spoke again all his heartiness was gone and he sounded tired. Resigned.

'Why don't we go across the street for a cup of tea?' He looked around the room and Anna understood that he didn't want to talk there, that someone might be listening. It would be better to go somewhere neutral. Somewhere public.

'Sure,' Anna said pleasantly. 'A cup of tea would be nice.'

Nel's fingers fumbled with the keys as he locked his office. They rode the lift in tense silence and crossed the street to the Imperial Hotel, a graceful old building that was part of the city's colonial heritage. They sat at the bar near the ground-floor atrium. A pianist tinkled contemporary classics on a baby grand in the corner. A waiter in smart uniform and startlingly white gloves asked if they would like to order refreshments. The Brigadier ordered a double brandy. Then he cleared his throat, rubbing his hands together as he attempted a smile. 'Now, this is a bit more conducive.'

James took out his tape recorder, pressed play and put it down on the bar. Nel looked down at it as the spools began to turn.

The brandy arrived and he downed it in one. Anna watched the jiggle of his Adam's apple as he swallowed gulp after burning gulp. She wondered if he'd lied about his sobriety at the amnesty hearing. Or if he'd just fallen off the wagon. He lit a cigarette and met her stare, his eyes narrowed to dark slits. 'I know you hate me,' he said bitterly, 'but *I'm* not the one.'

'So who is?' she said steadily.

The Captain laughed sourly and ordered another drink, the same again, apparently intent on obliterating the sharp edges of the situation. He drained that one too and launched into his story.

'Nineteen eighty-seven. Joe Dladla was a Captain then, like me, and like you say, he was Paul's Handler. Paul worked with my unit, but he reported to Joe. Don't ask me who Joe reported to – I think it was the guys in Section A, but I never knew. That was the way it worked in those days. Need to know. I didn't need to know who Joe reported to, so I didn't.'

James sat quite still, only his eyes darting now to the Brigadier, now to the cassette player. Anna listened, as with Sherry Nel, as if she were some kind of vessel for the words to be poured into. 'So, me and Joe were technically the same rank, except that I was a straight Security Policeman and Joe was an agent, a double agent. That made him my senior on the operation. It was Joe who planned it and who gave the orders.'

'Which orders?' Anna interrupted.

'To kill Lewis and Oliphant.'

Silence. The room seemed to spin around them, like a kaleidoscope, a drunken vortex of colours. Nel lit a cigarette off the one that was in his mouth. 'Well, now you've got your truth,' he said.

'Yes, now I've got my truth,' Anna repeated.

And the truth was more awful and more familiar than she cared to know. The truth was no acid pellet of knowledge delivered to the Commission for sanitising and sealing and disposing in the dustbin of history. It was a dull mirror, which showed the dirt that clung to everyone, instead of cleansing and absolving all.

'Tell me what happened. That night.'

His eyes were like those of an animal in pain.

'How did Paul die?'

Nel held his head in his hand, his cigarette burning between his fingers. 'We drove to Mafikeng ahead of Oliphant and Lewis, just me and Joe. We checked into a motel and waited, like I've said before. I was scared. I'd never done something like this before. And I knew Paul, he'd been to my house, we'd been friends. We'd had our differences, but in my books that was no reason to kill him.'

Nel sucked hard on his cigarette. 'I'd been drinking heavily that day. I had a couple of bottles in my bag and I was trying to keep it from Joe, I dunno if he could tell or not. Sometimes it's hard to know what he's thinking. Anyhow, by the time we left that motel I was vrot. I mean – I was *gone*.'

Anna felt James's eyes on her and she was glad he was there, however distorted and fever-like everything felt. Details stuck out, like the dark hairs sticking out of the Brigadier's nostrils and the gravelly tone of his voice. 'Joe drove and we picked up the targets on the Vryburg road, trailing them at a distance. We were looking for somewhere quiet, a remote stretch of road where we could do the job without any fear of interruption. All I wanted was to get it over with and I suggested a few places before Joe decided on the right spot to pull them over.

'It was dark – there were no lights on the road. We were the only two cars. When we came up behind, Paul was driving and they tried to get away, but that car didn't have a chance. We could out-drive them easy. So we pushed them over, drew up alongside them and nudged them off the road.

'The plan was to shoot the guys dead and burn the bodies in their car. Easy. Not the first time I've done that, but the first time it was someone I knew. When we pulled Paul over I couldn't move. My legs just would not move. I was that drunk and that scared. So it was Joe who got out of the car and went over to them. I remember he had his pistol drawn, a Makarov so it wouldn't be traceable. I was so far gone I have to tell you that I can't remember a whole helluva lot of detail, but I remember that it was fast. He got the guys out the car, hands up, the whole toot.' Nell illustrated this by raising his hands as Jacob and Paul had done. 'I don't think there was much conversation, there wasn't time. Joe wasn't messing around. One thing I do remember is that Oliphant was laughing – he didn't seem to know what was going on, maybe he thought it was a joke.'

Anna closed her eyes. She didn't have to try to imagine. The pictures came to her so vividly it was as if she were there, hearing the clap and gurgle of Jacob's laughter.

'Then Joe jabbed the pistol in his back and he wasn't laughing any more. Marched them both over to the bushes and then fired. Jacob went down like a sack of potatoes.' Anna saw Paul's bewilderment and sudden fear. 'Paul wasn't laughing. He was quiet. Never saw him so quiet. He looked dangerous to me. I was fuckin' poeping myself. Joe levelled the Makarov, getting ready to fire again when Paul turned and just went for him. By the time I got myself out the car they were down on the ground and I swear I had no idea who was who. Two shots went off and still they were fighting. Then somehow Joe got on top of him, got the gun up against Paul's chest and another shot rang out and it was all over.'

Anna imagined the tangle of those two bodies, those men she knew so well, who'd loved each other so well, engaged in a fight to the death. Blood and sweat and rage. The kind of rage that kills. She couldn't imagine that.

She opened her eyes. Before her was Nel, slugging back yet another double brandy. And James. And somewhere close by the piano played something old and familiar. She had lived so close to the truth for so long. It had seemed so impenetrable and now it was as easy as sitting down to tea in the Imperial Hotel with Frans Nel.

Of course it wasn't so simple. The moment had come. Structurally, when the pressure is right and is properly applied in the correct place, the building collapses.

'Did he die immediately?'

Nel shook his head. 'It took a little while. Maybe ten minutes. I could see that much from the way the body moved.'

Nel's tone grew more and more vicious as he talked, as he spat the truth at her, taking pleasure in proving her wrong. He wasn't the bad guy. He'd been carrying it for Joe all these years. He was the wrongly accused putting the story right at last.

'Joe poured a bit of petrol around the scene, but not enough to burn it clean, just enough to leave some doubt. Then he got in the car and drove us back to Mafikeng. I passed out, woke up in a parking space at the motel. Joe was gone.'

'Why?' Anna asked, her tone thin as a razor.

Nel looked into the bottom of his glass. He looked like he might cry: his face was a mess. 'You see, what happened to Paul is that he changed. All that stuff he was spouting about the struggle and the liberation movements, et cetera, et cetera. It went to his head. The reason Paul was going to Vryburg was to hand himself over to the ANC. Jacob didn't know the first thing about it. He just thought they were on a regular operation. He had no idea what was coming.'

The room seemed to come back into focus. Anna's eyes were wide and for the first time during the conversation she wanted to cry. Just when there seemed to be no room left for amazement, she was amazed.

'One of the senior people from Lusaka was making a secret visit,' Nel explained. 'We were watching him all the time of course, but for whatever reason, Headquarters didn't want us picking him up. Paul was going to hand himself over and tell them everything. They would take him out of the country, debrief him and use him against us. Joe wouldn't have that. That would have been the end of him.' Nel drained his glass again. 'Jacob Oliphant was just in the wrong place at the wrong time.'

At last Anna understood Paul's note on the shower curtain: 'There is no fear in love; but perfect love casteth out fear.' And his depression and weird excitement the night before that day. There was a piece of Paul that really had been hers all along. Some of her faith in him and in herself was restored.

'What happened during that last detention? Why did you pull him in?'

Nel flicked ash onto the floor. 'To provide cover. And to kak

302

him out. We knew what was going on with him. It had been coming for a long time.'

'But he told me a story. About a limpet mine detonator?'

Nel shook his head, making a face. He didn't understand.

'He told me that you set off a limpet mine detonator, during an interrogation, like a test.'

Nel scowled, still shaking his head. 'Ag no. No. That wasn't Paul. That was some Indian guy. I told Paul that story. Shit. It was a youngster. ANC military. We had that guy in for a long stretch around that time. Fuck, that was one crazy guy.'

Pieces falling into place. The picture in the puzzle becoming clearer. Anna ran her fingers back and forth across her forehead, an unconscious, distracted movement as she listened. 'Paul was in bad shape that time. I didn't think he'd make it, and that was fine by me then. That's the truth. If he'd just hung himself or jumped out the fuckin' window ... There were days when I wanted him to do that.'

James interrupted the silence that followed. It was the first time he'd spoken in hours. 'Do you have any idea why Joe Dladla became a policeman?' The tape rolled round.

Nel shrugged. 'He's a complicated man, Joe. Don't ask me to explain. I've never understood him. He plays a different game to the rest of us. But I've always believed that he's a good guy at heart. He was a brave fighter. Fearless, ruthless. When things started changing he was one of the first to see it. He believes in the new South Africa. He made *me* believe.'

'Was it him who suggested you apply for amnesty for the murders?' Anna asked.

Nel laughed bitterly. 'That's one way of putting it,' he snorted. 'He wanted to put a lid on the thing. Stop you investigating. I mean, the Truth Commission investigations people couldn't find a Castle in a brewery; they weren't going to get anywhere. You were the problem.'

Nel was drunk and suddenly realised it. He stood up, swaying dangerously. 'So that's the truth. The whole truth and nothing but the truth,' he slurred. He swayed, turned white and slimy with sweat and then vomited, a stream of brandy-coloured spew jetting from his mouth and splattering over the bar and floor.

And it was at that moment Joe appeared. Anna looked up to

see him standing in the atrium, light shining down on him through the glass dome. Nel saw him too and his knees buckled. He swayed a little too far forward, then just too far back. James caught him and dragged him, still retching and spitting, out towards the toilets.

Anna looked down at the stinking brandy bile slopped onto her shoes. Then she looked up at Joe. She didn't know what to do. She felt soiled by him. Contaminated.

He looked up into the light, and then he turned on his heels and strode out through the lobby.

thirty-eight

Anna flew from the hotel, the vomit splashed on her shoes and up her jeans. She caught up with Joe on the street, less than a block away. He wasn't trying to run. He was walking away with his head down and his hands in his pockets. She raced towards him, grabbing him violently as she came up alongside. The momentum of her running and pulling at him spun both of them round. At last they were face to face.

Confrontation with Paul's killer was something Anna had rehearsed over and over in her mind, but to a script that didn't fit this scene. Nothing fitted. How to describe the feeling of disorientation? Later, when asked, Anna couldn't articulate it. It was so many feelings. Her heart like a hammer inside a chest so tight it felt it had to burst. Her mind reeling like the swirl of colour and noise seen from a roundabout in a drunken fairground visit. She didn't want to know this and yet knowing it was like knowing the blade that enters your chest in that space between your ribs. Part of you now.

She had no idea what to say. She didn't even open her mouth. She just stood there on the pavement, legs apart, eyes wild. People strolled around them – couples, families with babies in pushchairs, old ladies with shopping, and a group of blue and white robed Zionist Christians with crosses to bear.

She wondered if he had any idea, if he ever thought of the price they'd paid for whatever it was he wanted. The price that she and Rachel and the children, not to mention Paul and Jacob, paid for him?

Joe glared back at her. 'Happy now, Anna?' She shook her head. Tears welled up but she swallowed them down, she wouldn't let them come, not in front of him. 'You?' She flung the question back at him.

He stuck his chin out defiantly. Then he laughed. A horrible sound, a cruel explosion of self-pity and bitterness and rage all rolled into one.

'Why couldn't you just leave it alone?'

Anna took a step towards him, to be close enough to observe the set of his mouth and the look in his eyes. She felt the cold weight of her gun in her jacket pocket.

Joe saw the shape and flinched. 'You want me to explain, don't you? You want me to tell you why.'

'Do you think you can?' She spat it back at him, but there was also a quiver of hope in there, a crazy ribbon of optimism and need that thought perhaps he would be able to explain. That there would be a credible, logical answer and somehow it would all be all right.

He looked up and down the street. There was movement and sound and colour around them, but it was just that. There was nothing else that was sharp, that mattered, but the two of them and that stretch of concrete pavement between them.

Anna slipped her hand inside her pocket and closed around the Beretta, because she needed to hold onto something. He saw the movement and understood. Or he thought he did.

'And what about *your* culpability, Anna?'

'*Mine?*'

'You saw what you wanted to see. You heard what you wanted to hear. I never lied to you. Not once.'

Anna shook her head, very slowly, the madness, the evil of what Joe was saying hitting her like a hail of birdshot. She knew that she'd seen what was presented to her, what was offered, and she'd not wanted to see behind that, not wanted to see deception. But who the hell would?

'That's not the kind of excuse I expect from you, Joe. That's not good enough.' Words came rasping from her throat like sandpaper, dragged out from deep inside, scraping off flesh. 'Don't pretend you didn't have a choice.'

He started to say something. His hand flew up to his head. The gesture was sudden, but he wasn't reaching for anything. He rubbed his hand over the smoothness of his scalp. He blinked. He had nothing to say.

Anna wanted to kill him in that moment, to strike him, hurt him, break him, humiliate him, and reduce him to the pleading wreck that was Paul on the ground when he pumped the third and last bullet into him. In her imagination she howled and scratched at him with tornado-like violence.

She took her hand from her pocket, holding the Beretta tight and steady. Joe lifted his hands in the air. He didn't look scared; he looked like he was acting the role he deserved. She almost laughed when she realised that was how he was thinking. It was so petty, so ham. She closed both hands around the gun and raised it so it was level with his head, stepping forward to push the cold nose of the .38 Special into the space between his eyes. He flinched for the second time. Just barely. But she saw it. The fear and also the relief.

He closed his eyes. His lashes quivered against his skin, as she'd seen them do so often on the nights she lay beside him, curled up against the warmth of his body. 'Is this what you think you deserve, Joe?' It was almost a whisper. He said nothing. She looked at that face, its supplication, its resignation and crazy heroism. And she knew this was exactly what he wanted. Her finger jerked against the trigger, a tiny spasm, but not a pull. It was just the sensing of it, the possibility of it that she wanted to feel; she wasn't going to shoot him.

She shoved the gun into Joe's raised open palm. His eyes opened in surprise as he took it. And in that moment she knew she'd never known him at all. They were someone else's black eyes staring at her, a stranger. She turned away and walked back towards the hotel.

She was tired; she needed to sit down on that big red sofa in the lobby. Just as long as her feet would carry her there, just as long as exhaustion didn't overwhelm her, take her under. She felt arms around her, she felt her breath heaving hard against someone's warm wool-covered chest.

James.

thirty-nine

Rachel couldn't believe that Anna didn't kill him. She wished him dead. She was lying in her bed, where she'd been since Anna phoned to tell her about Joe. Her kids were with her. Temba quietly brought trays of tea and comforts. Anna sat amidst the blankets and pillows while Rachel clung to her sons, her body wracked with sobs. 'They have to know what their Uncle Joe did to their father. He has to know what he did to them. That fucker has to know!'

Anna cried too, hot silent tears coursing down her cheeks. Joe had disappeared. His phone was cut off, there was no one at his apartment and he'd not returned to his office. Rachel had looked for him everywhere, dragging her children around with her. Raging, weeping, banging on the door. But he'd run away. 'Maybe he'll do the job for us and kill himself,' she cried. Anna shook her head, she didn't think so. Joe was not a suicide.

Willem Swanepoel was more shocked by the news of Joe's betrayal than he had been by that of Paul's. It took him some time to recover after Anna broke it to him. 'So,' he said heavily, 'the past comes back to sabotage the present again.'

He went round to the house later on, to see them all and to discuss a possible legal course of action against Joe. Joe had not applied for amnesty for the Mafikeng Road Murders and the application deadline was long past. They could take legal action against him. Willem felt there was an important political and judicial point to be made out of the case. But Anna had balked at the idea of a court case and the pain of going over it all again. Rachel just wanted revenge. She wanted Joe to hurt as much as she hurt.

All three felt a powerful desire to apportion blame. There had to be a cause, something they could point to as an incontestable, unequivocal reason for what had happened. But of course there wasn't really any such thing. The truth had a complex of causes and the blame was too widespread to be meaningful.

So they'd dropped the idea of a case against Joe.

Rachel was railing against the injustice of it all. 'Does it help you to know the truth?' She sniffled into her tissue, looking at Anna with more than a hint of accusation. Her eyes were red-rimmed and swollen and bloodshot.

'I'm not sure,' Anna answered, looking down at the bedspread and its swirls of flowers. 'At least there are no shadows any more.'

Rachel snorted. 'You're telling me.'

'All I know is I want to live in the present. I'll settle for nothing less than what is real.'

'How do you know what's real and what isn't?'

Anna smiled wryly. 'I'm planning to think about that. A lot.'

And at last Rachel laughed. Only a little, but it was definitely a laugh. It was Bram who said the words that got her out of bed. 'Daddy's dead, but he's still a hero. And you've got us and we've got Temba now.' Rachel looked at her son with fresh tears in her eyes. Then she kissed him on the forehead and sat up. 'I should think about making supper,' she said and she hauled herself out from under the covers.

Anna stood with her at the end of the garden, looking out across their city. What did Paul's voice sound like? Anna wondered. Was it gravel? Glass? Ice? Water? Wind? Music? Anna had lost him, she couldn't remember. But at least she truly knew him now.

She knew that the last detention had finally prised open his divided loyalties. Had exploded his split self and left him in a no man's land, longing to be on the right side. At least in the end he knew which the right side was.

Anna slipped her arm through Rachel's. The moment was laden with memory, but with a sense of the future too. 'You know,' she said, 'I feel so excited, I don't know where the feeling's come from, but it's bursting out of me.'

Rachel looked into her friend's eyes. 'It's the future.' Yes, it was *her* future. She had restored it to herself.

The stars came out. And there it was, the Southern Cross with its four bright pointers and the dust cloud in the middle clearly visible. The Coal Sack.

The next day was a Saturday. Anna wandered down Seventh Street enjoying the spring morning, enjoying the idleness of it. Passing a florist, the soft, musky scent of roses caught her and she turned back and went inside to buy herself an armful of the richest red blooms. She couldn't remember the last time she'd had flowers in the house.

Anna was filling vases at the sink, lost in the fragrance and colours of the roses, when the doorbell rang. She wasn't expecting anyone and she didn't much feel like conversation, but after a short debate she went to answer it.

It was James. She smiled, leaning against the doorpost. He said nothing as he put his arms around her, gently, like a lover. Her body felt like a flower opening towards the sun, fragile and vulnerable, but robustly loved.

James moved his face towards hers, as if to kiss her, but Anna stopped him with her fingers over his mouth. 'Hey, I'm seriously out of practice on the kissing thing,' she murmured breathlessly.

James laughed, his eyes narrowing just slightly. 'No problem,' he said and he took her hands in his, playing with her fingers, rolling them over and examining her palms. 'I have a special offer on this week. A fifty per cent discount on kissing for beginners, but you have to start now.' Anna looked down at her hands, which were locking and unlocking in his. She could feel the heat of his gaze.

'First, you look at me,' he went on quietly.

She did.

'Then our faces move closer.' He spoke softly and without a flicker of jest now. Anna's breath caught in her throat.

'Then our noses touch.' His voice dropped to a whisper as he rubbed his nose against hers, the silkiest, simplest sensation. His mouth was a fraction open, a little closer, and she could feel his breath on her skin. His lips curved upwards into the slightest smile as he said, 'You see, it's all in the moment *before* the lips touch.'

And she smiled and their lips touched, lightly at first, then harder and with more heat until they were lost in one another.

part eight

What's past is prologue
WILLIAM SHAKESPEARE

forty

Spring had come and jacaranda trees were in bloom all over the city. From a distance they were clouds of indigo, up close they arched over you like a magical, blue heaven. October in London sets the trees on fire, but in Johannesburg they turn a different shade entirely and colour the city with the blue of deep distance. The streets of Melville were carpeted in purple.

That week the TV weatherman stood in front of a map that was red and orange and yellow, outlining the bands of heat moving across the country. The radio warned of dangerously high temperatures. The whole country was caught in the grip of the heatwave, left panting and sweltering and clinging to shade.

James strolled into the office dripping with sweat and longing for the cool of an air-conditioner, but there was no such luxury at the *Sunday Chronicle*. He'd be lucky if he managed to commandeer one of the old fans that lay around the place in various states of disrepair.

'James!' Someone squawked his name as he picked his way across the newsroom. He turned to see Ilse McLean bouncing towards him. 'How're you, baby?'

He laughed helplessly as she leapt up and flung her arms round him. 'I'm fine. I'm fine. But you look *great*.' She really did. She'd put on a little weight and there was colour in her cheeks that didn't come from a make-up case.

'I'm here for a job interview.' James looked surprised. 'I quit the Truth Commission. Couldn't take it any more. Need to move on,' she smiled.

Chris Rassool ambled up behind her. 'Morning, Jim,' he

winked and then turned to Ilse. 'Why don't we do this the civilised way and go out for a coffee?' he beamed.

James sat down at his desk and looked at the heaps of junk that covered it. Time for a clean-out. He called Alison first. She sounded better, but she still took it hard. He felt sad for her, but sure that they were wrong for each other. Probably had been all along.

'You sound different,' she said. 'Happy.'

'Yeah. I guess I am.' The truth was James felt elated by the connection he'd made with Anna. He literally tingled with the delicious shock of meeting and being met. It was an affinity like none he'd felt before. It scared him a little, but that was part of the exhilaration of being with her. He loved Anna for her forthrightness, her integrity, her gentleness, her innocence – for the power and vulnerability that co-existed in her in such a raw mix. Most of all he loved her for the sure, wild gift she'd made of herself.

He picked up the phone, about to call and tell her that, when Chris's assistant popped her head into his cube. She slapped a pink message slip on top of a pile. 'Chris says you've got to do it. He's *busy*.' James smiled; I'll bet he is.

A body had been found in Hillbrow. From the urgent tone of the message it sounded like someone well known. James grabbed Guy Donaldson from the picture desk and they headed over there together.

Approaching the cordoned-off area at the far end of Banket Street, James had a terrible premonition. He broke into a run, pushing through the cops and bystanders to get to the scene. The blood-soaked corpse was sprawled in a corner of Joburg's rubbish heap, arms above his head, legs pulled up to his chest, as if he was curling into himself in those last seconds of his life.

It was Joe Dladla.

Killed by a single bullet to the back of the head. He'd been executed. If this new democracy had failed to clear out all the corruption at least there was a kind of justice in the criminal world Joe came from. In the end it took him back into its bloody embrace, meting out its punishment with a simplicity and a savagery that seemed appropriate.

forty-one

Anna dreamed of Paul again. It was that old dream. As always they'd found each other at sea, in a storm so violent Anna could barely distinguish between the water and the air. He was waiting for her on a larger craft, which Anna boarded easily, despite the heaving sea. He was sitting in the same chair wrapped in the same old sleeping bag, which he shed as he stood up to greet her. They didn't embrace this time; they stood at arm's length apart in the rolling cabin.

'It's time for me to go,' he said.

Anna nodded; this was something she already knew. It was to be their final leave-taking.

'I'm sorry, Anna. I let you down. I let us all down.'

'In the end it was yourself you betrayed.' She struggled for words, choking on tears. 'I do love you, Paul, I will always love you,' she said.

Then someone came to take him away.

Anna woke up crying and certain that she would never dream of him again. She felt like an accident victim coming round in hospital. Aching and bewildered, but alive. It was over. She went to the bathroom where she sat on the rug in the middle of the floor and wept until there were no tears left. Then she took a long hot shower and her skin felt new and lovely under the jets of water.

It was the day of Joe's funeral. James was still asleep, sprawled face down on her bed. Anna pulled on the dark linen dress she had bought for the occasion and went to make coffee.

James found her in the living room, staring out at the garden, the coffee cold in her hand. 'Does this mean that everything was for nothing?' she asked sadly. 'That there was really no difference between them and us?'

'Of course not,' James shot back emphatically. 'Look at your Minister, look at you. There were good people in the struggle who did what they did because they believed in justice, not because they wanted power or whatever it was that Joe wanted.' Anna knew that, but she felt contaminated by the lies that had surrounded her for so long. 'Good guys have always been infiltrated and corrupted by the bad,' James continued. 'Always have been, always will be. And it's crucial not to lose sight of that.' He put his arm round her. 'Perhaps more crucial now than ever because it's people like you who will conquer the corrupt and the venal, otherwise the struggle *is* lost. These battles are as old as time, they never end.' She nodded. Knowing that what he said was true, but feeling sad all the same. He took the empty coffee cup from her fingers, put it down on the windowsill and led her back to bed.

James made love to her entire body, his mouth and fingers testing, touching, caressing every cell of her being. He made love to her with his eyes open, sometimes smiling, sometimes serious, but always lost in the dance.

Afterwards Anna searched for her dress and found it creased up in a ball on the floor. James took it from her and laid it out on the ironing board near the window.

'What are you doing?' she cried.

'What does it look like?' he grinned.

Anna sat on the edge of the bed in her underwear and grinned back. 'Aish. Now I know I've seen everything. A *man*. A *white* man nogal. Ironing *my* dress!'

James was precise and efficient and completely absorbed as he stood naked at the board. There was something in the care with which he worked that moved her utterly. And when he was finished he brought the freshly pressed dress over and helped her slip into it, gently pulling up the long zip at the back.

He didn't want to let go of her, but she managed to pull herself away and climb into the car, rolling her window down so she could kiss him once more. 'Will you be okay?' He seemed anxious for her. She nodded, not sure at all. Then she drove away, the scent of him still clinging to her.

Willem and Rika Swanepoel held hands at the graveside. Anna stood a little apart from them and the small group of cops who'd turned up. Rachel had refused to come. She wouldn't dignify him with a proper burial. It was not how Joe would have wanted it, but nothing had turned out as he'd planned.

Perhaps that was the lesson, Anna thought. Perhaps the terrible lesson of life is that beyond the invincible, powerful time of one's youth there are only moments of happiness punctuated by the periods of shock and reaction as life delivers its blows without warning and with total abandon.

Joe would always remain a puzzle and that was the hardest thing for Anna to grasp. Right and wrong, action and consequence, logic and science, and psychology and explanation – none of them had any power in the face of what he'd done. She simply had to let it go.

She stood in the blistering noon heat, staring down into the dust as the Minister spoke the words that laid Joe to rest.

'Ashes to ashes,' he intoned from underneath a wide black umbrella.

'Dust to dust,' Anna whispered.

Thunderhead clouds blossomed on the horizon. The storm that broke in the afternoon was beautiful. The air was humid and the light steely. The sky was streaked with luminous golden yellow clouds that boiled against a blue that was the colour of shallow water over white sand. Anna drove through first the heat and then the sudden rain and crashing bolts of lightning. When the storm was past and the dust had settled and the sky was clear, the world smelled new.

Anna let herself in through James's front gate and walked into the house. She found him alone in the living room, stretched out on the sofa, a book in his hands. He put it down, smiling. A serious smile. She went over to him and he took her hand and kissed it.

'I love you –' he said.

Anna started, pulling her hand back, but he held on.

'– in that dress,' he finished, grinning impishly.

Then he sat up and put his arms round her. She leaned into him, closing her eyes, feeling his breath on her cheek.

'You know why I love that dress?' he whispered.

She shook her head, her face pressed against his neck. 'Why?' she murmured.

'Because it's easy to iron.'

glossary

AK47 Kalashnikov semi-automatic assault rifle.

ANC African National Congress. The liberation movement founded in 1912, banned in 1960 and then unbanned on 2 February 1990. Oldest political party in South Africa, which came to power after the first multi-racial fully democratic elections in April 1994.

Apartheid Literally 'separateness' in Afrikaans. Official government policy from 1948 to 1990 designed to ensure racial separation at all levels of society.

Bakkie A small pick-up truck.

Balletjies Nickname meaning 'little balls'.

Boerewors Spicy sausage.

Bok, bokkie Buck – a common term of endearment.

Braai A barbecue.

Braaivleis A social gathering at which meat is braaied or barbecued.

Castle Very popular South African lager.

Comrade A young militant activist affiliated to one of the liberation movements.

Contact Term used to describe the moment of contact with the enemy in a bush war.

Dagga Marijuana.

Hardegat Hard-core/stubborn.

Highveld High altitude grassland on inland plateau where Johannesburg is situated.

Jol and jolling A party, or to party.

Karoo The name of a vast semi-desert region of South Africa.

Kaffir Insulting term for black people.

Khakibos A common weed, thought to have been brought by the British during the Anglo-Boer war.

Klap Slap.

Koppie A small hill.

Lekker Literally sweet, but used to mean nice, good or even just to refer to sweets.

Liefie – Term of endearment meaning 'love'.

Makarov Standard issue Eastern Bloc pistol, widely used by liberation movements in Africa supported by Eastern Block countries during the Cold War.

Mandrax A heavy tranquilliser.

Mesa Small mountain.

Moffie Slang for gay man.

MK See Umkhonto we Sizwe.

Nando's South African fast-food outlet.

Nogal – As well.

Oker Bloke

Oros Orangeade.

Plak Mission.

Poeping Shitting.

PAC Pan Africanist Congress, established in 1959 by breakaway Africanist members of the ANC.

Poes Shitty or cunt.

Sonbesie Literally a sunbug. A beetle that makes a continuous high-pitched noise, especially when it's hot.

Sjambok A whipping strap.

Stoep A patio or veranda.

Steers South African fast-food chain.

Stompie A stump or a butt, often refers to the discarded butt of a cigarette.

Shebeen A place where alcohol is sold and consumed, an informal, sometimes illegal, bar.

Struggle Opposition to apartheid comes from 'the struggle to be free'.

Stywepap A local stiff, savoury porridge made from mielie (corn)meal.

Tannie Aunt. Used to refer to older, married woman.

Terrorist or terr White South African slang for Freedom Fighter or guerrilla.

Tsotsis Thugs, small-time criminals, troublemakers. Can be pejorative.

Toyi-toyi A militant and very stirring high-stepping crowd dance. During the struggle it was danced at funerals and protest marches.

Umkhonto we Sizwe Translated literally means Spear of the Nation. It was the name given to the military wing of the African National Congress – often abbreviated to MK.

Vrot Rotten, often used to mean rotten drunk.

Zionist Christian Church (ZCC) Very popular African Christian church whose members wear distinctive blue and green and white robes to weekly rituals.

thank you

To David Ferreira – for everything.

To Ed Victor, Rosie de Courcy and Kirsty Fowkes for believing that one day this book would be finished.

To my family. Particularly to my parents, Ken and Barbara Follett and my sister Kim Turner, Pamela Louw and Foszia Turner-Stylianou.

To David Jammy and Harriet Gavshon who were so generous with their space and time.

To Elize Viljoen for Rosendal.

To Fink Haysom, Wim Trengove, Mark Wale, Antony Altbeker, Anton Harber, Howard Varney, Dipak Patel and Janine Rauch for their expert knowledge and endless patience with my questions.

To Eugene de Kock and Schalk Hugo for trusting a writer.

To Barbara van der Want.

To my colleagues on the Truth Commission Special Report: Max Du Preez, Gael Reagon, Shenid Bayhroo, Benny Motau, Hanné Koster, René Schebie, Linky and Bronwen, and Jacques Pauw.

And to my girlfriends, for their love and insight and incredible support; particular thanks to Nantie Steyn, Sarah Forster, Gillian Kettaneh, Lauren Segal, Nicola Galombik, Anne-Marie Casey, Katty Kay, Solveig Piper, Kim Barlin, Justine O'Reilly, Lesley Cowling, Joanne Richards, Tanya Yudelman-Bloch, Sophie Balhetchet, Nicola White, Laura Fraser, Tanja Hagen and Leslee Durr.

To Kenneth Nkosi, Rapulana Seiphemo, Darrel Bristow-Bovey, Duncan Cremer, Craig Harwood, Shaun de Waal, Jim Flint, Robbie Thorpe, Guy Tillim, Barry Streek and Johnny Copelyn.

And finally to Drue Heinz, Amy Norton and Margaret, Jean and Kerry of the Hawthornden Castle International Writers' Retreat for the peace and seclusion in which to complete at last.